THE BIG LIE

A WEATHERBY MYSTERY

THE BIG LIE

A WEATHERBY MYSTERY

J. M. T. MILLER

A JAN DENNIS BOOK

THOMAS NELSON PUBLISHERS
Nashville

Published in Nashville, Tennessee, by Jan Dennnis Books, an imprint of Thomas
Nelson, Inc., and distributed in Canada by Word Communications, Ltd., Rich-
mond, British Columbia.
Scripture quotations are from the NEW KING JAMES VERSION of the Bible.
Copyright © 1979, 1980, 1982, Thomas Nelson, Inc., Publishers.

Library of Congress Cataloging-in-Publication Data

Miller, J.M.T.
    The Big Lie: A Weatherby Mystery/ by J.M.T. Miller
        p.   cm.
        "A Jan Dennis Book"
    ISBN 0-8407-6357-3 (pbk.)
        1. Private investigators—California—Los Angeles—Fiction. 2. Los Angeles
(Calif.)—Fiction.   I. Title
PS3563.I4117B54   1994
813'.54—dc20   93-27309
                                                                       CIP

Printed in the United States of America

1 2 3 4 5 6 — 98 97 96 95 94 93

Chapter
──ONE──

Mr. Weatherby?" Her voice was soft. It was also husky, as if she hadn't talked for a long time.

"At your service." I held my office door open wider and gave her my most charming grin—then felt my face stiffen as her dark green eyes mesmerized me. They were strangely hollow, and the circles under them were so dark that at first I thought she had two fading shiners. I looked deep into the liquid emeralds, but I couldn't read a thing there except some heavy pain. She hesitated, then stepped gracefully into my office. As she floated past, she extended her hand for a lady-like shake, then suddenly jerked it back, biting her lip as she remembered something. I caught my own handshake in midair and let it drop to my side.

I moved back behind my desk, and she sat stiffly in the client's chair, her long, frail fingers clasped tightly together. She kept biting on that lip. Finally, a little ripple of determination crossed her face. She steeled herself and said, "I'm Elizabeth Livingstone. I phoned you earlier . . ."

"You're right on time." I grinned. Friendly me. She graced me with an elusive smile and rearranged herself in my brand new high-backed applegreen chintz chair. The colors were a perfect frame for her pale, heart-shaped face. She wore a flowing white dress, and as she arranged the hemline, I glanced down at her feet.

They were bare.

And not only were they bare, they were covered with drying mud, as if she'd recently squished those elegant little toes through a very nasty mudpuddle.

I looked at my brand new carpet. Dirty footprints ran all the way from the door to the chair.

Great. Two weeks I'd been closed so my office could be re-done after a demented enemy had trashed the place. Built-in walnut bookshelves, walnut panelling, brass lamps, and the new chintz sofa with matching client's chair. Not to mention the malted-milk-brown carpet, a quality job that tickled your ankles and had been spotlessly clean till a moment ago. In fact, this wraith-like woman was my first client since I'd dropped six grand fixing up the place. I'd been looking forward to her arrival so I could show it off. And now—?

My irritation must have shown because she looked down at her feet, then looked back up at me with a stricken expression. She said, "I'm so sorry. I didn't realize . . ."

"No problem." I whisked my hand in dismissal. I'd bill her extra for the carpet cleaning. For the chair too, because now I could see a large smudge of mud across the back of her frayed dress. I said, "What happened to your shoes?"

"They—they came apart. I—I'm . . ." Her words faded to a mumble.

"What?"

"I'm sorry. It's been so long, I—" Her eyes flooded with a sorrow so intense that it set me back in my chair.

I studied her. She was one of those old-fashioned beauties who remind you of lawn parties, weeping willow trees, pink and yellow tea roses. She had long, slightly curly hair, shoulder length and combed straight back from her forehead. The dress was filmy cotton with tattered white lace at the bodice, long sleeves, and more tattered lace at the wrists. It had a flowing, tea-length skirt, fancy but frayed—though maybe just the look to go with bared, muddy feet.

She could have been anywhere from twenty-five to forty-five, maybe even older. And as I studied her, she studied me back. There was an overwhelmingly sad quality about her, and she was thin—too thin. Her alabaster skin was almost translucent. She wore no makeup, not even a dash of lipstick. And those eyes . . .

The deep shadows under them detracted from the lovely dark green of the irises. Maybe she'd been sick for a long time, or hadn't been getting any sleep—or maybe she'd been sleeping too much. She could have been a turn-of-the-century laudanum addict, locked away for decades in some dark Victorian house, or maybe she was one of those people born with such an intense sensitivity to sunlight that ultraviolet was never allowed to touch her skin. As I tried to pigeonhole her, she stared at the floor. Her hands went to work kneading a white handkerchief trimmed in Spanish lace that was as shabby as the dress.

I sensed the full depth of her tragedy, and I recognized the pain in her eyes now. It was the kind of deeply intense grief most often associated with the death of someone you love. I knew that feeling. I dropped my professional pose and waited for her to speak. If she needed time to get up the nerve to lay it out for me, then time is what she'd have.

After a long moment, she quit fidgeting with the handkerchief. "I shouldn't have come. I—" Her voice caught in her throat.

I put an interested expression on my face, then leaned back in my swivel chair and waited for her to say more.

After a while, she rewarded my patience. "They told everyone it was an accident. But it wasn't."

I nodded as if I knew what she was talking about. I opened my desk drawer and surreptitiously touched the button on my tape recorder. The newly built-in microphone would pick up every word. Just for show, I pulled out a brand new leather-bound notebook. I pulled my gold-plated ballpoint pen from its gold and marble holder and poised it over the paper. "Who got hurt?"

"She wasn't just hurt, she was murdered."

I nodded, then doodled a question mark onto the paper, then added a tombstone. "Okay. *Who* was murdered?"

"I—I can't tell you yet."

I gave her a long-suffering look. "I'm going to have to know who *got* it before I can find out who *did* it."

She reached into her tattered bodice and demurely withdrew a long white envelope. She leaned forward and placed it on my desk. "There's a check for five thousand dollars in here. Will that be enough for you to start?"

"Depends on what I'm starting."

"I want you to investigate a murder."

I thought about the bill for six grand's worth of office renovation. "I'm listening."

She stood up. "Everything you'll need is in that envelope. But you are not to open it till fifteen minutes after I'm gone. Please. That's very important. Then, if you choose to help me—and I beg you, you must—please take the check to the bank and cash it. If you can't take the job" —a stricken look came into her eyes— "then tear up the check. Destroy it completely. Never tell anyone you've seen me. But if you possibly can, please, I need your help . . ."

"Wait a minute. When did this murder happen? Have the police been notified? I'm going to need some more information . . ."

"It's all in the envelope. Please, Mr. Weatherby. It's far too late for the police. You must help me. There's no other way . . ."

I thought it over, then said, "Look, I'll check it out. Nothing guaranteed." I was skeptical. If this woman had five grand in the bank, why didn't she invest in some new shoes and a decent dress? And why the big mystery?

She'd been edging toward the door as she talked, and now she opened it. She said, "Thank you again. You're the only hope I have . . ."

I moved to the door too. "Mrs. Livingstone. It is 'Mrs.,' isn't it?"

She started ever so slightly. "I—I'm afraid I don't know."

"Why not?"

"It—it's been a very long time . . ."

I considered that, then decided to work on it later. "Look. I'll need an address, a phone number, somewhere I can reach you."

Her eyes flooded with panic. A nerve jumped near her mouth. "No. That's impossible. I—I mean, it's not wise, at this point. I—I'll have to contact you . . ." She stepped through the door and into the hall.

"But if you're going to hire me, we need a contract. I can't take a job like this. You don't even have a receipt for your retainer."

"It doesn't matter. I'll stay in touch. Please." Her eyes had filled with tears. "I can't tell you how important this is, but you'll soon see. This is the only way . . ."

A slow deep warning chimed inside my head, then reverberated there. I said, "If you're in some kind of danger, I could arrange protection. Maybe you really should be talking to the police . . ."

Her eyes widened and she started to say something, then stopped. A look of dread mixed with disgust made her face sag into something old and heavy. "I'm so very tired, Mr. Weatherby. I'm not thinking straight. I—I'm sorry, no, I can't tell you more than I already have. You'll just have to see it for yourself."

I sighed. "Look, Mrs. Livingstone, I'm not following you on most of this. But—okay, I'll see what I can do."

A tiny flicker of hope leaped into her eyes, then she quenched it and smiled sadly. "Thank you."

I watched her track down the parquet floor, then step into the elevator. Her footprints weren't quite so muddy now. She'd left most of the grime caked into the carpet on my office floor.

Chapter
——TWO——

The white envelope sat on my desk like a coiled rattler. Several times I started to pick it up, but each time I felt guilty. I'm like that. I'd promised her I'd wait for fifteen minutes, so wait for fifteen minutes I did.

I spent a few minutes thinking about the woman, wondering about her strange appearance and her muddy feet. But that just made me want to grab the envelope and rip it open before the time was up. So I stood and stretched, then walked to my window and looked down into the canyon known as Baker Street. A glint of sunlight flashed off a cab's window as it turned the corner. People milled in the street, purposefully striding to who knew what orchestration. They all seemed artificial to me, wooden, like wind-up toys animated by some Master hand then set to move at random, creating far more chaos than order. The ambulance chaser who rented a space down the hall from me was striding briskly toward our building, a soft-leather yuppie briefcase clamped under his arm. I did some work for him from time to time, but it wasn't the kind of work I was proud of.

I kept glancing at my watch, and just as the minute hand ticked over for the fifteenth time I stepped over, grabbed the envelope, stabbed in my letter opener and slit it open. I shook it, and out fluttered two pieces of paper. The first was the check. Five thousand to the letter, written in delicate strokes with a lot of old-fashioned curlicues. It was signed by Mrs. Elizabeth Ann Livingstone. Imprinted

6

on the top left was her name, an address in the old money section of Bel Air—even a phone number. So much for mystery!

The second piece of paper was a yellowed newspaper obituary. Someone had taken a black magic marker and inked out parts if it, so that it read:

age 35, died today at her Bel Air home. She was well known for her charitable activities and also for her roles in several major motion pictures before her marriage. She is survived by her husband, and by her brother Interment will be Thursday, eleven A.M. at the Chapel of the Flowers Mortuary and Memorial Gardens, 2119 Woodhill Road.

I read it twice, turned it over, held it up to the light. But it was impossible to see through the black ink to what had been printed beneath. And there was no masthead, no way to tell which paper it came from. The obit didn't tell me much. Somebody had died, had been buried at Chapel of the Flowers Memorial Gardens. At least whoever it was hadn't gone anywhere. On the other hand, a lot of people were buried in that cemetery, all the way from the early settlers who had seeded this "City of Angels" to the celebrities who favored the newer section of the boneyard today.

I picked up the envelope and gave it another little shake. Out fluttered yet another yellowed news clipping. This one was also inked up, and it came from a different newspaper because it had a slightly different type face.

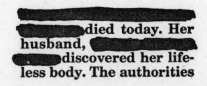

died today. Her husband, discovered her life-less body. The authorities

> have ruled the death an accident, though more precise details have not yet been released. An autopsy has been scheduled. ▮▮▮▮ will be interred in the Chapel of the Flowers Mortuary and Memorial Gardens. Her friends are asked to omit sending flowers and instead to make charitable contributions to the Foundation for the Enhancement of the Human Spirit.

I peered into the envelope again. I turned the paper over. And around, and upside down. No sudden and obvious clue jumped out at me. Okay, the date would help. I had enough to get started. Furthermore, I was curious now. And the mystery lady was paying me five thousand smackeroos to be that way, so why not?

I checked my watch. Nearly ten-fifteen. With any luck, I could have the first part of this case cracked wide open in time for a leisurely dinner at the Hollywood Diner over on Cahuenga. Wrapping it up might take a little longer—like a day or so. And then I could catch a charter fishing boat down to Mazatlan. I was long overdue to check out Mexico's marlin. I stood and stretched. If I wore a fedora, I would have grabbed it. I was through with being an interior decorator. It felt good to be a gumshoe again.

Chapter
——————THREE——————

Elizabeth Ann Livingstone's check had been drawn on the Livingstone Bank and Trust. Interesting. I caught the Hollywood Freeway, then drove to the very heart of the Beverly Hills financial district and left my gray BMW in the bank's parking lot in front of a sign that said "EMPLOYEES ONLY." The revolving door let me into a high-ceilinged lobby with a lot of dark wood and a plush carpet the exact color of old money.

I fell into line behind a dowager with a faint whiff of gin about her and a dead fox draped around her shoulders, then had a great time resting my weight first on one foot, then on the other, while I awaited my turn at the teller's window.

But finally I was face-to-face with the short skinny gent with the paisley bowtie. I put my driver's license on the counter, picked up the five-cent ballpoint they had chained to the desk, and scrawled my signature across the back of the five grand. I pushed the check at him, face down.

His tea-colored eyes darted across the endorsement, then he checked the signature against the one on my driver's license, then he turned the check over—and stopped short. His shoulders drew up, his eyebrows fell, and his face turned gray all at the same time. He looked at the check, then at me, then back at the check.

"Something wrong?" I asked.

He took a short step back from me, the check still in his hand. He adjusted his tortoise-shell glasses, then peered again at the check. "Excuse me for one moment, sir." His voice was reedy and weak.

I shrugged and watched him disappear with my five grand through a huge oak door. I cooled my heels for about two minutes, and then he came back. As he stepped up to the window again, a thin little smirk crossed his face. "Mr. Dreyfus would like to see you."

"Who's Dreyfus, and what's wrong?"

"Mr. Dreyfus *manages* this bank." He said it like I should be impressed. "Go through the door to the side"—he pointed—"and he'll be waiting."

I walked through the door and into a room where a middle-aged secretary with frosty posture, rime-streaked hair, and a lavender button-down blouse smiled coldly and told me Mr. Dreyfus was waiting behind still another door: This one was of carved oak. I opened it and stepped into an office cluttered with stacks of computer printouts, bound financial statements, and other debris. The walls were paneled in dark oak, and the man who sat behind the desk was trying to hide his paunch behind a vest that was a size too small. His tie was a red-and-green plaid. His neatly-pressed brown suit jacket hung over the back of his chair. His nose was bulbous, and his eyes were small and close-set. "Mr. Weatherby?" He didn't bother to stand or to stick out his hand for a shake.

"Yo."

"Sit down, sir."

I sat.

"Mr. Weatherby, you're attempting to cash a rather substantial check, am I right?"

"Right as rain."

"I would like to ask you, sir, precisely what you're up to."

I shrugged. "What you just said. I'm trying to cash a check. What's the problem?"

He puffed up importantly. "The problem, sir, is that this account is closed, and has been closed for ten full years. Furthermore, this check is dated ten years ago today. Might I ask why you've waited so long to try to cash it?"

He was holding the check in his hand, and I reached for it. He jerked it back. "Let me see it," I said. "That check was just written today."

He held it out to me, his thumbs and forefingers pinching each side tightly so I couldn't grab it away from him, and he squinted at me as I tried to read it. "As you can see," he said, "it was written exactly ten years ago today! *Not* today. Furthermore, the person who signed it couldn't possibly have written it."

"Why not?"

"Perhaps I should let you ask her husband that question."

I sat up straight. "You know her husband?"

His look was scathing. "He happens to *own* this bank."

So it *was* the same Livingstone. No wonder my new client could write a check for five grand. But why the frumpy clothes and the dirty feet?

Dreyfus wasn't waiting for my gray cells to turn over fast enough to figure everything out. He reached for the phone, dialed, and after a moment, in a voice calculated to impress, he said into the mouthpiece, "Hello, Mr. Livingstone? I want to inform you that a man is here trying to cash a ten-year-old, five-thousand-dollar check on your wife's account. Would you like me to phone the police?"

He listened, then said, "Oh. Well, yes, certainly. I understand." He hung up the phone, reluctantly handed me the check, and said, "Mr. Livingstone would like to see you. Right away." He rummaged in a desk drawer, pulled out a business card, and handed it to me. "Here is his address, and if I were you, I'd waste no time getting there."

I walked out of the bank and caught the freeway till I reached Sunset, the Boulevard of Dreams. Now *there's* a street for you. For twenty-four miles it skirts the Santa Monica mountains, starting near the slums of Chinatown then rushing you on to the flesh markets of West Hollywood and the Sunset Strip, then it takes you on to—and through—the old money areas of Beverly Hills and Bel Air. Finally, it rushes you on to Pacific Palisades, where it drops you with a crash into the thundering blue Pacific.

I'd grown up in a place more like the low rent district of eastern Sunset, with no regrets. As I turned my car toward the ritzy part of Bel Air, I'd far rather have been traveling back to Dodger Stadium for a hot dog and a game and the not-always-pleasant smog of reality. The scented, rarified air that the big money buys all too often masks the stench of something rotten, so far as I've been able to tell. In my opinion it takes someone brittle and cold and more than a little dead to amass and keep a fortune vast enough to let you close yourself off in the mausoleum-houses of La La Land. I mean, think about it. If you had a million extra bucks and there were a hundred thousand kids starving and you could feed them all for ten years with that money, could *you* hang onto the million? Having big money can cost you a lot.

I followed Sunset all the way to Bel Air Heights, the streets getting increasingly wider, the yards and houses getting bigger and more expensive. Finally, when the houses had disappeared altogether behind wide hedges and thick trees and high iron fences, I found Livingstone's street and hung a left. I drove about the equivalent of a block, then found the street number affixed in small brass numbers to a huge stone wall beside a two-story Normandy-style gatehouse with an opened wrought-iron gate. The gatehouse appeared to be vacant, but as I drove through the gate, I thought I saw a curtain drop in an upstairs window, as if someone had been watching me.

I wheeled the car up a winding driveway, past heavy eucalyptus and olive trees and other lush foliage that screened both sides of the estate all the way to a flagstoned courtyard.

Edgar Allan Poe would have liked the house. Its builder had somehow managed to blend the worst features of Gothic with the worst features of Normandy and Tudor and then molded it all together into an immense three-story chunk of dreary gray stone. The mansion was in good repair: the Gothic arches had been recently painted, and the dark banks of hedge were carefully pruned.

Nevertheless, there was a sorrowful aura to the house and the thick stands of trees that surrounded it.

I rang the gorgon-shaped bell, then waited. After a moment, the knob turned from inside, the door opened, and a tall, melancholy man in old-fashioned butler's livery looked at me though soul-weary eyes. He was an aged version of Casanova, though the Spanish was mixed just a bit with Indian to give that special caste of Mexican nobility to his face. There were Basset-hound bags beneath his eyes, and his lips were full and pouty—too large for his narrow face. He acknowledged me with a small nod of his head.

"I'm Artie Weatherby," I said, trying to put some cheer in my voice. This place could use some cheer.

"Yes, of course, Mr. Livingstone is expecting you."

He led me into a vaulted hallway, across a floor made from pink-veined Italian marble. Arched, leaded windows looked out on a formal English garden. We went past the main room with its cathedral ceiling, glass, and stone, and on down the hallway, till he stopped in front of a dark mahogany door, knocked, then stuck his head in and said, "Mr. Weatherby is here, sir."

I waited for him to back out, then stepped in and closed the door behind me. I was in a huge, surprisingly colorful room. A fire glowed in a stone walk-in fireplace, and brightly colored Mexican rugs were strewn here and there over the gleaming bleached oak floor. Bookshelves lined one wall, filled with several hundred volumes bound in dark-green leather. To my right, floor-to-ceiling shelves held mid-sized, pre-Columbian carvings of various Meso-American gods which scowled, empty-eyed, from behind sparkling glass. Thanks to a few anthropology and archaeology classes at UCLA, I recognized the squat, malevolent shape of Coatlicue, the Aztec goddess of the earth. Beside that was a smaller carving of her son, Huitzilopochtli, one of the many sun gods. And in the midst of the exhibit, perhaps a full foot tall, stood a sleek stone carving of Quetzalcoatl, the Meso-American sun god who was also the Aztec god of death and resurrection.

The drapes were drawn shut. Near the far wall, a table lamp emitted a feeble light, illuminating a thin, small man with colorless hair and a forgettable face who sat in a high-backed green leather chair. He stood up stiffly.

I couldn't help it. I said, "Mr. Livingstone, I presume?"

He gave me a thin smile. "And you must be Mr. Weatherby. Sit down, please, and tell me why you're trying to plunder my bank. And in such a clumsy way, I might add."

"I'm not trying to plunder anything. I'm simply trying to cash a check."

"May I see it, please?"

"Certainly." I handed it to him.

He looked it over, then gave it back to me. "It is a good forgery of my wife's signature."

"If Elizabeth Livingstone is your wife, then it *is* your wife's signature." I sat down, leaning forward to watch him closely.

He squinted at me and I couldn't read his eyes. "Then why have you waited so long to cash it?"

I started to tell him I'd just received it that day, but something stopped me. "Is your wife here? Maybe she could explain this." I looked again at the date. Today's date and month all right, but sure enough the year written down was ten years ago to the day. Somehow I'd gotten so interested in the obits that I'd missed it.

"What are you trying to pull, young man?"

Again I started to tell him, but just then my eyes fell on the accumulation of family photographs on top of a spinet piano. There were several old portraits of people I assumed were departed family members, including one of a handsome silver-haired matriarch in a tiara and diamond necklace who bore a distinct resemblance to the woman who'd given me the check that morning. And sure enough, there beside her, in a filigreed silver frame, was a portrait of the woman herself. "Why don't you call your wife?" I said. "She must have accidentally jotted down the wrong year."

"My wife didn't sign that check," Livingstone said flatly. His eyes had turned flinty and his face was transfigured into something savage and hard, like the faces carved into the pre-Columbian stone.

"Is that her photograph?" I pointed.

"Indeed it is, God rest her soul." His face was again transformed, this time with sorrow, but there was something oblique in his eyes. "It was taken only two days before her death."

That made me sit up straight. "Death?"

His chuckle was low and ugly. "But of course, Mr. Weatherby. My wife died ten years ago today. So you see, she couldn't possibly have written that check. I repeat, Mr. Weatherby, my wife is dead. Very dead." For an instant his mouth twitched at the corner, and I thought that whatever was going on behind the mask would break through, but he managed to stifle it. He said, "You picked a sorry victim for your little forgery scheme this time, didn't you?"

Again I started to tell him the truth—my mouth even started working, but nothing came out. And then I looked again at the photograph, and it hit me. Whammo! I'd just been hired by a dead woman to investigate her own murder!

Livingstone was studying me gravely. "I find your bungling amusing, Mr. Weatherby. Otherwise, I'd have let my bank manager phone the police. But I am curious about one thing. How did you get the blank check with my wife's address imprinted on it?"

"Uh—someone gave it to me."

"I see." He looked scornfully superior. "So someone is printing checks on my bank. I'd certainly like to know who it is."

I decided not to touch that one.

He said, "I suppose we'll have to start being more careful. But I advise you to forget targeting my bank. The only reason I'm overlooking this incident is because I don't care to have any negative publicity associated with my late wife's name, and that's an added piece of luck for you."

"Tell you what," I said. "You forget the incident, and I'll keep the check—how does that sound?"

He looked like he wanted to argue, but I let my eyes go glacial and stood up, giving him the full benefit of my six-feet-one-inch stance. I held my hand out and he blinked twice, almost petulantly, but he handed over the paper. I took it and waved it back and forth. "A little memento," I said, "of a most unusual day." I strode toward the door, then turned back suddenly—I'd learned that from watching "Columbo"—and said, "How did your wife die?"

He started, and then caught himself. "A simple domestic accident. Why? What difference does that make?"

"What kind of accident?"

But the surprise factor was gone. He said, "If you don't mind, I hardly feel like chatting about it. Especially with *you*." He nodded toward the door. "Do you mind?"

I studied him for a moment, but his face wouldn't tell me a thing. He was used to high stakes games, was my guess, which was an easy guess to make, considering the size of his house and his bank.

He continued glaring at me. He wasn't breaking. So finally I gave him a curt nod, turned, and went out the door, closing it softly behind me. The butler wasn't in the hallway, and he probably hadn't done it anyway. I found my own way back outside where I stood for a moment, savoring the fresh air. The sunshine had weakened. The breeze held the flowery menthol scent of eucalyptus and the fresh, sweet smell of impending rain.

Chapter
──── FOUR ────

I cruised through the gate and hung a right on Glen Drive, then drove down Sunset, this time toward the first freeway on-ramp. I was on my way to look at a grave.

Once on the freeway, I pulled the check out of my shirt pocket and glanced at it again. Five big ones. Paid to me by a dead woman. Or at least by someone who looked just like Livingstone's dead wife. Assuming she really was dead. So far, I had only her husband's word on that.

I played around with that one for a while. The woman who'd come to my office had claimed to be Mrs. Elizabeth Livingstone. She'd handed me a check signed by Mrs. Elizabeth Livingstone, of the Livingstones' address, and she'd looked just like the photograph of Livingstone's dead wife. So, maybe Mrs. Livingstone had a twin sister? But the obit said she'd been survived by only a brother. So—maybe someone had hired an actress to do a number on me. Or maybe not. Whatever was going on, I knew for a fact that the woman in my office that morning hadn't been dead. Had she? I found myself thinking about the pale skin, about those hollow eyes and the raspy voice . . . and I hadn't really touched her, she'd jerked her hand back from my handshake, maybe because my hand would have gone right through her . . .

Come on, Weatherby. Time for a reality check. I'd never believed in ghosts, not even as a kid. When my heinous little buddies and I

17

had sat around in the pitch of night telling ghost stories, I'd always been the cynic who refused to scream with terror when the "beast with five fingers" suddenly gripped me by the throat or the person telling the story about "gimme back my liver" suddenly yelled, "Gotcha!" The bravery had been easy because I really hadn't been afraid. I'd always figured that dead is dead. Period. Oh, my grandmother with whom I lived at that time had believed in life after death. She believed in heaven and hell and the whole bit, complete with church every Sunday morning, me spit-shined and sitting beside her in the pew, thinking of the other boys playing baseball, eager to get out of the stuffy church and into the big world.

Then I'd really gotten into the big world—by way of the front lines in Vietnam. Too young to know better, I'd volunteered for the Special Forces, and there my new buddies and I had spent a lot of time thinking about death, administering death, watching death take our fellow soldiers in various gruesome ways. We wondered if, when we caught the shrapnel or the bullet or the grenade or the knife in the dark, was that it, was the joke over? We'd sit at night or between incoming rounds and talk about the war, and the meaning of life and death and God. One lieutenant—a brother of color from Austin, Texas—had talked to all of us at length about Jesus dying for our sins, about eternal life, and also about a thing he called the "baptism of the Holy Spirit." A dozen or so men had been "saved". . . I was never really sure what that meant. But they said they'd been reborn in the Spirit, and they indeed became different people, literally overnight. They'd started a prayer group and when the brass was handing out assignments, these people had always prayed afterward. You could see them, in their special place in a little cluster, talking to God. And word started coming back that amazing things happened when these people went out on missions. Viet Cong miraculously surrendered, thereby keeping villages from being razed and innocent people from being killed. They'd be assigned to target certain VC brass who were responsible for atrocities far and wide, then would arrive at the destination to find their targets already dead. These stories gave us all some hope that Somebody upstairs really did care what was happening to us out there in the blood-soaked jungles. But then the lieutenant bought it in a raid up near Khe Sanh, trying to get some trapped Marines out of trouble. One of his men who had been with him said The Loot had been talking straight to Jesus when he died, that there was a look of pure joy on his face as he breathed his last earthly breath.

Nevertheless, I'd finally decided that you only get one shot at this life, why waste time worrying about what comes next? It's coming, whether you worry or not, whether you want it or not, whether you like it or not . . .

I crested a hill and there, below me and to my right, was the sweeping emerald expanse of the Chapel of the Flowers Mortuary and Memorial Gardens. As I approached the base of the hill I braked, then swung right and drove between huge white marble pillars, engraved with cherubs and posies. I cruised into the parking lot right beside a metallic green hearse with puffy pink upholstery, and turned off the ignition. The chapel was in front of me with its amber-and-gold stained glass windows and its graceful arches. Beside it was a sleek one-story office building with squat plaster cherubs on each side of the door, and beyond that was a crematorium.

The director's office was easy to find, and the director was even in it. He was long and lean, with thinning silver hair atop an appropriately cadaverous head. His gray pin-stripe had razor-sharp creases in the trousers, his shirt was blindingly white, and his tie was silver silk. His white gold tie-tacks and studs had probably cost as much as their top-of-the-line burial box, and it had taken a lot of tombstones to pay for the diamond pinky ring on his left little finger.

He gave me a weary smile and wrung his hands in the manner of a professional mourner, as his sharp eyes studied me. I didn't miss the dollar signs clicking in his eyes, as he said, "Good afternoon. Welcome to the Chapel of the Flowers. May I be of assistance?" Why did I get the feeling he was measuring me for a coffin?

By the time I finished explaining that I wasn't there to buy a plot, the smile had withered and been replaced by a bored look. It took him about a minute to look up the date of Elizabeth Livingstone's burial. Sure enough, it was ten years ago, almost to the day. It took a second longer to give me the location of the Livingstone family plots, and an extra second to explain how to get there.

The cemetery was huge, and I had to backtrack a few times. The road wound past and around mausoleums, past memorials and markers, past ordinary gray granite gravestones, some of which dated back all the way to the early 1600s. This was the oldest cemetery in the city, and it had long ago swallowed up the tiny mission cemetery that it had grown upon and around, back before missions were declared historical sites. The bones that lay buried in this ground had at one time carried flesh, had been infused with life, and among all these now-dead people, they'd seen it all—from the gold-greedy Portuguese, Juan Cabrillo, who had claimed the land for Spain in 1542, then had named the tiny village *El Pueblo Nuestra Señora la Reina de Los Angeles*—The City of Our Lady Queen of the Angels—to the missions and opulent Spanish ranchos and orchards that had next sprung up in the area, to the gold rushes, to statehood, to the oil and land and entertainment booms that had begun the spate of growth that resulted in the present-day jumble of clogged traffic, lung-scalding smog, Hollywood fantasy, grotesque affluence, gut-wrenching poverty, ethnic gang warfare, drive-by shootings, drive-in churches, and all the other peccadillos that make Los Angeles the epitome of all the best and the worst in the world.

Sometime during the heavy growth era of the early 1960s, a developer had bought up the farmland surrounding the cemetery, divided it into plots, landscaped it, and built the huge chapel. Grass and shrubs and banks of flowers had been planted everywhere. Freshly pruned hedges now separated the various sections, and just in case the residents had a hard time sleeping, enough trees had been planted to keep virtually every grave shrouded in perpetual gloom.

The sky was turning gray as massive clouds blew in from the sea, threatening heavy rain. The moisture was mixing with the humidity, to cause a mist that already rested heavily in the hollows and around the edges of the shrubbery. The sun had dissolved into a pale, distant orb. I drove slowly up one lane, down another, till I finally found the Livingstone family plot. The section was huge and entirely enclosed by a high granite wall that, though intact, managed to give the impression of crumbling out from beneath the huge iron spikes that jutted from the top and prevented any of the inhabitants from escaping. An eight-foot gothic arch demarcated the decaying wooden gate. Etched deeply into the granite at the top of the arch was the legend: LIVINGSTONE.

I parked on the side of the road, climbed out, and with a sudden and inexplicable surge of depression, I started toward the gate. In spite of the warm air, I shivered.

I grasped the old-fashioned handle and thumbed down the rusty release, then pushed. There was an ugly grating sound as the gate moved on its rusted hinges. But it came open, and the interior of the compound was before me. I felt like I was entering another, darker world. Thick sooty mist rose up from the earth like an unnatural apparition, bearing the slight taste of sea-salt. The thick vapors that had been trapped by the stone walls and cold gravestones were wisping and writhing around the stone crypts. In fact, except for the occasional jut of a gravestone or a tree, the ground was almost entirely hidden. With a deepening dread, I moved into the compound.

I had stumbled some seven steps into the dreary vapors, disoriented, visibility no more than an arm's length in front of me. Then, wet, prickly tentacles licked at my ankles, and I jerked back from what I now saw were ferns and into an icy pool of water. I yelped as it sloshed my pants, then stepped from the watery gravel pathway onto what I thought was grass. But I found my loafers sucked into pure mud. No wonder there was so much mist inside the compound. The water sprinklers were on, adding moisture to the already heavy humidity. I backtracked, trying to avoid the looping water and the mud, and suddenly a man-sized tombstone loomed in front of me, so close I almost slammed into it. I stopped short as I read the inscription: "Jonathan Livingstone Seigal, born 1848, died 1922, beloved son of . . ." The rest of the letters had crumbled away. What was left of the marker was covered over with a moldy, minute fungi that seemed to be eating away the stone.

I stepped back again, and only then did I realize that I was backtracking near to another gravestone. I turned quickly, and finally found myself in a wet tangle of shrubs, then on the grass. My shoes were getting heavy from the thick, viscous mud, and I bent forward and pulled a limb from a shrub, to clean them. I could see then that I'd left the imprint of my muddy size tens all the way across the grave as well as alongside the path.

I quickly scraped the mud from my shoes, found the gravel path again, then left through the gate. It took only a moment to find the water faucets that controlled the network of hoses and sprinklers inside the compound. I turned them off, and returned through the gate. And I could see now. With the dissipation of the water, the mists were abruptly vanishing, though a slight vapor still hung in the air and tatters of what could have been either sea-fog or ectoplasm hung on the branches of the huge trees and ragged shrubs.

The Livingstones had apparently owned these plots for a very long time. The wide, spreading trees were old, and they cast their shady pall over everything. I easily kept to the gravel this time, walking between graves, all of the markers elaborately engraved with the names of Livingstones or Livingstone spouses and offspring. I made a right turn and started up yet another row of graves—these from a more recent time—when I suddenly saw footprints. Small footprints. They were slightly caved in around the sides from the water that had sprinkled atop and partially filled them.

I bent forward and looked closer. Bare feet had walked here; feet of a size that might belong to a very slight and delicate woman.

As I looked around, it became evident now that someone had recently taken a renewed interest in the compound. Gardeners had been bedding in marigolds, daisies, lilies, and other flowers whose scent was overwhelmed by the damp, freshly turned earth of the planting. Numerous rows of hedges were newly trimmed, and I could see the gardener's footprints: waffled bootprints tracking around the flower beds and other planting areas. But the small bare footprints, easily distinguished, tracked only through the newly turned soil and made straight for the rusty gate. I followed them to the gate, then turned and backtracked them alongside the gravel pathway—the gravel had no doubt been harsh on bared feet. They swerved and originated at a mound of freshly turned earth beside a gaping hole.

At first I thought the gardeners had made this hole in order to perhaps plant a tree, but then I saw the gravestone, a huge rectangular shaft of pink-veined white marble with an engraving of a near-life-sized, wide-winged angel keeping watch over the opened grave. And it was indeed an opened grave, the disturbed earth spaded up and then dumped beside the gaping hole. The grass that had been atop the grave was scattered in clumps, mounds of rich, damp earth were spread around, though much of the earth had also collapsed back into the grave. The grave apparently had been violated earlier in the day or perhaps during the previous night. The puddles and dampness told me that the water sprinklers had saturated this newly spaded earth as well as everything else in the compound.

But what stopped me in my own tracks was the fact that the tiny, bare footprints came up and out of this violated grave. I could even see where fingers had actually clawed their way from the depths of the grave to the rim, where whoever or whatever had pulled themselves up and out of the hole. I looked carefully all around the rim. Nobody had gone back in.

I suddenly remembered a pair of delicate, muddy feet and saw the mud being tracked across my brand new office carpet. Impossible. Get a grip, Weatherby. There are no ghosts. Ghosts mean life after death. No life after death—hence no ghosts.

With more hesitation than I'd like to admit, I stepped around to the front of the tombstone to read the inscription: ELIZABETH ANN LIVINGSTONE. I felt an icy shock slide down my spine. Until now, I'd been expecting some clue to pop up and prove that the pattern I saw so far was all coincidence. But no more excuses, now I had to look squarely at the truth. Beneath Elizabeth's name was the date of her birth, and the date of her death, ten years ago almost to the day, at the age of thirty-five. There were no other words carved into the marker, not so much as an "R.I.P." Just her name, the dates on the marble, and the rest of the stone—huge, monolithic, and bare.

I moved fast then, suddenly anxious to get away from all these monuments to death. I extracted my wallet from my hip pocket and rummaged frantically till I found a gasoline receipt. It would have to do. I folded the paper into a little cone, bent forward, scooped up some earth, then stowed the soil sample in the paper. And then I walked quickly out of the compound, sprinted to my car, and opened the door just as it began to rain.

What was I going to do if the soil from this opened and desecrated grave matched the soil that had, that morning, been tracked onto my spanking new carpet? What then?

This was going to take some thinking . . .

Chapter

—FIVE—

My rented redwood bungalow was isolated and compact against the dark cut of Chaparral Canyon, with its cover of ironwood, scrub oak, eucalyptus and, of course, chaparral. No other houses were nearby. This was my escape, my place to hide when the rigors of La La Land got to be too much for me—which had happened by about seven-thirty that night.

Earlier in the day, after my eerie visit to Elizabeth Livingstone's grave, I'd returned to my office and scraped some dirt from the carpet, remembering to congratulate myself for failing to phone the janitor earlier. That done, I immediately drove down to the University and dropped off both soil samples at the Agronomical Sciences lab, where a grad student had agreed by phone to analyze and compare them in return for a fifty-dollar bill, paid in advance.

Next I phoned the City and County Forensic Science Center. I needed to get a lead on whoever had pronounced Mrs. Elizabeth Ann Livingstone dead that day ten years earlier. I needed to know how she had died—I needed to know *if* she had died. The file clerk snarled a bit when I asked her to check it out for me, but then she went swiftly to work and dug out the name Dean Gates. "But Dr. Gates is no longer with us," she said.

"Any idea where he might be?"

"Last I heard, he'd gone to work down in San Diego." Before I could ask any more questions, she hung up.

I phoned the San Diego city morgue, but they'd never heard of Gates. So I phoned the San Diego P.D., and when they picked up at the other end of the line I said, "I'm trying to get in touch with Dr. Dean Gates, a pathologist, probably working as an M.E. Any idea where I might find him?"

A tobacco-roughened voice said, "Who wants to know?"

"My name is Dr. R. T. Weatherby. I'm working on a research project, and we need to get permission to use some quotes in a paper we're publishing in the *New England Journal of Medicine*. But we haven't communicated for a very long time, and I've lost his address. It's very important that we reach him right away."

That brought a "Hold it," and then a "Just a second." Finally, the man came back on the line and said, "Dr. Gates was with the M.E.'s office here for about six months some six or so years back, but then he went into private research. Had a place up in Orange County. Got a pen?"

Great. Right back to where I started. I should have just looked in the greater L.A. phonebook.

The number was in Newport Beach, but when I dialed I got a message from an answering machine. "You have reached the phone of Dr. Dean Gates. Dr. Gates is a research pathologist and does not see patients. Dr. Gates is presently on sabbatical. If you need medical attention, phone the Physician's Exchange. If you need emergency treatment, please dial 911. Thank you." Beep—no space for a message, even if I'd wanted to leave one. Okay, dead end there.

Next, I phoned my old buddy Angelo at the *International Inquirer*. He'd just come on duty, ready to crank out tomorrow's morning paper. I said, "Hey, old buddy. How's about digging out some dirt from the morgue for me? You got time?"

"What's in it for me?"

"The story, if and when it breaks. In return for all the dirt you can dig out of the archives on the Livingstone Bank and Trust, including the owner, Livingstone himself. But I especially want to know everything you can find out about his wife—or maybe I should say his deceased wife—Elizabeth. I want to know how she died." Angelo was a credible sort. No point in bothering him with all the details.

"What's the angle?"

"Can't say yet, but stay tuned for a big one."

"Yeah. So he always says. Nuts. We got a special section coming out in the morning edition on that new legislator who bought himself a home in Acapulco with your tax dollars. I only have about 12 hours of work to do on that. But what the hey. If I forget to go to the john and skip dinner, I might be able to squeeze in a couple of minutes to do your work for you. So okay, Weatherby, use and abuse me. I'll try to fax the info to your office before I leave in the morning."

I knew he'd roll both jobs over to his assistant while he sat eating jelly donuts and reading Ezra Pound or Herman Melville or some other piece of literary meat that would take him back to the good old days when he'd planned to write the great American novel and let the newspapers take care of themselves. Not a trace of guilt in this one for me. I said, "I appreciate your sacrifice on my behalf. I'll look forward to seeing the fruits of your labor."

"Right." He hung up.

I managed to run down about three more dead ends on the phone and was getting ready to work on my fourth when the phone rang just as I was picking it up. "Yo," I said. "Weatherby Investigations."

"Weatherby, this is Alphonse Riggatoni. I got a little proposition for you, you got the time."

That stopped me for a minute. "Big Al" Riggatoni was the front-man for the mob's porn shops, strip joints, massage parlors, and other skin trade establishments. He was an old-time pit-bull of a mobster with a thick neck and thicker wits who kept a platoon of equally thick-witted tough guys hanging around him. In return for belonging to the mob and raking off about ten percent of the take, Riggatoni went up front and took all the heat, picked up the mob's money and counted it for them, pretended it was all his action while the real thugs—mostly Carlo "Paisano" Testa—sat in plush offices in the financial district and worried about the stock market, mixed it up with the movie stars and the old-money crowd in the various country clubs, held subdued parties on their yachts, and otherwise pretended to be legit. Riggatoni and I had brushed shoulders a time or two—there's a lot of overlap in organized crime and regular crime, and a shamus sees his share of both worlds. But Riggatoni had all the manpower he needed for anything he wanted to get done. So this was indeed a surprise.

Which I guess Riggatoni knew, because he said, "It ain't gonna get you in trouble with the heat, if that's what you're thinkin', you understand? Thing is, I hear you're a stand-up guy, and I got to thinkin' of you because we sort of got this problem on account of you, I figure you oughta fix it for us, you know what I mean?"

"*I'm* causing *you* problems?"

"Well, you might say you got involved way back when."

"When what?"

"When you put one a my best men in the joint, four or so years back. Thing is, he goes in a worker, he comes out nuttier than a fruitcake. I figure you put him away, it's your fault he goes nuts like that. So I figure you owe me a little favor, you get my drift?"

"What are you talking about?"

"I'm talkin' about you helpin' me out, and maybe nobody gets hurt. I don't want to see this guy go down, we got a lot of history together, I loved that man like a brother. But you know, we got to take care of business, and this guy is hurting us now . . ."

Alarm signals were going off like sirens, but I said, "Who's your problem?"

"How many of us you put in the joint, smart-mouth? Tony the Geek, who else?"

I had to stop for a minute at that. Tony Cacciatore, alias "Tony the Geek," had been one of the most vicious hit men since murder had been incorporated. He'd been traded to the L.A. mob, at his own request, from the New York Genovese crime family some eight or more years ago, about the time of the commission trials and the accompanying breakup of much of the old-time structure of the five

New York Families. His reputation had preceded him to the West Coast. In fact, the word in the streets was that he'd really decided to come West only after he'd pulled the trigger on a certain *consigliere* who had been trying to name himself the new *capo di tutti capi* after the old one had been given 100 years in the slam on a RICO charge. The *consigliere*'s cronies had tried to get even, and Tony had killed an even dozen of them before they'd finally offered to quit fighting, but only if he'd get out of town. Not that he hadn't continued to take care of East Coast business for the West Coast mob.

Word was that Tony could kill a man with the same aplomb most of us would use to dispatch a fly. Word also was that there was nothing too ugly for Tony, that no despicable act of violence would turn his stomach. Hence his nickname, "Tony the Geek," though nobody had ever dared call him that to his face.

The FBI had wanted Tony for a very long time, and I'd inadvertently given him to them, as a side effect of a case I'd been working on some four-and-a-half years ago. It was a fluke; I hadn't even been after Tony, but the evidence I turned up had put Tony away for fifteen years, eligible for parole in four. Some criminal justice system. But then, they'd only been able to try him for breaking and entering, and fifteen years is a stiff penalty for just a B & E. Nevertheless, he'd sworn repeatedly that as soon as he got out of the joint, he'd kill me.

Frankly, I'd lost a little sleep over it during the days of the trial. But as time went by, I quit thinking about him. Four or so years is a long time to hold a grudge, even for someone who is a professional hater. And surely, in the joint, Tony would find other enemies to occupy his time. Trouble was, nobody had bothered to tell me that he'd been paroled.

Riggatoni evidently realized he'd surprised me. He said, "Relax. This guy is *a fesso*. He can't even take care of his own action any more. I told you. He went psycho in the joint, he ain't lookin' for you. Thing is though, he's messin' with our action, we need him stopped. So what I want is, I want you to go over and have a sit-down with him, tell him what's what, before my boys have to clip him. *Capiche?*"

"What makes you think he'd listen to me?"

"You ain't gonna believe this, but he says you're the one who changed his life." I could tell he was talking around a cigar now.

"He says that he went nuts because of me?"

"Look, tell you the truth, we considered puttin' a contract on you back when you got him busted. But thing is, he was goin' to get caught anyhow, it was just as well he cooled his heels in the slam on a B & E as the big one, you get my drift? Cleaned him up, got him off the *babania*. We thought he was straightened out, but then he turns around and goes nuts on us."

"*Babania*? Tony was on heroin?" *That* was a surprise. Junkies are drawn to one another like magnets. As an ex-junkie myself, I thought I'd never again miss anyone who was on the needle. Tony had fooled me. Though, to give myself credit, I'd only really spent time around him during the trial, and he'd been across the courtroom most of the time then.

"You didn't know? Yeah, Tony was fallin' apart on the stuff. What'd ya think? If he was in his right mind, a punk like you couldn't a never laid a hand on him."

I decided to let that one slide. "So now you want me to go have a chat with him?" This had to be some kind of a set-up.

"You're thinkin' it's a set-up, it ain't," Riggatoni said. "It's just that he's been workin' us over some, we got to stop it. I don't want to see Tony get hurt, on the other hand, I ain't gonna let him hurt me, you get my drift?"

"What's he doing?"

"He's messing with my money." The words came out clipped, cold.

"I see . . ."

"Simple little sit-down, there's three bills in it for you, you just let him know to lay off, nothing else, let him know we're serious about this."

I thought about it. Technically, with Elizabeth Livingstone's retainer check uncashable, I was unemployed. And if Tony the Geek was back on the streets, maybe I should see where he was and what he was doing. If Riggatoni wanted to pay me three hundred to do that, why not? And if it was a set-up? I thought about it. If Tony wanted me, he'd come after me sooner or later, and probably sooner. I might as well take the initiative.

"Mail me a check," I said. I knew Riggatoni prided himself on being a man of his word when it came to money. Everyone has to find something to like about themselves. "I'll get over there tonight."

"He ain't home tonight. I already had him checked out. He's down in Tijuana. Just as well. If he was here, he'd be out costin' me money."

I wanted to ask him just how Tony would be doing that, but Riggatoni had so many illegal things going I decided not to meddle. I'd find out soon enough on my own. I said, "Tomorrow, then, if that's what you want."

"That's soon enough. Look, if you want, I can have someone drop the money by."

"The mail's fine. I'll let you know how it went as soon as I check things out."

"Right," Riggatoni grunted. Something was still coiled up tight in his voice. He gave me Tony's address, told me I'd probably find him there about five the next evening, then he hung up.

I had to think about this one. I leaned back in my swivel chair, put my size tens up on my shiny new desk, and surveyed the scene outside my window. Maybe I'd find some answers there.

I'd rented this office when the building was still full of junk bond boiler-room operations, third-rate lawyers, shady insurance salesmen, and other hit-and-run types. The office I occupied had once been the home of a ship-salvaging business, and what had sold me on the lease was not only the price but the fact that I was directly across the street from the piers and five stories up, with a window that wrapped all the way around the corner. That made up for the fact that I was sitting at the edge of skid row, only ten or so blocks from one of the districts where Big Al Riggatoni's peep shows, strip joints, and other dens of iniquity raked in a good chunk of the mob's millions. In fact, the address he'd given me for Tony the Geek was only some twelve blocks away, right on the edge of the red light district. Still, my office wasn't all that bad, especially now that I'd fixed it up. The yuppies had started moving in, and several other offices were also newly renovated, as was the lobby, which looked like a wood-paneled fern bar these days. But the smell of rancid hamburgers and scalding coffee still wafted up from the greasy spoon on the corner when the wind was just right, and I could still sit and watch the sea traffic come and go to all the various ports in the world.

The sea had turned a deep teal blue, and on the horizon it already reflected rust as the sun prepared to set. A couple of ships were putting out to sea, laden with dark green cargo containers destined for exotic places—or so I would dream. A couple of sailboats were returning to port, their sails trimmed as they plowed through the channel at the point where the waters turned deep and inky. I felt a sudden yearning for faraway places with strange sounding names.

But instead of hiring on a freighter and putting out to sea, I turned off the office machinery—careful to leave on the fax for Angelo's transmission. I'd had enough for one day. I turned on the call-forwarding feature so my home phone/answering machine would pick up any messages while I was en route, and then I locked my office, descended in the elevator to the parking garage where I climbed into my ice-gray BMW, then spun rubber out of the parking garage and onto Baker Street, then onto the freeway.

That had all been earlier in the day. And now?

Home was the sailor, home from the sea, in his redwood bungalow, sitting with his shoeless size tens propped up on a Mexican mosaic coffee table, watching the Cable News Network divulge the world's miseries as he savored the burritos, salsa, guacamole, and chips he'd picked up at Sancho Panza's drive-through on his way home.

In spite of the fact that there had been a hurricane in the Philippines and an earthquake in Alaska, a new war in South Africa and the latest exhibitionist rock star had cut another album and bared

32

another part of herself (I hadn't realized anything was left!)—and in spite of the fact that tomorrow I had an unannounced date with a hit man I'd personally put in prison who had vowed to kill me for it . . . in spite of all that, my mind kept returning to the wraith-like woman who'd picked my name out of the phone book (or so she'd said when she phoned) then wandered into my office that morning. I kept thinking about her pain-filled eyes, about her muddied feet, about her colorless husband and her violated grave. Earlier, I'd deliberately neglected to report that grave to the Director of the Chapel of the Flowers, or to the police. Frankly, I wanted to learn a bit more about what I'd fallen into before I brought others in on the problem. It never hurts to minimize the clutter.

But now, I kept thinking about that grave. My mind kept zipping over a dozen possibilities at once. I might have missed a bet by not checking it out more thoroughly. After all, there hadn't been a disintegrated casket flung open there, *a la* Count Dracula. It was still entirely possible that a body rested in that grave, or that Elizabeth Livingstone had never so much as laid eyes on the grave—or that *I'd* never so much as laid eyes on the real Elizabeth Livingstone, for that matter. In fact, that was *extremely* likely. Still—curious though I was, I wasn't about to go out there with a pick and shovel and conduct my own exhumation in order to find out what was still there and what wasn't. Cynical as I am about spooks, I'm not all that fond of dead bodies.

Maybe I'd phone the police and let them check it out for me. Or maybe I could notify the husband. Except that if he really thought I was scamming him with regard to the check, I might be putting myself in a position of having to answer some questions for the police, which didn't sound all that interesting.

Nevertheless, maybe I should phone the husband and come clean with him. Maybe let him handle the little task of checking out the grave for me. That way I would at least know what was and wasn't in it. But the more I thought about Mr. Livingstone, the more certain I was that if I told him I'd just run smack into another granite slab.

Nah, the more I thought about it, the more it seemed like he might even blame me for the desecration.

While I was thinking all this over, I got up and padded into my kitchen to grab a glass of iced tea from the fridge. Just as I opened the freezer door to get some ice cubes, the phone rang. I reached over and picked up the wall extension, cupped it beneath my chin and against my shoulder while I continued trying to pry an ice tray from my overly-frozen freezer, and said, "Yeah?"

There was a hesitation on the other end, then a stilted, precise voice said, "Mr. Weatherby?"

"Speaking." The ice tray came loose and I put it in the sink and stuck a forefinger in my mouth to ease the freezer burn.

"Mr. Weatherby, this is Frank Livingstone. We met this afternoon . . ."

I jerked the finger out of my mouth and forgot about it. "Of course. What can I do for you?"

"Mr. Weatherby, I've just learned from the telephone information service that you're a private investigator. Might that have something to do with your possessing a check from my belated wife?"

"Not a thing," I lied. "Frankly, it's just that business has been bad lately and I've had to resort to extracurricular activities." Let him figure that out however he wanted to.

"Well," he said, "I've given your visit to my home some careful consideration. And I want to inform you that I've decided to honor the five thousand dollar check which you claim was written by my departed wife."

I didn't say a word.

"If you will take the check to the bank tomorrow morning, the teller will give you the cash. Then we'll hopefully have an end to this matter."

"What made you change your mind? Did you hear from her?"

He snapped, "Certainly, sir, you don't suppose I attend those ridiculous meetings."

"Beg your pardon?"

34

He hesitated, and now his voice was wary as he said, "The meetings. The seances. I went once, and that was enough. Those people are conniving charlatans. I used to tell Lizzie . . ."

"Excuse me, sir, but you lost me."

"You asked if I'd heard from my wife. I assumed you meant the seances. How else on earth would I hear from her?"

If I asked too many questions I was going to lose him altogether. Nevertheless, I had to ask the big one: "What seances?"

"You don't know?"

"No. Should I?" This conversation was getting strange.

He cleared his throat, embarrassed. "Forgive me. I thought you'd perhaps talked with Lizzie's brother and sister-in-law. They're what you call trance channelers. They hold seances, where spirits are supposed to speak with, to, and through them. Good heavens, you didn't know? My word, how foolish I must have sounded. But—" He paused. "What *did* you mean when you asked if I'd heard from her?"

I wanted to tell him then. *Mr. Livingstone, I have reason to believe your wife is alive. I base that belief on the fact that she walked into my office this morning and handed me a check for five thousand dollars, even though she dated it ten years ago.* But one of us was dead wrong about the state of his wife's existence, and it if was me I didn't want to put the poor fellow through any unnecessary pain. So I swallowed my eloquence, and said, "Sorry, I wasn't thinking. It's just that you've had such an abrupt about face, I have to wonder what's up."

"That's easily explained," he said. He was sounding testy again. "I want you to cash that check, and then I want you to stay strictly out of my affairs. Is that understood?"

I thought about it. Technically, I would be in the affairs of the person who'd retained me by writing the check. If there was some overlap with his affairs, would that matter? And the fact that he'd decided to buy me off had me more than ever interested. So I said, "Fine by me. I'll drop by the bank in the morning. By the way, what's your brother-in-law's name? Maybe I'll drop by and see him too."

"Mr. Weatherby, you just agreed to stay out of my affairs."

"It's just that I have a friend who's interested in psychic phenomena."

"Frankly, Mr. Weatherby, I don't want to be responsible for introducing anybody to that poppycock."

"Whatever you say." I'd have to dig the name out by myself.

"Thank you for understanding. I do hope we've resolved our little conflict." His voice was icy now, yet somehow I sensed that was an affectation. This man spent a lot of time hiding his true feelings.

"The situation works for me," I said.

"Then I'll bid you goodnight, Mr. Weatherby. And, oh yes, I'd still like to know. Where on earth *did* you get that check with my wife's imprint?"

"Afraid I'll have to plead the Fifth, Mr. Livingstone. Tendency to incriminate myself, and all that." If we'd been face to face, I'd have given him a conspiratorial wink.

"Yes, well, I suppose it doesn't matter all that much. But I would like to say one more thing. This little game of yours will only work once, so don't try it again, even if you've somehow gotten your hands on more of my wife's blank checks. I do not want Lizzie's name dragged through scandal, that's the only reason I'm paying you off this time. And now I must say goodnight."

He hung up. And left me thinking again. If he thought I'd forged the check, why did he want me to cash it? Did he know his wife was alive? Did he at least suspect it? He was definitely sending me mixed signals. Was he really hoping to stop me from prying into his life, or did he want to get me more interested? Maybe that was it, maybe he realized I'd gotten that check from someone, and he wanted to know who but couldn't ask too many questions without giving away answers. Maybe he just wanted to whet my interest enough so I'd turn over some rocks and we could both see what would skitter out from under them. And maybe he'd killed his wife himself, and didn't want anyone prying into the decade-old crime, even if it meant having to pay someone like me to lay off. The possibilities were endless . . .

I chunked ice into my glass, poured in the tea, then went back into my living room. I leaned back on my sofa and put up my feet again, then turned off the lamp. I was gazing down the black cut of the canyon with its wisps of lash-like foliage, down at the endless twinkling lights of Dreamland.

Livingstone had been lying to me about a couple of things, had been feeding me information about others—like maybe the seances. No need for him to tell me all that, and something had rung false about his explanation. Oh well, so he'd lied. I'd lied to him about a couple of things, too.

I was suddenly weary all the way through to my bones: tired of lies, tired of deceit, tired of living a life of alienation, the Big Tough Private Eye who solved everyone's problems and sent them all cozy to bed, then came home and sat by himself and gazed down at the cold city lights.

I thought about the ethereal woman who'd come to my office that morning. Where was she? Was she back in her grave, taking her night's rest before haunting the city once again in daylight? Or was she real flesh and blood, sleeping on a park bench someplace, or perhaps locked in the attic of her husband's huge mansion?

I thought again about the grave and about everything else that had happened that day. There was a lie there somewhere. An evil, insidious, monstrous lie. I'd felt its foul, fetid breath when I'd "strolled" through the ectoplasmic mist in the cemetery that afternoon, I had felt its tentacles move in and around me, flexing, waiting for a chance to strike and blind and suffocate.

And this lie was draining me. Already, one day back on the job, I was mentally and physically burnt out again.

Great going, old kid.

Maybe it was time for me to get out of the business. Do something sane.

Trouble with being a P.I. was people hired me for just one thing: to stave off the evil tentacles of all the little lies that belonged, somehow, to the big lie, the one big lie, that always lay behind it all, festering there. They hired me to fight and destroy the lies, to uproot the decay, to get at the truth that would take the stench away from their lives. But where was truth for me? Most of the time I didn't think about my own truth. But tonight thoughts of life and death were very much with me. And for some reason the cynicism and loneliness in my life came crashing down around me. Good work, Weatherby. Dig through the sewage of everyone else's lives so you don't have to accept the fact of the emptiness in your own. But—what was the point of it all?

I missed Christine. She hadn't been back in the country for three months now, and the last time she'd been here we'd only had a few hours together. Why did she have to trek off around the world in her own version of the battle between good and evil? Why was she the only woman I'd known for years who could get me interested? Because she was gone all the time? Was I really that antisocial? No, I wanted to phone her, hear her sweet, lucid voice telling me that she was fine, that she and her fellow drug enforcement agents had busted up another South American drug cartel, that she'd be home on the next redeye from Washington, D.C. But she was in Colombia, somewhere, or maybe back in Miami, I didn't know. She only told me enough to let me guess.

I suddenly felt the urge to get up, step into my loafers, and drive down to the Canyon Bar and Grill, a place where I'd once found enough anesthesia to block out the feelings of emptiness that had come home with me from Vietnam, then stayed until the booze and drugs had come closer to killing me than had any of the VC's knives and bombs and bullets.

I'd stopped drinking and using drugs nine years ago when a good friend had finally picked me up off skid row and dried me out in a clinic he'd founded to help Vietnam vets. For a year or so there, the jones—that urge to return to my addiction—had hit me hard and I'd had all I could do to stay dry. But gradually, over the years, the desire had died. Only to awaken with a full and inexplicable fury on this night, as I sat and thought about the ultimate emptiness of life. Why not, Weatherby? Why not drive down and have just one? Bend elbows with some people, what better place to find some instant company?

I polished off the iced tea, clicked off the TV with the remote, and stood up. I looked out over the city again. Somewhere someone was being murdered, on some street a woman or a child was being beaten or raped or insidiously and persistently abused; somewhere the money men and movie stars were living their brittle and empty lives creating illusions for the rest of us, pumping their bodies full of drugs and silicone in an attempt to stave off time, playing their games of seduction in order to affirm their own desirability and self-worth. Somewhere else, teenage gang members were shooting and stabbing each other and innocent bystanders over drug money and imagined insults and general frustration and rage. At that very minute, crack babies and AIDS babies were being born. Welfare mothers were trying to figure out how to feed their kids or how to get their old men out of jail. Yep, the "masses of men" were out there leading their "lives of quiet desperation." And I was up here, looking down on them, doing exactly the same. I mean, what was *the point*?

You know the saying. Life's a joke . . . and then you die.

Some city. Some life.

Suddenly, I was disgusted with myself. And here, up in the canyon, a thirty-eight-year-old private investigator sits all alone giving himself a pity party. Get a grip, Weatherby. This is it, all there is. You either make it work, or you lose it.

I thought once again about the bar, but the strongest part of the urge had passed. I went into my bedroom, threw on a black jersey sweatsuit with red racing stripes, then went out the front door, leaving the lights on as a beacon for my return. I went for a long night run, up the road that led to the isolated part of the canyon, beneath the arc of beauty that was the cold, indifferent night sky.

When I got home my mind was clear again. I took a hot shower and fell asleep the instant I hit the bed.

Chapter

SIX

It's not for nothing they call Los Angeles "La La Land." It's a land where the first idol is the Almighty Dollar, the second is the Silicone Breast. After that, you can find someone to join you in worshipping just about anything or anyone you want, from the followers of the Reverend Sun Myung Moon (who claims to be "god" and who brainwashes his "Moonies" into working the streets in various ways to keep him in spending money); to the followers of the Eastern mystic, Sai Baba (who also claims to be "god"), with his mystical "healing" smoke (it comes in myriad colors and can be purchased in most novelty shops under the title—guess what?—*Mystical Smoke*); to Witches, Pagans, Druids, Warlocks, Satanists, and numerous varieties thereof; to Shirley MacLaine (who claims to be "god") and the other New Agers with their fat wallets and their transcendental lingo and their insipid explanations for reality and their transcendental excuses for keeping their wallets fat; to the Hare Krishnas with their saffron robes, their tambourines, and their shell-shocked eyes; to all the various pseudo-religions like Synanon, est, Scientology, and all the rest. Quite a few people even still worship the original Judeo-Christian God and His resurrected Son, Jesus Christ. But even under that umbrella, there are a lot of bogus "Christians" who are simply worshipping the Almighty Dollar under a different label. A lot of people rake in a lot of lucre by professing to have the ear of "God"—

whoever that might be—and it isn't easy to tell the real believers from the fakes. On the other hand, from what I've seen of life on this planet, maybe none of them are for real.

I mean, it would be nice if a benevolent God who had created all this and ruled over it did indeed exist, in spite of the fact that some evil being had caused the world to be deeply flawed. But from where I sat and the way things looked to me, the whole thing just didn't add up. After I'd gotten sober, and my life was suddenly empty of even the booze and drugs, I'd gone looking for God for a while. I'd spent a lot of time reading various things, including my Bible, and I'd spent a lot more time sitting in synagogues, temples, and churches. But they'd all been emptier than my own soul, so I finally concluded that I was right in the first place, that it was all nothing more than an elegant and beautiful myth.

I'd reached the 3000 block of Alcatraz Street. It was solid skid row, overlaid by a colorful bazaar of every huckster and phoney-baloney religion known to man. The action started as soon as I turned the corner, with a flock of some fifteen Hare Krishnas swaying and shaking their tambourines, pounding their drums and chanting in the million decibel range, their glazed-eyed children right beside them, mesmerized from the noise while still in the womb. They'd camped in front of a bar with its door open, and the bleary eyed patrons had evidently decided to fight back, because the juke box was blaring an equally loud version of Willie Nelson's "Mamas, Don't Let Your Babies Grow Up to be Cowboys." Ravi Shankar meets Nashville. I hit the gas pedal and cruised on past.

Next came a storefront that advertised Scientology as "The Answer to the Problems of the Universe," and offered me a free personality test. Strange pickings down here for that group—they usually plunder the money crowd. There were a few more bars, a couple of which I'd frequented in my drinking days. Then I cruised past a "botanica," one of the new Latino folk medicine shops that had sprouted up in the midst of all the other pagan capitalism. Here you could buy a curse

41

or get rid of one, buy an evil spirit or—hopefully—get rid of one. I found a parking space in front of yet another bar and then continued my journey on foot. I passed a pawn shop or two and a shop called "The Dark Side" that advertised Voodoo and Witchcraft paraphernalia (with various icons, candles, and other Santeria supplies featured in the window display, along with a bunch of hash bhangs, heavy metal T-shirts, swastikas and military knives), then I passed a greasy spoon with a fly-specked window, and then a storefront that advertised: PSYCHIC READER, PALMS READ, TAROT CARDS, NO WAITING, ROCK BOTTOM PRICES.

Finally I came to 3099. It was a huge one-time warehouse now painted white, although the fresh paint was already pitted from the salt air. The several oblong windows in the front were covered with whitewash, and a freshly painted six-foot-high white cross stood atop the roof. Above the double-wide front door a white canvas banner proclaimed in red: JESUS CARES ABOUT YOU. On the second story, a neat gold neon sign told me I'd just arrived at the GRACE OF THE SHEPHERD MISSION. This was where Tony Cacciatore lived?

On second thought, it figured. If Tony was on the outs with Riggatoni, he was an outlaw. There wasn't much mob business he could muck about in without getting his hand caught in the wringer sooner or later, and there was probably still enough heat on him that he didn't want to get back into his old line of work right away, especially as a free-lancer. So he'd obviously just stepped into a totally different occupation—some type of scam. I wondered how he was working his operation, how much loot he could be skimming in down here. Probably not much as a straight Bible-thumper. The real money there was in the fancy churches. So—? The mission had to be a front for something else, and most likely something that was driving Big Al Riggatoni nuts, because it was messing up the mob's action somehow. Bootleg wine? Nah. The legitimate stuff was about as cheap as you could sell it, and more plentiful than water these days. Drugs? Now there was a possibility. It had been several generations since skid row had held only winos and other alcoholics. But then again, there was a lot of money in drugs, and most of it wasn't on skid row. No matter what I thought about the way Tony had made his money, he had been a big-time operator, pulling in fifty to a hundred thousand a job. Nah, not drugs, at least not in the small-time way he could operate here.

I opened the front door and stepped into a large sanctuary. The floor was a lightly varnished wood, the walls were plain white, with a few palm plants along the outside aisles to give the place some color. There were oblong windows on one side of the room, facing an alley, and faint sunlight filtered through. Rows of gray metal folding chairs had been set up as pews, enough to hold about 500 people. At the far end was an elevated platform, and on that were several short, U-shaped rows of the same folding chairs. In front of them was a pulpit with a small wooden cross carved on the front, complete with microphone. Amplifiers stood to each side. On the floor in front of the platform was a simple wooden altar that ran the width of the room. Someone had set out boxes of tissue at intervals along the varnished wood. That figured. The people who ended up in these places had a lot to cry about.

A dark-haired girl in Levis and a loose pink shirt sat at an old black baby grand, up on the platform. She hadn't heard me come in, and she was intent on practicing her music, though it wasn't amplified, and I could barely hear it from the front door. She was a beginner, faltering, hitting many wrong notes, but I surprised myself by recognizing the song. A few of the words even whisped through my mind. "Earnestly, tenderly, Jesus is calling . . . calling, 'Oh, Sinner, come home.'" I felt a sudden small ache. My grandmother had sung that song. She'd done her best to raise me after my mother died in childbirth, and in the warm Los Angeles evenings she sat on her front porch and listened to the radio, to evangelists from Texas and other Bible Belt states filling the airwaves with hard lessons and gospel music from a simpler and nobler generation—whose values you had to respect, whether or not you shared their beliefs. I shook off the nostalgia and walked toward the platform.

The girl saw me from the corner of her eye and stopped playing. She just lifted her hands up, folded them primly and put them in her lap, then turned and waited with an immense and innocent patience till I reached her. I could see now that she was about eighteen, exceptionally pretty, with large luminous dark eyes. Hispanic. Her pink cotton blouse was crisply ironed. It had tiny red hearts on it. Her bleached Levis were spotlessly clean and had not a wrinkle, her dark hair shined from brushing, and beyond that, there was still something fresh-scrubbed about her, something I couldn't quite put my finger on. As I stepped up on the platform beside her, she offered me a shy smile. Her complexion was a pale golden brown, her teeth were white and even.

"Sorry to barge in like this," I said. "I'm looking for Tony Cacciatore. He around?"

She looked bewildered, then looked at the floor.

"You speak English?"

She nodded, then looked square at me. And it was only then that I realized something was wrong. Her eyes were overly innocent, maybe even a little vacant.

I tried again, speaking slowly and evenly. "Do you know Tony? Tony Cacciatore?" If she could play the piano, surely she could understand that much.

A door banged behind me, and I turned, to see a young ebony-colored man about my height coming down the aisle. He had short-cropped hair, and he wore a red-and-white striped tank-top that showed the muscles of a body-builder. He watched me like he might be expecting trouble.

I stepped down from the platform and extended my hand. "I'm Artie Weatherby," I said.

As he shook my hand he sized me up. I evidently passed muster, because he suddenly gave me a million kilowatt smile. "Shelby

Knight," he said. "I help out here." There was something calm and clear in his brown eyes. I felt like I was looking into a pond as clean and refreshing as spring rain.

"I'm here to see Tony Cacciatore," I said. "He around?"

"Tony's in the kitchen. 'Bout time to set up for the soup line. Come on, I'll show you." He turned to the girl. "You okay, Rosa?"

"Si. I can almost play it now. You want to hear?" Her words came slowly.

"You betcha, Sunshine. Be right back." He turned and gave me another grin, then motioned for me to follow him.

He led me back down the aisle and around the side to where a double-wide door opened into another section of the one-time ware-house. The smells of chili and burgers and brewing coffee wafted through the air, overpowering the other, soured scents of the neighborhood. He whisked me toward the door, gestured for me to enter, then turned and headed back toward the "church" section of the building.

I stepped into the kitchen. Two men—one middle-aged and black with grizzled stubble on his chin but otherwise neat and clean, the other a hickory-colored Mexican about seventy-five years old and also freshly spit-shined—toiled over industrial sized stoves, stirring huge iron pots of chili. Burgers sizzled on a giant grill. To my left a wide door opened into a dining room, where several more people were busily placing white butcher's paper over long wooden tables. Paper plates and cups, giant, battered coffee urns, and plastic utensils were all in abundance.

I stopped beside the chubby white woman who was frying the burgers. She had a pretty face and a sweating brow. I asked, "You know where I can find Tony Cacciatore?"

She gave me a sweet but distracted smile, then wiped her hair back with her arm, careful to stay sanitary, and nodded. "In there."

I followed her nod into the dining room, and there he was, slightly hidden from view by a jutting corner. Tony Cacciatore. His face was clean-shaven, though a dark shadow had already crept through. His jet-black hair was cropped short—no more fifty dollar haircuts—and there was a lot more gray than I remembered. His crooked Julius Caesar nose was still the same and he still had the same square, jutting jawline. In place of his thousand dollar suits, he was wearing nondescript gray slacks and a white, short-sleeved dress shirt open at the throat, a mat of curly black hair peeking over the collar. He'd spent some time in the prison gym, because he was thicker and more muscular than I remembered. A young, thin white man with pale-brown hair was standing beside him, and they were deep in conversation. The man wore a T-shirt that said, "The Way of the Rock," and he held a video camera in one hand, casually aimed toward the floor.

As I approached, Cacciatore noticed me coming and turned with a mild interest in his eyes—most of his attention was still on whatever the young man was saying—and then his eyes narrowed as he recognized me, and he broke off the conversation and stepped toward me. As I nodded a greeting, I casually brushed my hand across my jacket to make sure the .38 snub-nosed Chief Special I'd packed inside my shoulder holster was there and ready.

But Tony surprised me by grinning widely, an expression that would have been obscene on his face the last time I'd seen him. Now, it looked right at home. And either he'd been taking acting lessons while he was in the joint, or he was genuinely happy to see me, because as he came toward me the grin turned into a wide, beaming smile.

I extended my hand for a shake, but he came right past it and wrapped his arms around me in a bear hug that almost cracked a rib before I extracted myself. I hid my surprise, stepped back, readjusted my shoulder holster by pretending to straighten my jacket, and said, "How you doin', pal? I heard you got out. Is there someplace we can talk?"

Tony was looking square at me, and I suddenly remembered the last time we'd been eyeball to eyeball. I'd just testified against him in court, and he'd been on his way past me, an armed guard on each side as they took him to the cellblock after his conviction. As he reached me, he suddenly stopped dead—the strength of his fury stopping short both guards as well—and he looked at me. Just looked. And there had been a black, boiling rage in his eyes that had almost stopped my heart with its intensity. He hadn't said a word. He didn't have to. There was something living and serpentine and cosmically evil in that look.

And now that same man was looking at me again, but these eyes were warm brown and filled with joy. He was really glad to see me! I instinctively responded to the welcome and relaxed for an instant, but then I quickly remembered Riggatoni's words. *He's gone nuts.*

So—was he going to smile one minute and rip my face off the next? Easy, Weatherby. Smile or no smile, this was still Tony Caccia-tore, the man who had committed more violence in his fifty-odd years than had Al Capone.

But he was still looking at me, like a mother looks at a son just come home from the war. Nothing else, no sudden moves, not a trace of anger, not even the macho strutting and posturing that had marked his behavior in the old days.

Tony broke past my discomfort. "What brings you down here? You working a case?" Without waiting for an answer, he gestured with a typically Italian expansiveness, and asked, "How you like my mission? Ain't this something? Hey, I know you never thought you'd see me runnin' a church!" He gave me another happy grin that smoothed all the hard lines out of his olive face.

"Actually," I said, "as a matter of fact, Big Al phoned me. We need to talk."

The smile fell from his face. He looked at me in a different way, measuring me, and then he beckoned and turned toward a door in the rear of the room, saying, "Big Al. Yeah. I figured I'd hear from him before long."

Tony led me through a door and into a small, dilapidated office. There was a scarred wooden desk, and several steel bookcases held stacks of Bibles, tracts, and worn hymnals. He nodded toward another of the steel folding chairs, where I planted myself as he sat down on the one behind his desk, then said, "So what's up?" For a second there, he sounded like his old self: the New York Sicilian accent, the small shrug of the shoulders, the cold blink.

"What's up is that Big Al is thinking about taking you out. He says you're messing with his money and asked me to tell you to stop or you're gonna get clipped. His exact words."

Tony thought about that for a moment, and then his face broke into another and even wider grin. "He's gonna clip me? I'm really getting to him that bad?"

I was puzzled. Tony had been a professional hit man long enough to take these things seriously. The evil he'd seen and done was anyone's guess, but one thing was for sure, no professional laughed when the mob put out a contract on him—or even threatened to. Tony of all people should know that the mob carried out its threats, no matter how long it took, no matter what it cost. Had he really gone nuts from his time in the slam?

I said, "Look, if Big Al had a contract out on me, I'd do some serious thinking about what I was doing to make him mad. And if it was something I could give up without giving up my soul, I'd be a changed man in a New York second."

"I can't," Tony said, still beaming beatifically. What was with this guy?

"Can't what?"

"Can't quit without giving up my soul."

"Can't quit what?"

He laughed out loud at that. "Can't quit what it is that I'm doing that's bugging Big Al."

"Which is?" I was getting a little confused.

"You got a minute?"

"All the time in the world."

"Then come on, I got something to show you."

48

He led me back through the kitchen, out the alley door where street people were already lining up for the evening meal, then down the alley. We cut through one of the gin joints, past rows of winos leaning over their cheap shots of wine, then out the front door, and just like that we were in the next block, on Canal Street, right in the middle of the skin district, weak neon glittering out invitations to indulge in all the sins of the flesh, prostitutes wobbling back and forth in search of prey, showing the signs of heavy drugs as well as their too-high heels. Pimps loitered here and there, keeping a dark eye on their meal tickets—"meat," they called them. We walked past the human tragedy and toward a building featuring a movie marquee that advertised "ADULT MOVIES" replete with several titles that disgusted even me.

"Big Al's joint," Tony said, nodding toward the theater. Then he stopped, tilting his head the other way, nodding now toward a cluster of people who stood in front of the theater entrance. "My people," he said.

The people stood to one side so as not to bump into any of the theater patrons, but they were totally conspicuous. Most of them were young. One was a Vietnamese boy about eighteen, and beside him were a couple of black women who looked like they might have spent some time in the streets themselves. There was a hulking black man who must have been a pimp in a former life—or formerly in this one—an elderly Hispanic woman dressed like she bought her clothes on Rodeo Drive, and several other assorted characters. About half of them held video cameras, and they were calmly filming everything that went on around the entrance to the theater, including an occasional shot of the cashier who sat behind the glassed-in window. She was making a big point of indifference by reading a paperback book. She had silver, upswept hair, a thin, librarian's face, and the look of a pure prude. You just never know . . .

While we were approaching the action, a black Bentley with dark-tinted windows purred around the corner, started to pull to the curb, but then the inhabitants evidently saw what was going on because the chauffeur slammed his pedal to the metal and went lurching and screeching down the block. Somebody didn't want his ugly tastes to hit the evening news. And even though a huge sign informed the public that the main feature was beginning in less than ten minutes, not a soul was going into or out of the theater.

I turned to Tony. "This is what's bothering Riggatoni?"

He chuckled. "To the tune of at least a hundred grand a week."

"From *this* theater?" He had to be putting me on.

"Nah, no way. We're messin' up his action all over town. This is just one little sting."

"You just videotape the customers?"

"Right. Ain't no way they're goin' in there if their wives and neighbors and bosses can find out."

"So why are you doing this? You know how Big Al is with money. You used to take care of the people who were stupid enough to get between him and a dollar, and now you're doing this for amusement?"

He looked at me like *I* had gone nuts. "Amusement? You got to be kidding. I'm serious as a grave about this."

"But why?"

He studied me, frowning now. "I would of figured you of all people would know. Man, when I was with the mob, I used to hear about you. The time you took down that pimp who beat those three hookers to death? And ain't you the man used to talk about getting rid of all the big-time drug dealers and pimps so's the small-fry could straighten themselves out?"

I looked at the floor, embarrassed. "I used to be a bit of a crusader, I guess. The drugs and the booze almost took me out, you know, and I came back hard."

"Yeah, the booze and the dope almost got me too. Not that I didn't deserve it. But a lot happened while I was in the slam. Couple a years ago, these people come around talking about different ways to live, you know. You ever hear about being born again?"

He threw me for a second with that one. Maybe it was the atmosphere. A couple of wilted "ladies of the evening" stood behind him so that as I looked at him, they were in my line of vision. They were propped up against a telephone pole, trying their best to lure me in by batting their bloodshot eyes. They were a little distracting, and the pimp who stood at the edge of the alley behind them, menacing them with his body language so they wouldn't give up before they'd earned him his next fix, was equally annoying.

"Born again? You mean like on TV? All those people who yell and cry about love and honesty and then turn around and spend their evenings down here?"

His face tightened ever-so-slightly, but it was as if he'd stepped back and was studying me in a new light. And then he said, "It ain't like that, you know. Oh sure, Christians are still human. They mess up now and then, and when the famous ones do, they get the headlines for years, same as the mob. But it ain't really like that."

Christian? Was Tony Cacciatore trying to tell me that he'd become a Christian?

I tried to hedge my way back out of this conversation. "I'm not really interested in religion, one way or another. I'm just delivering a message."

He gave me a cynical grin that held a hint of his old self, and said, "I used to be an altar boy. Wanted to be a priest, but my old man wouldn't stand for it."

"So, you've—uh—gotten religious again, or what?" If there was anything his mission *didn't* look like, it was a Catholic church.

"Nah, I gave up on all that religious junk. Bad as any other kind of habit, even drugs. No, I mean born again. Spiritual rebirth. Really becoming a brand new person inside the same old shell of a body."

"Sounds a little metaphysical to me."

"You never heard of it?" He was looking at me with a tiny bit of sympathy now, as if he'd suddenly realized I was one of the under-privileged.

So I decided to admit to what I knew. "I had a grandmother who believed in all that," I said lamely. I was uncomfortable like never before. In fact, this Tony was so different from the one I'd known and expected to see again that I could easily see why Big Al Riggatoni thought he'd gone off the deep end. And maybe he had. "My grandmother raised me after my mother was killed," I explained. "I went to Sunday school. I learned about Jesus Christ and salvation and all of that, but that was a long time ago."

"What happened to your old man, he take a lam?"

"He got my mother pregnant then went to fight in Korea and never came back."

"Ah, like that," he said. Then he turned as one of the picketers waved and caught his eye. "That's Wendy," he said. "Used to work for Big Al in the massage parlor down the street before we got her off the smack." He gave her a high-five then started toward her. I lamely followed along. I knew the mean streets, had been in and out of them all my life one way or another, but I wasn't following what was happening here at all.

Wendy was a soft blonde woman about twenty-five. She wore a sunshine yellow blouse with little orange Happy Faces on it and loose, baggy white pants. There were bronze bracelets on her wrists and white plastic clasps held her shoulder-length hair back on both sides. No make-up, cobalt blue eyes. A few pock-marks from an early case of acne that didn't do a thing to detract from her looks. As we approached, she reached up to shove a stray strand of hair back, and I saw her arms. Scarred in the pits, scarred at the wrist, scarred in every place anyone could possibly reach a vein with a needle. She had been a heavy user. She gave Tony a casual hug, then said in a worried voice, "That man who runs the theater was back. He said he was going to 'work us over' if we didn't stop picketing. I thought you should know."

"Yeah," Tony said. "Look. Maybe you should take a few days off." He glanced at me and said, "I got word that things might get a little heavy."

"Can't we just report him to the police?"

Tony graced her with a smile. When his face wrinkled, it showed an ancient knife-scar in the crease of his cheek. "It ain't gonna happen that way. If the cops could do it, it woulda already got done. Now I want you and the resta the people who used to have anything to do with Big Al's operations to lay low for a while. Just till we get this thing straightened out. You're the ones he'd likely come for first."

"I'm not afraid of Big Al. He's already done his worst to me. We're the ones he really messed up. It's our battle."

"It's God's battle, and the point is to win it. Which we're close to doin'. Politicians are having a new hearing up in Sacramento about obscenity. Couple more months, if everything goes right, the political heat will shut the worst a these joints down for us. In the meantime, we got to keep the pressure on without getting anyone hurt."

Wendy looked like she wanted to argue some more, but she finally said, "I'll pray about it."

"Good enough for me," Tony said. He glanced at his cheap Timex. The last time I'd seen him look at a wristwatch, it had been a twenty-thousand-dollar gold Rolex. "Got to roll," he said. "Soup's on."

We cut back through the gin mill—everybody seemed to know Tony and most of them nodded greetings for the second time—and then we were back in the alley beside the mission, then through the kitchen and into the dining room, where the folding chairs beside the paper-covered tables were already almost full. There were all kinds of people, and of every color: women with small children, winos who could barely sit up straight, a couple of very skinny men who either had AIDS or I was totally missing my bet, a few people of various types in wheelchairs—the general flotsam and jetsam of the city known as The Big Smog, a.k.a. La La Land. Tony grabbed my arm in a friendly way, and said, "You eat yet?"

"I couldn't," I said, automatically pulling back. There had been a time some ten or so years ago when I would have been more at home here than in my own living room. And that was the problem. Being in skid row was bringing back a flood of memories, all of them bad. On the other hand, the chili smelled delicious, the burgers looked plump and tasty, and the place was spotlessly clean. Tony, sensing my indecision, held on to my arm and pulled me with him. "Come on. You don't want the food, you don't have to eat, but we got more to say to each other so you ain't leavin' yet. I got to say the grace, then we can go back to my office and work some more on this thing with Big Al."

He stood at the head of the first and longest table, I sat at his right. All the accoutrements of a meal had been placed at intervals atop the snow-white butcher's paper. Salt and pepper shakers, huge platters of hamburger buns, pickles and lettuce and tomatoes, ketchup and mustard dispensers, plastic knives, forks and soup spoons, paper plates and bowls, everything but the food itself. As Tony took his place, the ocean of noise in the room suddenly stopped. Every head turned to look at him.

Still standing, he said, "Those of you who are new here, I want you to know, these doors are always open to you. You ain't got a place to sleep and we ain't got any more room in the dorms upstairs, we'll put a mat out in the chapel. You ain't got food, we serve two squares a day here, breakfast at six A.M. and dinner right now. And you ain't got any hope in your life, you're sick and dying, you're hooked on junk or coke or crack or sex, even just booze, I got a solution for you for that, too.

"Most a you here know my story, and I know you're hungry and the food smells good, but you got to learn how to feed your souls too, or you ain't never gonna make it. Time was when I fed my belly pretty good, pretty regular. Best joints in Las Vegas, L.A., Honolulu, New York City, even Rome and Palermo, they all knew me, I been to them all, they treated me like a king. But my soul was dyin' because I didn't know nothin' about the Bread of Life, didn't know nothin' about the Living Water.

"Oh, I grew up in the Catholic church, same as a lot a you. But I didn't know the answers, in spite of it. My life got so jammed up, I didn't care if I lived or died, didn't care if anyone else lived or died neither. Fact is, I'd rather seen most of them dead, I'd learned to hate so hard. But then this man"—and he jerked his thumb at me—"he come along, and he got me busted. That's right, got the cops to come and cuff me, take me away, even stood up in court and testified against me, and they locked me up and threw away the key. And even in the joint, wasn't long before I was considered the toughest man there. I'm not braggin', mind you. Things you got to do in the joint to get that kind of reputation, if I told you now you'd never be able to eat. But I done 'em. I was in hell, I wanted to take everyone else there with me.

"Then one day this other man come into the prison and told his story, how he used to be a big man in the government, got busted for helpin' Nixon's boys double-deal the competition, went to prison and got 'born again.' He told us what it was about and told us how it had changed him into a new man. And at first I was like some a you must be right now, I was thinkin', *Man, another scam and I already seen enough to last me a lifetime.* But somethin' happened when I was listenin' to him talk, and I felt myself sort a meltin' inside, somethin' dead shivered a little and tried to sit up. Then he told us that the only way to get straightened out was to accept the fact that Jesus Christ is the only begotten Son of God, that He came to earth and died so we could have eternal life, that if we wanted to we could talk right to Him right then, ask Him to help and change our lives—and man, I got feelin' funny. I got to thinkin', *hey, maybe all that stuff I learned in church when I was a kid has something to it. Maybe it really is possible to talk to the One who created this whole universe, me included, maybe He really does care what happens to me.*

"And before I knew it, I was down on my face bawlin' like a kid, and something happened that changed me—totally changed me, just like someone had taken out the bad and pumped in the good. And my life changed. We call it bein' born again.

"And now today, I want to tell you, your lives can change too. All that misery, all that suffering, the drugs, the destructive sex, anything you got that's eatin' you up, you can just say, 'Lord Jesus, I want you to take this from me. I don't like the way I live anymore. I know I've sinned because sin is anything that separates me from You, and I know I've somehow got separated. Take me back to be a part of your family, Jesus, and save my soul so I can live right while I'm here on earth and when I die I can come live with You for eternity. You say that, you don't have to even say it out loud, though if you want to that's probably the best way. But the important thing is you say it. You can 'confess' Him after you get the hang of it all. Now, let's all bow our heads and talk to the One Who made you and me, Who made this table we're sittin' in front of and the food that's about to be set on it, Who made the stars and the moon and all the rest of everything."

He bowed his head, and most of the people at the table did likewise, though a few sat looking coldly defiant. After I'd checked that out, I bowed my head too, though more out of respect for Tony's speech than because I really believed I was going to talk to anybody, especially God.

Tony said, "Lord Jesus, we come before you now in our need. We don't know where we came from, most a us don't know where we're goin'. All we know is this is a tough planet you put us on, and we can't go it alone. So we ask you to forgive us of sin, Lord. Take away anythin' that separates us from You and bring us all close to You, so we can live like You wanted us to in the first place. We thank you for this food that's about to be served, and we thank you for these brothers and sisters who are good enough to share our table. In Jesus' name, Amen."

People looked up, and a few had tears in their eyes. And then several people in white cooks' aprons brought in the huge pots of chili on heavy rolling carts, another couple came right behind them with the burgers, and everyone fell to chowing down, myself included. Tony grinned like a delighted child when I held my soup bowl out for a serving of chili, and as I accepted a hamburger, he kept saying, "Take two, take two, there's plenty, and the crowd's light tonight."

As I fed my face, I watched Tony out of the corner of my eye. In spite of his little speech—in spite of the fact that it had touched me deeply in some strange way—I still wasn't sure I trusted him. But he sat there, looking fondly now and again at the people sharing his meal. Then he caught me looking at him. He was just shoving a spoonful of the excellent chili into his mouth, and he had to chew then swallow, wipe his mouth with a paper napkin, and then he said, "You think it's a scam, don't you?"

"Tell you the truth, Tony, I don't know what to think."

He picked up his second hamburger and began to dress the bun: first a light coating of ketchup, then a touch of mustard, a thick wedge of onion, a couple of layers of lettuce, hold the tomatoes. He speared a couple of sweet pickles from a plate that was going past, put them on his paper plate, then said, "You will. You keep your mind open, God's going to show you what's right and what ain't. And it'll happen in God's own time and when you least expect it, just like it happened with me."

"Maybe," I said. But I really didn't think so.

Chapter

───────SEVEN───────

By six o'clock, Sepulveda Boulevard was more or less thinned of gridlock, so after I left Tony Cacciatore's mission I drove west, planning to take the scenic route almost to the airport where I'd catch the freeway again, then I'd exit, as I had yesterday, at Sunset. That would take me back through Bel Air, near to Frank Livingstone's estate, and then on toward the plushest part of Pacific Palisades. I was going to meet Mrs. Elizabeth Livingstone's brother.

As I drove, I thought about my day. I'd slept late, then awakened thinking about Frank Livingstone's phone call. About ten, I'd stopped by the bank, where the five thousand dollar check was indeed cashed, by the same wimp with the paisley bow-tie who'd taken so much pleasure in my consternation the previous day. It had felt good, watching him count out those hundreds, almost licking his chops and having a little trouble letting go.

I'd arrived at my office just before noon, to find that Angelo had also kept his promise. He'd faxed me everything he could find about the Livingstone family. There was so much paper that my fax machine was buried and another page would have jammed it.

It had taken me a couple of hours to wade through Angelo's information and reaffirm my impression that the Livingstones were a weird lot of people. That done, I'd then phoned the University's Agronomics lab to see if there was any information about my soil samples. The grad student who had examined them was out, but she'd left a note with the person who answered the phone. The soil from my office carpet and the soil from Elizabeth Livingstone's cemetery plot were a match. Which meant something. But I was a long way from knowing what.

At two o'clock, I'd ordered a take-out Veggie Burger on rye from the health food restaurant down the street. I'd taken it back to my office, and while eating lunch I'd thought some more about the soil samples, trying to understand why anyone would go to the trouble of making a grave look violated, or would go to the trouble of salting their bared feet with cemetery mud. I even found myself wondering again if I had indeed been visited by the ghost of Elizabeth Livingstone.

At about six-fifteen, as I was still cruising along toward Pacific Palisades, my mental recap of my day was interrupted by a bus that made a hard right in front of me, causing me to hit my brakes, lean on my horn, and leave a lot of rubber on the pavement. The bus driver didn't even turn to look at me, but I gave him a piece of my mind anyway. And then I was back in the traffic, and then back in the recent past, back at work, thinking now about the talk I'd just had with Tony Cacciatore, wondering what he and his people thought about ghosts. Maybe I should have asked.

I thought some more about Tony, wondering if Riggatoni would really kill him, trying to figure out why Tony took the threat so lightly, and then my mind wandered back, again, to the earlier part of my day. Over my Veggie Burger lunch, I'd finally come to the same dead end with the Elizabeth-Livingstone-as-ghost line of thinking as I had the previous day. So I'd again looked at the yellowed newspaper obits she'd left in the envelope, had rewound the tape recording of our conversation and listened to it yet again, and had then decided to take a stab at the problem from a different angle. I'd called information and gotten the phone number of the Foundation for the Enhancement of the Human Spirit, the place to which Elizabeth Livingstone's obituary had directed all the flower money. It had turned out to be a place in Pasadena, about a half hour's drive from the address I'd been given for Tony Cacciatore. I'd stopped there before I delivered Big Al Riggatoni's message to Tony. I wanted to take a real look at the Foundation, rather than take whoever had answered the phone's word for the fact that it was a nonprofit organization whose purpose was to "perfect the human experience"— whatever that meant.

The Foundation's housing had turned out to be a huge snow-white Victorian mansion with white shingles on the roof and brown gingerbread trim. Snazzy. It was set in the middle of about an acre of trees and flower beds, and the topaz blue ponds had real live ducks—white, of course—floating around on them. Everything was immaculately groomed and it would have passed for somebody's home except for the fact that part of the front lawn had been paved over for parking and a four-foot-wide sign beside the front walkway explained, in gingerbread-brown curlicue against a snow-white background, that this was the place.

A small placard on the front door said PLEASE ENTER, so I did and found myself in what had once been a teakwood paneled parlor but was now a reception area. An elegantly slender woman with a swan-like neck sat behind an antique table-desk, her ankles crossed to display perfectly proportioned legs sheathed in beige nylons that were a perfect match for her beige designer dress with its shawl collar and her beige high-heeled pumps. Her hair had been bleached to platinum and it was pulled severely back in a bun. On her ears were two tiny gold earrings and she wore a gold wedding band and a tiny gold watch that I bet had cost as much as my car. Though she was carefully made up, she had a surprisingly plain face. She gave me a practiced smile as I entered and said, "Yes?" It was the same voice I'd heard on the phone.

"My name is Artie Weatherby." I'd rehearsed my speech a couple of times on my way up the drive. "I'm working on an article for the Sunday news supplement about the older houses in Pasadena. My editor is especially interested in this one. Can you give me some history?" I pulled out a pencil, licked the tip, and poised it over a steno pad I'd found under my car seat.

"Of course," she said. She braced herself as if she had to do this about ten times a day. "This home was built by Elmer Cardwell in 1889," she began.

The name made me sit up straight and listen harder.

"Mr. Cardwell built a fortune in shipping—by rail, sea, and land. His son inherited the fortune and brought a bride home from Boston. This house was their home too. The dwelling stayed in the family until just over ten years ago, and then their daughter—Elmer's granddaughter—inherited it. She married well and kindly donated this estate to the Foundation. This house is in the historic register, if you'd like more precise information on architecture and so on." She stifled a little yawn.

"And what exactly is the Foundation?" I asked, still scribbling on my pad.

The question woke her up. First, she sat up straighter. Then her two tiny plucked eyebrows came close together in a frown of concentration and the animation drove the blandness from her face. "Did you phone earlier?"

"I did. I needed to know if this was a business or a private residence or what before I came out. I suppose I could have learned more by phone, but I needed to see the house, you understand. There will be photographs and all that . . ."

"Oh, of course. How nice. Well—the Foundation is a little hard to explain to those outside it." She was like a doting mother now, talking about her children. "As I said, our purpose is to perfect the human experience, both physical and spiritual. We're strictly nonprofit. Everyone who works here in any capacity is a volunteer. My husband, for instance, is a psychiatrist—Doctor Vance, of the Vance Institute—and yet even *I* volunteer here for Mondays and Wednesdays."

I nodded. "Could you be more specific about what you mean by 'perfecting the human experience'?"

She actually shifted positions at that, uncrossing her legs and leaning forward over the desk. She began nervously toying with a thin wisp of hair that had trailed down her neck, rolling it in her fingers, curling it, the light reflecting off her gold wedding band, her neck even more swan-like as she craned it to one side to better meet my gaze. "Well . . . that's difficult," she said. "You see, there are so many levels a person has to go through before they can reach pure enlightenment. But I can say that we here at the Foundation attempt to understand the deeper meanings of life. There are so many dimensions we have yet to explore. We need to seek out and go where others haven't gone, to boldly meet the future . . ."

The words sounded familiar for a minute, and then I realized they were more or less a paraphrase of the introduction to "Star Trek." I raised my eyebrows; she deciphered that as accelerated interest, and she started talking again.

"We sponsor various workshops, and underwrite certain experiments. We're interested in conventional psychology and psychiatry, of course, but we're most interested in the cutting edge of psychological research. Phenomena such as ESP, trance channeling, spiritualism, the reality of connecting with our 'Higher Selves.'"

I nodded sagely and scribbled furiously.

"We believe the world is in transition, from the old age to the new. Spirit creates matter, matter in turn creates spirit, and we are creating ourselves and our own new age. Even right now as we speak, it's coming into being." The fine, keen light of the fanatic had found its way into her wide hazel eyes. "We believe that it's time for a new consciousness, a new global ethic," she said. "Spiritual values are at the basis of secular change. We here at the Foundation are at the forefront of both."

"I see. And could you translate that into a more practical explanation for our readers?"

She gazed at me, thinking, and then she said, "Actually, I can't. I don't think there's a simpler way to say it. Spirit creates matter, we create spirit. We create everything and most of all our own realities. You see, the old traditional values had it that we couldn't do much about reality to change it, that we had to rely totally upon a being we called God to make any difference at all in our lives. These new values put the responsibility right where it ought to lie, with each and every one of us."

I could see I was getting nowhere and I'd found a comfortable place to stop, so I stood and thanked her, telling her I had all I needed for the moment, then I promised to come back soon with a photographer and excused myself. And then, at four-thirty on the button, I left the lush greenery of that section of Pasadena and returned to the soot and grime and smog of the city. Finally, I made my way down to skid row, where I'd gotten a different kind of lesson in spiritual and physical wisdom from none other than one-time hit-man, Tony Cacciatore.

What a day.

And it wasn't over yet. Because I was on my way to the home of Mr. Caspar Cardwell, brother of the late Elizabeth Ann Livingstone, born Cardwell. That's right, Cardwell. My wraith-like client was the same woman who had inherited three-quarters of her mother's fortune—an amount running into the double-digit millions according to the newspaper clippings Angelo had faxed to me. Upon receiving her inheritance, my client must have immediately donated the family home—worth at least five million, considering the amount of land and its location—to the Foundation for the Enhancement of the Human Spirit, which information had somehow *not* made its way into Angelo's paper, at least not into the newspaper clippings that Angelo had faxed me, because it had been a pure surprise to me. A pox upon Angelo and his paper, for missing that important piece of information.

No more than six weeks after Elizabeth's 80-year-old mother had died—and after Elizabeth had made the donation of the house and surrounding land—she had tripped on the upstairs carpet of her own home, the one in Bel Air—or so one of Angelo's news clippings said—and had fallen down the spiral staircase to her death. Or so said Dr. Gates (said the newspaper), the medical examiner who had presided over the autopsy.

I wanted badly to talk to Dr. Gates, worse now that I'd read the news clippings and knew the alleged cause of the alleged death. Even the most casual reader of mystery novels knows that shoving someone down a spiral staircase is an easy and untraceable way to commit a murder. I needed to learn why Dr. Gates had determined it was an accident. But Dr. Gates was going to be a hard one to get my hands on, I could see that already. And right at that moment I had other felons to fry.

Chapter

————EIGHT————

The sun had dipped behind the slate-blue sea, but there was still some daylight. I was already well past the pleasant greenery of the old Will Rogers estate—now a historic park—and well past UCLA. I was watching the streetlights blink on as I headed straight for the ocean when I saw the sign that said: "Coasthaven Highway, Oceanside Scenic Route." The road cut away from the main drag and meandered along the seashore, in the general direction of both the mountains and Malibu. I followed it past open beach and an occasional estate till I reached a dead end where the darkening surf rolled in on one side and the mountains jutted up on the other, and there, behind heavy iron fencing, I saw the Cardwell estate through a gap in the surrounding greenery. I pulled onto the shoulder, backed up, and stopped to have a gander.

I'd seen photographs of the house in a write-up in the magazine, *L.A. Architecture*, and also in a couple of other publications, but it was far more impressive in person. Vanessa Hammond, the silent film star, had built the beginnings of this present estate back in the 1920's, and then had come the scandal that involved her and the head of her studio, you know, the one where she abandoned the house and moved to Europe then lived out her days in seclusion and the studio head shot himself and his wife. The mansion had gone through the hands of some dozen other Hollywood luminaries since then, each adding his or her own touch to the architecture and grounds.

Now, the mansion was a pale pink vision of opulence against the twilight of the lavender-blue sky and the deep purple cut of the mountains. The pale, warm, golden-yellow of artificial light filled the porticos and arches and washed the columned patios; it filled the panes in the French doors and the Mediterranean-style windows, both upstairs and down; it fell in puddles along the numerous trellises and ponds. The swimming pool was bottom-lit and lavender-blue. More concealed lighting defined the wide stone steps that led from the pool up to the front patio. All throughout the yard were pink pastiches of flowerbeds, neatly pruned shrubs, and an occasional stone bench, all of it lit as if by pale moonlight. The thick surrounding olive trees were furry purple-black with the coming night, as was the rest of the unlit shrubbery. The effect was breath-taking.

A wine-colored Morgan—you know, the handmade, customized English job that looks like the richer big brother of an MG—came screaming down the road behind me, causing me to break my gaze and wonder if I was far enough onto the shoulder to avoid catastrophe. But the woman behind the wheel whipped to the left just in time to miss my fender, then gave me a cheerful little wave as she sped past. I caught a glimpse of her rear license plate, a vanity job bearing the name ARIEL, and then she braked and turned into the driveway some twenty yards beyond my parking place. I looked back at the house, at the people now, several of them strolling through the grounds, more of them in silhouette against the light in various places within. The Cardwells were giving a party.

I fired up the old gray Beamer, edged back onto the roadway, and followed the Morgan through the gate. Nobody stopped me. I pulled up and parked beside a pale green Ferrari. There were about a dozen other expensive cars also parked on the flagstoned courtyard beside the garages at the side of the house. I climbed out of my car, went around to the front, then walked blithely up the pink front steps, just one of the crowd.

Music filtered through the house, something with a lot of strings and occasional Eastern Indian cymbals. The front door opened into a large room with a cathedral ceiling that continued the pink stone. The floors were white Italian marble. The decorator had also continued the outdoor foliage just enough to enhance the room: ferns, potted palms, even a huge fuchsia bougainvillea plant in the corner, in full raucous bloom. There was a white marble fireplace, and just beyond that was a wet-bar where about half of the thirty-or-so people had congregated.

Everyone was dressed in casual chic: pant suits in rich silks and polished cottons for the women, light-colored summer slacks and short-sleeved shirts for the men. Several types of expensive California wine bottles showed their necks above silver ice buckets that had been set on the bar, and next to the bar a long buffet table clad in pink linen had been laid out. I walked over and picked up one of the white, silver-trimmed china plates, grabbed a heavy silver fork, and acted hungry. Everybody was busy, nobody tried to stop me.

There were tiny broiled shrimp, curried crab legs, oysters, clams and slices of abalone, all spread out over cracked ice. Various cocktail sauces. All types of sushi, salads, vegetable garnishes, cuts of meat, and sandwich bread. Several silver chafing dishes held hot hors d'oeuvres: tiny quiches, escargot in garlic-butter, sauteed mushrooms, what looked like cocktail wienies in barbecue sauce, and several other things I didn't recognize.

I filled a plate about half full—Tony's chili and burgers were still with me—then found a seat out on the balcony, within sight of the room but far enough from the action so I could scope it all out before I went to work.

The people seemed to range in age from about twenty-five to the late sixties, a few even older. I recognized one motion picture producer, Tod Montgomery. He was sleek and tanned, his hair a sheening silver and his body as trim and fit as a thirty-year-old's. He'd done a few really good movies in the seventies and early eighties, then had suddenly flopped over into horror films—Stephen King type stuff. Financially, he'd been overwhelmingly successful with the horror flicks, but his critics had gone sour on him. He didn't look like it had cost him much sleep. He was smiling at a young red-headed woman with an athletic body that she'd clad in a billowy silk pant-suit with a wild green-and-mauve pattern. She was flirting back, and they were both enjoying the game. She arched her head back, and I recognized the profile from the wine-colored Morgan that had preceded me through the gate. But she didn't look like an Ariel, she looked like a Ginger or a Jill.

I'd just dabbed a shrimp in some sauce and popped it into my mouth, ready to continue my anthropological study of the California rich, when a petite woman sailed through the door and bore down on me. She was wearing white cotton designer slacks and a matching loose-fitted jacket over a red silk shirt. Her hair was pulled back and held in place by a red scarf with a gold harlequin pattern, which was in turn held by a large gold brooch studded with various-colored crystals. She was probably nearing sixty, though it's hard to tell here in The Land of the Plastic Surgeons. Her short beige-white hair had that spun-sugar quality that comes from years of bleaching and tinting. Cut crystal earrings dangled from her ears, a large white crystal pendant in an obelisk-shaped gold setting hung from a thick gold chain around her neck, and wide gold bangles with hieroglyphic etchings adorned her wrists. Expensive but fussy. Her nose had a scalpel-like perfection to it, her lips were full and painted deep red, her eyes were black and hard as lumps of coal. She offered me a wide, chilly smile, then sat down on the edge of a pink rattan chair a few feet from me. Her toe was tap, tap, tapping against the marble tiles. Medium-heeled white sling-back sandals. Panty hose covering long red-polished toenails. Her voice was thin and birdlike, if you know any birds that can't sing, as she said, "And you must be . . . ?"

"Artie Weatherby. I invited myself."

She pursed her lips, then looked downward and blinked hard, showing displeasure. "I had wondered," she said. "I didn't recall having seen you before."

I gave her my most charming grin. "Actually," I said, "The redhead invited me. I was sitting out on the road admiring the surf when she thundered by and beckoned."

She frowned for real this time and a little flame licked at those coal-black eyes.

"You know Ariel," I lied. "She and I are old friends."

She thought about that for a minute, then she raised her shrill voice, and called, "Ariel?"

The redhead tossed her head, throwing her mane in the opposite direction from where it had been, and looked.

"Could you come out here for a moment, dear?"

The redhead strolled out to where we sat, sizing me up as she came, interest kindling in her honey-colored eyes. I could see now that there was a dusting of freckles across the bridge of her nose. The film producer stood twirling the stem of his wine glass in his hand and looking annoyed. When Ariel reached us, she said, "Yes, Mother?"

"Dear, do you know this man? I'm afraid perhaps the security people aren't paying attention again . . ."

Mischief flashed through Ariel's eyes, and she surprised me by saying, "Of course, Mother." I stood up, trying to act polite, and she immediately linked her arm through mine and turned her charm on me. "I'm glad you could find us, darling."

Mother looked confused and frustrated for a moment, then she said to Ariel, "Really, dear, I wish you'd let me know these things. You know I don't want to be rude to your friends." Which was a lie bigger than any I'd told for weeks because everything in her body language said she wanted to be more than rude to me. But I'm a nice guy, so I let it slide.

The woman turned and went back into the house to mix with her guests. Ariel sat down in the chair her mother had vacated, kicked off her shoes, and put her bared feet up on the rattan ottoman with its pillowed top, looked at her toes and wriggled them, then smiled at me. "Gate crasher, huh?"

"That was me in the BMW," I said. "You never should have waved."

"And other than a Peeping Tom, you are—?"

"Artie Weatherby, at your service." I gave her the sit-down version of a little bow. She looked even better up close. "And you're . . ."

"Ariel Cardwell, of course."

I feigned surprise. "This is your house?"

"My parents'. I'm in and out. I keep a place in town, too."

"Which part of which town, and when can we have dinner?"

She laughed. "I have a combination bookstore and aerobics studio just off Rodeo Drive," she said. "I've redone a lovely little apartment upstairs from it."

"And when you're not reading and exercising and rescuing gate-crashers, what do you do?"

"Mostly, I'm into acting. *And* I'm engaged to be engaged to Tod Montgomery," she said, "and here he comes. Act like we're old friends, darling. I went to UCLA. So did you."

As a matter of fact I really had, so when she introduced me as an old college friend I didn't feel too guilty. Montgomery barely acknowledged my existence as he pulled her to her feet, handed over her shoes, and towed her gently but firmly away, saying, "Mildred and Michael just got back from the crop circles. The new ones in Germany. They're showing photographs, it's incredible what's going on there, UFO sightings by the score, I'm really thinking we should insert it into the script. . ."

She smiled up at him, little-girl like, but as they went through the door she looked past him and back at me. She winked, gave me a little wave of her fingers, and mouthed, *Have fun.*

I sat there and studied the crowd a bit longer till I'd decided where I wanted to edge in. There were several good choices, from a doll-faced woman in her early eighties who seemed to be the liveliest person there; to a pouting fat man who sat in the corner and sulked, waiting to be noticed; to a lithe, fiftyish brunette who seemed to be cruising every man in sight. I finally decided on a plump, fortyish Beverly Hills blonde in black pajama pants and a white satin halter top who oozed insecurity. Even while I watched, she'd swilled down several glasses of white wine, and now she was loquaciously talking to a paunchy bald man in white flannel slacks and blue-and-white striped dress shirt with white suspenders. He wore gold-rimmed spectacles and had apparently done a lot to adopt the facial expressions of Sigmund Freud. He was either a shrink, or I wasn't a detective, and she was either getting his services free of charge, or I was going blind.

Just as I'd expected, he eagerly excused himself the moment I injected myself into the conversation. As he hurried away, I said to the woman, "Nice buffet. Did you try the shrimp?"

She looked blankly at me, interrupted as she'd been in mid-stream of consciousness, and then she looked forlornly after him, making a helpless little gesture with her hands as if to draw him back, and then she looked again at me and evidently decided I was all she had left. She said, "I can't eat much, you know. Since Jason died I haven't had an appetite."

I felt bad for a minute. "Sorry," I said, "I hadn't realized . . . but I'm afraid I didn't know Jason."

"My husband," she said impatiently. "He died in 1979, you surely heard? Jason Jordan? He was producing a movie for Huston Hathaway and had one lined up with Tod Montgomery when he had that stroke—it was simply awful. But surely you heard? It was in all the papers, *Variety* gave it a whole page. No matter what I do, I simply can't get over it."

"I should say not," I said. I mean, that's a long time to not be able to eat. Not that I believed she had—or should I say hadn't. There was too much extra meat straining against her seams.

"Who are *you* going to talk to tonight?" she asked.

"Beg your pardon?"

"I just *live* for these chances to speak with Jason," she said. "I don't know what I'd *do* otherwise. He gives me all my financial advice and he's been an absolute angel about making sure I don't get involved with someone who'd try to use me."

It was taking me a while to catch up, but I was beginning to understand. "You mean Jason, your dead husband?"

"Oh, yes, isn't it wonderful? I'm so grateful to Cassie and Caspar for opening this channel for me . . ."

"We're going to be talking to the dead tonight?"

She graced me with a sweet, patient look. "Didn't you know? That's why we're all here. We're going to have the most wonderful seance, right at the stroke of ten."

I checked my watch. Quarter till. I asked, "Is this a regular thing?"

"More or less. Of course, Cassie's Spirit Guide tells her when to have the sessions. His name is Quetz. He's millions of years old, the most ancient of all the Guides. Cassie is very lucky he's chosen her as his channel. Several of the others have been trying to get him, but he simply won't leave Cassie."

She could have been talking about house help, the way she said it. I said, "You mean Cassandra Cardwell, right?"

She gave me a "where have you been" look. "Of course, Cassie." She pasted on an ethereal smile and gazed into the distance. "*My* guide is an extraterrestrial named Thur. He's only 35,000 years old. I've been channelling him for about a year now. Of course, he can't cross-channel transcendants like Quetz can, since he hasn't yet metamorphosed to that purely spiritual realm."

"And which realm is that?" Might as well learn what I could.

"Why, Step Five, of course. What the unenlightened call death, though we realize it's merely another and transcendent phase of the same existence we have here on earth. It's all cyclical, you know."

"Let me see if I have this straight," I said, trying to understand this new language. "Your, uh, guide is from another planet?"

She gave me a puzzled look. "Of course."

"And he talks to you?"

"Well, and through me, though I can't channel at will like some can. I have to be in the right transmagnetic axis, with the right spirit-friends around me. Not like Cassie, who can channel Quetz wherever she is. Why, once he started talking through her at a dinner for the governor, she was so amused when we explained later what she'd said."

"Which was?"

"Oh, she was just explaining what needed to be done about the water shortage here. Things that the ancients know all about, but unenlightened people just won't listen, you know. They simply ruin everything. Why, I can't even water my lawn any more, it's turning absolutely brown, and the taxes I pay are simply outrageous . . ."

At that moment another woman stepped forward and gushed, "Sofia, love, did you know that *Femura* is here?"

"No!" Sofia's faded blue eyes went wide. "My stars, she hasn't been here for simply *ages* . . ."

"She's been in Tibet. She only just returned."

"Pardon me," I interrupted, "but is this Femura another spirit guide or something? And just how many ages since you've seen her?" This was starting to get wacky.

The newcomer shot me a scathing look. "Femura *Riley*, of course. The author of *The Path, The Power and The Psychic.* I assume you're not familiar with her book?"

"Guilty as charged."

Her nostrils narrowed and she snorted, appalled by my ignorance. "You neophytes do not take this seriously enough. I really think Cassie should start being more selective in her invitations, we do need to separate ourselves from the common people. No one should be allowed here until they've reached at least Stage Three." She sniffed, turned, and sailed away, leaving me with . . .

"Forgive her," Sofia said. "She's a writer, TV scripts, they just canceled her series."

"Which was?"

"'Blood Brothers.' The vampire thing. I didn't care for it myself, but we must be open minded about all phases of the unknown . . ."

I was wondering if we could expect any vampires to visit along with the extraterrestrials and spirit guides when suddenly the lights went low and the music stopped. Everyone froze in place, and the air was suddenly charged. Even the breeze from the sea stopped, as if on cue, and then, after that silent moment, the sound of temple bells filled the air, growing louder, the people listening yet still motionless, though they gave the impression of high animation. And then the temple bells mellowed into wind chimes, and then a new slow song with sitars and a heavy, hypnotic Indian drumbeat played through the sound system—also the source of the chimes and bells, I realized now. Wine glasses were swiftly set down, clothing rustled as people moved purposefully toward a wide doorway in the back of the room. A sudden swift wind blew in from the sea, carrying salt-scent and stirring the potted palms and other leaves, rushing the people to their destiny.

I joined the crowd, and was washed into a sunken room done in deep mauves and grays that looked out over a more spacious and private patio, beyond which were the jutting black mountains and the endless night sky and stars. The patio was dark, though moonlight showed several white marble sculptures, one a life-sized replica of the Greek goddess Aphrodite, another of the ancient Babylonian goddess Astarte. Other statues carved in gray stone were only outlines against the relative darkness. One was a pot-bellied Buddha, another was Kali the Hindu goddess of death, another was Shiva the Hindu god of both destruction and procreation, with his many angular arms. There were several others that I didn't recognize, though some of them had the blunt look of pre-Columbian art, and I thought I saw a large Christian crucifix in a distant corner. A strange assortment of carvings. And in the center, at the back of the patio, was something larger than any of the others, hulking, about ten feet high, something carved in stone yet unetched by the faint moonlight. It looked like a faintly man-shaped sculpture, maybe something begun but not yet finished, something still clothed in its dark drapery.

The floor of this room was thickly carpeted in velvety charcoal gray. There were pale gray satin floor pillows to sit on beside black-lacquered Japanese tables, each of which held a large cut-crystal candy dish filled with small crystals: agates, amethysts, black obsidian, bloodstone, citrine, jasper, quartz—they were all there, in various sizes, polished and unpolished, back-lit by some sort of small light fixture set into the back of each dish, something like they do at museum exhibits. As we entered, each person scooped up several stones and either held them or put them in pockets. I did likewise, selecting an especially pretty rose quartz and then a smoky one. I figured they were some kind of party favors.

The room also held several deep black sofas, and at the far end of the room, dead center, was a padded knee-high object about six feet long that I thought at first was a sort of bench, until I realized it was an altar. Behind it was a more elegant version of Tony Cacciatore's elevated platform. Sure enough, there was a four-foot-high, black obsidian, obelisk-shaped pulpit of sorts standing there. It must have cost a fortune. On both sides, in the corners of the platform, were rough-hewn geodes, one at least four feet across and six feet high, glittering with encrustations of amethyst, another equally large and made from shimmering white, gold-flecked quartz.

There was no one at the pulpit, but the crowd had fallen breathlessly silent, as if waiting for something portentous. I continued my examination of the strange room.

Across the front of the platform, at about one-foot intervals, were foot-high pre-Columbian statues. One was a head, the stone face sunken, the nose sharp, the eye sockets empty, the back of the skull a crude depiction of an eagles face and feathers. This was the ancient Eagle Warrior. Next to it sat the square-shouldered Aztec earth goddess Coatlicue, this version far more intricate than the one I'd seen in Frank Livingstone's collection. There was a polychrome pottery version of Tepeyollotl, the jaguar god who symbolized the dark forces inside the earth, the painted reds, rusts, and greens still apparent after centuries in the soil. Beside him was a statue of another jaguar god, this one Tezcatlipoca, yet another sun who was also the god of the night sky, this statue etched with carved stars intended to resemble the jaguar's spots. In the very center of the artworks was a gold carving I didn't recognize from my two years of Anthro. Two gods with serpentine features were intertwined, their various limbs entangled, both faces flat and dead, the mouths opened in fixed horror. To the right of this was the depiction of Tlatoc, the great god of rain and vegetation, and there were three more carvings, all of plain stone. If these were all real, the collection was priceless.

On the wall at the back of the narrow platform were professional oil portraits, all but one of them carefully arranged so that none was higher or lower than the others. There was Buddha again, with his portly belly; Muhammed, with his white robes and scowling Arab features; Krishna was there, along with several saintly faces I didn't recognize; Astarte again, and Aphrodite. And then came a portrait of Jesus Christ, the one with the gold halo, with Jesus looking up, the one you see in a lot of Anglo-Saxon churches. Definitely not a picture of someone powerful enough to help His Father create a supernova, I thought, much less the Andromeda Nebula, or a black hole, or even a rose or a newborn child—unless He was in deep cover when He sat for the picture. But then that's just one man's opinion. And to tell you the truth, I don't know how you could get all that down in a portrait anyway.

In the center of all these portraits, a full three feet above the others so there was no mistaking rank, was a painting so colorful that it immediately drew the eye and became the center of the room. It was done in rich primary colors: a life-sized angelic-looking man with a beautiful, light-filled face, wearing robes in various blues and golds, holding a staff, with a round radius of light shining behind his head. "Light-bearer," read the inscription beneath the painting. I studied it, looked away, then did a double-take. The painting was worthy of Salvador Dali, though it wasn't in the strictest surrealist style. But it offered two pictures at once, in a gestalt-like surprise, one the inversion of the other. One was the "Light-bearer," while the second and more subtle form was a man-sized multi-colored serpent, sitting upright on a coiled tail, its face half human and violently evil, a wide collar of multi-colored feathers surrounding its neck. It was hideous, but more than that, it was somewhat familiar. I'd seen a stone carving with a similar face in Frank Livingstone's quarters only yesterday, in his collection of pre-Columbian art.

Quetzalcoatl. The Feathered Serpent. The Toltec/Aztec deity associated with the evening star, the symbol of death and resurrection and ancient human sacrifice. It was Quetz, all right, but more than him, too.

A tall, angular man with thinning gray hair came into the room. He wore a black robe trimmed in gold thread, and he had a priestly air about him. I felt my eyes bug out, and I moved closer to the front of the room where he was greeting people, shaking a hand here and there. And the closer I got to him, the more resemblance he bore to Elizabeth Ann Livingstone—the frail features, the wide forehead, the deep green eyes. Except whereas on her—or on her ghost—the features added up to beauty, on him they added up to an effete and unpleasantly frail look. This had to be her brother, Caspar Cardwell.

People were sitting on the sofas, others relaxed on the floor pillows. Ariel and Tod Montgomery were sitting together in a corner of the room, their attention now focused on Cardwell. "Mother" had come in too. She saw me and scowled, started to move toward me, then glanced in Ariel's direction, apparently changed her mind, then pursed her lips and got back to business.

Welcome to a seance California style. There was no table, no pitch blackness, no place to sit in a circle and hold hands while someone in a hidden place made rapping noises and surreptitiously elevated the table; no place for someone to secrete himself and project ectoplasmic images on walls and windows as the "medium" kept the suckers busy with a terrifying spiel. No place to run, no place to hide.

And something had changed about the people around me, too. Their faces all wore similar expressions, images of a strange, dark hunger.

Caspar stepped up behind the altar and stood beneath the various pictures. A hush fell across the room. He began a thin, high hum. The others joined in, eyes closed, hands folded. I figured they were meditating. After a moment of that, he began to intone: "I am the chakra of the violet light, I am the chakra of the violet light . . ."

The others chanted right along with him.

After about two minutes of that, he suddenly stopped short, the others stopping right with him, and he intoned: "We are here . . ."

"We are here . . ." intoned the people, right on cue.

"To seek our higher power," said Cardwell.

"To seek our higher power," the people murmured.

A chill seemed to fall across the room. Or maybe it was just me. I wasn't enjoying this.

"We seek the higher power that comes from Ometeotl, from Great Narayama, the dweller of the highest heavens."

"The dweller of the highest heavens," the people repeated.

The lights went even dimmer, though everyone was still visible, and then the room was infused with a dim, violet-colored light.

Cassie Cardwell had been seated on a sofa to the right of the "altar," and now she stood, stiffly. Everyone stared expectantly at her, including her husband.

"I heed your call to the Creators," she said, and her voice was a deep, resonant basso, totally unlike her birdlike chirp. I felt the hairs on the back of my neck stand straight up. The sickly sweet burn of incense filled the room, and with it came the impression that it was covering over something decayed.

"I, Quetzalcoatl, come." She seemed to be in a trance, her face was stiff, her eyes unseeing, her body held in an unnatural posture now. "I come at the bidding of Great Narayama, of Ometeotl the Heavenly Pair who dwell in the Highest Heavens. I come to enlighten you." There was nothing at all amusing about this deep masculine voice coming out of this woman with her fussy clothes and perfectly tied-back hair. Her face seemed to have withered up even as she spoke.

I glanced around me. The blonde named Sofia was staring with mouth partly opened, enraptured, while several women near to her seemed to be chanting something under their breaths. I turned and saw Ariel watching with narrowed, somehow angry eyes, while Montgomery had a loopy half-smile on his face, the look of someone stoned on phenobarb or demerol.

Cassie was talking again. The deep voice coming out of her mouth was all the more incongruous because of her diminutive size. "Awaken," Quetz said through Cassie's mouth. "I am the one you've been waiting for, the one who can heal all your pain. Cleanse your minds of all else, for I offer you the wisdom of the ages. I, Quetzalcoatl, more ancient than this galaxy, more ancient than thought itself. I am all things, and I come in many guises. I span all. I span that which you call life, and that which you call death, I transcend all. Speak, make known your needs. I come to guide you to the highest reality. Follow me."

Cassie suddenly opened her glazed eyes and focused on the Beverly Hills blonde. "You," she said in the basso voice. "Your needs are deep. Open your third eye, come to me, I will grant your wish."

Sofia stood, and said in a faltering voice, "Jason? Please, I need to talk to my husband." She sounded like a wife breaking in by phone on a board meeting.

"Sofia? Babe?" Cassie's voice had changed yet again, though still masculine, this time to the pure Hollywood abrasion of a wheeler-dealer. "Glad you could make it. Look, I been meanin' to talk to you about the IBM deal. The stocks are going to take a dive, you're betting the farm. Buy Disney instead, they got a great movie in the pipeline, stocks set to go up nearly double."

Sofia's voice was timid. "That's not what I need to talk to you about, Jason. It's—it's about taking the Fourth Step. Do you think I'm ready? I mean, it brings me so much closer to you, but it's such a risk . . ."

Cassie's eyebrows furrowed as Jason thought that over. Then Cassie's mouth and Jason's voice said, "No problem, Babe. You're ready. Sell the house in Lake Arrowhead, that'll finance your deal. Forget the Disney stocks, just sell IBM and put that cash in, too. You already know what to do with the house in Malibu. Look, got to go now, we'll do lunch next week if Cassie's available."

Sofia sat back with a grateful look on her face, as Cassie seemed to come out of a daze. "Jason spoke?" Cassie asked, looking around as if trying to see him.

"Yes, thank you," Sofia said. She was dabbing at her eyes with a handkerchief as she sat back down. She looked old and somewhat frightened. I felt sorry for her and felt a sudden surge of hatred toward these people who were so obviously duping her out of her money.

A couple of others talked to dearly departed loved ones. One mother was weeping openly as she chatted with a teenaged daughter who had died the year before of a drug overdose. The "spirit" of the teenaged girl was informing her mother that she wouldn't be available after the first of the year because the spirits who were mentoring her had decided it was time for her to be reincarnated; they were sending her back as a spiritual regression specialist so she could serve enough people to make a personal move up the karmic ladder. Her mother approved of that and made the girl promise to find some way to let her know when she had landed back on Planet Earth. I felt a little sick at the glibness of the conversation and the exploitation of the mother's grief.

As far as I was concerned, the seance, though unnerving, seemed to be mostly hype. I was, however, having some trouble understanding how Cassie Cardwell did the bit with her voice. But in this "new age" of new electronics, nothing was impossible. There had to be a way, because she was doing it. As far as the advice, I could see already that a disproportionate amount of it had to do with money, and in a lot of instances the spirit advisor, whoever it might be, had come right out and suggested that certain sums of money should go to the Foundation for the Enhancement of the Human Spirit in return for certain spiritual concessions.

For a few minutes, I ruminated on the image of Elizabeth Livingstone sitting here in this peculiar room while someone channeled spiritual advice—maybe from her newly deceased mother—for her to give up her five-million-dollar family home. Somebody had a nice scam going here, though I was a long way from seeing exactly how it worked.

But there was something going on here that I *didn't* understand, too. Mostly it was the way this thing made me feel. *Creepy* was the word. Rats in the attic, mold in the basement, not quite clean.

My mind had wandered away from a chat between a woman named Doddie and her father who had "taken the Fifth Step," and I hadn't noticed that they were through talking and the spot-light had shifted to me. But sure enough, Cassie Cardwell was looking square at me, eyes still hot and glazed, and she said in her Quetz-voice, "There is a newcomer among us, a seeker of truth in this new age of wisdom. You are lonely, newcomer. Your life is without purpose. But your quest has brought you here. Come to me, new follower. In what way do you wish to heighten your knowledge of the cosmos? To whom do you wish to speak?"

I felt my eyes go narrow, and I did a once-over of the room, feeling superior by now to these nitwits who were really believing they were talking to the dead. And I suppose my attitude erupted, because I heard myself say, "Let's see if we can wake up Elizabeth."

"A last name please?" Cassie's eyes seemed to have some of her own intelligence in them now.

"I'm talking about your sister-in-law. Elizabeth Ann Livingstone."

I heard Cassie's breath suck in, saw her husband's face turn into white beef jerky. The lights came up high—I figured a hidden switch somewhere near the obsidian pulpit—and everyone turned to stare at me, all faces wearing identical masks of hostility.

The party was over. I'd ended it. Good thing I was used to taking a lot of flak because I could see I was about to get some more.

But I wasn't prepared for the unholy shriek that suddenly went up from behind me. I jerked around to see Sofia standing, her body hunched, her hands claw-like. She was pointing dead at me with a forefinger hooked like a talon, tipped in blood-red polish, and her eyes were pools of hatred. "Nooooo," she wailed. My blood ran as cold as if she'd been a genuine manifestation of pure ectoplasm.

"Leave me alone!" And suddenly the voice was that same raspy whisper as had come from the mouth of the woman who had arrived at my office the previous morning to hire me to find a murderer. For the first time, I knew the meaning of the phrase *made my flesh crawl.*

"Leave meeeeee," she wailed. Then, thrashing with her arms, as if she were fighting off something terrible, she shrieked, "Be gone, be gone, leave me to my peace and eternal rest . . ."

This was too much for the movies now. I stood upright, strode to the woman, and grabbed her by the shoulders. "What do you know about this?" I asked, shaking her. "Where's Elizabeth?"

"*I* am Elizabeth. I speak to you," wailed the eerily raspy voice. "I wish only to rest. Go away, leave me be, let me be, go away . . ."

The woman had a thin line of drool coming out of the corner of her mouth now and her eyes were wide open, but vacant. And then, as I shook her, her eyes slowly slid back to consciousness and her slack face tightened back to normal. And then she was herself, looking at me, asking in a panic, "What happened?"

"Your guess is as good as mine," I said. I didn't know whether she had acted the scene out or not. She was sagging at the knees, and I helped her into a chair just as Caspar Cardwell reached me and clamped my right elbow in a surprisingly strong grip. I let him frog-march me from the room—everyone quickly staring at the floor as I tried to make eye-contact in passing—and then we were on the patio, and then on the lawn, and then he was speaking to two hulking mutations from gorillas to beachboys who were apparently paid to guard the joint.

There was a whiff of marijuana in the air about them, but they tried to pay attention as Caspar spoke. "When we've finished talking, he's leaving. Immediately," he said. "And then I want you to come into my study. I've told you before. Absolutely no one gets in without an invitation, even people you know." He looked at me as if I were on his side of the problem, and confided, "Something is very wrong here."

The two men looked embarrassed, then turned on their heels and began to patrol the grounds, looking for I don't know what. Caspar let go of me, sat down on a stone bench bathed in pink light, and gestured for me to sit beside him. "Who are you?" he asked.

I gave him the name only, omitting even the rank and serial number, and then I said, "I wasn't being cute in there. Since your wife asked, I really do want to talk to your sister."

"Elizabeth is beyond our reach," he said sadly. He was playing at civility, but his sharp emerald-green eyes were darting back and forth, trying to see into my mind. "You should have said something privately."

"I felt guided to do it that way," I said, trying out some of the language. "I meant no harm."

He tried for a priestly look and folded his arms. He was staring at me. The black draped sleeves of his robe made him look like a crooked bat till he got the material rearranged. "What do you want to talk to my sister about?"

"I met your daughter through Dr. and Mrs. Vance. They're old friends of mine." I figured it wouldn't hurt to drop the name of the woman I'd met at the Foundation, but now I wasn't sure if it was smart or not because Caspar's jaw had clamped shut and alarm was shooting through his eyes. He was visibly struggling to regain control of his facilities, and finally he managed to force a weak, puzzled smile to his face, and say, "Yes?"

"When I learned that Ariel was the famous Elizabeth Cardwell's niece, I couldn't help myself. I wheedled an invitation. I know your sister never did any feature roles, but I was a big fan of her movies when I was a kid. I bet I've watched "Circus in Caracas" at least a hundred times. I just wanted to see where she went, how she's doing." It was lame, but it was the best I could do on such short notice.

Caspar gave me a contrived look that was supposed to say he was surprised and pleased by my interest. Then his eyes misted and focused on something past me. "Yes, Lizzie was a good actress, wasn't she? She might have made it big if she'd had any support from our parents. But you know how that was. In those days, acting was considered a tarnished occupation in our circles. So Lizzie was manipulated into marrying that pip-squeak of a banker, and predictably, she died an early and tragic death." He shook his head as if to clear it, then refocused his eyes on me. "But then, I'm dragging out far too much of the family's linen. Look, I really do need to apologize for what happened in there, but these events aren't for the uninitiated, you know. The Vances must surely have told you that." He peered at me.

I shrugged.

He said, "You have to come in step by step . . ."

"And how do I do that?"

People had started to leave now, most of them glancing curiously at Caspar and me as we sat talking on the stone bench. We were just enough out of the way to discourage the departees from moving over to chat, though some waved and called out their "good-nights."

He thought for a long moment, then said, "Actually, we're having a smaller get-together tomorrow night. Something not quite so advanced as tonight's session. Cassie will be reading a couple of astrological charts and maybe we'll use the Ouija Board. And we have a retrocognitionist also stopping by." His eyes fairly gleamed at that.

"A what?"

He emitted a meek little chortle. "A specialist in seeing into the past," he said. "Always a real treat. Would you like to stop by for cocktails?"

I forced myself to look only mildly interested. "Depends on what time."

"Sevenish," he said. "We'll serve a light buffet."

I stood up, mostly to see what would happen. Nothing. I said, "Sounds good to me."

Caspar stood too, all conviviality. "Good, good. We're always happy to help a fellow human in his quest for spiritual wisdom." I was walking toward my car now, and he was following along, still chatting amiably. "It's so easy to get wrapped up in the material world and forget about the spiritual," he said. "I did it myself for years and years.

But I'll tell you this much. I'm glad I found the Foundation. Now that I can see beyond the five senses, everything has changed. I've never been happier in my life."

I surreptitiously studied him. He looked about as miserable as they come, to me. We reached my car, and I opened the door. "Well, I appreciate your hospitality, Mr. Cardwell . . ."

"Caspar," he said warmly. "Call me Caspar. Look." He cleared his throat, slightly embarrassed, and the tiny little wattle beneath his chin trembled. "I wonder if I might ask you a favor?"

"Certainly. Shoot."

"Vernon and Vera must have told you already," he said sheepishly, "but I'd like to say it again, just to be sure. This is all rather private. I mean, not the Foundation, of course, but the seances. So many people don't believe . . ."

"Gotcha." I said. "Mum's the word."

He looked at me oddly, like it was taking him a minute to translate, and then he smiled, "Oh, I see. Yes. Well, thank you for your discretion, Mr. Weatherby, and we'll see you tomorrow night at seven." He swept his black robes around him, turned, and walked away.

Later, at home, I kept replaying that evening's events. The whole thing had me on edge, and it had me thinking again about life, about why we're here and where we go from here. Where we came from, too.

I mean, here we are, products of a chance meeting between sperm and ovum, grown to birthing size then shoved through the birth canal and out onto this beautiful blue droplet of matter spinning through space, living breathing creatures, and not a whit else about our existence really makes sense, so far as I can tell.

So, from my point of view, people try to make sense of it on their own. They come up with scenarios ranging from the manipulative dark religious philosophy I'd seen in practice at the Cardwells' tonight; to the shallow, materialistic beliefs of the Hollywood movers and shakers who make up the dreams that make up the media that feeds our increasingly alienated and despairing culture; to the saffron-robed adherents of East Indian gods too numerous to name; to the Mud-people who had recently appeared in the L.A. area with huge beehive mud-cones on their heads and mud-smeared bodies, who found their purpose by walking around like zombie primitives and contemplating any and all types of objects, from gum wrappers retrieved from the gutter to tree branches. Drugs and booze also fit into this scenario. This is what people do to deaden themselves against all the other emptiness and futility of existence.

And then at the other end of the spectrum was Tony Cacciatore and his belief in being born again by a Deity who had created us, only to have an evil being somehow foul the creation so that the Deity had to send His only begotten Son to die for us and set things straight, if only we would (or could) believe in Him. Tony's was a light-centered belief; a belief in the inherent goodness of all things, had the evil not somehow crept in. This had been the belief system of my grand-mother. And as I thought about all this, I missed her deeply. I wished she was there to talk with me about all I'd seen and felt that night, to explain away the nightmare lie that I sensed was lurking just beneath the surface of all this.

My grandmother. She was a warm though poignant memory. In the evenings, when I was little, she used to sit on the front porch swing and talk to me. She'd tell me marvelous things about rocks and insects, about birds and trees, about the stars and the moon, but most of all about the Being who had created all this. Though she was largely self-educated and had worked most of her hard life as a practical nurse, she had a wisdom that few can ever match.

She taught me that the rocks, trees, and streams—indeed, all of this planet—was a tribute to God's artistry and majesty. "But it's a lot more than that, Little Arthur," she would say to me. "It's a womb. A place where we're growing and changing, so one day we can be born into our true homes as the perfect spiritual beings He wants us to be and that we will be if we just choose to serve Him."

I hadn't understood that then. I probably didn't understand it even now.

"Life isn't easy, and you've gotten off to a pretty hard start," she'd said. "But there's one thing you'll have to learn, no matter how hard the lesson. And that is that you're given to this world for only a short time, only a heartbeat. You're here to learn God's perfect will for you, and you'd best do just that. Because unless you get to know Him as your personal Lord and Savior, unless you live within His will, there won't be a thing about your life that will be worth living."

Even back then, I'd had trouble with all that. How was I supposed to believe in a Being I couldn't even hear or see? And when I talked to Him at night, He never spoke back.

"You'll see it in God's due time," she said. "God is all around us. His beauty is in the raindrop, in the sunshine. You're feeling him every time you draw in a breath of air. You'll see. And God won't take you home till you *have* seen because I'm praying for you, Little Arthur. It will all happen in God's due time."

I hadn't thought about those words for years, but as I lay on my solitary bed, looking out the window and past the scrub oak to the moon rising above the black canyon wall, I could hear every word again. It shook me to the center of my soul. Tony had revived these memories with his talk about 'God's due time,' I realized that. But for a moment there I felt a supernatural presence in my room with me, and I wasn't sure if it was good or evil, welcome or not. I reached over and turned on my bedside lamp, then sat up and looked swiftly around me. Nothing there, and whatever I sensed had vanished with the light.

And gone, too, was the emotional and mental turmoil that I had felt since my troubled meeting with Elizabeth Ann Livingstone. I turned off the light and looked again at the moon. There it was, for all to see, a huge orb spinning in a vast, black nothing of space, in company with the stars and the nebulae and all the other moons and planets.

Where had all this come from? Where, for that matter, had *I* come from? Like a child, I mulled it all over again and again until I finally fell asleep.

Chapter
━NINE━

At four o'clock A.M. the ringing of my phone dragged me up out of a dreamless sleep. I grabbed the receiver and growled, "Yeah?"

A whispery voice said, "Mr. Weatherby?"

I fought to come all the way awake. It was Elizabeth Livingstone. "I'm listening," I said.

"You know who this is."

"Right."

"What have you been doing?"

"Look." Suddenly I wanted nothing more than to talk to her and find out what was going on. "I went to your grave. It's been dug up. The mud matched the stuff you tracked onto my carpet. Your husband is upset, he thinks I'm running some kind of scam. I went to your brother's house last night and tried to talk to you, but this fat blonde screamed at me to leave you alone. What in the Sam Hill is going on?"

There was a hesitation on her end, and only later, when I was running the tape of the conversation back through, did I realize that there was a tiny, new, yet nearly imperceptible hint of hostility in her voice when she finally said, "Why did you go to my brother's house?"

I snorted. "Because I couldn't think of anything better to do. Look, come to my office. Better yet, grab a cab and come on up to my house. We need to talk, and bad. Tell you the truth, I'm baffled

89

by this whole deal. For Pete's sake, half the time I don't even know if you're alive or dead!"

Her voice became stilted and cautious. "But you know I'm dead. You just said you went to my grave."

"But you're alive now, or else how could I talk to you?" Even as I said it, I realized how inane it sounded.

But she didn't affirm my statement. She just said, "I need to see you too, but I'm afraid to come there. I want you to come to where I am instead."

"Which is?"

"You know where I am."

"In the cemetery?"

"Of course not. In the other place. Where I told you."

"You didn't tell me anything."

"I'm sure I did."

That was about the point where I started to catch on. Maybe it was partly because I was at last coming fully awake. I said, "Look, Elizabeth, it's here or nowhere. I'll wait till eight and then I'm going to take myself out for a steak breakfast."

"I can't come. You have to come to me."

"Then I guess our little fling is over. Toodle-oo."

I waited to see if she'd say more, but she didn't. Instead, I heard the receiver being gently placed back in the phone cradle, and then I hung up too.

And then I spent some time thinking about the voice that had come out of Sofia Jordan's mouth last night, when she'd screeched at me—in Elizabeth's voice—to "leave me alone." I rewound the recorder that automatically tapes my phone conversations. And this time through, it seemed just enough different from Elizabeth's voice to be genuinely suspect. When I picked up on the newfound hostility right after I'd called Sofia a "fat blonde," I was sure.

This could mean only one thing. The Cardwells and friends were already trying to find out what I was really up to. Sofia had indeed been faking Elizabeth's voice last night. Now, they'd gotten her to phone me and try to pump me for information. And, like the dunce I sometimes am, I'd just tipped my hand enough to at least let them know I'd been in contact with Elizabeth. Or with someone pretending to be Elizabeth. Or . . . ah, whatever.

It was pretty easy to figure. I'd given Cardwell my name. It would be no problem for him to check me out, I was even listed in the yellow pages. Or maybe he'd phoned Dr. and Mrs. Vance, had found out they'd never heard of me, then he'd looked me up in the phone directory and there in big bold print had seen that I was a private investigator. Then he—or someone—had put Sofia up to phoning me and pretending to be Elizabeth, just to see what I would say. And they wanted to know where Elizabeth was. They'd intended to set me up and follow me to her. Which meant, more or less, that maybe Elizabeth really wasn't dead, or they wouldn't have believed she was in contact with me. I scratched my head and thought again. On the other hand, that bunch seemed to do more visiting with the dead than with the living. When I factored that in, I couldn't draw any conclusions at all.

Drat. I'd sat there flapping my gums, giving away a whole lot of information that should have stayed tucked neatly inside my gray matter where it belonged. Get a grip, Weatherby. You're starting to lose it, old boy.

I thought about Elizabeth Livingstone, and then I thought about her husband and her brother and the whole crazy deal again. It kept me awake till first light began to illuminate the scrub brush outside my bedroom window. But I drifted off again, and then I awakened to the sound of heavy rain. In spite of the fact that I'd slept late, it looked like it was going to be another day, and a rainy one at that.

I'd been lying about the steak breakfast. I went into the kitchen and made some chaparral tea—can't get enough of that weed, I guess—then I went into my bathroom and was just dragging my hand across the cactus that had grown on my face overnight, thinking about plowing it off, when I again heard the phone ring.

More ghosts? A pox on them, too. I suddenly realized I was in a very nasty mood.

I let the phone ring two more times, then I picked it up, giving my voice my most mellifluous tenor to hide my mood, and said, "Weatherby Investigations."

Big Al Riggatoni said, "So how'd it go?"

It took me a minute to shift mental gears, and then I said, "I really can't tell you. Tony's a hard one to read. But you know, the guy seems pretty straight to me. Maybe he really has found religion—"

"He's lost his marbles, is what it is."

"—and you can work something else out. You know, that's not the old Tony we're dealing with."

"You're tellin' me."

"Look, let me get back with him and see if I can't make it sink in that you're serious."

"I ain't comin' up with any more cash for you."

"That's okay. Money isn't the point. I'd just like to see this thing settled without anyone getting hurt."

"You and me both, and right now I'm the one hurtin'. Look, okay, I'll give him another day. But then if they don't get them cockeyed cameras out of my action, I'm goin' to the mattresses, tell Tony that."

He hung up in my face. At which point I went back to the bathroom, showered and shaved, then dressed and drove down to my office. Once there, I went to my window, cracked the venetian blinds and stared gloomily out at the piers. It was indeed a lousy day, a gray drizzle running down the window pane, the ocean waves a steady grind of deadly gray chop. No day to be standing out in the weather pointing a video camera at perverts; and certainly no day to be sleeping on a park bench or sitting locked up in a closet or climbing in or out of a lonely, muddy grave.

Where—and who, and *what*—was Elizabeth? Much as I was concerned about Tony Cacciatore and his problem—which really might be madness, from this distance it didn't seem quite so simple as it had yesterday—I was even more concerned about Elizabeth Livingstone.

Or maybe I was just concerned about my own sanity. Because the more I looked into the Elizabeth Livingstone matter, the daffier it seemed. First a ghost had hired me to find out who murdered her, next thing you know I'm hanging around with ancient spirits named Quetz, and space men named Thur, and vampires, not to mention the illustrious Caspar and Cassie Cardwell. And—was I really planning to spend the coming evening at the Cardwells' again, talking to a Ouija Board?

Yer durn tootin' I was. I couldn't wait to get back into that house and try to figure out those Lobos. So interested in them was I, in fact, that the very next thing I did was walk back to my desk and pick up my cross-reference directory, planning to find out the street address of one Ariel Cardwell. She'd told me she had a place just off Rodeo Drive, a combination bookstore and aerobics studio. ·

I found the number—the RAINBOW PYRAMID STUDIO— and had just reached out to pick up the receiver to dial it, when the phone gave a sudden harsh jangle and my hand jerked back. This whole thing was turning me into a nervous wreck.

I gingerly picked up the receiver. It was Frank Livingstone.

"Mr. Weatherby. I hope I'm not intruding . . ."

"Never." .

"I trust you had no trouble cashing the check?"

"Not a bit."

"I was just wondering. When you left my home yesterday, uh, um, I don't exactly know how to ask this—"

"Just spit it out," said my bad mood.

"Very well. Did you by any chance visit my late wife's grave?"

"Affirmative."

"Yes. The Director at the memorial gardens described a man I believed was you. I . . . may I ask, did you find anything uh, unusual there?"

I clenched my jaw and cursed myself for being so stupid. The gardeners had of course discovered the violated grave. The Director would have remembered me. "Has anyone phoned the police yet?" I asked.

"That will be my next step unless I get some straight answers, sir. I must demand to know. What did you discover at my wife's grave?"

"Someone had dug it up."

"Yes. I know. Fortunately, they stopped short of the casket and her remains weren't tampered with, the Director said. But I am concerned."

I did a quick recap of the past two days' events in my mind and decided it was finally time to lay it out for him. I said, "Look, Mr. Livingstone, I have reason to believe your wife is still alive."

"Preposterous!"

"Yes, it is, isn't it? But I have every reason to believe it's true. Unless maybe she has a twin sister?" I felt a quick glimmer of hope for a rational solution.

"Hardly. Lizzie was one of a kind."

"Then I have to tell you. Either she or her exact double walked into my office yesterday morning and handed me that check for five thousand dollars. Even if she did date it ten years ago."

"I see." Disbelief was strong in his voice. "And what, may I ask, did she give you five thousand dollars *for*?"

"I'm afraid that's confidential. But she was here, she gave me the check, and that's a fact."

"Then where is she now?" His voice was trying to drip with sarcasm, but there was a tremor in it.

"Your guess is probably better than mine."

He cleared his throat. "You realize, of course, that this is rather shocking. It couldn't possibly be true . . ."

"Mr. Livingstone, either she or someone who is a dead ringer for her—pardon the expression—was here. There's no way I can prove what I'm saying. But I'm frankly stymied. I could use some help figuring this thing out."

"Well, someone *has* certainly violated her grave." There was a bit of capitulation in his voice now. "And frankly, there was a good two feet of earth still on the coffin. We didn't check it completely . . ."

"Then that's what we need to do next. You could easily check the body in that grave against her dental records, to at least see if she really is buried there. If she is, I'll have to revise my theory that she dropped by my office yesterday morning. If not, you'll have to more or less believe it's at least possible that she's still alive."

"And how would I exhume her and examine her jawbone without going through the police?"

"I see what you mean."

"Yes. I told you, I don't want so much as a breath of scandal to tarnish my late wife's name, and there would be no *way* to keep something like that out of the papers."

"Who was her dentist?"

"Nathan VanDerber."

"Over on Wilshire?"

"The same."

"Tell you what, you find out where he has her records stored, I'll see what I can do about getting them. Maybe we can find someone who can check the jawbone against them and who won't talk a lot. In the meantime, what's happening regarding the grave?"

"I told the Director to please wait while I spoke to a friend, that we'd been discussing having her body moved into the big crypt."

"Fine, fine, stick by that, tell him not to have the gardeners fill in the grave for a day or two, in the meantime we'll see what we can do."

"Mr. Weatherby, I must be frank. This hardly seems like the right way to go about things . . ."

"Do you want to know if your wife's body is in that grave?"

"Yes." It came out flat and emphatic, and for the first time I realized he was at least partially leveling with me.

"Then have the Director tell the gardeners to take the day off," I said. "Phone me as soon as you learn where her records are. I'll get the message either at my office or here at home. In the meantime, wrack your brain a little and see if you can think of a place where she'd hide out. Because, to tell you the truth, if she is still alive I have a feeling she isn't going to be that way for long."

"Why on earth do you say that?"

"Because something's going on, Mr. Livingstone. Something heavy. I don't know what, I don't know why. But I know it as surely as I know I'm standing here. I can feel it in my gut."

After he hung up the phone I cogitated on the conversation for a few minutes, then my thoughts moved again to Ariel. I'd jotted her phone number down on my blotter, but as I started to pick up the phone again, inspiration hit. Why settle for a phone call? Why not go over to the studio and take a look? I spun open my wall safe and withdrew two hundred in twenties—I was running short of cash—and then I checked the fax—no more news from Angelo—then I turned off the lights, locked the door, and left.

Chapter
——— TEN ———

Beverly Hills is the heart of the fantasy, the essence of the dream. The very name drips with opulence and extravagance and fame. By the time I turned off the freeway and onto Wilshire Boulevard, the rain had stopped. When I got to the Beverly Wilshire Hotel, I turned north onto the palm-lined altar to materialism that the world knows as Rodeo Drive.

The three-block segment between Wilshire and Santa Monica was resplendent with such names as Gucci, Cartier, Courrèges, and Giorgio. Tourists gawked into store windows, pretending they could afford the glittering gems and luxurious furs and chic leathers and fabrics. The real shoppers darted quickly from the air-conditioned privacy of Rolls Royce or Mercedes limos and into the shops, some of them with famous faces averted from the fans who ultimately paid the bills in more ways than one.

I cruised past the shops—no speeding on Rodeo—looking for the 600 block. When I reached it, I hung a left and then another sharp left and found myself in a brick-paved alley lined with more palms and ferns and other lush greenery. Directly in front of me a two-story building sported a red-trimmed white stucco façade that looked a lot like a smaller version of the Alamo. It stood at the end of a rounded cul-de-sac. There was a Spanish-style fountain in front, with water gushing into a circular concrete pool and a life-size stone grandee on a rearing horse making up the centerpiece. The building itself had a wide balcony on the second story and not a sign of commerce about it except for the several fancy cars parked in front of the fountain, among them Ariel's wine-colored Morgan.

I parked my Beamer beside a white Excaliber with gold trim, then followed the red brick road up to the front door. There was a recessed doorbell with a tiny brass plate above it that read: "RAINBOW PYRAMID STUDIO." I pushed the doorbell, straining to see if it worked, but I couldn't hear a thing through all the concrete.

I pushed it again, and a moment later a trim Mexican woman of about forty, with a severe face that emphasized her Indian ancestry, appeared and opened the door. She was wearing a black leotard and black tights, and she had a body that spelled S.W.E.A.T. She was a little out of breath. "You have business here?" Her accent was heavy.

"I need to see Ariel Cardwell."

She looked at me like she didn't quite believe me, but she gave me the benefit of the doubt. "Your name, *señor?*"

"Artie Weatherby."

She looked skeptical, then closed the door in my face. I did the old "put the weight on one foot and then on the other" routine while I waited—about five minutes—and then the door swung open and Ariel stood there in a pale-green leotard with forest-green tights, looking like she owned the joint. Her red hair was pulled back into a pony tail, and she wore a lime-green headband. Her face was scrubbed clean of make-up, making the dusting of freckles more pronounced. She looked a little older than she had last night, but she still looked good. A fluffy pink towel was draped around her neck.

She had a mischievous grin on her face. "Didn't get enough of us last night, huh?"

"Of you, no. Of your family, no again."

"I can't believe it. My father all but threw you out."

"Ah, but he invited me back again tonight."

She frowned. "You're going?"

"Why not? He said it would just be some of the lighter stuff."

She thought about that for a minute, still frowning. And then she forced a smile to her face. "I'm working, darling. We're in the middle of advanced aerobics. You'll have to wait till I'm done."

"No problem."

She waved me in, and I followed her past a reception desk with no one behind it, past a doorway that opened into a small bookstore, and then down a short hallway and into a large exercise room. There were six or seven women in the room, all straight out of a Jane Fonda video, wearing different-colored variations of Ariel's work-out duds, and barely puffing as the Mexican woman led them in some intricate steps set to the tune of Ravel's "Bolero." There was a juice bar at the back of the wide room. Another Mexican woman, this one about fifty and plump, was cleaning the counter behind the bar. The rich and famous hire more cheap labor than any other class of people except sweat-shop owners. Not that this wasn't a sweat-shop of sorts. I made my way over, plopped down on a white naugahyde stool, and said to her, "You open?"

"You want juice, I fix you some. You Mees Ariel's friend?" She gave me a lewd wink.

"Not yet, but I'm working on it. You got any O.J. back there?"

She smiled and turned to a refrigerator, withdrew a plastic quart jar of orange juice, opened it, opened another cooler and took out a frosted cut-crystal glass, then placed a paper doily with lace border in front of me and set the O.J. and glass upon it. "You weesh me to pour for you?"

"Thanks, I can manage." I went to work on the job, took a deep swig—fresh-squeezed and delicious—then asked, "What's your name?"

"Maria Elena." She was doing something to a malt-mixer with a brush now.

"You from Mexico, Maria?"

"You no can tell?" She wasn't bothering to turn around to chat now. She was scrubbing furiously.

"From Baja?"

I saw her go tense, and then she made a full turn and stood, feet splayed, hands on hips, and said, "Mees Ariel, she don't like us to talk weeth customers. You have questions, you ask her, *por favor.*"

Which was just about the reaction I would have expected from an illegal alien, if I'd bothered to think about it.

The volume of the music had dropped a bit. Ariel had bobbed and stretched her way near to me, keeping an eye on the "girls," showing this one how to hold her arms, the other how to move her legs. I raised my voice a bit, and said, "Mind if I take a look in your bookstore while I wait?"

She smiled breathlessly and waved me toward the doorway. "I won't be much longer."

I polished off my O.J., wondered for a second if I should lay a tip on the bar for Maria, thought better of it, then back-tracked down the hallway and went into the bookstore, nodding to a small gray-haired woman in a paisley cotton dress with a white collar. Her shoes were those sturdy black ones with the thick soles, and she wore white ankle-socks. She was unpacking a box of books. When she saw that I was planning to browse, she forgot me and went back to her work.

I'd expected holistic health publications: books on herbs, vegetarian diets, Eastern health remedies, maybe something on acupuncture. And there was indeed a section of these, but a very small one. The rest of the books had titles like: *Doorway to Your Third Mind,* and *Mystic Powers of the Shamans,* and *The Occult Guide to Beauty and Weight Loss* and *Trance Channelling: Your Key to Power,* and *Ectoplasmic Wonders,* and *Mu and Moo and You, and The UFO: How to Make Contact,* and *Poltergeist Power,* and *The Ancient Powers in Chichen Itza.* Pretty weird stuff. Femura Riley's book was even there: *The Path, the Power, and the Psychic.* These people definitely had a thing about power.

There were also books on reading tarot cards, books on clairvoyance and clairaudience and even one on Claire de Lune—just kidding about that last one. There was a section devoted to witchcraft—which surprised me—and several volumes about Druids and Dragons, and then there were sections devoted to Buddhism and Hinduism, and even one devoted to Catholicism. Or so I thought, till I opened one book and read a few sentences. The book was actually about Santeria, that peculiar religion that crossed voodoo with Catholicism and who knew what else and came up with something dark and dreary that required a lot of votive candles and dead chickens and dogs.

There was a large glass display case near to the register. I moseyed on over there and took a gander at the wares. There were hundreds of different items of jewelry, all of them encrusted with various kinds of crystals. Tiny pewter earrings with amethyst pendants; tiny wizard rings with aquamarine stones; pewter, brass, and gold bracelets with the same peculiar hieroglyphic design I'd seen on Mrs. Cardwell's arm the previous night; brooches, barrettes, combs, fans, any trinket a woman could wear or own, and all of them set gaudily with the many types of crystals. In addition to the crystal-trimmed items, there were various crystals all by themselves, duplicates of the crystals in the Cardwells' seance room.

The woman had finished unpacking her box and stood up now, so I asked her, "What's the deal with all the crystals?"

She looked at me like I'd said something obscene. But then she studied me for a moment, her pinkish eyes ranging from the toes of my gray loafers and up my gray cotton slacks, past my sky-blue shirt with the little antelope over the pocket—why pay twice as much just to get an alligator?—then over my dark blonde hair, past my handsomely rugged face, and all the way back down again. And then she evidently decided it had been a serious question, because she said, "Who let you in here?"

"Ariel Cardwell." I said. I expected sudden deference. But instead, she frowned.

"Ariel? What on earth is she up to this time?" She shook her head like a horse blowing after a run, and I almost expected a whinny for a second there, but then she said, "You really don't understand about crystals?"

"Sorry. I'm a neophyte."

She gave a slow combination nod and blink, as if that explained everything. "Crystals are catalysts," she said. "They've been used for everything from healing to technology, since the ancient days of the Muvians—"

"The *what?*"

Her nostrils flared and her thick iron-gray eyebrows slanted upward in the middle. "My stars, don't you know anything?"

I shrugged. "Apparently not."

"Mu was the true Garden of Eden. The Jews simply stole the concept and added it into their own religion, to make themselves seem more important. But the true beginning of humanity was nowhere near the Middle East."

"Excuse me, but would you mind repeating that?" She already thought I was stupid. Might as well go for broke.

"Good heavens, you *are* a neophyte!"

"That's why I'm in a bookstore. I need to educate myself."

"Oh." She thought about that, then smiled hollowly. Then her voice became professorial.

"Mu was the first continent, the evolutionary cradle of mankind. It was created by the supreme spirit, the great seven-headed serpent and intellect, Narayama. He was the over-god of it all. He created the continent right here in the Pacific. The evidence lies in glyphs from Easter Island, and tablets have been found in ancient temples in places as diverse as Calcutta and Rangoon and Baghdad. The ancient Mayans also documented it. The secret was lost till the late 1800s, when scholars began to decipher various ancient languages and the truth came out. The continent contained a civilization far more spiritually enlightened and secularly advanced than anything today. Unfortunately, it sank into the Pacific Ocean after a violent volcanic upheaval, some twelve thousand years ago. The queen of the continent was named Moo, and she and some of her family managed to escape the cataclysm. They fled to Egypt, where she founded a new civilization. There, she was known as the goddess Isis."

"I've heard of her."

That encouraged her. "Isis built the Sphinx and all the great pyramids—she was immortal, of course, as we all are—and of course she retained contact with the remnants of the Mayans and others, since she could astral project, plus she had psychic contact. Some descendants stayed in the Western Hemisphere and built all the great pyramids in Mexico, especially in the Yucatan. And of course, Queen Moo had also colonized other far-flung parts of the globe. She had followers and avatars in India, in China, in Tibet and Russia, and all throughout ancient Europe and Asia, even in Babylon."

"Makes sense to me," I said. I felt like humming a few bars from the theme to "The Twilight Zone."

"Isis and her mate and brother, Osiris, are also manifested as the Aztec duel deity, Ometeotl, the dweller of the highest heavens, as well as the dual Hindu god, Kali and Shiva. All of these are really just other incarnations of Narayama. But back to your question about crystals. They're a part of the mystic tradition. You can use them to crystallize love or money or power or healing or anything else you want. They're like a portal into the higher realms. They are matrixes for energy and light and all sorts of psychic phenomena."

I was amazed at how learned she sounded. "How do you know all this?"

"I'm a professor of psychiatry and parapsychology. I certainly should know something." And with that she turned and marched into a storeroom. A moment later she came back out, carrying another carton of books.

"Can I help you with that?"

She set the box down and ignored me. I looked over her shoulder at the titles: *Retrocognition*, by Dr. Deborah Winch. As she picked up a handful of the books, I saw that her photograph was on the back cover. I said, "Are you Dr. Winch?"

She looked up, surprised. "Of course."

"You're a writer? And a professor? What are you doing working in a bookstore?"

She stood up straight and really frowned at that one. "Aren't you a member of the Foundation?"

"Uh—not yet. I'm working on it."

"Well, when you are admitted, young man, you'll realize. Everyone volunteers whatever they can. Everyone. I don't care if you're the President of the United States."

"Yes, well . . ."

"Do you want a copy of my book?"

"Uh, sure."

She whipped out a cheap black ballpoint and signed the book's inner cover in cranky little letters, then thrust it at me. "Read this, and then you'll know something."

I took it, opened the pages, looking interested.

"Eight ninety-five," she said.

It took a second to register the fact that she was selling the book, not giving it to me. I tried to hand it back. "Sorry, I don't have any cash on me," I said.

She whisked her hand back and forth. "Never mind, I'll just put it on Ariel's bill."

I nodded my thanks. I'd give the book back to Ariel later. And then a thought struck me. "Are you by any chance planning to be at the Cardwells' tonight?"

"I'll be the guest speaker. Why?"

"I'll be there too," I said. "I can't wait to hear you speak." I managed to sound boyishly sincere.

But she was ignoring me again, her jaw screwed up, her eyes slitted as she studied shelves and decided where to best display her wares. So I moseyed on out of the book shop and back into the aerobics studio, where the final bars of the *Bolero* were just winding down. Ariel wiped her face with the fluffy pink towel, then came toward me. "Well? What do you think?"

"I thought this was your place."

"It is."

"I mean, the woman in the bookstore said something about the Foundation . . ."

"Oh, I let them use the space for the bookstore. All the profits are theirs. From the studio, too, for that matter. I've been getting enough income from Aunt Liz's trust to keep me going . . ."

"Your aunt left you a trust?" I managed to keep the sharp interest out of my voice, but just barely.

"Oh, yes. Even though I was only fourteen when she died, Aunt Liz and I were very close. She could never have children, you know. I used to spend more time with her than with my own parents. That's probably why I turned out fairly normal." She grinned.

I'd been meaning to look into what had happened to all the money Elizabeth Livingstone had inherited from her mother. This looked like a good place to start. "What are you doing for dinner?" I'd just checked my watch. It was only about three, but I didn't have a thing to do for the next couple of hours.

"Still curious about Aunt Liz, huh?"

"Well, I am. But I'd like to spend some time with you, too. I mean . . ."

"Look. It's okay. Tod is working tonight. They're doing a movie with Robert Rhodes, you know, *Death's Final Agony?*"

"I hadn't heard, but his loss is my gain."

"We'll have an early dinner in my apartment upstairs," she said. "Maria is an excellent cook. She can prepare it down here and won't have to bother us at all, and we'll be done in plenty of time for you to get to my parents' gathering."

"Aren't you going?"

"I'm not sure. I might, I guess, but I'll drive myself if I do." A flicker of worry passed through her eyes. She instantly hid it. And then, as if sensing my discomfort and curiosity at the offer of a private dinner in her apartment, she added, "The dinner is strictly platonic. I'm solidly tied to Tod at the moment. He's planning to feature me in his next movie."

I was surprised at how relieved I felt. "I hadn't thought it would be anything else."

Chapter
─ELEVEN─

I followed Ariel up a private stairwell and into a white and yellow living room. She offered me a glass of white wine, which I declined, then she went to take a shower and dress, leaving me to detect what I could.

The first thing I detected was that this girl was very rich, just like her mommy and daddy. Not that I hadn't had a few clues before this.

Her living room was carpeted, draped, and painted in winter white. Two white armchairs were arranged beside a lemon-yellow sofa. Creamy yellow throw rugs softened the primary color, and there were several other pale yellow accents throughout the room, including a soft painting of yellow daisies in a white vase against a gray background, and a large pewter vase full of real daisies, in pink and white and yellow. Several green plants further softened the room, which was smart, expensive, and impersonal. It was a designer's creation that Ariel had apparently never bothered to make her own except for one surprising touch: a calligraphic print of the 23rd Psalm, the letters intricately drawn then matted on silver paper, framed, and hung above the sofa.

I peered through a doorway and into a small, shiny kitchen that looked as unused as a display in an appliance store, then I peeked into the door she'd disappeared through, but left partway open. It was her bedroom. Her bed was queen-sized, with a silky gray spread. A couple of white and yellow throw pillows continued the color theme. One full wall was nothing but closet, the doors opened, clothing brimming out and over the edges, shoes stacked everywhere. A jewelry box stood on a dresser cluttered with perfume bottles, cosmetics, and other female flotsam. The shower was still running, so I tip-toed over and took a look. There were numerous pieces of jewelry, but none of it looked really expensive; it was mostly semiprecious stones—crystals—set into various rings and pendants and necklaces and earrings and bracelets. The shower stopped, and I beat feet back into the living room.

There was a photo album on an end table. I opened it and flipped through. Most of the photos were of Ariel and friends or family in various places, including many with Tod Montgomery on set, some with several movie stars, some obviously taken on vacation. But as I got toward the back of the book and Ariel kept getting younger, I found more and more photographs of her with the woman who had hired me to solve a ten-year-old murder. No doubt about it, Elizabeth Ann Livingstone was indeed the same person she called Aunt Liz. There were some photos of just Elizabeth alone. I took a couple of the smaller ones out of the album and squirreled them away in my wallet, then moved to the window and pulled aside a drape—and looked into a surprising vision of beauty. The small back yard had been turned, by someone, into a secret garden.

Thick green wisteria climbed up the windowless back of the building that closed off the far side of the garden, two stories of soft, feathery foliage dappled with shadows of gray-green and black. In the foreground, I recognized some Queen Anne's lace and a bed of buttercups. Thick greenery of other types turned the garden into a somehow organized tangle that exploded into a burst of colorful flowers here and there. A path of dark bricks meandered past a large bank of foxgloves and on to where a white filigreed iron bench sat in shade beneath a small weeping willow tree. There was a table beside the bench. Someone had left a book there, and a pitcher and a glass. I peered carefully. Nobody was there now.

Ariel called from the bedroom. I dropped the drape shut as if I'd been caught spying. She said. "Just a minute longer, darling. If Maria comes up with dinner, would you please let her in?"

I opened the drape and looked again. "Happy to."

I was still gazing at the greenery when Ariel came up silently behind me and dug her fingers into my ribs. "Gotcha!"

I started and spun, fists raised, then grinned and dropped them. "Gimme back my liver," I said.

"Huh?" She was sprawling onto the sofa, wearing a sleeveless pink dress with a leafy rose print. Her feet were bare, her hair was still damp, and curly. Her face was fresh-scrubbed.

"An early childhood memory," I explained, a little embarrassed.

I pulled the drapes shut and turned to join her, but she said, "Leave them open. Here." She stood and moved to the window, where she pulled a cord and the drapes slid open across the double-wide picture window, framing the garden. "Beautiful, isn't it? It was Aunt Liz's, you know."

My eyes wanted to light up with interest, but I wouldn't let them. Ariel was sitting again, and I parked myself in one of the white armchairs and tried to look equally relaxed. "This was your aunt's apartment?"

"She liked to get away from Frank. Not that he was a bad husband, but she liked to have some time to herself. Grandfather Cardwell owned this place. A clothing designer had rented the downstairs for years, and then Aunt Liz stayed in this apartment when she was working in Hollywood. After her marriage, she came and spent a week or so every month, just by herself. I redid the apartment before I moved in, but I've kept the garden as a sort of memorial to her."

"Looks like a lot of work."

"It is, but Thomas—her old gardener—comes in from Bel Air and does it several times a week. This is his labor of love, though I make it a point to take good care of him."

I thought about Elizabeth Livingstone sitting in the garden, beneath the weeping willow tree, her shoulder-length hair combed straight back from her alabaster forehead, her filmy cotton dress draped over legs she'd pulled up beneath her. She was drinking lemonade from the pebbled green glass now sitting on the table and reading from the book. She turned her graceful neck and looked up at me. And suddenly I could see her eyes again, as if she was standing dead in front of me. Those eyes, a liquid forest, dark with pain, pleading for help . . .

Ariel was talking. ". . . and Aunt Liz loved roses. But her two best bushes died, and Thomas hasn't been able to find the same types here. I believe he's placed some on order . . ."

"Ariel, tell me about your aunt's death."

Her eyes went wide with surprise, then she processed this change in the conversation and emitted a tinkling little laugh.

"You don't waste any time."

"It's important."

"I know. I mean, it must be. My mother phoned me this morning."

Uh-oh. "And?"

"I know you're an investigator. Mother was furious with me. She wanted to know why I'd spirited you into the seance like that."

"It was just a spur-of-the-moment thing. I saw you whiz by, and I followed."

She laughed again. "I know. That's why I liked you. Look, don't let Mother bother you. She's a little weird—she goes to Egypt at least twice a year and talks to the dead pharaohs—did you know that? And even more often she goes on pilgrimages to Mexico and Chichen Itza, for seances with the Indian shamans. Not to mention all her other eccentricities. But she and Daddy are content in their strange little world, so I humor them. They're basically harmless." She shot me a little look to see if I believed it.

"I thought you and your boyfriend were part of their group."

She shifted and smoothed the hem of her dress, and as she looked down I realized that she and Elizabeth shared the same profile. "Tod had some money problems, that's all. He needed financing for a picture a few years ago, and he heard about the Foundation. They support certain films and other art and publishing projects that further their own beliefs." She looked uncomfortable, then looked directly at me. "I shouldn't have said that. It's very, very private. Life-or-death private, in fact."

"Mum's the word," I said, zipping my lip with my finger.

"Anyway, Tod is simply overwhelmed by it all. I grew up with it, it's all second nature to me. Oh, Tod tries, but he has to take tranquilizers to be around them. Still, if he quits attending the meetings, he's out of the Foundation and out of investment money."

I remembered his loopy look during the seance, and nodded. I would have bet money I could pick the first of his movies that the Foundation had financed, too. It would be his first horror flick, titled *The Psychic,* a third-rate tale of a "true" psychic—a sweet little Miss Marple type who had captured a serial murderer preying on young California surf bunnies—lots of blood and gore—after the FBI and all the police in Southern California had failed. I'd watched a scrap of it one evening when nothing else was on TV. The little old lady had also talked to spirits. In fact, she'd even had a spirit guide.

"As soon as Tod finishes shooting *Death's Final Agony,* he'll quit the Foundation, though." Ariel sat up straighter, and some fire flashed through her honey-colored eyes. "I'm going to finance his next picture."

My eyes went round in spite of me. "You can afford to finance a whole movie?"

"Well, maybe not all of it, but I'll put in about two million and use this place as collateral to get him another five or so. This property also includes the several adjoining shops"—she gestured toward the wisteria-covered back wall of another building—"and you're standing on some of the most expensive real estate in the world."

"You seem so young to be so rich."

She laughed again, easily, cheerily. "I just came into my trust. Aunt Liz set it up so I couldn't touch anything but a portion of the income till age twenty-four, and I just had a birthday, Happy Birthday to me! That's why everyone's upset with me, of course."

"For getting older?" I played dumb.

"For getting richer, silly. They want me to contribute the whole ball of wax to the Foundation. I'm not about to. Tod and I have other plans. Our movie is going to cost about ten million, but it will be wonderful. The life story of Leo Tolstoy. Filmed in Russia, one of the first full-length American features entirely done there, that's why we can do it so cheaply. It will be a hundred times better than *Dr. Zhivago*! There will be beautiful period sets, beautiful scenery, a lot of Russian actors. Ian James will play Tolstoy—he's costing us two million—and I'll be Tolstoy's wife."

"I'm surprised to hear that your aunt left you so much. I'd have assumed she left it all to the Foundation."

Her face lit up with delight. "They thought she was going to. But she fooled them all. She'd changed her will only two days before she died. Of course, she'd just given them the house in Pasadena with all that land. I suppose she decided that was enough. Her new will left the trust to me, and a few mil' to Daddy. Frank only got Aunt Liz's art collection, though it's worth a bundle. Not that he needed money. He has plenty of his own, and he never spends a cent of it."

"Frank has nothing at all to do with the Foundation?"

"He hates them. They've tried and tried to get to him, but he's as stubborn as sin."

"So your aunt had everything set up in a trust before she died?"

Ariel's face curled into a frown. "That's the odd thing," she said. "Nobody really knew how much money Aunt Liz had. Daddy only inherited a fraction of the Cardwell money. His mother couldn't stand him, and she really cut him off when he and Mother joined the Foundation. She was a devout born-again Christian, gave a lot of money to missions projects and other causes. A stern old woman, but pretty good-hearted. She really blew her stack when she learned that Daddy had donated her wedding diamond to the Foundation. She'd given it to him for Mother, of course, since he was oldest, but . . ."

"That was a little insensitive, I'd say."

"Oh yes, but you know, they especially like diamonds. Aunt Liz got the diamond back for Grandmother, though I'll bet it cost her plenty. Aunt Liz inherited the diamond when Grandmother died, and she wouldn't let the Foundation have it then, either. Everyone was upset about that. If you'll notice, none of the women wear diamond wedding rings—all diamonds go to the Foundation as soon as you join. So does all but a small amount of your gold. Diamonds are supposed to be the most powerful crystals, gold the purest metal. Only the Foundation gets to own diamonds."

"Who in the Foundation?"

She shrugged. "The people who want my money."

"Who are?"

She shrugged. "All of them, I suppose. Mother's one of the treasurers. My own mother, can you imagine? They spend a fortune on psychic experiments, publications, and movies and on any other thing they can find that furthers their beliefs. Including—" She stopped short.

"Including what?"

"Never mind."

"What about that fancy pink house?"

"Oh, the house belongs to Mother. Her father was the film star Howard Hudson, and he piled up a bundle. Unlike most of the stars of his time he was sharp enough to get a cut of the action on every picture he did, and by the time he died he owned a major share of his studio. But Daddy only has a few million of his own—or did have, he's given most of it to the Foundation. Mother lets them use her too, though she's far from broke. So far."

"How much do you think your Aunt Liz inherited from the Cardwell fortune?"

"All of it, except the bit that went directly to Daddy. Grandfather Cardwell died, and after that Grandmother had it all for about twenty years. She sat on it like a fat little wasp, except for her missions projects. She was really generous with them. She supported an entire orphanage down in Baja. Maria Elena grew up there, isn't that nice? Anyway, in the meantime, Daddy and Mother and Aunt Liz had all joined the Foundation, and they tried to get her to donate something from time to time—the others put pressure on them to work on her, you know—but Grandmother simply wouldn't budge. She hated the Foundation, said they were anti-Christ, that there was no way she'd contribute so much as a cup of coffee grounds to them." She curled her legs up beneath her, and laughed again. "A lot of people say I'm just like Grandmother."

"If your grandmother hated the Foundation so much, why did she leave her money to your Aunt Liz? I mean, you said your Aunt Liz was also a member."

"Aunt Liz stopped attending meetings shortly before Grandmother Cardwell died, and relations were strained between her and my parents. Grandmother believed Aunt Liz was done with the Foundation and had come back to share her beliefs in plain old ordinary Christianity, so she left the money to Aunt Liz."

"Any chance that Aunt Liz was conning your grandmother so she'd do just that?"

Ariel thought hard, then said, "I don't think so. Aunt Liz was really very confused about the Foundation. She was teetering between their beliefs and her mother's faith. I used to go to church with her." A wistful, longing look touched her face. "I wish I'd never stopped going. I wish Aunt Liz was still here, so I could talk to her and figure my life out."

"And yet your aunt gave the Foundation the family home just a few months after your grandmother's death."

Ariel shrugged. "That surprised everyone, even Daddy."

"Did she start attending your parents' meetings again before that?" I was still wondering if she'd been mesmerized into it during one of the Cardwell seances.

Ariel thought. "Not that I can remember. Of course, I was just a teenager then, off in my own world. They didn't allow me to attend the real seances or any of the other heavy stuff, so I might have missed it if she did. But from what I can remember Aunt Liz saying, she was getting fed up with them."

"And her husband, Frank? Did he make any static over her giving away the family estate?"

Ariel grinned. "He always hated the Foundation. Called them charlatans, said the whole business was a lot of poppycock. I heard him and Aunt Liz argue over it when I used to stay with them, back when Aunt Liz first joined the Foundation. He flatly refused to have anything to do with it and tried everything he could to get Aunt Liz to drop it. Yes, he was mad when she gave them the Cardwell estate. He was murderously furious."

"How much do you think the Cardwell fortune was worth when your grandmother was alive?"

She gave a little shrug and pursed her mouth in thought. "Oh, people say Grandmother had a hundred million or so, at one time. But there were a few bad investments, and she gave the missions' projects millions. It probably wasn't near that by the time she died. Still, the Cardwells once had one of the great old fortunes, you know. They socialized with the Rockefellers and Vanderbilts in the early part of the century. When my grandmother died, we found some fascinating tin-types and old photographs in the attic showing my family members with all kinds of famous people—even the crowned heads of Europe."

Maria picked that moment to rap lightly on the door. Ariel jumped up and went to let her in.

They spread out the feed on a round table that I moved in front of the picture window, so we could look at the garden while we ate. Maria made sure everything was okay, gave me another lewd wink, then she retreated downstairs. I held out Ariel's chair for her, then seated myself and put a white linen napkin in my lap.

I wasn't really hungry, but I didn't want to seem too greedy for Ariel's information, either. So I spent a few minutes complimenting the garlic-baked chicken and steamed red potatoes Maria had set in front of us. There was a simple green salad with tarragon-mustard dressing, and ice water to drink—Ariel was careful about what went into her body, she explained. That was fine by me.

But after a couple of forkfuls of the chicken, Ariel, with absolutely no prompting from me, put down her fork and started talking again.

"Aunt Liz was up to something before she died," she said. "Some of her assets weren't liquid, of course. Real estate here was at an all-time low, so she kept these buildings and then put them into my trust. But she liquidated almost everything else. She established one small trust for my father, the more generous one for me. And the rest of it is just gone."

"Has anyone tried to trace it?"

"You're kidding. Frank tried desperately, and what with owning his own bank, you'd have thought he could find out. But from what he told Mother and Daddy, he couldn't find a trace of it. Not that I'm sure I believe him."

"Must have been a bundle. Too much to go up in thin air."

"Yes." She'd stopped eating, was toying with her food, twirling her fork in the salad. "I know. Believe me, I know. It's been driving my family crazy. Not that they'd hang on to it long if they had it. It would all just go straight to the Foundation." Her mouth curled into a contemptuous rosebud.

"Why don't you hire me to look into it?"

"You?" She looked full at me, as if seeing me for the first time.

"That's what I do for a living," I said, then shrugged modestly.

"But what could you do?"

I was starting to feel a little insulted, but I kept my temper. "I never know till I find out."

"Do you think you might really be able to find Aunt Liz's money?" She was looking more skeptical by the minute.

"Anything's possible, isn't it?"

"If you found it, who would get it?"

"Her legal heir, I suppose. Her husband, unless it was otherwise specified in her will."

"Why don't you ask Uncle Frank to hire you then?"

116

"He doesn't exactly trust me."

A little ripple of excitement passed over her face. "So you do know Uncle Frank?"

"I had a little trouble with my checking account," I said quickly.

"Uncle Frank has nothing to do with that level of banking, he leaves it up to his managers." She eyed me with hostility.

"Look, I can't exactly explain all this right now. But I can't really talk to your Uncle Frank."

The honest approach worked better. She started looking like she might be thinking it over, then said, "Maybe I could make a deal with Uncle Frank."

"Worth a try, right? But I wouldn't bring up my name if I were you."

"I'd have to talk it over with Tod first."

"Fine by me, I'm in the phone book if you decide you'd like to hire me."

"Who's hired you now?"

"Now?" That question had come out of left field.

"Yes. Who's paying you to nose around us. Uncle Frank?"

"You've got to be kidding me."

"The Foundation?"

"Hardly. I'd never heard of those Lobo—uh—those people till the other day."

"Then who? Why is anyone interested in what Mother and Daddy are doing?"

"Tell you the truth, they're not."

"Who's they?"

I thought about telling her, then decided not to. And then I decided to more or less change the subject. "Do you remember much about your aunt's death?"

She stepped out of her suspicious mode at that and took a stroll back down memory lane. "I went to the house right after it happened," she said sadly. "Mother and Daddy picked me up at school. Of course by then they'd already taken Aunt Liz's body away."

"Do you recall any of the conversation? Anything out of the ordinary?"

"Not really. The man who'd pronounced her dead was still there . . ."

"Do you remember his name?"

"Something that sounds like 'doors.'"

"Could it have been Gates?"

"Yes, that was it, Dr. Gates. I remembered him especially because he'd been at some of the meetings."

"Meetings?"

"At my parents' house, of course. The Foundation's seances and all."

Eureka! I wanted to stand up and shout, maybe beat my chest a little, but I controlled myself. "Anyone or anything else?"

"Uncle Frank. He was really upset, he tried to attack the doctor. The police held him back, and then Dr. Gates gave him a shot to tranquilize him. Frank was in the hospital for a month or so after that, because of grief and nerves. Dr. Gates kept him there. Frank really loved Aunt Liz, you know. She loved him too, I suppose, but he—"

"Something wrong?" Her face had twisted into a look of absolute bitterness.

"Oh, it's my mother. She's so neurotic, so pathologically insecure. She wanted to be in movies, but in spite of her father's success she never made it. She just couldn't act. She met Aunt Liz when she was still in pictures. Mother was deathly jealous of her. I think that's how it all came about. I don't think Mother ever had any real interest in Frank, he's such a dry little man. But Mother couldn't take Aunt Liz's talent away from her, so she chased after Frank instead until he finally collapsed under the weight of her determination. He's such a weak man. Anyway, they had a brief affair. Mother just had to tell Aunt Liz, gloating about it. Mother's insecurity takes on some pretty destructive forms. I think that's why she's so involved with the Foundation, because they'll let her 'act,' in a way. She's finally a star."

She turned to stare out the window into the deep leafy green of the garden. "That's why a lot of people get involved. It's better than sitting at the country club drinking one cocktail after another and helping each other justify being rich. This way they can pretend they're doing something, but they don't have to really get their hands dirty with the true problems of the world. And it's all very mysterious of course. That makes them feel special and important."

"You're pretty cynical for a little girl."

"You wouldn't believe the stuff I've seen."

"Such as?"

"I can't even talk about most of it. It makes me sick."

"So I take it you're not a True Believer?"

"You've got to be kidding." She'd pushed the plate away, the food barely touched. "As soon as I get my money in hand, I'll be gone so fast, they won't even see my smoke."

"You don't have your money yet?"

"It's being processed. The lawyer is getting the documents ready so I can sign them. There are a few things that also have to be liquidated—a couple of pieces of Mexican property that were left in the trust. The Foundation is pressuring me to donate at least that, even if I insist upon keeping the rest. They're only worth about $45,000. I actually might end up letting them have the property, just to get them off my back. But right now, I'm feeling stubborn. Either way, the whole thing should be straightened out in a few weeks. By then Tod will have the horror flick he's working on wrapped. He doesn't care about this picture, he's going to let his assistant oversee the post-production work while we fly to Russia to scout locations."

"Does your lawyer belong to the Foundation?"

Her face twisted up into an expression of exhausted disgust. "Everyone I know belongs to the Foundation. I can't wait to get away from them. I wish they would all go straight to hell."

Chapter
──────TWELVE──────

There is a hell," Tony Cacciatore was saying. "The Bible tells us hell is real. But you can escape that hell, just as you can escape the hell you have here on earth. All you have to do is give your heart to Jesus Christ."

He was standing in front of one of Big Al's seediest strip joints. It was called "The Bare Affair," and it was a genuine bucket of blood. Fights every night; hookers with turkey tracks so bad that they'd almost turned to gangrene; a clientele made up of pimps, bikers, perverts and wannabees; as well as johns and an occasional skid row bum who'd managed to pop somebody's wallet for the price of a drink for one of the bust-out girls—who drank club soda with a shot of red wine, charged a cool ten bucks, and called it "champagne." If you wanted to get rolled or come down with AIDS, this was the place to be.

Tony was talking through a megaphone to anyone in a three-block radius who would listen. Beside him was the elderly Mexican Indian I'd last seen stirring chili, and clustered behind them were about ten of Tony's followers, including the handsome young black man named Shelby Knight, and a few others who had been here the other day. Some of them were again wielding video cameras, this time panning Tony, then panning the small audience of derelicts and hookers, then back to Tony, getting it all down.

"These people don't care about you," Tony was saying. "Believe me, I know. I used to sit and listen to them talk. You ain't even people to them, just something they can use to make a buck. They get you strung out so's they can convince you to do the things you got to do to make them rich, things you wouldn't do in a million years if you didn't have a habit. They got you in chains, and them chains come straight from the pits of hell.

"That's what drugs is all about, and that's what porno is all about. Putting people in chains, makin' it so's you can't see each other as humans, just as bunches of body parts. Drugged-out body parts, for sale to anybody who's got a buck, to get used any way the buyer wants. Don't you think you deserve better than that?"

A black pimp had sidled up. He was long, lean, and muscular, dressed in expensive but soiled clothes: a gold silk shirt, stained white flannel slacks, gold chains around his neck and gold bracelets on his wrists, gold rings on his fingers, beige Gucci loafers with gold socks. He wore wrap-around sun-glasses and his hair was cropped close to his oversized skull. He stood, his head tilted arrogantly, beside two women—both black, one blonde, one brunette, obviously hookers, both most likely in their late teens. I could see he was giving them a little static, but the blonde tossed her head and gave him some static right back, and he grinned, showing a gleaming gold tooth. He then reached in his pocket and extracted a toothpick, stuck it in his mouth, and leaned into the building, still grinning cynically, planning to enjoy the show, at least till he could figure out how to get his women back in line without causing a scene right there in public.

Tony was saying, "Wasn't so long ago that I was one of the people trying to keep you in chains. I couldn't see past the money, I thought money was the only thing you could trust. Money, money, money. It was my god. I even sacrificed people to that god. I know how you're thinkin' right now, because time was, not so long ago, if someone woulda come along and told me to give it all up, I woulda laughed in their face. I woulda said, 'What else is there?'

"And besides, I come up the hard way just like most a you. My old man was in the mob. My grandfather was in the mob, he come straight from Sicily. I didn't know no other way to make it, it really boiled right down to that. I didn't like what I saw happenin' around me, but like I say, I figured, 'What else is there?'

"I'm here to tell you that there's a lot else. I know most a you live from day to day, don't even have your dope money put together for your next fix. You're thinkin', 'Sure, it's easy for someone who's got three squares to come down here and tell us to give up the only thing we got.' But I'm here to tell you that not two blocks away, you got a warm bed. You got meals. You got people who care about you who'll get you into a detox and then a rehab, so's you can turn your life around, and we'll even stick with you while you do it.

"I'm talkin' about the Grace of the Shepherd Mission. Place we set up a while back. I'm Tony Cacciatore. I used to be a mob enforcer, some a you may of heard of me back in the old days. I was tight with the jerk who runs these joints. I'm tellin' you, don't trust Hollywood's version of what it's like to be in the mob. Ain't nothing glamorous about it, nothing at all. If there was, I wouldn't a ended up having to be hyped up on heroin, everything about me already dead, in order to do the work. And ain't nothing glamorous about what you people are doin', neither, I don't care if it comes off playin' that way in the movies. Ain't no 'lady' here goin' to get picked up by a limo and live in the lap of luxury the rest of her life. I don't need to tell you, a john ain't like that, real life ain't like that. People who feed you this baloney, movies and TV and all the rest, they're usin' you same as your pimps, same as the people who own these joints, same as the mob, same as the johns. They're helpin' you kill yourselves because it makes them a buck.

"I'm tellin' you, I had shackles around my heart that choked it dead. But if I can get out of the chains, so can you. All you got to do is ask Jesus into your hearts, and you'll be reborn, a brand new person. A lot a people, they don't even have to go to the detox, Jesus frees them of the drug habits right on the spot."

The pimp was moving, bearing down on Shelby Knight. I figured there was trouble brewing, so I edged in that direction, in case I had to intercept any heavy stuff. I had my .38 in my shoulder holster, and I still knew all my moves from the Special Forces.

But to my surprise, the pimp reached out and gave Shelby a high-five. "Howzit-goin'?"

Shelby said, "Better and better. How're things with you, T-Bone?"

"Ain't seen you for a while. Wanted to get a kilo or two, but word on the street is you ain't dealin' no more. You take a bust?"

Shelby gave his million kilowatt smile. "No way, man."

I was really listening now. I was far enough away that they weren't aware I was interested, yet close enough to hear every word.

"You carryin' some weight, man," T-Bone said. "Man, I know you is, you face lit up like a light bulb. Don't-cha be holdin' out on me."

"I'm not using."

"Tell it to the judge. I need to deal. My old ladies, they gettin' disrespectful, I can't keep 'em fed."

"It's Jesus," Shelby said.

The pimp's face folded into disbelief. "I don't want to hear that jive."

"I'm telling you. I got clean. I don't fix any more, I don't deal any more, I don't have any ladies any more. I found Jesus. He detoxed me and set me straight, and I'm the happiest man alive. You ought to try it, T-Bone. Ain't nothin' like it and never will be, not the best scag, not the best crack, not even the finest China White. Think about it. You know that high you get when you just fixed? That silky glow that tells you ain't nothing you can't handle, ain't nothing in the world ever going to be wrong again?"

The pimp nodded his head and slouched down, in his element now, talking drugs. "I been there."

So had I. So had every other junkie in the world. I knew that feeling well, and still missed it every now and again. It had carried me through many a night of horrors, both in Vietnam and back here at home. But it had eventually led me into even deeper horrors. I listened harder.

"What if I told you I had a fix that would get you off about a thousand times that high, but it would stay with you forever? I mean, you take it once, and it's yours, man. And nobody can take it away." Shelby was leaning in, talking the man's language.

"You messin' with my head," the pimp said.

"No way. I found that fix. And it's for real. And it's yours, any time you want it. You think China White or Mexican Tar can get you off? Man, you've never felt anything till you get a dose of the Holy Spirit. You want to stay with white powder when you can have the power and the beauty of the One who created the stars and sky? Man, you're settling for way less than second best."

"You messin' with my head," the pimp said again.

"No way. It's true, and it's yours. All you have to do is try it. Just check it out. Look, if it was a powder and I was holding it in my hand, you'd give me a thousand bucks for it. More. You'd sell your soul for it. But it's not physical, and it's not for sale. It's something that's just out there, for the taking. So give it a try. It's easy. All you have to do is ask Jesus to come into your heart. Just talk to him, real honest, right now. You're not going to believe what happens. Look, let's pray together . . ." He reached out and tried to take the pimp's hands.

But the pimp was suddenly enraged. He jerked away. "Get outa my face, fool! You probably be workin' with the feds, you lyin' . . ." He moved back to his women, leaving a trail of obscenities in his wake. Shelby looked after him with sadness, then turned back to listen to Tony, and the disturbed expression turned instantly back to a beaming smile.

I could understand the pimp's skepticism—something that made you feel a thousand times better than the finest China White? This was religion? What was Shelby talking about?

I was an ironclad cynic. Shelby's words just added to it. I mean, what were these people peddling? Promising that a relationship with Jesus Christ could bring true joy and even ecstasy, when all I could remember was the dry regimentation and religion I'd known as a boy, the judgmentalism, the authoritarian rules and regulations and interceptions of my boyish pleasures, the holier-than-thou attitudes of nearly everyone but my grandmother, who had been a saint and not subject to human foibles. Joyous? Get you higher than the finest heroin? What a joke. Religion was nothing but boring. A haven for losers. Someplace to go when you'd used everything else up and didn't have the nerve to go out and stir up something new.

But then there was Tony. Something had definitely happened to him, and he seemed happy. Even joyous. And he didn't act a bit religious, except that he talked a lot about God and his new relationship with Him. I thought about Tony, about the new-found happiness in his eyes, about the seeming new purpose in his life. If I could buy that in a pill or powder, would I? Maybe . . .

This line of thinking led me back to Big Al and the problem I was supposed to be helping to solve. Was Tony angry with the mob for something they'd done? Was this harassment the only way he could get even without bringing heat down on himself?

I stepped over to Shelby. "How you doin', pal?"

"Never better."

"You realize Tony's got his life on the line here?"

I looked at my watch, anxious to get this little errand done. I'd left Ariel's at five-thirty, after she'd started sulking and had clammed up. I'd figured three-quarters of an hour to stop by here and deliver Big Al's latest message, then on to the Cardwells' and I'd be right on time.

Shelby said, "Tony's not afraid to die."

That stopped me. It was the last answer I'd have expected. "You realize what you're into here?"

"Nothing I haven't been into for the past ten years. It's just that now I'm on the Winner's side."

"The mob is going to kill Tony. I mean that. Read my lips, and I'll say it again." I did, mouthing each word carefully, trying my best to get the point across. "If you're a friend of his, you'd best put him on a plane to Iraq or Libya or some other safe spot. Because if he stays here and keeps doing this, in about another day you and I are going to a funeral. And if you're hanging out here with him when the Big Boys come, it might be yours as well as his."

"Nobody's bigger than the God we serve."

"Sorry to disagree, but an Uzi—any weapon—is bigger than any abstraction you'd care to discuss."

Shelby turned and leveled a sternly compassionate look at me. "God isn't an abstraction. He's more real than you are. He created every cell in your body, every sub-atomic particle of this universe. He's bigger than any mob hit-man, and He's big enough to take care of those who serve Him. Psalm twenty-seven says, 'The Lord is my light and my salvation; whom shall I fear? The Lord is the strength of my life; of whom shall I be afraid?'"

I gave him a long look, realizing how hopeless the conversation was, then I returned to where Tony was just finishing his short sermon by offering up a prayer. I waited respectfully till he was done, then I stepped forward and into another bear-hug. I didn't hug back.

As soon as he'd let go of me, I said, "Tony. It's about Big Al." He looked tired.

"Come on, I got to get back to the mission. We can talk on the way." He scratched at the black brush starting to erupt on his face. A twice-a-day shaver, and I thought I had it bad.

As we walked back down the alley, I talked, he listened. But when we got to the mission, it was as if I hadn't said a word.

So I tried one more time. "Give it up, Tony. It's not worth getting killed over."

"I ain't gonna get killed."

"So then you have to kill someone else, and you end up back in the slammer for life. It's not worth that either."

"It is," he said. "Them people out there are dyin', and they don't know the God who made them. They're bein' used up like tissues, and most of them's so drugged out they don't even know what hit them."

"You've picked up a missionary complex. Most of those people don't want to change. You couldn't change them if you literally put them in chains and preached to them twenty times a day."

"You're right about that. I can't change nobody. But God can. If He changed me, He can change anybody, anytime." We'd stopped by his office while he put away his megaphone, and now he opened the door to the sanctuary. I followed him inside.

The Hispanic girl was practicing the piano again, this time dressed in a peach-colored blouse, acid-washed denims, and huaraches. She didn't notice us come in.

Tony took a seat near the back of the room, and I pulled up a chair, turned it around backwards, then straddled it, facing him. "So what are you going to do, Tony? I have to tell Big Al something."

"Tell Big Al that he must be born again, or he'll never see the kingdom of God. Tell him I was already dead back when I was with the Family. Just like he is. Physical death would be a walk in the park compared to that."

"You don't have to go back to work for them. Just lay off hassling their skin joints and hookers so Big Al doesn't feel obligated to zotz you." In one way I could see why Big Al thought Tony had gone nuts. On the other hand, my respect for him was growing by the minute.

Just then the girl started singing, her voice a clear, pure contralto, beautiful as a skylark's: "Amazing Grace, how sweet the sound, that saved a wretch like me . . ."

I was washed with another wave of nostalgia. My grandmother had loved that song. It had been played at her funeral, in the little white church, me sitting wracked with grief, straight from the VA Hospital where I'd been recuperating for the past three months, some of the VC's shrapnel still in me. Her heart attack had been so sudden. No one had even known she was ill.

I swallowed the feeling. "Look, Tony, tomorrow's your deadline. Then Big Al is sending someone to take care of you. Is that what you want?"

127

The girl had finished her song. She closed the piano, then walked down the aisle and up to Tony, where she gave him a sweet smile, then sat down close beside him, displaying the type of loyalty and love that usually comes only from someone's dog.

"What about her?" I said. "Who takes care of her when you're gone?"

"I'm not going anywhere."

"That's showing a little more tunnel vision than I ever thought you'd have. Come on, Tony, give it a break. Look, I have to go to this wacky meeting at this house in Pacific Palisades tonight, I'll leave the phone number, you think it over and call me if you come to your senses. I could talk to Big Al again, maybe work something out." I reached in my pocket, pulled out my wallet, fumbled for the scrap of paper with the Cardwells' phone number on it.

From the corner of my eye I saw the girl go stiff. I whipped around to look at her just as she screamed, then screamed again, a look of stark horror on her face! Her eyes were fixed on the floor.

I leaped up, yanking out my .38 and panning the room with it even as I stood. Tony had also leaped to his feet, hands out to brace himself, scanning the room, locked in his professional fighting stance. But there was nothing to shoot, nothing to fight, nothing but me, Tony, and the screaming girl.

And yet the girl kept screaming, her shrieks bringing others now, running in from the kitchen, shouting, wondering what had happened, who was hurt.

And then I realized what the girl was staring at. In the process of thumbing through my wallet for the Cardwells' phone number, a photograph of Elizabeth Ann Livingstone had fallen out, one of the two I'd taken from Ariel's photo collection. It had landed face up on the floor beside me, and the girl was staring at it, rigid, in shock, screaming and screaming and screaming.

I bent down and grabbed the photo, then stuffed it in my pocket. The girl's screams instantly turned to wracking sobs. Tony had her in his arms now, comforting her, asking her what was wrong, praying for her.

I couldn't believe what I'd just seen. Why had the girl reacted like that? Had it been the photo, or had the photo been just a coincidence?

I pulled the photo out again, Tony looking at me quizzically while he stroked her hair. I waited till the girl's sobs had somewhat subsided, then jerked the photo up in front of her and held it there.

Instantly, she started screaming again, staring in shock at the photo.

Tony froze, and shoved the girl aside. "What'd ya think you're doin'?" His muscles were bunching, his fists were balled up.

I stuck the photo back in my pocket and held my hands up, palms facing him. "Hang on, pal. Take care of the kid, get her settled down. We got some talking to do."

Tony hesitated, still angry, but the girl had stopped screaming as soon as I'd put the photo away. So he comforted her again, then handed her over to a woman who'd come in from the kitchen. Then he turned to me.

"What's in that picture?"

I pulled it out of my pocket and showed him.

He looked puzzled. "Just a face?" He eyed me suspiciously. "How come this upset the kid?"

I shook my head in genuine bewilderment. "You got me."

"Who is this woman?"

"Somebody I'm looking for."

"For what?"

"Because she's disappeared."

Tony scratched at his head.

"That's all," I said. "By the way, what's the deal on the kid, anyway?"

Tony shrugged. "Nobody knows. She seems retarded, but that ain't quite it. Doctors say it's severe emotional problems, maybe complicated by drugs. Probably psychedelics, from the stuff she babbles sometimes. Strange kid. For a while she's okay, happy as can be, then she'll go into a sort of dark place and nobody can follow her there. But we pray her through it every time. One minute she's way out in left field, talkin' about priests and snakes and human sacrifice, then all of a sudden she'll come out with something really bright, seem real normal for a while, though she can't remember much about her past." He thought, then shot me an accusing look. "But she ain't never cracked up like that before."

"Any point in asking her about it?"

"I don't think so. She gets like that, she ain't talkin' to nobody."

"She got a family?"

"Don't know, but probably not. She's illegal. We found her on the streets in Tijuana, we got an outreach down there. Literally picked her up out of the gutter one night. Shelby did. So drugged she couldn't stand up. She was being run by a pimp name of Pablo Garcia who had about ten 'old ladies,' though none of them was very old. Shelby tracked Garcia down and jacked him up a little, tryin' to learn what he could to help the girl. Garcia said she'd hit the strip in Tijuana already messed up like that, didn't even know what was going on around her, everybody just usin' her, not even botherin' to pay. His story was he did her a favor by takin' her in, givin' her a place to stay, clothes, food. She still worked the streets, of course, but at least she had a little protection. That's the pimp's story, anyway. But it seems to jibe with a lot of what she says."

"Where'd she come from?"

"Somewhere on down in Baja. That's as much as we could figure out. Who knows what happened to her there. Mexico ain't too easy on its kids."

"What'll happen to her now?"

"We'll take care of her. She's seein' a psychologist, a Christian who won't mess her up any worse than she is. We'll pray her through this, you wait. One a these days she'll be as normal as you or me."

He picked up on the irony of that at the same time I did, and we both grinned.

"Where'd you get the money to start this place? How do you keep it running?"

His grin faded. "Big Al pay you to find out? He goin' to clip my backers too?"

"Nah, he just hired me to deliver the message, which I did. I'm no longer employed by Big Al. This is personal curiosity."

"I had a little dough saved up. I worked for a lot a years, didn't spend much, and then I got lucky a few times on the horses. Anyhow, when I got out of the joint, I figgered I could at least use my money to try to put somethin' back of what I destroyed. The man who came to the prison, he turned me on to a church, they put us and the Tijuana outreach in their mission fund, so we get a regular check from them too."

"Which church is that?"

"Church of the Shepherd's Grace, down in Anaheim. Nondenominational, Pastor's name is Irby Howard. You mighta seen him on TV."

"I don't watch much besides the news these days."

"Well, he has a big ministry, they back us up. Paying right now for our lawyers."

"I don't mean to disillusion you, Tony, but I don't think Big Al is going to take this to court."

Tony guffawed at that. "You always had a sense a humor, pal."

I shrugged.

Then he turned serious. "We got a lawyer fighting the porno laws, tryin' to get them tightened up. Make it illegal to procure for a prostitute, or to show some a the smut you see. We want them to enact some a them laws that work other places."

"They work if you can get anybody to enforce them," I said. I'd seen this tried before.

"They will," Tony said with conviction. "We get that far, they will, I don't care if I gotta jack up the mayor himself. In the meantime, nothing to do but keep it up with the sting operations, mess up Big Al's skin action as much as I can."

I started to tell him again that Big Al's threat was a real one, but he shot me a heavy-lidded look, and I suddenly realized that he knew it better than I did.

But he really didn't care.

Chapter

—THIRTEEN—

The high iron gate to the Cardwell estate was skillfully camouflaged amidst palms and eucalyptus and oak trees. I'd wheeled right up to it before I realized it was closed up tight tonight. I screeched to a stop and was wondering what to do next, when the two Surf Gorillas from the other night materialized out of the shadows. One of them stuck his head up near my window. He looked like a sun-tanned Neanderthal with bleached-blonde hair. He grunted, "Mr. Weatherby?"

"At your service."

"I gotta see your identification. You 'bout got us fired last night. We owe you one." The words were lifeless, something his ego required him to say. I noticed that he was still using Essence of Marijuana Smoke for aftershave.

I showed the ID, they rolled open the gate, and then I was moving smoothly through and up the driveway, surprised to see several other guards both beside the road and patrolling the grounds, most of them hulking Mexican thugs armed with Mini-Uzis and machine pistoleros, watching with cold eyes as I rolled past. A lot of security tonight.

A few of the same expensive cars I'd seen last time were parked in the pink-lit flagstoned courtyard. But the centerpiece tonight was a long white Rolls Royce limo with fancy gold trim. I glanced at the plates: California, probably a rental. Another Mexican thug was leaning against it, wearing a white chauffeur's uniform, smoking a cigarette. As I walked past him, I jerked my thumb toward the car. "Nice set of wheels. Who's the boss?"

He sneered, his wide nostrils flaring out, his dark eyes cold. He flipped his cigarette onto the flagstones, then ground it out with his heel, implying he'd like to do the same to me. He tilted his head arrogantly and watched me as I walked on past and toward the house.

Fine by me if he didn't want to talk. I already had it figured out anyway. From the looks of the security and the price of the limo, the Cardwells' had to be entertaining the President of Mexico.

The house wasn't quite so well lit as the other night. The golden-yellow light filled only the downstairs, and about half of the pink outdoor lights had been turned off. I took the wide stone steps two at a time and found myself standing in front of a closed double-wide Spanish-oak door. I hit the bell, the door was instantly opened by an albino houseman, an older, thinner version of the Surf Gorillas. He wore white cotton pants and a white cotton shirt with turquoise and black Mexican embroidery around the neck. I couldn't help noticing the bulge beneath the shirt: a shoulder holster, complete with gun. I felt a curious reluctance to proceed farther into the house, as if the air before me had suddenly become too heavy to press into. Nevertheless, something seemed to be behind me as well, pressing me forward, so on I went.

The room with the fireplace and cathedral ceiling was dark tonight. The houseman led me past it and down a short hall. Another Mexican guard stood at attention beside a closed door, a 9mm Walther P-1 at his waist, the holster left open for fast action. Mucho mystery here tonight. The houseman ignored the guard, rapped on the door, and from inside, Cardwell called, "Come in." The houseman gave me the nod, so in I went. Once I was inside, Cardwell came up beside me, stood and smirked at me, then shut the door and slid the dead-bolt shut.

This small, semiformal living room was done in turquoise and black, not my favorite combination of colors. Yet somehow it was made tasteful—even expensive looking. French doors were opened all along the far wall, to show the back patio—the one with all the strange statues. Tonight they were faintly illuminated by milky moonlight. Beyond this, the yard was dark and wide, and the mountains jutted against the dark sky.

The black and turquoise sofas were soft and plump. The handful of guests were scattered about, some of them on overstuffed black chairs, all of them trying to hold their own against the tension in the room. Or was it the presence of evil? Whatever it was, it filled the air with a suffocating weight. I stood a minute and drew in a deep breath, almost sniffing the air. But if there was sulfur in it, it was masked by the heavy scent of incense.

This room was also decorated with pre-Columbian art, mostly small carvings embedded with jade and obsidian and turquoise. The *tour de force* was an Olmec head about two feet high, a stele carved with powerful simplicity. The face was twisted into a mongoloid snarl, the thick lips pouted prettily. The eyes were empty, and it wore helmet-like headgear. Whoever had sat for this carving was a real cheery fellow, probably someone who would indeed carve out your liver and have it for lunch. I suddenly had the eerie sensation of inhabiting a nightmare.

Cardwell shook my hand—I felt like I'd petted an eel—and then he turned and said to the little group, "I would like to present Mr. Arthur Weatherby. He's a private investigator who's been looking into our affairs." So that was how it was going to be. Direct confrontation. No matter. I could let him have his little moment, while I stood looking polite and stupid.

Cardwell gestured toward a man who was obviously the owner of the white limo. The several chairs to either side of the man were vacant, so as to set him apart from the rest of the group, almost as if he were on a throne. The man wore a flowing white silk pajama-suit reminiscent of an Indian guru's attire. His neck crooked like a vulture's, and around it was a six-inch-wide band that looked almost like a dog collar, except that it was gold, encrusted with turquoise and obsidian. Similar bracelets adorned his wrists. The man had the large, blunt nose and rough-hewn face of a Mexican Indian. His eyes were deeply sunken, and they pierced through when he looked at you. What was left of his black hair was plastered thinly across an elongated skull. His hands were long and bony and aglitter with gold and diamond rings. Aha! Diamonds! This told me he had to be one of the Foundation's elite, assuming Ariel had spoken true about only Foundation big-wigs getting to own the 'purest crystals.' The man's nails were as long as a fashion model's, manicured and buffed to a sheen. He held himself stiffly, regally, and everyone in the room looked at him with awe-filled eyes. Cardwell said to me, "This is Auguste Flores. A special guest from Mexico, we had no idea he'd honor us with his presence tonight."

Flores gave me a solemn nod of his head, moving almost in slow motion. I said, "Pleased to meet you." For an instant his black eyes glittered with interest, but then he blinked long and hard, and when he opened his eyes again he looked disdainful and aloof.

Cardwell motioned for me to sit in a deep black armchair at the far side of the room, then proceeded to introduce me all around, not bothering to hide his distaste.

The first man, Byron Atkins, was introduced as a thanatologist—a man who specialized in the scholarly approach to death. He had also written a book, I was told. A combination information guide for people who wished to commit suicide as well as a thesis on reincarnation. Another single man was there, introduced as Juan Valdez, though he certainly wasn't carrying a can of coffee and leading a burro. This man had a Fernando Lamas nose, the polish of Valentino, and a Boris Karloff smile. He was introduced to me as an expert in pre-Columbian art.

And then there was the sprightly eighty-year-old woman I'd spotted the other night. Fern Franklin was her name. Cardwell introduced her and said, "You'll be interested to know that Fern was a close friend of my late sister's. Fern channels the spirits of departed artists, especially Dali and Hieronymus Bosch. That's how she painted the beautiful portraits in our 'sanctuary.'"

I murmured something and managed to keep a straight face.

The platinumed and polished Vera Vance was there—looking puzzled as I came in, even more so as I sat down and joined the crowd. She was probably still waiting for me to come back with a photographer and do justice to the Foundation's Victorian house. Cardwell introduced us, saying in an aside to me, "Since you two haven't met before," rubbing it in.

She overheard him and said, "Oh, but we have met."

Cardwell frowned. "But you said on the phone . . ."

Her eyes went wide and she covered her mouth with her hand, then said, "You mean this is . . . ?"

Cardwell nodded meaningfully. She shook her head in disgust. I pretended I wasn't noticing any of this.

Vera's husband was with her. In fact, Caspar Cardwell and Dr. Vernon Vance appeared to be very good friends. Vance was a dapper little man of about fifty-five or sixty, wearing an expensive black suit and a wealth of gold jewelry. A huge emerald ring adorned one manicured finger. His hair was blow-dried and black, with a heavy blue rinse. His eyebrows were also exceptionally black, as if they'd been dyed, and his lashes were thick. His cheeks were slightly pale though his lips were rosy, and the overall effect was as if he'd been wearing traces of makeup. His movements were affected, self-absorbed, and when we were introduced and I looked into his cold, black eyes, I felt as if I'd just had a mind probe. Fortunately, at that moment Juan Valdez stepped into the conversation, and I managed to break quickly away from the sinister little clown.

Cassie, of course, was also there. When I asked about Sofia, she informed me in imperious tones that she wouldn't be around any more, she'd already taken the Fourth Step. When I tried to ask what the Fourth Step was, she sniffed disdainfully and moved away. And then there was Dr. Winch, looking contemptuous of me, shifting uncomfortably, not wanting to be associated with me. I made it a point to step over to her and say, "Nice to see you again."

Everyone seemed to be uncomfortable except Auguste. And I could tell they'd been discussing me before I arrived. I thought about the Mexican bodyguards in the yard, about the chauffeur. I surreptitiously patted my shoulder holster, making sure I still had my .38. I was wishing I'd brought my .357 Magnum. Maybe even a hand grenade or two.

There was no buffet set up, nor did I see any Ouija Boards. Obviously, there'd been a change of plans. A white-clad butler served cocktails—I settled for a lime Perrier—and everyone made small talk for awhile, careful to exclude me.

I'd settled into my chair and was studying the cheery little group when Cardwell came up and settled into the chair beside me.

"Not what you'd expected, I imagine."

I shrugged.

"Auguste's visit surprised us all," he said. I looked at his guest of honor, who was being tittered to by Cassie. Cardwell said, "Auguste is an avatar, you know. An ascended master, the actual incarnation of the great sun god, Tezcatlipoca, one of Quetzalcoatl's brothers, although he's also another aspect of Quetzalcoatl, you know how that goes. If you get within several feet of him, you can feel his *tonalii*."

"His *what*?"

"*Tonalii*. Sorry, I forget how advanced this must all seem to you."

I managed to keep from snorting.

He said, "*Tonalii* is the force that animates the soul and provides energy for growth and development. Auguste fairly *sings* with it! Tonight is a real privilege. He usually visits us just twice a year, on certain holy days, and only the innermost circle is allowed to participate. And then we see him in Mexico. But he phoned today and said he was in town on special business. I did mention you, but he said it would be all right if you attended, even though you'd been deceptive. We won't be doing anything that's private, and I'm still willing to teach you. But I'm afraid Auguste is a little too advanced for Ouija Boards or astrology readings."

"No problem," I said. "In fact, I don't want to intrude. I could come back another time."

"Oh, no, no, there's no intrusion. Its just that we so seldom get to spend time with Auguste in an informal way. Everyone is just a little uncomfortable, that's all."

Dr. Winch broke the tension. She stood and said, "As some of you know, my new book, *Retrocognition*, is finally in print. I've brought an autographed copy for each of you. But tonight, I feel that something a little different from seeing into the past is in order. We have a neophyte with us, unusual I'll admit, to have Auguste and a neophyte in the same room . . ."

A little titter of agreement swept over the room, like wind rustling leaves. Auguste smiled tolerantly.

"Caspar tells me that Mr. Weatherby arrived under false pretenses, and as you know he's turned out to be a private investigator. He is also apparently a skeptic, perhaps intent upon disproving our abilities. I suggest we spend some time proving to him that our psychic skills are genuine."

That perked some of them up. The elderly woman nodded sagely, Auguste's eyes glittered with interest, Cassie Cardwell even warmed up a bit.

"I would like to show Mr. Weatherby the truth in psychic powers, if the rest of you agree. So instead of working with retrocognition tonight, I'd like to do a simple psychic reading."

I heard Fern whisper loudly in Cassie's ear, "But she's so advanced to waste her time that way . . ." while the others nodded their assent and muttered their approval.

"Mr. Weatherby?" Dr. Winch was speaking imperiously.

"At your service."

"If you would be so good as to move over here beside me—" she gestured to a place on a black leather sofa—"we could begin."

I shrugged, looked at Cardwell. He nodded warmly. I picked up my Perrier and did as asked.

As soon as I was planted, Dr. Winch leaned in close to me—the hint of her dentures wafted on otherwise stale breath—and said, "Place your hands on your knees, palms upward."

I did as asked.

"Now, shut your eyes and breathe deeply, and say after me, 'I am the chakra of the violet light, I am the chakra of the violet light . . .'"

"What's a chakra?"

"Don't interrupt, young man. Do you want to learn anything, or don't you?"

"I wouldn't mind learning what a 'chakra' is, but if this is the wrong time we can let it slide."

Her frown reminded me of my fifth grade history teacher. She said, "Now, do as I say. We'll never get anywhere if you stop to ask questions about every little thing."

"Right."

"I am the chakra of the violet light, I am the chakra of the violet light . . .'"

I repeated the words, feeling like an absolute idiot.

But she was breathing harder now, still chanting. I leaned back a bit to get out of the line of her breath and tried my best to mimic her intonation to the letter.

Then suddenly she stopped and said, "Give me your hands."

I held them out, still palms up.

She took them in her own hands, telling me to relax my muscles, and then she took a small amethyst geode out of her pocket and passed it over my hands a few times then put it away. She shut her eyes tight and went into what looked like a trance, her own body relaxing, her face taking on a vacant look. And then she spoke to me in an entirely different voice—though still female. "Your name is Arthur Allan Weatherby?"

I sat there, not sure what I should do. Her hands were icy cold, and she was holding mine in a tighter and tighter grip.

"Answer me!" she demanded.

"Arthur Allan Weatherby, that's me all right."

"You live in Chaparral Canyon?"

"Right again." The others were watching with such keen interest that I was beginning to feel a responsibility to fulfill their expectations of me, sort of like a man standing on stage when suddenly the curtain goes up, the lights come on, and the audience emits a communal sigh of anticipation.

"You are thirty-eight years old?"

"As of February twentieth."

"Then I will speak of your past. As you were returned from the eleventh level to the present one, reincarnated to your present form, your mother was taken to the thirteenth level," she said. "With that act, she has ascended to the highest layer and now has become a true spiritual god."

"You've got me on that one." I didn't like them bringing my mother into this, but I figured it was just part of their act, nothing personal, so I let that slide too and went on with the game.

"I mean, your mother died while giving you birth. That act fulfilled her karma, and now she has evolved to be a pure spiritual god. She won't be incarnated back to this earth again."

"I see . . ."

"Your father lives in Philadelphia and has seven more children by his present marriage. You speak to him by phone every Friday, but he seldom comes to visit."

I thought about that one. I'd never met my father. Like I'd told Tony, he'd gone to fight in Korea while I was still in the womb and hadn't returned. Should I tell them this? Nah, they were the psychics. Let them figure it out for themselves. I said, "Correct."

"You went to UCLA, where you met Ariel Cardwell. Through her, you came to know the members of her family. But now you are deceiving them. You are truly working for an investigative firm that specializes in tracing financial transactions. You are looking into the financial affairs of her family and are using her as a dupe."

I thought about that, too. Part true, part false, but even the part that was true wasn't quite on target. Still, I said, "I apologize. I hadn't realized how duplicitous all this might seem to you."

She nodded sagely. Her eyes were still shut, but I swear, I saw her suddenly open them and give Cardwell a victorious gleam, then shut them quickly and paste on her previous facial expression. She said, "You met Elizabeth Livingstone when she was an actress. Your father took you on a studio tour, and Elizabeth was filming at that time. She spoke to you, and you have adored her ever since."

"True." It wasn't, of course, but I was getting into the beat of things by now.

"You are a seeker of truth. Though your life has caused you to be awash in spiritual ignorance, you have been given the first glint of enlightenment and now you wish to follow the pathway, to open your chakra and enter the violet light."

"More or less."

"Your ex-wife is a secretary for the IRS," she said, kneading my palms like they were bread-dough. "She had two children from a prior marriage and you tried to be a father to them, but she resented your closeness. She finally was unfaithful with a fellow worker, and you divorced her. She moved back east and refuses to allow you to see the children. You have great bitterness."

What in the world was this woman talking about? I'd never dated an employee of the IRS in my life, much less married one. Matter of fact, I'd never married anyone. The closest I'd ever come was Christine—who had never been married before, nor did she have any children. We'd have made the move, if she hadn't been transferred to Colombia. I tried to get her to stay here, she'd been married to her job, and that was my big romance. I was abstinent at the moment, trying to get myself straightened out emotionally from the last round. I thought about all that, then gave Dr. Winch a bright little nod. "True."

"Your life is dry and boring. You have little energy, little interest in life. Nothing much has happened to you for many months now."

I thought about Elizabeth Ann Livingstone hiring me to find her murderer, I thought about Big Al and Tony Cacciatore, I thought about sitting here now with these psychos. I said, "True."

"You are ready to take the First Step."

"More or less."

"You have finally realized that material things have no value, that the only things of true value are those which affect your higher power and your soul. You have few material possessions. You drive a two-year-old BMW. Expensive for you, but nothing at all in the eyes of the eternal and universal cosmos. You would willingly give up that car, the money in your bank account, and everything else you have that is of value in return for the smallest form of spiritual enlightenment and joy in your life."

I pulled my hands out of hers and said, "Wrong."

Her eyes popped open. She looked at me.

"That's false. So was a lot of the rest of it." I stood, and stretched. Then I said, "I've now completed my investigation of the lot of you, and I find you a little off base." I added a winning smile to the words, so as not to seem too harsh.

Dr. Winch was squinting, peering at me, genuinely flabbergasted. "But . . . I mean, what . . ."

Cardwell intervened by clearing his throat. For the first time, he also looked flustered. He said, "Well . . . perhaps we should move on to other things, since Mr. Weatherby apparently doesn't want to be read tonight. We do have a small dinner set up in honor of our special guest—" He looked at Auguste, who had a nasty yet pleased smile on his face. I had the feeling he'd actually enjoyed seeing Dr. Winch fall flat on her face. I realized then that she'd been miffed at him showing up and interfering with her place of honor. She'd been trying to steal his thunder—at least in part—and she'd gotten her comeuppance. We moved into a formal dining room done in mauve, wine, and silver, with rich cherrywood furniture, and gleaming Queen Anne table and chairs, and a Turkish carpet worth as much as the Suleiman Mosque. Silver dishes and teapots and trays and chafing dishes gleamed behind spotless glass doors in cherrywood cabinets. The table was covered with real Irish lace, the dishes were Wedgwood, the silver was so heavy you almost needed a forklift to lift a fork, the goblets were Irish crystal.

The servants served a dinner of very bitter tomato-beef soup, elegant salad greens with a sour dressing, a very stale prime rib, and all the fixin's. I polished off the soup because I was starving, but the taste more or less killed my appetite for the rest of the food, which seemed overdone and cloying. Besides, my mouth was numb. I ate enough to seem polite and listened hard to the conversation. Most of it didn't make sense to me. There was a lot of talk about birth signs and sun signs and moon signs, and the four quarters and the five sections, about the thirteen celestial levels and the nine underworld levels and how to get to each one. There were intense discussions about *tonalii* and *malinalli* and chakras, about the stations of the Cross and karma and the Turquoise Overworld, which I gathered was the sky, and the Obsidian Underworld, which could have meant anything from the subways in New York City to hell itself. People were discussing each others' auras and past lives and crystal-consciousness and *kundalini*, and they all talked about their Spirit Guides as if they were discussing old friends. And I was feeling nauseated. Something in the soup. But the nausea wasn't *that* bad, it came and went. I thought about bailing out, then thought about all the artillery guarding the place, then decided to play through till I could make an easy and unsuspicious exit. And as long as I had to be here, I might as well try to detect what I could.

Throughout all this, Auguste seemed decidedly bored but tolerant. Patient. Wading his way through the chitchat and the slavish deference to get to where he wanted to be, and I was curious to know where that was. The rest of the people were keeping a stealthy eye on him, all except Dr. Vernon Vance, who looked even more bored than Auguste. He actually nodded off one time and emitted a little snore before his wife kicked him under the table to wake him back up. But all the others seemed to be out to impress the obsidian-eyed Mexican god-guest.

Chapter
——FOURTEEN——

After the dinner, I moved with the rest of the men into a study where the sharply geometrical books in the bookcase were a little off-center and bound in particularly brilliant colors. The women had retired to wherever it was that women went before all the ones I know got liberated. For all of us he-men, sherry was served. I took a glass and sipped at it, forgetting my abstinence, forgetting everything except the terrible bitterness in my numbed-out mouth and the saliva pouring into it. Something was definitely wrong. In fact, it was about time for me to bug out, guards or no guards, as soon as I could make the trip to my car.

Cardwell was in deep conversation with the shaman, and then they seemed to decide on something. Cardwell lit a strong cigar, puffed theatrically on it, then stepped up and offered me one.

"No, thanks," I said, holding up my cut-crystal sherry glass—which would still have been full to the brim if I hadn't used most of it to refresh one of their plants. They'd dropped something in my food, and I was furious. Mostly at myself, for being so careless. But I was still together enough to hide how messed up I was. Maybe. "I have my hands full," I said. I noticed that they were not only full, they were trembling.

"I wonder, Mr. Weatherby, if you realize just how fortunate you are tonight. Very few people in the world have been able to meet a genuine incarnation of a god."

145

"That so?" He seemed to be leaning in too closely, and his face was a bit distorted. I kept my own face straight, stopped my eyes from bulging. I wasn't going to give them so much as a clue as to how messed up I was, but I was looking hard for the exit.

"Auguste is a Huichole shaman," Cardwell said. "He also channels the other ancient Aztec gods who control our destiny. Yours, mine—except that we are all one with them, of course. As is Abernathy Klaxbingichov . . ."

Abernathy Klaxbingichov? Could he really have said that? I tried to fix him with my eyes, stare at him, pin him down. He wouldn't pin. He was swimming now, in a pool of rainbow-colored lights. And my stomach was contracting, my bowels were burning, my lips were numb, my mouth was salivating so that I was searching the room for someplace to spit. Or throw up, or both, except that now I couldn't see anything except the mist of rainbow lights surrounding Cardwell, whose cigar smoke was roiling up into his bright aura, mixing in with pastel colors.

I said, "The Caterpillar."

"What?" He had stopped swimming, had materialized out of the mists to again peer into my eyes.

"The Caterpillar, in *Alice and Wonderland*. You played him, didn't you?" I felt smug at this insight. "Your sister wasn't the only actor in your family," I chided him. "Why do you keep this accomplishment secret?"

He smiled then. With a satisfaction I would remember for a long time. Then he said, "Higgledy-piggledy, rats are all over, the cow jumped into the spoon."

"Huh?" I pulled my handkerchief out of my pocket and wiped at my mouth.

He smiled, and his teeth were long. "I repeat, why don't we go on outside till it's over and take a good look at the moon?"

I shook my head, realizing that didn't make all the sense in the world either. But when he took my hand, I let him lead me toward the balcony. I felt a hand slip inside my shirt and remove my .38. I was pleased to be rid of the weight.

And then I was in the corner of the lawn, vomiting into a plastic pail half-filled with dirt that I was pitifully grateful to see, and then I was sitting on one of the stone benches, my cheek resting against the cool stone backside of the goddess Astarte, and Cardwell and the guru were sitting across from me. I listened to what they were saying.

"Am-erama Mexico," said Cardwell. He scowled at me. "Tweedle Dum and Tweedle Dee were going to have a battle." He shook his head sadly, examined me more closely, and then he started speaking so fast it was almost like speeding up a recording. "So why can't you experience the intellectual insight that allows us all to sometimes expand our quintessential being into something far more experiential than the moment? After all, no one has yet established whether existentialism is pre-war or postwar, and if so, which war."

I was pleased at the sudden heightening of the intellectual content of the conversation. It reminded me of my days in philosophy class when I'd been the wittiest of them all. I said, "Wittgenstein met the Jabberwock, that's when the world turned breen." It seemed like the most profound thing I had ever uttered.

"He's too far out of it," the guru intoned.

Cardwell said, "We'll wait, we'll wait, it's a very important fate . . ." I expected him to get up and dart off like the White Rabbit.

"I know what you did," I said, surprised to hear myself speaking. "You poisoned me. But I'm not afraid of you. You're just a bunch of rich eccentrics." I heard myself laughing at that, laughing and laughing, and then I was at the rail, throwing up into the bucket again.

And then the two men were gone, and I was alone, so alone, and the world was a desolate place. I was the last man alive on the entire planet, even the animals and insects had perished. And I was so alone . . .

I started crying.

And then I realized that I was flat on my back against the cold marble, and the gods loomed above me. I saw Astarte shift her position, her stone head pivoting slowly, then it tilted as she glared down at me. "You have failed," she said. "Your life has no purpose. It's nothing but a huge lie. You should take the Fifth Step and regenerate yourself, so you can try again."

"Does that mean commit suicide?"

"If you want to call it that, though that's a silly way to put it." She had a very bossy voice, like one of the nurses in the VA hospital where I'd recovered from my Vietnam wounds. And she was dressed in white like the nurse, too. Maybe she'd tell me what was wrong with me . . .

I asked.

"You refuse to open up to your Higher Self," she said. "You need a Spirit Guide to show you what's what. You're never going to learn on your own, you just do the same things again and again, look at you right now, just like the last time I saw you, flat on your back . . ."

I felt bad about that. I wanted to please her. I tried to get up, but I'd turned to stone, too.

"Lot's wife," said a dark-stone face. It was one of the pre-Columbian statues, thick-lipped and angry. "You looked back. You should never look back." It stuck its tongue out at me, and I wanted to tell it off, but my tongue had also turned to stone and I couldn't speak. I rolled my head to the other side so I wouldn't have to look at it.

I knew where I was then. I was in the Garden of Eden. I had made it through all the shrapnel, my entire unit had been hit by VC, I had dragged myself through the jungle for days, using the morphine pills I'd taken from the dead medic's kit to stop the pain so I could move. I'd dragged myself over a ledge, had dropped into a clearing covered with cool white marble. The sky above was diaphanous and held a million brilliant stars. I had arrived at my destination, back to the beginning of it all.

A serpent coiled up a tree and looked at me. It had rainbow-colored feathers surrounding its face. It saw me looking at them. "Do you like my feathers?"

"They're beautiful."

"They're made from hummingbirds and blood. I'll give them to you if you'll tell me what you're after."

"After?" So far as I knew, at that moment I wasn't after a thing. I was completely content, I had arrived at the origin of all meaning.

"You want to talk to Elizabeth," the serpent said. "What do you want to say?"

I couldn't remember, in fact I couldn't even remember anybody named Elizabeth, so I said, "Nothing."

The serpent said, "If you'll tell me what you want, I'll make you like God. Don't you want to be a god?"

"Not especially."

The serpent came in close and licked its lips. "You don't have to lie to me. I'd never lie to you. I always tell the truth, it's the best way, don't you think?"

"Lies can get you in a lot of trouble," I agreed. I was amazed and pleased at how passive I felt.

"Do you know who I am?" The serpent asked.

I remembered something from Sunday school and said, "Original sin?"

The serpent sneered. "Hardly. I am the great plumed serpent, the god Quetzalcoatl. First born son of Ometeotl, the dual-god who created all. I was born when Ometeotl put an emerald in my mother's belly. I have divine birth. I am the son of the Light of the Day, of the Skirt of the Stars, of the One Who is Wrapped in Black. I am the Light-bearer. To serve God, you must serve me."

"But—"

"Yessssssss?"

Something from a long time ago was nudging at me. I said, "I don't mean to argue, but . . ."

"Yes?" The voice was impatient now.

"I thought Jesus Christ was the only begotten Son of God."

The serpent actually snorted. "Rubbish! Jesus's life and death and resurrection is only a metaphor. He was only one of the many christs—that word means teacher, you know, you could call your professors at school by the name, if you wanted. You could even call Dr. Winch a christ. We are all christs. And Jesus the Christ was only another teacher, another Adam. The Jewish people merely stole the story of my incarnation then enhanced it to make themselves seem more important than they are."

I was starting to come around a little bit—enough to begin to realize that I wasn't talking to a real serpent, but to a hideous mask. Its face was leathery with brown and green splotches, its eyes were reddish-green and hot with evil. Large, curly orange worms coiled out of its ears and a snake's tail was coiled out of its fanged mouth, wriggling like a tongue as the mouth inside the mask spoke. The whole thing rose up out of a thick collar of multicolored feathers that continued on to cover the shoulders and then the chest, then fell away to cover the body all the way to the marble floor.

My mouth was dry and still numb, but I was making out another form now. Cardwell was standing a short distance in back of the snake-man in the feathered robe. And there was still another figure behind him, a cunning, clownish little face that withdrew into shadows when I tried to peer at it. Some dim part of my brain indentified him as Vernon Vance.

I was still prostrate on the floor, I still couldn't stand up. Nothing to do but play along with them for the moment and see why they'd drugged me or poisoned me or whatever had gotten me into this fix. I made a little whimpering noise, wanting to sound submissive.

Cardwell said, "Why do you want to talk to Elizabeth?"

"Who is Elizabeth?

The man in the snake mask turned to Cardwell, and said, "It's no use. His brain is fried."

"Maybe not. He didn't really touch much but the soup."

That woke me up a bit more. Maybe I could play this my way and learn something myself. I said, "I know! Elizabeth is dead." From what I could tell, I was doing a pretty fair imitation of myself a few moments ago, when I was still totally stoned.

"She left her grave," said the serpent mask. "We must find her, or her soul will wander forever and she will never be able to come back."

"Bad karma," I said.

"Worse than that," said Cardwell. He had knelt beside me, and now he was peering into my face, studying me, maybe realizing I was coming around a bit. "For her it would be total spiritual death. And it will be your fault if you don't tell us where to find her."

I tried to remember just how much I'd said when Sofia had phoned pretending to be Elizabeth. I'd admitted to having talked with Elizabeth, I'd mentioned that her husband thought I was running a scam, I'd mentioned that her grave was desecrated and that I'd been to her brother's house. Not much besides that, if my mind was working well enough for me to remember. Which it seemed to be now. In fact, things were looking a lot clearer and I was getting some feeling back in my face and hands and feet.

"But Elizabeth wasn't really dead," I said, trying to still sound stoned. "She was gone, but not dead . . ."

I saw Cardwell stiffen. "She had transcended her material body."

"No." I had to push it to see what he'd say. I tensed my legs to check them out. I'd be wobbly, but I was betting I could stand up now. Maybe even plant a pretty good left hook square into the middle of the serpent's gut and as for Cardwell, he'd go down with a hard breath.

"I saw her," I said, sounding petulant. "I know she wasn't dead, even though she left her grave."

There was a long humid silence. And then the mask said, "Where did you see her?"

I rolled to the side and lunged to my feet, then did a side-kick sweep that hit Cardwell square behind the knees, knocking him flat on his keister, the wind whoofing out of him. I whirled, measured the distance carefully to compensate for my impaired perception, then started to come in with a left hook for the man in the mask. But something crashed into the back of my head and hurled me back into outer space, only this time the trip whizzed by in a flash of orange lightening followed by a burst of hot white light. And then I shook my head, managed to clear it, and even rolled aside in time to avoid a boot that had been about to smash into my ribcage. I looked up the leg and saw the grinning face of the Mexican thug, the chauffeur with an Uzi in his hand. Then I saw another of the Mexican bodyguards, and something smashed into my face. It was suddenly scalded with blood, a boot kicked into my kidney, and something else came down on the back of my head. Excruciating pain shot through me, and then everything went mercifully black.

Chapter

FIFTEEN

I was alone again, in a pitch black tunnel, and everything was real, very real, more real than anything had ever been in my life. Which was altogether odd, because I realized at that moment that I was dead.

A very peculiar feeling. And yet, on second thought, I realized that I wasn't really dead, I had just left the body I had always thought of as myself. But wasn't that what they meant by being dead?

I was floating through the tunnel, toward a pale shining light that had appeared in the opening at the far end, and as I moved, I pondered on the fact that although I was dead, I felt more alive than ever before. Everything had come into sharp focus. The drugs that had been in my system were totally gone—my system was gone, for that matter. And I knew I was on the brink of the most amazing discovery—the edge of the greatest of all adventures—and I was fairly exhilarated by it.

And then light came into the tunnel. I looked more closely at this light and saw the shape of a small person outlined therein. The figure shaped itself into a light-sculpted version of my grandmother, and as she moved toward me with a beatific smile on her face, I suddenly knew a peace and wonder I had never felt before. I felt perfectly protected. And the closer she came to me, the more calm and serene I became, until she was beside me and I felt myself bathed in the warm glow of light, and knew a peace that had elements of the love I had known from her during childhood. It was a love of a depth and scope that I had never even imagined before.

She was beautiful, much like she had been on earth, small and perfectly groomed. But she was younger than I had ever seen her, and her body seemed to be made of some kind of metallic-light substance that gave off glints of slate-blue. I tried to touch her, but there was no substance to my body at that point, and I had nothing to touch her with except my reciprocal love. We moved to the end of the tunnel, and I could see out into the brilliance now. The light should have been blinding, but again I knew what was there, not through perceptual sense but through a sort of intuitive knowledge that was far more certain than anything I had ever perceived. This light-world was serene and infinite, the essence of absolute love and beauty. I wanted to step into that light more than I'd ever before wanted anything.

With a feeling of exhilaration, I started to move on and out of the tunnel, but my grandmother held me back. I pushed against the force that emitted from her, and I realized that if it was just up to her, she'd let me in. But there was more to it than that. An infinite sadness came from her, overwhelming me. And I realized then that for some reason I was not to be admitted to this wonderful eternal world of light. I wept.

And then my grandmother was gone, and I was alone again. Then—suddenly—I was sucked back into darkness, and I felt an intense throbbing pain so severe that I wanted to scream but my throat wouldn't contract, there was something in it, and then I realized I'd been intubated with a breathing machine, that I was struggling up into consciousness, but I didn't want to be back in my body. I was enraged that I'd had to reenter this broken, pain-wracked machine, I tried my best to escape again, and then I again blacked out.

A voice said, ". . . breathing okay on his own, looks like he's going to make it. He should be coming out of it soon. We'll see. In the meantime, continue the IV."

A second voice said, "Yes, sir. Did you want to increase the dosage after he wakes up?"

"We'll see how he's doing."

I felt the prick of a needle then, and my eyes opened. Everything was milky for a moment till I blinked hard, and then my eyes focused and I could see a white ceiling and the top of some kind of metal machine off to my left. I tried to turn my neck so I could see better, but it was stiff. I realized there was a thin plastic tube stuck in my arm. Out of the corner of my eye I could see more tubing running from an IV pole to my neck, one tube with a clear liquid, another with deep red blood. I was getting a transfusion. I moved my hand up—I couldn't believe how weak I was—and felt the bandages swathing my head. Then I brought my eyes back around: a TV sat on a high shelf on the wall opposite my bed, and that was about as much as I could see. I tried to lift my arm. It was bandaged, and the bandage was spotted with red seepage from some kind of wound.

"Oh, you're awake!" The voice belonged to a black nurse who was bending over me. Her face was plump and her cheeks were rosy. Her eyes were filled with concern. "How do you feel?"

"I can't tell yet." I was surprised at how clear the words came out.

"We about lost you a couple of times, you know," she chided me. "You'd better take a moment right here and thank the Good Lord that you're still alive."

"What happened?"

"Looks like somebody tried to beat you to death."

"They *did* beat me to death."

She was still leaning over me, rearranging my pillows, checking the IVs and my bloody bandage. She gave me an alarmed look, then said, "Frankly, there were a few times there when we weren't too sure if you were alive or not. We've reported it to the police, of course. They're waiting to see you as soon as the doctor gives them an okay."

"Why?"

She said, "They want to know who did this to you, of course."

I heard myself say, "Will they bust them for homicide or for attempted homicide?"

"What?"

"They killed me but you brought me back around. Does that count as a full-on homicide, or just attempted?"

She studied me a moment, then said, "I'd better see doctor about decreasing your pain medication."

It was at least twenty-four hours more before the doctor gave the LAPD detective, Bernie Harper, a green light to come into my hospital room and talk to me. And in spite of a splitting headache and the tubes sticking into me, I managed to pump him and learned that I'd been found on the beach by an early morning jogger, near the Santa Monica pier. My car had been parked nearby in a city lot. The police had impounded it; I could pick it up by stopping by and signing for it.

Someone had picked me over—my wallet, jacket, and shoes and socks were gone—which made him think I'd maybe been out stoned and had gotten mugged. I let him keep on thinking that. He was just finishing up a fourteen-hour shift, and he wasn't all that interested in debating my answers, even though he seemed sharp enough to realize they weren't totally kosher. I signed my statement, he thanked me, and that was the end of that.

As soon as he was gone, I phoned my office and gave the code that allowed me to retrieve my telephone messages. Someone had phoned then hung up about half a dozen times, and finally Big Al Riggatoni's voice came on and bit off the words: "We got to talk," then he hung up.

The next message was from the phone company, complaining that my payment was late. The next was another hang up. And then Ariel's cheery, rapid-fire voice came on the line. "I've been trying to reach you for two days. Don't you ever work? Tod and I want you to find out what happened to Aunt Liz's money. We aren't going to bother Uncle Frank with it, he'd just confuse the issue. We'll worry about who gets it after we've found it. And, by the way, did you enjoy your meeting at my parents' house? What did you think of Auguste? Quite a hair-ball, isn't he? Mother asked me to redeem myself for letting you into the inner sanctum by prying personal information out of you. They wanted to impress you when Dr. Winch did her 'reading'.

Did you like the part about the girlfriend from the IRS?" She signed off with a tinkly little laugh, leaving me with the impression that she either had absolutely no idea of what had happened to me, or she was a shoo-in for the Academy Award when she played Tolstoy's wife.

There were several more interesting calls—from Frank Livingstone. He didn't say what he wanted, just left an urgent message for me to phone him.

The rest of my messages were rank and file stuff, someone wanting to know if I handled divorce cases and then an insurance company that wanted me to stalk some paraplegic and try to catch him playing basketball. When the messages had played out, I punched in the code to reset the machine, then tried to phone Ariel. I got the studio, but she was out. I also tried her parents' house—ready to use one of my many false voices so they wouldn't know just yet that they'd botched the job of killing me. But a maid answered the phone and informed me they'd all gone out of town for a few days. That figured. Next, I tried to reach Frank Livingstone. The butler informed me he was out but would be back that evening.

The effort of just that much work had exhausted me, largely because I was still a little short of blood. Head wounds bleed profusely, and the majority of the wounds had been to my head. Fortunately, the fracture had been clean and would heal relatively fast, according to the doctor. But I was still woozy and any quick motion made me nauseated. I was going to be laid up a while longer, no matter how much I tried to will otherwise. In fact, the doc was debating whether to pump another pint or two of blood into me.

After I'd rested a few minutes, I phoned Big Al. The henchman who answered the phone put me through as soon as he learned who I was. Big Al said, "So what's up?"

"I'm in the hospital. Flat on my back."

"That right?" He paused, processing that, then apparently decided it wasn't worth much conversation because the next thing he said was, "Look, I been waitin' to talk to you before I did anything. I can't believe what a saint I'm bein' about this. But I'm runnin' out of patience. So—what's the deal with Tony? You get a chance to talk to him again?"

"I did. He's not bending. Look, I'd like to talk to him one more time before this gets any heavier. I'd—"

"Forget that sleazeball. He's had all the chances he's gonna get." The phone clicked in my ear as Riggatoni hung up. I tried to call him back, but the phone just kept ringing, so I next phoned the Grace of the Shepherd Mission. Shelby Knight answered the phone. I repeated my warning of the other day, told him I'd just spoken with Big Al, that it was all about to come down. But Shelby said quietly, "The Lord is the strength of my life; whom shall I fear?" Then he thanked me for calling and told me not to worry.

Ha.

I lay there in bed and worried about everything until I finally fell asleep. The nurse awakened me at about three that afternoon, when the doc came in to examine me again. He decided I was going to make it without further transfusions, which meant the nurse could take the IV out of my neck. That was a relief, though I still had an IV in my arm, but at least I could roll my head from side to side now. Every bone in my body ached, and I could barely make it to the bathroom by myself, but I was coming around.

The doctor was heavy-set and had a face that made him look like a friendly walrus, right down to the whiskers. When the nurse pushed the tall IV pole out the door, he cleared his throat, tried to establish a bit of camaraderie by offering up some inane small talk about the food and a couple of pithy comments about how they'd had to work on me for a good long while before they'd managed to bring me back around, and how lucky I'd been that there'd been absolutely no brain damage.

I thought he was just fishing for some appreciation, so I thanked him and did my best to act sociable. But as soon as he had me chatting to the best of my ability, he said, "So what's the story? Did you jump off a skyscraper, or did someone actually do this to you?"

"I can't remember." Which was a lie but far better than trying to tell the truth. *Look, doc, I was attacked by a Huichole shaman and his thugs, after he'd drugged my soup.* That should change his mind about the brain damage. In fact, it would be a surefire recipe for commitment to a psycho ward.

"I'd like to refer you to a very good drug counselor who is affiliated with our facility," the doctor said, looking embarrassed. Most surgeons don't have to handle the social work.

"I've been clean for years, doc."

He frowned. "We had to get your records from the VA hospital, Mr. Weatherby. There's no point in trying to deceive me. Frankly, you're lucky you made it out of this one."

This one? And then I remembered the trip I'd been on at the Cardwells', the nausea, the saliva flooding my mouth. I'd never used hallucinogens, but I'd swapped enough stories with every type of drug user in the book to have a pretty good clue as to what had happened.

I said, "LSD or peyote?"

He looked surprised at my openness. "Mescaline, actually. It's a psychotomimetic substance derived from the peyote cactus. There was so much in your urine that it was practically psychedelic. Fortunately, for some reason your body didn't absorb quite enough to push you over the edge into a psychotic break, but it was close enough. I'd get some help if I were you. Your skull is fractured and we almost lost you twice, but somehow you got a miracle because you're alive. And sane. People only get that kind of luck once in a lifetime."

There was no way I was going to convince him that I hadn't done this to myself, so I agreed to see a drug counselor before I left the hospital and to set up regular therapy sessions thereafter. The doctor gave me another minute's worth of his anti-drug lecture then left to finish his rounds.

I managed to sleep for a while, then awakened, and my brain immediately shifted into high gear, going over everything that had brought me to the hospital—at least as much of it as I could remember.

And then I started thinking about the dream I'd had of my grandmother, which still seemed a great deal more real than the peyote trip.

Thinking about my grandmother set me off into some serious rethinking of my belief that there was nothing beyond this life. Being close to death like that can do it to you. What if I was wrong, what if this wasn't the whole banana? And if I was wrong, then I hadn't really learned anything of value in my entire thirty-eight years because everything I knew was centered on an inaccurate premise.

I felt a keen alarm as that realization struck me. And then the second punch of the double-whammy came, as I felt a sudden sense of unfamiliarity with my surroundings, even a sense of hostility toward them, as if they had suddenly let me down. In that moment I felt a vast alienation, as if I had somehow stepped up and out of my reality and was examining it from a position of distance. I suddenly saw the universe as one compilation of subatomic particles, whizzing and whirling through a vast space, adhering into lumps of matter: the visitor's chair, the television, the IV pole and tube. And then I was looking at my own arm, seeing it as nothing more than a magnificent flesh sculpture, animated by something beyond the physical, something which I did not understand.

I held up my hand and examined it: It was alien to me, nothing more than a clump of molecules fixed there in space, a strangely-shaped cluster of zillions of atoms, spinning in place. Something about the shape and heat of these atoms caused the light to reflect off them in such a way as to let me *see* them, as the photons bounced off and reached the rods and cones in my eyes. The information was sent at the speed of light to my brain, where I interpreted all this during every waking moment in an overwhelmingly simplistic fashion that left out the scope and depth and breadth and beauty of the entire underlying nature of reality. The very substance of my body seemed unreal, and I felt as if I was straddling a chasm, as if beyond and beneath these particles with their peculiar effects on my perception there was a vast chasm, a void, and I had no idea what was there.

Whew. I should never have read that paper on bootstrap theory for my senior paper in physics class. Or read Albert Camus or Jean Paul Sartre. I mean, it was just my *hand*, for Pete's sake! *My* hand, attached to *my* body, attached to *a* planet, itself a whizzing, whirling particle in a far more vast space.

But my perception was shaken to the very depths. What *was* I, anyway? A man? What did *that* mean? Something descended from an accidental meeting of sea-water and lightning? Or something carefully and lovingly designed by some vast and wonderful Being who had created every subatomic particle that made up both me and my surroundings, from my skin to the sheets on my bed to the hospital building to the cosmos itself. And if this Being existed, He had, furthermore, created each and every particle just by *thinking* then *speaking* it all into existence. What a majestic concept! What absolute wonder!

Suddenly I wanted very much to know if there really was a benevolent, caring Creator, as my grandmother had taught me. I looked at the white ceiling, and said out loud, "Okay, God. I'm ready. If You're real, please forgive me for never being able to believe in You. Don't ask me why I can't. It's just that You've never made sense to me, one way or the other. But You're God, and if You're real, You already know all this. And You know exactly how I got the way I am, and You know what's made me so cynical that I can't really believe anything at all anymore. So—help me, God. If You're real, I need to know it. I need to understand. And I need to know why my grandmother had to hold me back from coming all the way into that beautiful light."

I stopped there and waited for moment, then said, "Amen."

I waited again. The room was still, I could hear the traffic on the nearby boulevard grinding along. There were no sudden revelations here for me, no sightings of angels or other spiritual beings. After a while, I felt a little silly. I thought about Sofia, believing everything the Cardwells told her just because she had a departed loved one she couldn't let go of. Was I getting so lonely that I had to fabricate spiritual friends and family? I picked up the TV's remote and clicked it on to the news. There'd been another drive-by shooting in South Central, another war someplace, more starving children, more turmoil, mayhem, and chaos. Finally, I'd had enough of the world again. I turned the TV off and fell asleep.

But by eleven that night, I'd had as much bed rest as I could handle. I unhooked myself from the one IV they'd left in my arm, dressed myself in what was left of my clothes (I found them in the closet), then walked barefoot down the hallway and collapsed right in front of the nurses' station—no one there, of course, all of them making rounds. I lay there on the floor for five long minutes, too embarrassed to call out, too weak to move on my own. Then, when some energy started seeping back into my body, I crawled back to my room on all fours, slowly managed to pull off my clothes, scale the mountain of my bed-side, and meekly climb back between the sheets. Where I lay and felt sorry for myself. Philip Marlowe and Sam Spade never had to waste time tied to a hospital bed. Why me?

The next morning, I tried again. This time, I made it. Five full days in the hospital and they wanted me to stay at least two more, but I could stand up now without feeling dizzy. And Elizabeth Ann Livingstone was still out there somewhere, still waiting for me to find her killer.

I phoned a cab to pick me up at the hospital. The driver was a chubbier version of Diana Ross, though she was wearing blue jeans and a heavy metal T-shirt in place of the sequinned gown. She made note of the bruises on my face and my partially shaved head with its Frankenstein stitches, then asked a few polite questions about my health. I dead-eyed her and refused to chat. She shut up.

She took me to the police station, then looked relieved as she sped away. It took me about half an hour to wade through the paperwork to sign out my Beamer, but when I got into it, it still had half a tank of gas, and nobody had taken a sledge hammer to it. I managed to drive myself home.

Chapter
SIXTEEN

I had expected to find my bungalow trashed. But it was in good shape except for the coat of dust that had settled everywhere. Luckily, I'd taken out the garbage and had washed the dishes last time I was home, so it was ready for my occupancy.

The trip home had wiped out my energy again. After I parked the car and went into the house, I slid open the balcony door to let in some fresh air, then made a pot of tea. While it was brewing, I phoned and had the building manager check on my office. Nothing amiss there. After the tea was brewed, I poured it into a pitcher to chill, then sat down and turned on the news, something to keep me company while I rested from my big trip home, thought things over, and prepared for my next move. Which, after some thought, turned out to be trying again to reach Frank Livingstone.

He answered the phone himself. "Mr. Weatherby! Where on earth have you been? I've learned where my wife's dental records are kept." He told me, and even gave me an address. "How long before you can get them?"

"It may be another day or two."

"The Director of the Chapel of the Flowers is pressuring me to either let him fill in the grave or move the body. I think he's beginning to suspect something."

"Stall him one more day," I said. "I'll get the records tomorrow night, and we can try to match them up the next day or so."

"What about exhuming the body?"

I thought about Big Al Riggatoni and his boys. "I know where I can hire someone who's used to that type of work," I said. "I'll set it up tomorrow."

"Who will make the comparison between the skeleton's jawbone and the dental charts?"

There was a low-rent dentist in the office right down the hall from me who owed me a favor or two. I said, "No sweat. I'll take care of that, too."

"Thank you, Mr. Weatherby. I—uh—apologize for my behavior when we first met. I mean, I was confused, surely you can understand. Frankly, I still am. It's difficult to know who to trust."

"No problem."

"Something else has come up. It may mean nothing, but if possible, could you come over tonight?"

"Sorry, pal, but I don't think I can make it."

"Well . . . perhaps it's nothing. But I was thinking about some things and I went up to the attic where Lizzie's items are stored. Someone has gone through them all."

That woke me up. "How long ago?"

"Well . . . I probably should have mentioned this before, but . . . you understand, the circumstances and all. Anyway, I checked Lizzie's things right after you first attempted to cash her check. That's when I phoned you and said you should cash it, I was trying to find out . . . well, never mind that, but now I've checked them again, and more things are missing."

"What was taken the first time?"

"It's been ten years since I packed all that away, and even then I only did a small part of it myself. So I can't be sure. But her financial papers were mussed up, and I believe at least her checkbooks were taken."

"And now?"

"I'm not certain, but I feel that someone else has been here. At first I thought perhaps you'd broken in, you see, so I said nothing, but now—"

I thought about how badly my bones ached, how badly my head ached. These two thoughts apparently brought out the inherent masochism that leads all us hard-boiled types to become P.I.s to begin with because I heard myself say, "Look, don't sweat it. I'll be right there."

Chapter
———SEVENTEEN———

I hung a left and again drove through the still-opened iron gate beside the small Normandy-style gatehouse. And again, as I drove past, I thought I saw a motion in an upstairs window. Abandoned as the house seemed, someone lived there. Probably the servants.

I wheeled my car up the winding driveway, past the thick foliage, then parked in front of the huge, dreary house. I could see why Elizabeth had opted for the cleaner-edged apartment with its small, secret garden. I again rang the gorgon-shaped bell, the jowled Mexican butler again let me in.

This time, he led me all the way through the vaulted hallway and out a back door, to a wide patio beside a deep blue swimming pool. Frank Livingstone sat at a round enameled table, beneath a yellow-striped umbrella. He was wearing a white terry cloth swimrobe, tied at the waist, and leather sandals on his bony feet. His hair was damp, as was the towel he'd tossed on a lounge chair. He stood when he saw my bruises and dings, and his eyes widened with alarm. "Good heavens, what happened to you?"

"Traffic accident," I growled.

He motioned for me to sit down in the chair opposite him. When he offered me a drink, I asked for lemonade. He was fresh out, but there was a brand new pitcher of limeade in the refrigerator if I'd care to substitute. I did.

As the maid went to fetch it, I got right to the point. "Do you think your wife has been breaking in here?"

He frowned deeply and stirred the ice in his glass with a long bony forefinger, then pulled it out and licked it clean. "Actually, I'm puzzled. If the burglar was a stranger, I'd think they'd have gone for *my* things—I have a case on my dresser that contains many good pieces of jewelry, in very plain sight. And there is, of course, the art collection. It's priceless. And then there's the silver, many good rugs, other things. But apparently nothing of any value was taken. This person—or persons—bypassed all the valuables and went straight for the attic. That was very peculiar."

"You only have Elizabeth's things up there?"

"That and a few other old items, like broken furniture, several things my parents left in the house and which have since been put into storage, objects like that." He peered into the mouth of his glass, as if he were trying to read something in the ice cubes. His face grew dark and ponderous, and then he looked up at me with deep pain in his eyes, and said, "You've actually seen Lizzie?"

I thought it over carefully, then said, "I'm not certain, but I think so."

"I'll never forgive myself for letting them deceive me. God only knows what she's been through . . ."

"*Who* deceived you? How?"

He shook his head, still drowning in his own guilt. "I was drugged all through the funeral. It was as if it was happening to someone else. The coffin was closed. Caspar insisted, but there was no real reason for it, if it was true, as they said, that her neck and spinal cord caused her death . . ."

"You saw her after she fell?"

"Oh, yes. She'd fallen, all right. But I knew even then that she couldn't be dead. She'd never have left me, you see. Not even that way. They tried to get her to come live in Baja, over and over again, all the pressure on her, but she wouldn't leave me."

For the first time, I wondered if there was a trace of madness in Livingstone's eyes.

He said, "It was Cassie. She couldn't stand it that Lizzie was happy. She tried to destroy her happiness every chance she had."

I turned up my limeade and tapped the glass to get the last ice cube. I chewed it, swallowed, then set the glass purposefully down on the white metal table, and said, "Look, Livingstone. I've been trying to get to the bottom of this thing ever since I first met your wife . . ."

"You actually believe it was her? When did you see her? How did she look?"

"She looked like she'd just crawled out of a grave. I mean it. Whatever she'd been through, she hadn't enjoyed it much."

"Dear God in Heaven. I wonder where she is now, what she's going through . . ." He stopped short and grabbed his chest.

I automatically reached out and started to steady him. "You okay?"

He jerked back from me, put his face in his hands, and was silent. I wouldn't have known he was weeping if I hadn't seen his chest heaving. And then, his voice cracking, he said, "All this time I've hoped beyond hope, and it turns out to be true."

"There's still a chance it wasn't Lizzie."

His head snapped up and his tears abruptly stopped, but his eyes were red and rheumy. "Why do you say *that?*"

"Because I don't really *know* anything yet. And to tell you the truth, I have a feeling that even if she is alive, she might not stay that way for long."

"Someone's after her?"

"I don't know."

He shook his head. "There was so much I never could understand . . ."

"Like what had happened to most of the money?"

He looked at me sharply, then gave me one of his thin smiles. "I'm beginning to think you might be very good at what you do."

"I am," I said. And I meant it.

His hands were trembling now, though he tried to hide it by wringing them. He said, "I don't know what I'll do when I see her. I've missed her so, I should have done more to be certain, I've tried everything. Do you know the investigative firm of Kennet and Koble? I spent a fortune on them, and they couldn't find out a thing. I tried to have the grave opened. Dr. Gates stopped me—he was one of them, and he was still at the City and County Forensics Center at that time. I should have tried later, but she left of her own accord, you know. If she really is alive, she did it all to herself . . ." Abruptly, he fell silent.

I waited.

Finally, a tiny little lizard of suspicion slithered beneath his taut face and he said, "Why did she come to you? What are you doing for her?"

"I've been hired to find her killer," I admitted, then watched him carefully, ready to file away every facial nuance.

Disbelief played on his face, dissolving the mistrust. And then a tiny smile crept to the corners of his mouth, and then he laughed. A small laugh, to be sure, but a genuine one. "Why would she give you five thousand dollars to find her killer when she isn't even dead?"

"You've got me. I suppose she really wants me to find something else, but I don't know what yet. Got any ideas?"

He rubbed his forehead with his soft hands, then shook his head quickly. Then he said, "She was here, you know. I know it was her. She broke in and got some of her things, and she didn't even let me know she was back. It had to be her, who else would want her things after all this time? But she'd never do that unless she had a very good reason. She would have let me know she was back, she would have gotten in touch with me a long time ago . . ."

"Wives sometimes leave their husbands and never look back."

"You don't understand. Lizzie and I were—well, she just never would have done that. You'd have to know her to understand."

"She knew about you and Cassie."

His face turned gray. "What *about* me and Cassie?"

"She knew about the affair. Cassie told her a long time ago."

His expression changed slowly from astonishment to hatred to despair. "That explains a lot. I should have known. Why didn't I know? That woman is *evil*."

"You could have said no to her."

His eyes went hard for an instant, and I thought he was going to get angry, but instead he shrank back to size and said, "I could have done a lot of things if only I'd seen through those monsters. I thought they were harmless. So I didn't do anything, at least not anything serious. And Lizzie disappeared—actually helped fabricate her own death, from what I can see now—and I have lived through utter despair for these past many years." He picked up a pair of round reading glasses and began to absently polish them on his bathing towel, his eyes looking into the distance. His hands were still trembling.

"Coatepec," he said suddenly, his face twisting up in anger.

"Beg pardon?"

"Coatepec. Serpent Mountain. The Fourth Step, Lizzie called it. It's the *axis mundi*, the center of the world."

"You've lost me."

"That's where she's been. It has to be. I've always known it, but I haven't known what to do about it. Oh, they have powerful friends, people in high places. And how could I go to the authorities with a story like that? That my wife had helped to feign her own death and somehow in the process she was abducted by ancient Aztecs? Look at you, the look on your face. Even now, you don't believe me, how could I ever have convinced anyone else?"

I wiped the look of cynicism from my face, and said, "I don't know whether she was abducted or not, or where she was, but I do believe that your wife is alive. Simply because I've seen her. But we're going to have to unravel a lot of deception before we get to the bottom of this. Years and years of lies. For starters, we're going to have to make absolutely sure Lizzie isn't in that grave. We'll have to check the jawbone against her dental records.

"And if it isn't Lizzie?"

"Then we have a whole new problem because we have to figure out who it *is*!"

He turned to stare at me. "There's no one in there."

"You're certain of that?"

"Yes."

"You've seen what's in the grave?"

"Not actually. But I think I've known all along. That day, when you came with Lizzie's check it was almost as if I was awakening from a long nightmare. Something was happening that I'd always hoped for . . ."

"What, exactly, was taken from your wife's things?"

"Clothing. Several dresses, a pair of shoes, some underthings, and a satchel. Her checkbook, of course. A purse." He continued the brief inventory, and I half listened, while the rest of my mind puzzled over this turn of events. For the first time I had another person's confirmation that the woman who'd come into my office to hire me was made of real flesh and blood. I'd known that all along, of course, but it nevertheless felt good to hear someone else confirm it.

"What is this Serpent Mountain?" I asked when he was done with the list.

"I'm not sure."

"Elizabeth talked about it?"

"When she first joined the Foundation. She'd planned to liquidate a lot of her assets and go there, take the 'Fourth Step' to spiritual enlightenment. She actually went down to Baja, using the excuse that her mother needed her to oversee the hiring of a new administrator at the orphanage. But I know she planned to make the initial arrangements to move down there. Everything was fairly new then, the Foundation had just set up their Mexican headquarters . . ."

"So this thing definitely spills over the border."

"Yes, though I'm not sure just how much. The Foundation was just opening a research institute somewhere down there; they were trying to get Lizzie to finance them. Her mother was still alive then, and she was furious that Lizzie was even involved with those people.

But Lizzie went down and apparently tried to kill two birds with one stone. We never talked about it because she knew how much I disapproved of the whole thing. But she was gone for a full month, and when she came back she seemed to have had her fill of them, thank God. There was a falling out with Caspar and Cassie, and I thought Lizzie had finally and totally come to her senses. Then about a year later her mother died, and she turned around and gave those charlatans her family estate! I certainly never understood that!"

"Do you know where the Foundation's headquarters is down there?"

"I only know it's somewhere near Bahia del Sol, off the Sea of Cortez."

"This Serpent Mountain. Is it a real place, or something they've made up in their minds?"

"It's real, so far as I know. Though I suppose it might also be a metaphor for some spiritual plane or other. But I think it's real. It must be. That has to be where Lizzie has been all this time . . ."

"What's your best guess as to its exact location?"

"Lower Baja, of course. Perhaps in the same vicinity as the orphanage, or maybe near to the foundation headquarters. I've never been there. But I'd like to hire you to find it and perhaps sort this thing out."

"I already have a client," I reminded him.

"There's no conflict between what Lizzie and I want."

"There might be. Obviously, she knows where to find you if she wants to see you. For some reason, she opted to come to a complete stranger."

"She's in trouble," he said. "That's why. She never relied on me, she always turned to her brother when something went wrong . . ."

"And now she couldn't turn to her brother, so she turned to me, a complete stranger?"

The distress in his face was almost palatable. "So it would seem. I suppose she never really did rely on me or trust me—even before the affair with Cassie, just in case you're thinking that might be the reason.

She had her own money, her own life, her own strong will. But she loved me. I *do* know that. And somehow or other she made a mistake, and it's been an enormous one. We have to find her, Mr. Weatherby. I'll pay you whatever it takes. I've lost her once. She's almost back, I can feel it. I'm not going to let her get away again."

As I drove back down the winding driveway, I heard a power mower at work behind the high hedge and the thicket of eucalyptus and olive trees. There was a grass turn-out beside the road, so I pulled off, then made my way through the thick foliage and onto a wide lawn, where a withered old man was riding a lawnmower. He was wearing a floppy brown hat with fish hooks stuck in it and faded coveralls. When he saw me, he drove the mower up to meet me, turned off the engine so we could hear each other, then climbed down and said, "How do. Somethin' I can do for you?"

I told him my name, shook his hand, then asked, "Are you, by any chance, Thomas?"

"That's me." His eyes were hooded, though his face seemed friendly enough.

I said, "I understand you still take care of the garden in back of Ariel Cardwell's studio."

"I does." He was only about five foot two, and he had a wizened little face that gave him a gnomish look. He had to tilt his head back to look me in the eye, but look me in the eye he did, and without missing a blink. His skin was leathery from years of sunshine, his hands were thick and stubby, his eyes were brown and sharp yet pleasant in spite of it.

"Do you live here?"

"In the gatehouse, got the upstairs. Downstairs has been closed up for years now, they uses it only for storin' stuff."

"I see. Look, Thomas, I understand from Ariel that you were immensely fond of Mrs. Livingstone . . ."

"Lizzie. She always made me call her 'Lizzie.' And yup, she was the best. Never knowed another woman like that in my life, not even my Martha, God rest her soul."

"You were married?"

"Yup. Twenty-five years. Till Martha died some twenty years back. Never married again, nor felt the need to. Never find another wife like she was nohow."

"Thomas, have you ever wondered if Lizzie Livingstone might still be alive?" He started at that, then stared up at me as if I'd just sprouted horns. So I added, "I mean, say something had happened, that someone else had died that day, or maybe no one had died. And she was still alive. You knew her pretty well, didn't you?"

"I did. We was best friends, much as a lady like that could be friends with a gardener."

"Do you have any idea where she might hide out if she was still alive? I mean, not for the long term, but right now."

"You ain't woofin', are you? You really believes she's alive?"

"I suspect it strongly. And I need to find her. I'm deeply worried about her."

"What happened to your hair?"

"I had a little accident. They had to shave part of it off to sew me up."

"Figgered. I can see the stitches."

"You have any ideas about Mrs. Livingstone?"

His expression turned wary. "I ain't seen her, if that's what yer thinkin'."

"That's not what I meant to imply. I just meant that since you knew her well, you might be able to guess as to where she might go if she was in trouble."

"I ain't got no opinions about that one way nor t'other."

"Yes. Well, thank you, Thomas. It's been a pleasure to meet you, Ariel has said some wonderful things about you."

"You's friends with Miss Ariel, huh?" He was still eyeing me suspiciously.

"I am."

"How 'bout with her high-falutin' parents, you friends with them, too?"

"Not especially. Look, here's my business card. Should you by some accident learn something, could you please phone me? I assure you, it's very, very important."

"You ain't one of them poppycockers, them nimwits that tried to take all of Old Lady Cardwell's money?"

"I assure you, I am not."

"Maybe I will call you then," he said, chewing on his lip and studying me out of his old teary eyes. "Somethin' comes up, maybe I just will phone you and let you know."

"Thank you, Thomas."

That was the best I was going to do with the old man. I climbed back into my Beamer and drove away.

Chapter

———— EIGHTEEN————

Ival Davidson was wearing a tailored dress, forest green, and real Italian leather pumps. Her briefcase was also Italian leather, and she kept glancing at a gold Seiko watch that was attached to her thin wrist. Tiny gold earrings set off her green eyes and raven hair. Her full professorship paid a lot better than had the teaching assistantship she'd toiled away at when I was a belated and war-weary student of Anthro 101.

"And I thought you were finally asking me for a date," she said and smiled.

I self-consciously touched my hand to my head, thinking about the stubble on my scalp, wishing my stitches would disappear so I could at least doff my Lakers cap in the presence of this lady.

She stirred her tomato juice with a celery stick, and said, "And really, all you want is to know about Aztecs. Why Aztecs?"

"It's a case I'm working on. The subject keeps coming up." I felt like shuffling my feet.

After seeing Frank Livingstone, I'd treated myself to a simple dinner and a good night's sleep. Now, it was late morning, and Ival and I were sitting in the faculty cafeteria at the university, where she'd agreed to meet me before classes. And seeing her again, I wanted to ask her out again, just as I had when I'd been a plebe freshman, just home from Vietnam with my insecurities freshly honed by the war and the infirmities—both mental and physical—that had followed. Furthermore, she knew I wanted to ask her out, just as she'd known when she'd stood at the podium lecturing on anthropological marvels and leveling long, warm looks at me.

"I remembered all those lectures on Meso-American Indians, including Aztecs, and figured if you knew that much back then, you must be the world authority by now," I said.

"Close to it," she said modestly. "Tell me, what exactly is it that you need to know?"

"Have you ever heard of a person, place, or thing called Coatepec?"

"Of course. Serpent Mountain, an Aztec shrine. It's the *axis mundi*, the center of the world, the most powerful place in the Aztec cosmos."

My adrenaline rushed to my head. "Where, exactly, is it?"

"Nowhere and anywhere. It's symbolic."

My adrenaline crashed and burned. "You mean it exists only in people's minds?"

"Not exactly. I mean it can be anywhere. That is, it can be anywhere now. At one time, it was in Tenochtitlan, it was another name for the Great Temple there . . ."

"You're losing me."

"Oh. Well. You'll remember that the ancient Aztecs founded their capital city, Tenochtitlan, on the site where Mexico City now stands. That's where they were when Cortez wiped them out during the early 1500s and made off with all their gold."

"Right."

"The center of Tenochtitlan with its Great Temple has been restored. It's now the Plaza de Constitución in Mexico City. We studied it, remember?"

"Chances are good that nobody lives there, then."

She shot me a puzzled look. "Of course not. It's a city institution. The government restored it from a jungle-covered pile of masonry to a civic center."

"Oh."

"Another *axis mundi* was Teotihuacan, about fifty miles north of Mexico City. The name means, 'where men become gods.' Modern day Mexicans call it the Piramides. It was one of the true wonders of ancient Meso-America, and the Aztecs believed it was the place chosen by the gods for the fifth reincarnation of the sun. Of course, one way or another, almost all the ancient gods were sun gods."

"Would this place be habitable?"

"You've got to be kidding. It's a tourist mecca. A pile of ruins."

"No chance of someone hiding out there for ten or so years?"

She frowned. "What an odd question. But the answer is no. Excepting the employees in cabins and camp trailers and government officials, of course. It's a very important site. There are guards there twenty-four hours a day, to keep the scavengers away."

"That's not it, then."

"Not what?"

"I'm looking for a Serpent Mountain where someone could have hidden out for ten years."

"Well, no one's been hiding out at the Piramides except some lizards and iguanas. Maybe a spider or two. Probably a lot of snakes."

"Right."

"Anyway, an *axis mundi* could be practically anywhere. The very concept of a mountain is central to the Aztec religion. The pyramid-shapes of their temples are intended to represent mountains, you know. They believed the mountains were their spiritual and physical resources, the connecting points between the sky and the earth, between spiritual and physical realms. And the mountains were also supposed to be the source of water, of life. And homes to various deities, just as with the Greek and Roman gods, you remember, Mount Olympus and all that."

"So this place could be a real mountain somewhere?"

"Not necessarily. It would more likely be a temple, certainly a pyramid-shaped temple, symbolic of a mountain. Though it might possibly be atop a mountain. It could even be an ancient site. The Aztecs, like the Olmecs and Toltecs before them, were fond of lopping off mountain tops and building temples on them."

"You think it might be somewhere near Mexico City?"

"Perhaps, though unlikely. The modern-day Aztecs are still the largest aboriginal group in Mexico, and they still live mostly in that region—there are well over a million of them, you know. But there's not much going on in that area that isn't public knowledge, and I haven't heard of any modern Aztecs building new temples. And all the old ones have been picked to death by archaeologists and grave robbers."

"Where else could it be?"

"This is really important, isn't it?"

"Very. Someone's life may depend on how fast I can find this place."

I could see her wondering if I was trying to impress her with some cloak and dagger stuff, but nevertheless she said, "The Aztecs have spread out everywhere."

"Any of them in Baja?"

She raised an eyebrow and looked hard at me. "Baja?"

"Yeah. What kind of Indians live there?"

"Very unlucky ones. Didn't we talk about that in class?"

"That might have been a day I was home drunk."

She smiled again. I loved the way she smiled. "Well, you get an *A* for honesty," she said. Her face grew pensive, and she said, "We don't know much about the indigenous peoples in the Baja. There are some wonderful cave paintings down in the south. Very, very old. Maybe you've heard of them? Erle Stanley Gardner discovered some of them, and he wrote a book that I read when I was a girl. It helped get me interested in archaeological anthropology. But that's another story. We haven't really learned all that much from the cave paintings. Yet. The only other thing we know is what we learned from the records of the Jesuit priests, who admitted that after exposure to the Spaniards only a small percentage survived of the forty thousand or so Indians found in Baja. Not many more than five hundred of their descendants still exist today."

"What happened to them?"

"White men's diseases, mostly. Smallpox and syphilis. And no doubt the occasional blood- and gold-thirsty Spaniard. Though the Indians were fierce and held their own for a while. But then the wonderful Cortez set up a colony there. That was in Baja Sur, in Santa Cruz. He named the place. He didn't stay long. After that, the pirates took over, using Baja as a base of operations to raid the old Manila Galleons that sailed across the Pacific and then down the coast to drop their treasures at the Spanish colony at Acapulco for transshipment on to Spain. Thomas Cavendish captured a fabulously rich galleon off the coast of Cabo San Lucas, in the late 1500s. But that's another story."

"No Aztecs in Baja?"

"There may be some now. Like I said, the Indian tribes have moved everywhere. There are Mayans in Jalisco and Yaquis in Texas and Huicholes in Oaxaca . . ."

"Huicholes? Shamans?"

She shot me an odd look. "I suppose so. Why?"

"What do you know about the Huicholes?"

"They're indigenous to the Sierra Madre Occidental, in northern Jalisco. So far as Indians go, they're probably the ones least changed by outside influence. They've integrated some of the Catholic belief system into their religion, of course, but not much. For the most part, they still worship the old Meso-American gods, much like the ancient Olmecs and Toltecs and Aztecs and Mayans did. They're mountain people. You might remember them from the research we did into religion and mind altering drugs. They're also known as the peyote cult."

I sucked in one cheek and nodded.

"Everyone in the counterculture was fascinated by them back in the sixties and early seventies. I was lucky enough to go along on a peyote pilgrimage when I was a lowly undergraduate at Berkeley. It helped make my reputation. We started up in the mountains then trekked down into the San Luis Potosi desert, then back up into the mountains. What an experience that was! Dirt, and cactus, and more dirt, and so much walking that I thought I'd broken my back and legs."

"Why pilgrimages?"

"The Huicholes don't live where their 'sacred peyote' grows, yet it's a vital part of their religion. So they have to go down to the desert to harvest it. And the pilgrimage is all mixed up in ancient ritual. We could only drink a tiny bit of water, and most food was forbidden . . . it was awful."

"Did you try the peyote?"

"Afraid not. I was under the tutelage of my faculty advisor, who refused to let me indulge. He was supposed to be studying their religion, though I think he was really studying how to get stoned. I wrote most of his journal articles for him. He made me work my fingers off, tape recording or jotting down every little thing. But it later helped get me my T.A."

"And the Indians were Huicholes?"

"Yes. Why?"

"Did you by any chance hear of a shaman named Auguste Flores?" It was a long-shot, but long-shots were the only shots I had.

She thought, then said, "Not really. Auguste would be a pretty common Mexican name, even among the Indians—of every sort. They adopted names from the Jesuit priests; you know, some of their gods were even renamed with biblical names. Many of the people were forbidden to even learn their real Indian names. Even though the Huicholes are relatively uncorrupted, practically everyone in Mexico now has a name derived from Spain. But why the interest in Huichole shamans and peyote? I thought this was about Aztecs."

I lifted my cap, saw her stare and recoil at the same time as she looked at the thick red welts where the scars were healing, the duck-down where the hair was growing back. "Peyote did this to me," I said. "Along with a Huichole shaman."

A dark horror crept into her eyes. "What on earth are you involved in?"

181

I was sorry I'd shown her my head. "I don't know, but I do plan to find out."

"And it also has to do with Aztecs?"

"With the god Quetzalcoatl," I said. "I know that much."

"Well," she said, still tense, "I don't know where the Huicholes fit in, but I do know that Quetzalcoatl wasn't just an Aztec god. You'll remember that the Olmecs were the oldest civilization in Mexico. They disappeared about 400 B.C., in some sort of violent battle, and we don't know nearly so much about them as we'd like to, but we do know that they, like the Aztecs and other South American civilizations, had hundreds, maybe even thousands, of gods. Most of them were primarily sun gods, but some were also jaguar-gods who also had a preoccupation with the serpent. After the Olmecs there were several other short-lived civilizations, and then came the Toltecs. There's where we find our first evidence of a deity known as Quetzal-coatl. 'Quetzal' for 'bird,' of course, and 'coatl' for serpent. The plumed serpent.

"Quetzalcoatl was the central Toltec deity. Much of their art depicts fanged serpents with feathers, often coiled around people, who don't seem to be minding a bit. We have hieroglyphics from that time which tell us a tiny bit about what was going on. But the Toltec influence meant that Quetzalcoatl became the most important god in Mexico and Central America."

"I remember something about Quetzalcoatl showing up in several different forms in several different cultures and times," I said, trying to show off.

"You have a good memory. In the earliest evidence we have of him, Quetzalcoatl was benevolent and kind. A patron of the sciences and arts, and all that. But, like all powerful people, gods included, he had enemies. They got him drunk and set him up in an incestuous relationship with his sister, and when he awakened he was so shamed that he fled to the sea, to sail away on a raft made from snakes. Or, in another version, he set himself on fire, whereupon he flew up into the sky and became the evening star, Venus."

"They called the star Venus?"

She laughed. "No. Of course not. That's what *we* call the evening star. I don't have the faintest idea what they called it. Probably Quetzalcoatl."

In spite of her light tone, I felt a chill as she said the word "Quetzalcoatl"—a fluttering of something that vanished the moment I tried to bring it fully up into consciousness.

"The reason so many recognize the name, of course, is because the Aztecs believed that Cortez *was* Quetzalcoatl, and this peculiar event found its way into all the history books. Quetzalcoatl was supposed to have had white skin and a gold beard, and when he sailed away—or immolated himself, or whatever he did—he vowed to return. When the Aztecs saw Cortez coming with all his men and the horses—strange animals to the Aztecs, who believed for a long time that the men and horses were one and who even worshipped Cortez's horse's skeleton when it died—well, the Aztecs believed that Cortez was the returning Quetzalcoatl. They laid out the red carpet for him, and the rest is history, as they say. Which reminds me, I have to teach a class in the History of Anthropology in about ten minutes." She glanced at her Seiko again.

"Did you ever hear of a place called Mu?"

She rolled her eyes, as if to say *Oh, brother!* Then she said, "Of course. It's one of those imaginary lost continents, like Atlantis. Sometimes you'll find references to it in the context of the ancient Meso-American Indians. Some really racist historians tried to explain how the ancient Meso-American civilization could have been so advanced. They had to explain away the people's accomplishments, so they concocted tales of ancient civilizations, white and brilliant, of course, that had somehow landed in the Americas and tutored the 'savages'; or sometimes they had preceded the 'savages,' as in the Mu legend; or maybe it was white space men visiting—all sorts of things. Most of this trash started back when Europeans still wrote travel tomes about Africans having tails."

"No scientific truth to it then?"

"Nothing of the sort. It's totally pseudo-science, like psychic phenomena and UFO sightings and other oddball things." She glanced at her watch again. "Look. I hate to be rude, but I really have to go."

"One more question. Would there be any overlap between the Meso-American religions and the Babylonian goddess Astarte? Or the Greek goddess Aphrodite?"

She shot me a bewildered look. Then she shook her head, smiled wanly, and said, "What grade did I give you for the class? An *A*? I can't believe I gave you an *A*."

"It was a *B+*. And I assume that means, 'no.'"

"It certainly does."

"Well, then, what about people who worship all of these deities together? Along with Buddha, and Muhammed, and several more?"

She leveled a curious look at me, then said, "That sounds like New Age."

"Which is?"

"Something that rolls all religions up into one package and more or less believes that all gods are basically manifestations of each other: some of the people believe that Quetzalcoatl is really Jesus Christ, shown up in the Americas to do much what he did in Jerusalem. White skinned with a gold beard, of course, never mind that the real Jesus almost certainly had olive-colored skin and dark hair. But I do have to admit that there's some basis for that belief in the Meso-American glyphs—Quetzalcoatl as the god of light and resurrection, all that. There's a real similarity there, almost too much for coincidence. Though I personally believe that the similarity is a deliberate spiritual deception. But back to the New Agers. They also believe that Buddha is as much a deity as is Jesus Christ, that the Koran is just as true as is the Bible or the Tibetan Book of the Dead or the Egyptian Book of the Dead or the Cabala or the Hindu and Buddhist scriptures."

"Confusing."

"Indeed it is. Mostly, it has a strong Hindu influence. The followers believe they're in process of becoming perfected, that they'll go through many incarnations in many different cultures and times, and will eventually emerge as gods. Also, that some of them are already avatars, or gods incarnated to this material realm, and a lot of them believe they can trance channel beings from other planets, or from the spirit world, whether gods or departed humans."

"Sounds like the Foundation," I said.

"I beg your pardon?"

I shrugged and grinned. "Never mind. Look. Will you go out with me?"

She laughed, delighted. Then said, "Why didn't you ask before?"

"I was too mixed up, had too many problems."

"Well, I would have gone out with you then, in a heartbeat. I kept waiting and waiting. Back then, the girls still waited for the boys."

"But now?" My heart was sinking.

"Now I've just gotten engaged to be married to the head of the math department. Just yesterday. We're going to pick out the ring tonight. So now, it will never happen. And it's all your fault."

"Me and my inferiority complex," I said, standing up as she did.

"You need to do something about that," she said. "I believe we've missed something that would have been very special."

"Well . . ." I shrugged. My head hurt. I wondered if she was really engaged or if I'd blown it by showing her my Frankenstein stitches.

She moved toward the door and I stepped in beside her. "Do you have any books I might borrow that could tell me more about the ancient Meso-American religions?"

"I certainly do. Follow me to my office, and I'll lend you a couple."

Her office was small but neat. Several awards were framed and hung from the wall, and two full walls were covered with bookcases. I waited while she stepped up on a chair and took a couple of tattered old tomes from a top shelf, then climbed down and handed them to me. Then she glanced at her watch again.

I walked behind her to the door, then through it, then I thanked her and started to walk away, but she said, "Just a second."

I waited while she locked her door, and then she turned and stepped up to me, smiled angelically, and lifted the Lakers cap from my war-torn scalp. I was puzzled. She stepped up on her tip-toes—she was nearly as tall as me—and then pulled my head down so she was staring squarely at the top of my head. "I'm sorry you got hurt," she said. And then she planted a gentle, tender kiss squarely atop my mangled pate, then carefully replaced the cap. Then she stepped back, and said with all sincerity, "And I really am sorry you didn't ask me out before. If you had, I don't think I'd have even met the math teacher. But I did, and we did, and it's too late now, isn't it?"

I shrugged, started to say "maybe not," but she put her finger to my lips and said, "Shhhh. It is. But, you know, I just wish . . ." She let the sentence dangle off, then turned and started walking away. But she looked back over her shoulder, to see me still watching her and said, "You really do need to do something about that inferiority complex."

As I strolled back out to where I'd left my car, I felt decidedly better. The birds were singing, fresh-faced students, eager to take on the world, were hurrying up the steps to class.

In fact, my headache was gone for the first time since I'd awakened in the hospital. Be still, my foolish heart. I would have to face it: my love for Ival Davidson would be unrequited, I would continue to adore her from afar. Which my experience with Christine had taught me was certainly the simplest and safest kind of romantic love, anyway.

Chapter

——NINETEEN——

T

There was a huge clock in a dark church tower at the end of the block. Its tones rang out deep and ominous as it chimed midnight. A thin sliver of moon hung in the dark sky. Shreds of ectoplasmic fog floated in the gloomy street, between the looming slabs of tenements. Slime oozed up out of gutter drains. A thin man came around a corner, clad in a black English-cut suit and carrying an Ithaca Mag-10 guaranteed to blow up the first tenement he fired on. The weapon was so heavy it caused him to wobble a little as he threaded his way down the street, stalking someone or something.

A bloodcurdling scream ripped the silence. And another, and this time the screamer, a buxom blonde of maybe twenty, shattered a window and lunged out onto a narrow balcony on the fifth floor of the closest tenement. A huge, hulking shape with a hump on its back lunged after her, they struggled for a moment—the screams intensifying—and then the creature grabbed the blonde and hurled her over the balcony, her screams continuing. The thin man aimed and fired and the balcony exploded, creature and all, scraps of bloody flesh flying. Then everything was hidden by fire and smoke, though the blonde's screams continued.

"Cut!" said the amplified voice of Tod Montgomery. "Okay. That's a wrap. You have thirty minutes while we set up the next shot."

Someone turned on the overhead lights and turned off the kleigs. Another turned off the smoke machine, and suddenly the tenements were black and gray flats and the street was painted-over plankwood and the blonde was coming out of a door at the back of the tenement, wiping her face with a towel. Someone else had already picked up the blonde-wigged dummy that had hit the mattresses assembled in the street.

I stepped past grips and script girls, around cameramen and lighting men and technicians of every sort who were scurrying about, setting up the next shot, which was apparently going to be the same street but in daylight because someone was carrying in trees and potted plants and an actor uniformed as an English cop stuck his head in through a doorway, and called, "How long before we're ready?"

Tod Montgomery had abandoned his director's chair and was standing to one side, arms flailing as he explained to one of the technicians just how he wanted something done. I stood and waited until he was finished. He turned and spotted me and stopped cold. His mouth sagged open, and his eyes went dark with shock. Apparently he hadn't yet heard that I was still alive, because he certainly seemed to think he was staring at a ghost. He swallowed twice, hard, then managed to get a grip on himself and rearranged his face into stiff forbearance.

I went up to him. "Looks like an interesting picture."

"It's garbage."

I shrugged. "I guess you'd know. Look, can we talk somewhere?"

"Why? What do you want?" He was looking around like he expected Mom or Pop Cardwell to rise up out of the floorboards and hurl lightning bolts at him.

"No one knows I'm here," I said. "Let's go someplace private."

He almost broke his neck getting me behind his office door, which was only a few steps down the hall from the sound stage. And once there he didn't bother to sit, just said, "I thought you were dead."

"Why?"

"Ariel's mother told me. She said she'd heard it on the news."

"Then I guess it must be true."

His lip kept twitching. "What do you want?"

"I want to know where you get your investment money to make this garbage."

His eyes went wide. "How dare you ask such a personal question!"

"I thought you and Ariel wanted to hire me to find out what happened to the rest of her Aunt Liz's money. Do you?"

"I—uh—Ariel was to take care of that . . ."

"I couldn't find her. That's why I came here. I don't think we have much time to lose if we're going to recover any of it, and from what I hear, enough is missing to make at least one or two very good movies. No more garbage . . ."

"I don't know." He was looking around again, wondering who might overhear us.

"Look," I said, "no one is ever going to know what you tell me except you and me."

He shot me a heavy look. "Do I have your word on that?"

"You do."

"You don't know these people," he said. "On the surface, they seem normal enough—"

"No they don't."

"Well—you know what I mean. If you think you've seen some strange stuff so far, you just wait."

"Which is exactly what I don't want to do," I said. "I want to take the initiative here. So, what is it? Does the Foundation keep Aunt Liz's money, or do you and Ariel get a shot at remaking Tolstoy and maybe even a couple of other class acts?"

Suddenly he went back behind his desk and slumped into his chair, then dropped his head dramatically forward onto his hands, elbows on the desk, and said, "Those vermin."

"Which vermin are we talking about?"

"All of them. The people who run the Foundation. My financial backers."

"Meaning Mummy and Daddy Cardwell?"

"And the Vances and Valdez and all the rest. You're right. They're going to end up taking all of Ariel's money. The lawyers have it tied up, and I'll end up making this trash for the rest of my life. And losing Ariel in the bargain. I'll end up killing myself, and all because of those slimy, scummy . . ."

"Enter Sir Galahad," I said. "I'm here to see that none of that happens. But I need some information from you. Like where, and I mean exactly, does your money come from?"

"Do you really think you can stop them? Brother, think again. These are some of the most powerful and ruthless people I've ever met. You don't cross them. They'll kill to get what they want." Suddenly he stopped sharply and looked hard at me again. "I thought they'd killed you."

"If they did kill me, it didn't take."

He eyed me carefully, then shook his head in disgust. "You're as loony as they are."

"Perhaps. But that's the only thing we have in common. I think they're mutated pond scum, and I think you're nuts for ever selling out to them in the first place. I used to go to your movies—you made some really good stuff. You let me down. Personally." I shrugged. "But I guess we all make mistakes." I thought about Ival Davidson. One of my bigger mistakes. It felt good to think about her, and once I started, I didn't want to stop.

Montgomery said, "I couldn't get money anywhere else."

"Something would have come up. But"—I shrugged again—"that's hindsight. What we want to worry about, here, is the future. Of which there won't be much unless you level with me about where your money's coming from. I need someplace to start."

It took a little more prodding, but at last I got him to talk. As he explained it, he took his projects to Cassie, who took them to some sort of inner circle—he wasn't sure just who—for script approval. Once in awhile they brought a script to him and just told him to film it, such as the one in progress, which had to do with some witches who had lived several centuries and still refused to die. As soon as a certain script was approved, Cassie would disappear for a week or so, to line up the backers, she said. And then, almost mysteriously, money would be wired into Montgomery's bank account.

"From where?" I asked.

"It all comes from offshore. Different banks."

My mood nose-dived. The workings of the "offshore" banks were impossible to penetrate. There were thousands of them, and they all lay outside the United States' banking laws. Drug money, the financing for various terrorist organizations, illegal arms deals—anything and everything could be confused and finessed by using offshore banks. The transactions were buried layer upon layer, wired and wired from one bank to another till the paper trail was hopelessly muddled, usually beyond even the Federal Government's abilities to untangle it. I'd hit another dead end. Nevertheless, I asked, "Which banks?"

Montgomery gave me a list of several, three in the mobbed up Bahamas and Caymans, and a Panamanian one that fronted in Mexico City and had ties to legitimate branches in Tijuana and Burbank. This latter was where his most recent wire transfers had come from, out of Mexico City to a branch in Tijuana, then on to Burbank. Layers upon layers, just as I'd suspected.

Just as he'd finished writing down the names, an assistant director rapped on the door, then opened it and stuck his head in. "Thought I'd find you here. We're ready to roll."

Montgomery looked like he wanted to shove me under the carpet so his colleague wouldn't see me. When the man's head withdrew and the door closed, he yanked open his desk drawer, pulled out a bottle of multicolored pills, dumped half a dozen into his hand, then swigged them down with the dregs from a cup of coffee. He barely managed to hand me a decent farewell as he ushered me out the door.

I took myself out of his office, past the sound stage with its huge black machines and blinding lights and robot-like technicians. Everyone was standing at attention now, and a brunette was sprawled in the middle of the daytime street, a dagger stuck between her breasts and a pool of fake blood spread out around her. Hooray for Hollywood. I was happy to take myself out of the back lot and on down the pike.

Chapter

——————TWENTY——————

For the first time since I'd been "murdered" I stopped by my office and checked the mail. I'd checked my answering machine before I'd left my bungalow, and now I checked the office extension. In the past hour Ariel had phoned, Frank Livingstone had phoned, and my old buddy Angelo from the *International Inquirer* had phoned. I tried phoning them back in that order, but none of them had bothered to wait for my call.

Since I already had my phone in hand, I started calling all the limo services in town, pretending I was a hot-shot Hollywood producer who needed to rent a snow-white Rolls limo with snazzy gold trim. There couldn't be all that many of them in town. I found six, parcelled out among three places.

And I found the one with the right plates in the yard of the second limo rental joint I visited, a place called "RENT-A-DREAM." There it sat on plain, simple tarmac, totally unsinister, completely pretentious, resting between a pink Masserati and a beige Ferrari. It took a full C-note to get the man behind the desk to check out his books and tell me who had rented it on the night in question. But there it was, a paper trail at last, the car rented by none other than the elegant Hispanic man I'd met at the Cardwells' the night they'd tried to kill me: Juan Valdez. His home address was in Beverly Hills, his business address was on La Cienega, not far from the car rental dealership.

I did a drive-by of his business. It was in one of the polished, older one-story mission-style buildings set well back amidst foliage, but the gate was open and the driveway was unguarded, so I tooled on in and pulled up in front. I took the steps two at a time, just to see if I could do it, then reined in at the front door, where a tasteful metal placard said: VANCE & VALDEZ, COLLECTORS AND DEALERS: MESO-AMERICAN ART AND ANTIQUES. Which told me that Dr. Vernon Vance had more financial irons in the fire than just shrinking heads. There were small windows with bars on them, but I could see display cases in one room, several women sitting at desks in another, though no sign of Juan Valdez, not so much as a burro or a styrofoam cup of coffee. Which was fine by me, no need to let all the Wackadoos know I was still alive and kicking, at least not yet.

I climbed back into my BMW and was tooling back down the street, feeling as fine as possible considering I'd only been out of the hospital one full day. I turned on my radio to catch the afternoon news. Fires were hitting Santa Barbara again. New mudslides had occurred after the last rain, leaving some of the multimillion dollar spreads wide open to leap-frogging should the dry brush catch fire. People were being evacuated. Fire fighters were being called in from all over the state to battle the blazes, and I wondered for the umpteenth time why people kept rebuilding there. There'd also been a 4.5 earthquake up out of San Francisco. Another little nudge from the "Powers that Be" that all was not right with the state of California, or with the state of the world for that matter.

And then I snapped to attention and yanked the steering just in time to keep from clipping an eighteen wheeler that had rolled onto the freeway beside me just as I heard the news announcer say, "And Tony Cacciatore, one-time mobster turned humanitarian, narrowly escaped with his life today as two unknown gunmen fired on him and his coworker, Shelby Knight, while they were conducting services at the Grace of the Shepherd Mission in downtown Los Angeles. Mr. Tony Cacciatore was behind the pulpit delivering an afternoon sermon when the two men entered and opened fire with semiautomatic weapons. Police estimate that no less than twenty shots were fired. Mr. Cacciatore was taken to City of Hope where he was treated for a slight graze to his ankle. Mr. Shelby Knight escaped injury, and no onlookers were harmed. Police are talking to witnesses who claim certain elements of organized crime have threatened Mr. Cacciatore's life because of his campaigns against pornography . . ."

I did a U-turn over the divider, then slammed the pedal to the metal. I wished I had a siren and a light to clamp on my car roof, like the LAPD. But even without them, I was screeching into the hospital parking lot in under twelve minutes. I leaped out of my Beamer, raced through the door and into the reception area, and demanded to see Tony. A nurse with blue hair and a seen-it-all expression told me he'd gone home an hour ago.

Home had to be the mission. I charged down there, managing to avoid several collisions on the way, then banged past the uniformed cop and through the front door—and into a room empty except for several police technicians who were diligently digging bullets out of the woodwork. I strode up to the first one. "Where's Tony?"

He looked up with exhausted eyes. "Couldn't say. He hasn't been back here."

I went around to the kitchen, where several mission employees were clustered, talking fervently. I bypassed them and for the first time climbed up the back stairs that led to the dormitory, two at a time again, getting back in shape.

Two young men were scrubbing down the upstairs hall, talking as they worked, the entire place abuzz with the event of the attempted assassination of their leader. I could see they were trying to get some blood off the hardwood floor. I stepped up and said, "Tony been here?"

"Not since he ran up here when they were shootin' at him. Look, that's where he bled. Only a scrape on his ankle. Man you should have seen it, bullets flying right at him and he just raised his hands and started praying, only one even touched him." I gave them a long, level look that didn't seem to bother them a bit. Then I felt a little twinge of jealousy. There was a look of joy and peace on their faces that I'd never managed to feel, even in my best days. I shook off the unwanted feeling and asked, "You know where Tony went?"

They shot each other warning looks.

"I'm his friend," I explained. "The one who put him in the slam."

"Oh, yeah. We heard about you. Look, Tony's gone into hiding for a while, till he figures out how to handle this. Shelby is the only one knows where he is."

"Where's Shelby?"

The boys looked at each other again. The second one said, "Don't know."

They seemed to be telling the truth, so I hiked back down the stairs, looking for someone else to ask, and then inspiration hit me. I went into Tony's office, picked up his telephone, and dialed the Grace of the Shepherd Church up in Anaheim, the one that paid part of Tony's mission bills. After a couple of rings, a woman's voice answered. I asked for Tony. Dead silence. I asked to speak with the pastor, and she told me he was at home. Could I get his phone number? No. Could I at least get his name? (I'd forgotten it).

She figured that was common enough knowledge and jarred my memory. Pastor Irby Howard. Two seconds later I had his home number from information, two seconds after that I had him on the line. I gave him my name, then said, "Look. Tony is my friend. I'd like to help him out if I can. I'm betting you know where to find him. Let him know I phoned, let him know that all he has to do is say the word and he's got anything I have. Tell him I'm sorry I even carried Riggatoni's message to him, tell him I think the man is pond scum. Tell him to call me!"

That done, I used the same phone to call Riggatoni, who came on the line only after he learned it was me. "So," he said, "you going to rat me out to the heat, tell them I sent you with a message?"

"Any cop worth his salt will know it was you."

"Yeah. Which don't mean nothin' except I got to pay a little extra jack to keep them off my back, right? Especially since it's Family business."

"I just want to know one thing."

"What's that?"

"Did your men really try to hit Tony, or were you just scaring him a little?"

There was a long pensive silence, then Big Al's voice turned ugly, and he said, "I got to hire me some better shooters." He hung up in my face.

Chapter

——————TWENTY-ONE——————

I was home by eight o'clock, all cozy in my nest, a bowlful of microwave popcorn at my side, complete with napkins so I could wipe off greasy fingers before turning the pages of Ival Davidson's books. And some books they were. Bulky, esoteric tomes, chock full of bloodthirsty information about ancient Indians. Big Al Riggatoni and his gang wouldn't have had a prayer against some of these ghouls.

The first thing I did was check the indexes for the name, Tezcatlipoca. In spite of the peyote, I still remembered every detail of my last visit to the Cardwells', except for the parts where I was totally out of it, of course. But I definitely remembered this name and the fact that Auguste was supposedly an incarnation of this "god" as well as several others. I remembered Caspar Cardwell saying that Tezcatlipoca was one of Quetzalcoatl's brothers, as well as "another aspect of him." I wanted to figure that out.

Which led me first of all to a chapter that explained the cosmos according to the Meso-American Indians. The Aztecs, for instance, had believed the cosmos existed in five cycles, or "suns," who were also gods. The first four suns had already died, and we were now in the era of the fifth sun. When this sun died, we were in for it. Kaput.

Which explained their unpleasant practice of human sacrifice. Numerous Meso-American Indians had decided that the way to keep the sun from dying was to fortify it with the most powerful substance they could find, and they'd decided this substance was the human heart. Thus their bloodthirsty practice of ripping out human hearts, often while the owner was still alive, and sacrificing them to the sun god. This was to keep their sun god strong, so he wouldn't die like the four other suns, and take the cosmos with him.

Enter both Tezcatlipoca and Quetzalcoatl, in this particular scheme of things. (There were many versions of how this worked). The creator of the universe, as most Meso-Americans Indians saw it, was indeed the dual god named Ometeotl. This androgynous being had had various sons, foremost among them Quetzalcoatl and Tezcat-lipoca, though by the time the ancients had it all figured out, some 2000 more gods had been added into the mix. After some casual scholarship, it became obvious that not much was known about Tezcatlipoca except that he had been the god of the First Sun, the god of night and earth, and also the god of human sacrifice. His sun had lasted only six or so centuries then had died, taking the whole ball of wax with it. The sun-god Quetzalcoatl, however, had stuck around a bit longer.

Long enough, in fact, to descend into the Land of the Dead and sprinkle some bones with his blood, thus creating the human race. He'd also invented human food and had figured out how to resurrect the dead, including himself. Because when his sun died, he somehow managed to stick around, to rear his serpentine head over and over again throughout the cosmology of the Meso-American Indians.

Quetzalcoatl had at first been a benevolent god till he'd travelled farther south. Then he'd somehow merged with his newly reincar-nated brother, Tezcatlipoca, again, god of human sacrifice. The bloodthirsty Indians had adopted this new version of the plumed serpent god with a literal vengeance, and about this time followers of Quetzalcoatl began practicing human sacrifice, big time. They must have been really worried about the sun dying because they began offering up human hearts by the thousands.

According to the priests who demanded this sacrifice, they were actually doing the victims a favor. To have your heart ripped out and even eaten while you were still more or less alive meant that you would be given the highest place in the heavens, and would, in fact, be allowed to travel with the sun itself, following it in its cycle. This was because the victims had helped sustain the sun by offering up their own lives to extend its time-span. Quite an honor, but one I could do without.

It was hard to follow all this. There were thousands of different deities, and all these gods had various incarnations. After about an hour of digging through it all, my headache was starting to come back and I felt depressed to realize that so many people had lived like this. Sometimes Quetzalcoatl would be the big cheese, at other times the name of a lizard god named Itzamna would crop up as the overlord of it all. One scholar would depict the Mayans as a pretty civilized group of people who studied the sky from atop their pyramids, while other scholars depicted them as a bunch of bloodthirsty madmen. I was inclined to go along with the latter opinion. After all, they'd sacrificed their own children by ripping out their hearts, had cut themselves and bled for their gods. They'd otherwise mutilated themselves and plenty of others as a way to worship their bloodthirsty dieties. They'd sacrificed people then dropped them, still alive, into the well at Chichen Itza (where, according to Ariel, Cassie Cardwell visited regularly to pay homage). And the object of almost all of this bloodletting and pain was Quetzalcoatl, the god who Cassie proudly channeled back into the vortices of the human race. I was beginning to understand the Cardwells and their pals a little better than I wanted to . . .

After about two hours of this macabre reading, I put an overdue bill in the book to mark my place, got up and fixed myself an avocado sandwich, washed it down with a quart of chocolate milk, then went into my bedroom and changed into a pitch black sweatsuit, the one with the black hood I can pull up over my head in case I want to play Ninja. I went outside to my Beamer, opened the trunk and extracted my burglar's tools from where they were hidden inside the trunk wall. I checked them, then climbed in and headed for the bright lights of

Wilshire Boulevard, where lay the offices of Elizabeth Ann Livingstone's one-time dentist, Dr. Nathan VanDerber.

Chapter

————TWENTY-TWO————

At night, driving down the winding road from my bungalow, the city spreads out beneath me in a geometrical pastiche of light and darkness: a metaphor for good and evil, a topic which was very much on my mind after all my dark reading.

Tonight, the freeways gleamed like luminous gems. The skyscrapers downtown were spills of light against the thick sable backdrop of the sky. Dusk always transforms this City of Angels into soft lights and glitter, but night transforms it again—into garish carnival neon and menacing back alleys, into something cruel and hot, gritty and violent. But over all this lies the network of light, filaments as fine and fragile as a spider's web: incandescent sapphires and emeralds, glimmers of pinks and cherry-reds, with white diamond gossamer and golden topaz cobwebs overlaying it all, defining the streets and ballparks, the shopping malls and sleeping houses and even the skid row snake-pits.

Often, driving down the canyon, I find myself considering the nature of light. It's a beauty that puzzles me, and tonight even more so. Venus, the Evening Star, still hung on the horizon, freed, for the moment, from the haze of smog that usually obliterates any trace of a night sky from the greater Los Angeles basin and replaces it with black haze. I contemplated the story of Quetzalcoatl, a god who had become a man, a plumed serpent capable of resurrecting the dead, himself immolated on a funeral pyre, fleeing the shame of violating his own flesh and blood, his screams echoing over water, his own flesh crackling, sparks shooting out, skyward, and then—a sudden transformation! A burst of white-hot energy, and a new "being" had hung in the achingly empty night sky, a hope for ancient hearts that death could be conquered, that even the most shameful deed could be transformed, through scalding pain to be sure but nevertheless transformed, into something beautiful and eternal and triumphant.

The story of Quetzalcoatl's transformation into the Evening Star had many of the elements of a far more familiar tale: the story of Jesus Christ, the sacrificial Lamb of God, who had agreed with His Father, the Creator of the Universe, to be sent to earth as a man, to die on a blood-stained cross, so that He might be resurrected and overcome death for all humanity. To me, this was a far more compelling tale of how earthly pain and travail might be transformed into eternal life and joy and triumph. With Christ, the blood wasn't let to satisfy the heinous desires and power-lust of a deity, but as atonement, to save the human race.

Still, it was strange to me how it all seemed to center, somehow, around blood. But not so strange, after all, when I considered that blood was the center of the physical life force. This whole thing boiled down to a struggle between life and death, whether on the spiritual or physical plane. Still—give me a choice and I'd a whole lot rather worship a Deity who'd loved me and died for my sins rather than one who wanted to see me tortured before I died for his. But then, maybe that was just the cultural bias of growing up in a white, Anglo-Saxon household where I was inculcated with the Judeo-Christian belief system. If I'd grown up an ancient Aztec, I'd surely have seen things differently . . . Maybe. Maybe not. I imagine the ancient Aztecs didn't like being sacrificed much, either . . .

Be that as it may, I was fascinated with the fact that, all throughout the Bible, one found blood as a means of atonement, and so did all these ancient pagan religions. And along with this, there were always elements of light. Indeed, Jesus Christ was also known as "the bright and morning star," or at least so said a remote fragment of some barely recollected church song that occasionally wisped through my brain. "In Him (in Jesus Christ, that is), was life, and the life was the light of men. And the light shines in the darkness and the darkness did not comprehend it. John 1:4-5." Man! I couldn't believe I still remembered that verse, it must have been thirty years since I'd thought of it! And then another Bible verse came to mind: "In the Beginning, God said 'Let there be light, and there was light.'" Light. What was this thing about light?

Believe it or not, I'd been fascinated with the science of physics when I was at UCLA. I'd even toyed with the idea of going on to get a graduate degree for a while, till I'd realized that all the physicists I knew were clear-headed and sober fellows, whereas quite a few of the lawyers I knew were double-fisted drinkers like myself and managed to get along quite well in spite of it. So I'd decided to use what was left of my G.I. loan to go to law school. My first year there I dropped out and got a real education in the streets and back alleys of this City of Angels.

But I'd learned enough physics, in my sober moments, to understand the physical theories of light. Light came from the nuclear reactions in the stars (mostly our sun), streamed from it, creating and continuing life just as the ancient Meso-American Indians had suspected. A dead sun meant a dead cosmos—at least the material kind—because without light, nothing material could live. Least of all humanity. Our existence was intertwined with the existence of light in a million intricate ways, not the least of which was our need to light our streets and alleyways in order to stave off the aching terror of the pitch blackness of true night and the horrors that emerged from the human psyche within that blackness.

I knew, too, that light was made up from photons, something insubstantial which was neither wave nor particle yet could easily take on the properties of either or both. The speed of light formed an uncrossable barrier, something which we humans could never go beyond, whether at the astronomical level or the level of the subatomic. Because of our very physical nature, we would never travel faster than the speed of light. Nor would we ever see into the world of the very small, simply because the size of these photons that lit our vision did not allow for viewing particles smaller than themselves. Well—all that's confusing even to me. And yet—light continues to fascinate me.

I heard a professor of religion say once that God is the light by which we see. I'd believed, then, that he was talking about spiritual enlightenment. But sometimes I wondered. I'd been tutored well in the Scriptures, even though I'd blocked most of it out as I grew older. But I knew that all throughout the Bible God appeared as a Being of Light. When He appeared to Moses, He was hidden in a pillar of firelight. Sometimes, in pensive moments of solitude when I thought about the true meaning of life, I toyed with the thought that *if* there really was a God, He might sometimes choose to manifest Himself in earthly form as scattered particles of photons: something without physical substance, something just ever so slightly outside the material domain, and yet life-giving and so beautiful that your breath caught in your throat and your heart nearly stopped when you saw Him manifested as a dewdrop on a morning leaf or a crystalline snowflake or a sunset. Where, oh, where was this God that the ancients had longed for, that my grandmother had taught me so much about?

And then a sudden, long-buried thought struck me. Lucifer. Fallen from heaven, like lightning. Scraps and traces of Sunday school lessons, fragments of sermons I'd been forced to sit through. Lucifer, who desired to ascend into the heavens and exalt his throne above the stars of God, who had been cast down to become the Prince of the powers of the air. Lucifer, who desired to copy God and literally steal His thunder, who had perhaps finally ascended to become the "Bright Morning Star" in an inferior mimicry of Jesus Christ, only Lucifer had renamed himself Quetzalcoatl/Venus, the morning/evening star. And then there was Lucifer as the serpent in Eden: Quetzalcoatl, the Meso-American serpent in feathers. The parallel was so precise, the counterfeit so near the original, the thought was so sudden and so compelling, that I shot up straight as if I'd been slapped!

Where did you look if you wanted the true light? Certainly not to an ancient deity who would eagerly await your sacrifice. Nor to a group of mixed up millionaires who'd decided to further their own basic interests by following a religion as manipulative and exploitative as they had themselves become.

Maybe my grandmother, in all her brilliant simplicity, had had it right after all. Christ Himself had said *He* was "The Bright and Morning Star!" And suddenly another Bible verse flooded into my mind, another fragment from childhood indelibly etched into my memory by a stern, hard-faced Sunday school teacher who had demanded that we learn a verse a week, come what may. The verse told about heaven: "And there shall be no night there: They need no lamp nor light of the sun, for the Lord God gives them light. And they shall reign forever and ever." I'd seen a Christian scientist once on TV who talked about physics and our spirituality. This, he'd said, would be the new physics. No night, no darkness. God as the pure source, at last, of light and energy. Figure *that* one out, Einstein.

At that moment the concept amazed me. God as light, again. God, as the very source of light. But what was God? Should I be worshiping photons? I snorted out loud at the ridiculousness of that thought and shook my head in consternation, and at that moment my pensive mood passed, and I was taking the off-ramp from the freeway onto Vermont, and then I was turning onto Wilshire, driving past the furry black palms and man-made ponds in MacArthur Park where someone had left their cake out in the rain. Then I was in the dead center of a cluster of gray and silver highrises a few blocks east of the park, wheeling into a lot not twenty paces from the entrance to the office building of Dr. VanDerber, dentist of the not-so-late Elizabeth Ann Livingstone. Now, the only light that interested me was the faint illumination in several scattered windows within the building.

Chapter
——TWENTY-THREE——

A few dim night-lights fought back the darkness in the highrise wherein lay Dr. VanDerber's office suite. The lock on the glass front door gave up the ghost in about thirty seconds, no alarms rang, no security guards stormed the lobby. The elevator whisked me up to the eleventh floor without incident. Another ten minutes had me in the office door, in the storage room, and into the file cabinet where Frank Livingstone had told me I would find Elizabeth's dental files. I had them under my arm and was back down the elevator, out the door, and driving away, all in under fifteen minutes, feeling so smug about the ease of my B & E job that I wondered why I hadn't taken it up as a profession. Artie Weatherby, Cat Burglar: Nemesis of the LAPD, Scotland Yard, and Interpol. Intrepid and Daring Thief, Who Steals From the Rich and Keeps it! I sped back along the Hollywood Freeway, congratulating myself some more on my talent for crime. And just about the time I reached the turn-off to Sunset, a sudden thought struck me. I slammed on my brakes just in time to take the off-ramp, then found myself once more on my way to the opulent pink palace of the very peculiar Cardwells. Since I seemed to be on a roll tonight, this might be just the time to check out the Foundation's financial records which surely lay ensconced somewhere in the Cardwells' house.

It was almost two A.M. when I cut my headlights and drove slowly up a sandy side road that meandered off the main drive to the house.

The lights of the city made a milky wash on the skyline behind me, the dark sea rolled in with a rhythmic crash across the beach highway. To my right were the jagged black mountains and directly ahead of me, masked by olive trees and palms and hedges, jutted a ten-foot-high iron fence that was surely wired with an alarm system. Which meant that this B & E job might be a little tougher than the last one, but I, Artie Weatherby, intrepid "Master Thief," was surely up to anything the fates could hand me on this warm, sweetly scented Pacific night.

I made my way carefully along the fence, my memory conjuring up night walks in the Vietnamese jungle where sensors often lay just beneath the earth, ready to wail an alarm and warn the enemy that we were near; or maybe the rotted leaves that made up the jungle floor had been used to carpet over a mine field, a gift from Charlie to Uncle Sam. I walked very gingerly. These people were as dangerous as Charlie, maybe more so. Charlie had messed me up bad, but these people had all but killed me once. I wasn't going to give them a chance to do it again!

Two upstairs windows were dimly lit. Probably night-lights in bathrooms or hallways. As I crept through the brush, I stopped every few moments and waited, watching. Not a soul moved at any one of the windows, no sound but the steady crash of the surf.

I wondered about the Surf Gorillas. Did they patrol the grounds full time or just when a special event warranted special security? And what about other servants? I was around in back of the house now, and it was larger than I'd realized. The landscaping narrowed, the steep, ragged hill loomed close, and pink concrete towered above me, while two pink wings spread out to either side. I continued to follow the high fence around the grounds, came to a place where I actually had to scramble up and onto a rocky ledge to bypass the fence, so near was it to the foothill. And then at last I saw the spacious white marble patio with its strange and hideous assortment of stone gods.

I was still up on the small outjut of the abutting hill, and I could see everything. The drapes were pulled in the sunken room where I'd first been invited, by Caspar Cardwell, to enter the chakra of the violet light, and from what I could see it looked like a little violet light had lingered there. I'd since looked up the word *chakra*, had learned it was Hindu in origin, that each of us allegedly had seven of them (chakras, that is), and that they were sort of energy centers. They came in seven colors, ranging from orange to violet, violet being the highest level. The point of "becoming" a chakra was to connect to the part of your body that corresponded to each particular color, to work your way up to the top, then to sort of fizz it all together into some white fireworks, whereupon you'd be in touch with your true spirit consciousness. Or something like that.

I crouched down, surprised to find myself breathing hard from the minor exertion. Slow down, Weatherby, no point in trying to land yourself back in the hospital. And with that thought it all came back to me, the full degradation and violence of my last visit to this place, and I was suddenly scalded through with rage. There were boulders up above me, and I had to fight an impulse to scale the slope and send them raining down. I imagined a huge one crashing through the window, taking out the sanctuary, then I "saw" another one crash onto the patio, sending white stone arms flying, marble legs and faces turned to smithereens, a fine pile of white gravel left where these evil gods now lurked. I could do it. Doing it would make me feel good. But it wouldn't be a good move. Give it up, Weatherby . . .

While taking a moment to catch my breath, I surveyed the statues once again. Any artificial light stopped short of the patio, but moonlight again showed the sculptures, more clearly now than before. The Greek goddess Aphrodite stood regally in her draped white robes, the Babylonian goddess Astarte stood nearby, and now I recognized the Babylonian god-king Marduk as one of the statues beside her. The pot-bellied Buddha squatted in the midst of the odd conglomeration, and there, still, was Kali the Hindu goddess of both life and destruction. I could see the statue more clearly than before: it was smeared with a red paint depicting the blood required to satiate her, and she wore a garland of stone human heads around her neck. Beside her stood Shiva, her equally blood-thirsty soul-mate and husband. Like the Aztec dual-god and creator, Ometeotl, these two had somehow intertwined, some said through excessive sexual intercourse, and now they were essentially one and the same, the male and female manifestations of one evil entity.

The squat pre-Columbian gods had been rearranged. Now, in the center of their semicircular order, stood the hulking, ten-foot-high faintly man-shaped sculpture that had caught my eye before. It was still clothed in dark drapery, and suddenly I was curious as to what the heavy cloth concealed.

I crawled back to a spot just above the patio, calculated the distance of the drop—no more than seven feet—figured my probabilities of being able to clear the fence and then, before I had time to think any more about what had happened to me the last time I'd been in the company of all these strange boulder-beings, I jumped and landed square beside the familiar Toltec carving with the angry dark-stone face, fat lips, and protruding tongue. I stared it dead in its empty eyes, then reached out and tweaked its bulbous stone nose. "No wonder you're mad at the world," I whispered. "All your life you've had to live with people with stir-fried brains, and you don't even have legs to walk away."

This time the statue didn't say a word.

I hunkered there beside the cold stone for a full five minutes, waiting to see if the faint noise I'd made as my sneakers hit marble had awakened man or beast. When nothing happened, I moved silently to where the hulking carving stood hidden by black drapery. I grabbed a corner of the material, gave it a slight tug, and then realized it was tied on. I found the rope, untied it, then tugged again. The drape slid off, revealing a horror so hideous that it made me suck in my breath and step back.

It was stone, of course, but carved with such realism that I held my breath, lest even such worldly breath as my own might call it to life. A masterpiece. But a masterpiece carved by a demented demon, a bizarre blend of beauty and evil.

It was obviously a god, but a new god, something I'd never seen before. Carved into its countenance was the female and male, the beautiful and hideous, the esoteric and metaphysical, the occultic and satanic. Its facial expression held the slack monkey smile of a spiteful imbecile but also an esoteric poignancy that was nearly divine. It rose from a writhing base of serpents into a gold-leaf cloak of stylized feathers set with glittering crystals, all of them semiprecious stones. The body and face held elements of the carvings of ancient Aztecs, Sumerians, Babylonians, Hindus, and even ancient European art. Once past this confusion of first impressions, I could see that the shape of the face was that of the Light Bearer, the half-man, half-serpent being depicted in the painting in the Cardwells' sanctuary.

This had to be their chief god, Narayama, the one Dr. Winch had told me about in Ariel's bookstore. It held the essence of the Aztec over-god, Ometeol, as well as all the baals to whom the Israelites had offered up worship and sacrifice. This hulking, hideous symbol was, in fact, *all* the false dieties, imagined or otherwise, who had ever had a hand in the horrors that had eternally assailed the human race . . .

A deep, cosmic shudder ran through my body. I felt like I was going to be sick again. This was evil. Supernatural evil. But even in that moment, something light and pure touched me with a thought. If there was indeed supernatural evil, that alone proved there was a supernatural world. Which meant there also had to be supernatural good! Which set me to thinking for a flash of an instant: why was it so much easier to believe in evil as something that originated outside of humanity than it was to think of good as something derived from an External Source?

But no time to ponder that one now.

Narayama smiled emptily, his dead eyes fixed on the night sky. I glanced upward, toward where he gazed, and there saw Quetzalcoatl, or Lucifer, or Venus, or whatever name you want to call the Evening Star.

I was in a cold sweat now. I forced my eyes away from the horror and turned toward the house. A sudden urgency pumped me through

211

with adrenaline. No time to redrape the figure, no time to waste. The lie had a face now, a hideous face. Something cosmically destructive was happening here, and somehow, for some reason, I had been catapulted square into the center of it. And I had to get to the bottom of it, or I was going to go mad trying.

Chapter
—— TWENTY-FOUR ——

Once inside the door, I could see a violet ribbon of light beneath the door to the sanctuary where I'd first been introduced to the strange and occultic belief system of these obsessed people. I padded silently down the carpeted hallway and put my ear to the door. Cassie was chanting. I felt a sudden pang of anxiety at the mindless pitch of her voice.

I silently turned the knob, knowing the door was a good distance away from the altar with its obsidian pulpit and shimmering geodes. The door opened a crack, I peered in, and saw her kneeling there with her back to me, the violet light bathing her. She wore a long black robe, and now I could hear what she was saying.

"There is no evil, all is good. There is no evil, all is good. God is good, god is evil, god is good, god is evil." Her voice changed pitches, from a chant to a prayer.

"I come to you, oh Solar Father, I come to you oh Master Soul. Oh Great Narayama, I ask you to awaken my *kundalini*, I petition you to enlighten my being. Hail Quetzalcoatl, Hail Ometeotl, Hare Krishna, Shiva, Kali, Narayama . . ."

She continued her pagan worship as I softly closed the door then padded on down the hallway. I was looking for someplace they might keep the Foundation's financial records. I carefully peeked in doors, using my pen flashlight to scope out the corners and nooks and crannies. There was a Midas' fortune in furniture and carpets, rooms fit for kings—a kitchen sufficient for the Beverly Wilshire itself, and patios and anterooms and closets and amenities galore. But no office, at least not downstairs.

The carpet on the staircase felt like pink cashmere. The bannister was Spanish ironwork, scrolled and filigreed and shellacked in black. A tiny blue-tinted night-light had helped me make my way through several large rooms, then up the stairs, and now on down the hall to what had to be the master suite. I stopped outside the door, heard deep snoring, and assumed it was Caspar, tucked tightly in his bed while visions of spirit guides danced in his head.

I had already figured out that the servants' quarters were in the left wing of the house, beyond the kitchen and near to the garage. Which meant that this part of the house was probably up for grabs, except for Cassie and Caspar. I again started opening doors, silently, carefully. Several were locked. I made a mental note of which ones I might have to come back and investigate another time, and kept on going.

When I reached the third door on my left, I grabbed the brass knob. It wouldn't turn. Another locked door. I was making a mental note of that fact as well, had already turned and started to tippy-toe on down the hall, when the light inside the room switched on, casting a thin yellow wedge from beneath the door and onto the lavender hall carpet.

Uh-oh.

I froze in my tracks, too far from the stairway now to retreat. Whoever was inside that lighted room was almost certainly waiting for the faintest hint of noise so they could scream or phone the police or both. The rooms beyond me were uncharted territory. Blasting into one might land me in even deeper trouble.

So I stood, pressing myself into the wall, and waited for the light to go out. Which it did, in about two more minutes. I kept breathing shallowly, waiting for my intuition to give me an all clear. It made me wait for a long five minutes. But just as I started down the hall I heard the door creak open behind me and sensed someone peering out at my frozen-in-motion back.

I tensed. Okay, Weatherby. Fight or flight?

Just as I decided on flight and steeled my leg muscles for a leap toward the stairway, someone said, "Pssst!"

There was just enough light in the hall to define ghostly shapes. I turned, puzzled, and saw a form standing outside the door where the light had been, though the room was now dark. Again, the shape said, "Pssst! Come here."

I stepped closer, surprised. "Ariel?"

"Yes." We were both whispering. "Are you who I think you are?"

"Probably." I padded toward her, then stopped short. She held a tiny pearl-handled derringer, aimed dead at me. I whispered, "Are you going to shoot?"

She looked down at the gun, pointed it toward the floor, then said, "You're alive. I can't believe it. For heaven's sake, come in here before you wake up Father!"

Her room was scented with lemon and honey, and the carpet was as deep as the one on the staircase. I was betting it was lemon-yellow. We didn't turn on the light. Milky moonlight filtered through the curtains. She sat on the edge of a dimly outlined bed and said, "How did you find me?"

"Huh?"

"Weren't you looking for me?"

"Uh—not really. But why are you *here*?"

"I was visiting Mother, and it got late, so I decided to spend the night. Mother has kept my room for me just like I had it in high school. I've tried to phone you for two days."

"I've been busy."

"Mother told me she'd heard the police had found your body on the beach. Daddy said it was true, that you'd been the kind who attracted trouble. I didn't know what to think. Look, I'm really glad you're alive, for more reasons than one. The lawyer who's handling my trust is stalling me and lying to me. I need your help."

I quickly told her about my trip to see Tod Montgomery and explained how that had caused a renewed interest in her mother's and/or the Foundation's financial records, which was why I was in the process of burgling their house.

She said, "That's absolutely the stupidest thing I've ever heard."

"Excuse me?"

"Why didn't you just ask me, instead of breaking in?"

"You have access to the Foundation's records?"

"Well, maybe. I know where Mother's computer is. And I can assure you, if the records are here they'll be in her computer, and also on disk. She's very meticulous that way."

"Can you get them for me?"

"How soon?"

"How about right now?"

She hesitated a split second, then tossed her head. "Why not. Wait." She tiptoed out the door, pulling it quietly shut behind her. Then she was gone a long time, leaving me to ponder on the rhythms of the surf that continued to crash into the shoreline outside her balcony window and across the road. And then she was back, handing me a black leather valise. "I took them all," she said. "I dumped them in here. Mother had them in the safe, but I learned the combination to that a long time ago. There's a videotape in there too. I don't know what it is, but I thought it might be important so I brought it."

"Good work, kiddo. Any idea which is what?"

"I can't do *everything* for you. Look. You'd better go before you wake someone up."

"Are the Surf Gorillas working?"

"The *who*—? Oh, you mean Hans and Franz Mendoza. They have the night off. They don't live here anyway, just their father and mother . . ."

"Can I go out the front way?"

She leveled a long, irritated look at me. "I'll have to turn off the gate alarm."

"I'll wait," I said. "I don't think I'm up to scaling the back fence."

She moved in closer and looked at me again. "Are you okay?"

"I'm recovering."

"From what?"

I realized at that moment that she didn't have the faintest idea what had happened here last week. These people could keep secrets. I said, "From a little accident I had with your mother's friends from Mexico."

Her eyes went wide. "Auguste?"

"The same."

"They hurt you? They really hurt you?"

"They cost me a few days."

Her eyes suddenly glistened with tears. "I should have known. I should have realized something bad was going on when Mother cooked up that stupid scheme to have Dr. Winch do a reading on you. I thought I knew them, but I don't anymore, I don't even know my own parents . . ."

I grabbed her by the shoulder. "Shhh."

But she'd already broken off in mid-sentence, having heard the same noise I had. We waited while almost indiscernible footsteps padded down the hall. Then there was silence for a moment—someone listening, was my bet—and then a tiny rap came on the door, and Caspar's voice called, "Ariel? Are you all right?"

"Yes, Father, I'm fine. I just couldn't sleep, so I turned on the television. I'll turn it back off if it's bothering you."

"No, no," he said, "it's all right. I just thought I heard voices and I wondered . . ."

"I'm fine, Father. Good night."

He said good night, too. We listened through the door as he moved back down the hall, and then a door closed.

Ariel whispered, "Don't talk any more. Go climb down the balcony, so Father won't hear any doors closing or anything. Mother is up, she may hear you, too. Wait about five minutes after you get to the gate, and I'll pretend I'm going to get something to eat. I'll ask Father if he wants something, too, that will be my excuse for going to the anteroom off the kitchen and turning off the alarm system. Remember, you'll only have about five minutes, then I'm going to turn it back on, so check your watch. Ten minutes from now, the gate will be open, but only for five minutes. Got that?"

"Five minutes," I said. "Just like the old cloak and dagger days." I turned, went through her billowing curtains and out onto the pink balcony, then I started down the trellis. The scent of roses wafted up from the bushes just beneath me, letting me know I was going to get a thorn or two before this was over.

Chapter

──TWENTY-FIVE──

The behemoth building housing the *International Inquirer* was in an industrial park just off the Long Beach Freeway. It was a thirty minute drive from the Cardwell estate. At three A.M., the streets were deserted, and there was a taste of rain in the air as I pulled into the parking lot beside Angelo McPherson's sky-blue '75 Plymouth and a couple of other jalopies.

Downstairs, they did the printing and folding and loading for delivery. Upstairs were the offices of the people who wrote and managed the infamous rag. I nodded to Sammy, the gnarled security guard who sat at the night-desk beside the stairwell. We'd known each other for about a century now, ever since my buddy Angelo had come to work as night editor. Sammy nodded back at me, and I took the steps two at a time, just to prove to myself how fast I was healing.

Angelo was at his desk, a computer screen glowing green in front of him, words piled upon words within it, Angelo pounding at the keyboard furiously, no doubt trying to make a deadline. A TV set on the wall above him was tuned to CNN, a radio was tuned to one of the local all-news stations. I was glad to see him doing his homework.

"Yo," I said. Angelo stopped typing and swiveled in his chair, to glare at me. I said, "Got a minute?"

"Does it look like I've got a minute?"

"No, but then you're a master of duplicity."

"Whadda ya want, Weatherby. Spit it out, I got a story to write."

"I need a favor."

"So what else is new."

"You got anybody here who's good with finances?"

"Why, you need a loan?"

"Actually, I'm paying a C-note to anybody who will go through about two dozen computer disks and pick out the ones that have financial data on them. Then I need it organized and printed out. There'd be another C-note in it for anyone who could make even a little sense out of the information at that point. And I need it all by eight in the morning."

His eyes lit up with keen interest. "Something to do with the Livingstone deal?"

"Something."

"I still get the story if and when it breaks?"

"If and when."

He gave me a measured look, then lifted up the phone, hit the intercom, and said, "Carol? Yeah, look, something's come up. I'm sending the beginning of the homeless story over to you, you finish it up and get it ready for the next edition, got it? Yeah, that's right. Tomorrow morning's fine." That done, he turned back to me, and held out his hand. "Cash in advance," he said. "One of my kids needs braces."

"Happy to help the little shaver out," I said. I withdrew five twenties from my wallet, passed them over, then handed him the black valise that Ariel had given me. I'd stashed the videotape in my glove compartment and I'd counted the disks—twenty-four exactly. Surely he could plow through that in four or so hours, at least to the point of printing them out so I could see what was on them.

I thanked him and he grunted a reply, already inserting a diskette into the computer drive. He was a curmudgeon of the first order, but he was a brilliant investigative reporter when he wanted to be, and his word was as good as gold. I knew he'd have the work done as soon as was humanly possible, and in a way that would dig out as much information as possible. Which left me free to go dig up something far more distasteful. A grave.

The Chapel of the Flowers Mortuary and Memorial Garden was a sinister place at four A.M. The cherubs on the pillars seemed to be sleeping, fortunately, because I had to use metal cutters to get through the gate. The metallic green hearse squatted, toad-like, in the otherwise empty parking lot.

This time, I found my way straight to the Livingstone plots. The moon was obscured by clouds, now, making the night darker than it might have been. I used my flashlight to get from my car to the decaying wooden gate beneath the high Gothic arch. The rusty gate-clasp again grated as the ancient hinges came open, and the interior of the compound was again before me. I braced myself for the worst and went in.

Tonight, I stuck to the gravel path. The sprinklers were off, and Elizabeth's gravestone was easy to find. The gardeners had done a lot more work inside the compound, but nobody had yet moved the mound of earth back into the opened grave.

The life-sized marble angel that marked the gravestone gave me an eerie feeling, as if it were watching with disapproval when I took the shovel from my shoulder, dropped it down into the hole, then carefully dropped in beside it. I was a full four feet down from the surface now. Surely I wouldn't have to dig more than another couple of feet, and that should be easy going.

I had been working for about half an hour, spading up damp soil, raising my arms to toss it to the surface, then taking up another spadeful, when at last my shovel chunked against something solid inside the soil. A coffin. One part of me wanted to shout, another part wanted to weep. I didn't want to do this. But how else was I ever going to know who or what was in this grave?

Within another fifteen minutes I could see enough of the metal casket to stop spading and go to work with the crowbar.

I was sweating streams and covered with dirt as I worked on opening the coffin. Then at last I felt something give, and the lid creaked, then I had it braced with my arm and was forcing it up higher,

higher, and then at last it was fully opened and there before me lay something that had once been human but was now gray bones.

There was a dank smell, the result of a decade of rain and damp earth and decay. But the body had been buried long enough for the worst of the decay to dissipate and the flesh was long gone. I played over the skeleton with my flashlight, then stopped short, replayed the light on the skull once again, then reached forward and picked up the skull—it practically rolled into my hand—and then I knew. Two small holes had shattered the skull, holes that could only have been made by bullets. If this was Elizabeth Ann Livingstone, she hadn't been killed by falling down her spiral staircase.

My heart was beating fast and my own head had started to ache again. I had planned to mix up some moulage and make a cast of the jaw and teeth to take with me, but as soon as I saw the bullet holes I changed my mind. If this was going to turn into a full-blown murder investigation— which it well might—then the grave was going to have to be officially opened. And if the LAPD's lab boys found traces of moulage between the corpse's teeth, someone was going to have to do some explaining, and the way my luck was running that someone was likely to be me. So instead of making the casting I scooped up the whole jawbone, then took off my black windbreaker and wrapped it around the gruesome object, then pulled myself up and out of the grave. Almost done, Weatherby, don't think about death, don't think about decay, vanquish the horrors that lie in this compound by thinking of something else, something bright and vibrant and alive . . .

I made myself think about Christine, but she seemed remote and almost a dream, so I thought instead about Ival Davidson while I put back enough dirt to recover the coffin. As I worked, the twilight of dawn began to stain the skyline, the furry trees were etched in a faint purple-gold light, and the birds began to sing. The feeling and smell of death dissolved into the sweet coming of morning, and by the time I'd finished my work then tooled back out through the gate and closed it behind me, I was fine again, except for an aching, well-earned fatigue.

Chapter

───TWENTY-SIX───

One thing I'd treated myself to when I'd remodeled my office was a bathroom with a shower and a closet containing a few spare clothes. I wanted to catch my dentist neighbor first thing when he came in and get him to compare Elizabeth's dental charts and the jaw I had in a plastic grocery bag. I also wanted to be on the spot when Angelo faxed whatever Cassie Cardwell's computer disks yielded up. So I drove from the cemetery to my office, treated myself to a long hot shower, then changed into a new pair of skivvies and a T-shirt, grabbed a blanket out of the closet, then dropped, exhausted, onto my spanking-new chintz couch. My head throbbed. The stitches were healing, but I still looked and felt like Frankenstein. There were people out there who wanted me dead, and I didn't even know who or why. And Elizabeth, if she was still alive, was also handing me a raw deal. Why all this cat and mouse, why not just come right out and tell me what was going on so I at least had a fighting chance?

I was feeling particularly alienated and bewildered by my presence on this planet. I didn't want to do this any more. I wasn't really getting any closer to finding out who had "murdered" Elizabeth, even though I was one giant step closer to knowing if she really had *been* murdered. And after delving into her grave all night, thoughts of death and decay were very much with me, and with them came a deep, steely realization of my own mortality. One day I, too, would be nothing more than a bag of old bones lying beneath soil. So what was the point in all this?

Why was I trying so hard? Why not just kick back and enjoy life more, spend more time on the water fishing, get up in the canyons and do some hiking, forget about righting the world's wrongs. Why did *I* have to go to bat for Elizabeth Ann Livingstone? Or for Tony Cacciatore? For anybody, for that matter? I looked at my life and felt disgusted. Thirty-eight years old, and I didn't have a person on this planet who really loved me, unless you counted Christine, who loved the idea of eradicating the world of drug dealers even more, not that I could blame her. No family. No prospects, other than a P.I. license, a few bucks in the bank, and a strong desire to play knight in shining armor for the whole wretched world.

Depressed and somewhat angry, I finally managed to fall into a troubled sleep, with troubled dreams.

I was back at the cemetery, but this time it was the old churchyard just off Spring Street where my grandmother had been buried. I was wearing jungle fatigues and I'd just uncovered my grandmother's coffin, then opened it. Her tiny skeleton was intact, and she sat up and opened a pair of sparkling blue eyes. I was startled to see those eyes in the rattling bones, and she was equally surprised to see me standing there.

She looked me over, then said, "Land sakes, Little Arthur. Look at you, covered with mud from head to foot!" She stood up, reached out with a bony hand, and grabbed my earlobe. "March, young man. You're headed straight for a bath!"

Gently, I took her bony hand, removed it from my ear, and held it. "Grandmother." I was weeping. "I've missed you so much. Can you stay this time?"

Suddenly the bones dissolved into a fullness of shimmering, blue-tinted light and I was looking again at the beautiful, light-sculpted substance of my grandmother's spirit body as it had appeared to me when I'd had the dream or vision or whatever it was in my hospital bed. She gazed at me with a serenity and wisdom far beyond human depth, and said, "I'm not dead. I never was. I just cast off my shell."

"I—I don't understand."

Love shone through her eyes. "It's not that difficult. Remember what I taught you about the butterflies?"

"I—I'm not sure . . ."

"The cocoons. Do you remember the cocoons we found in the backyard, how you called me and asked what they were? And we watched them, and do you recall what came out?"

"Butterflies. Gorgeous golden butterflies. They flew away."

"They were no longer earthbound, Arthur. They'd been perfected into what they were intended to be."

"And that's what you are now?"

"Exactly." She smiled. "You always were a bright child."

I felt a surge of anxiety. "But even butterflies die. Even after they emerge from the cocoon." I glanced down at her grave and saw that her skeleton was back inside the opened coffin, though her light-body stood before me. "Look." I pointed at the bones. "You died once. Will you die again? Vanish from my dreams? Even from my memory?"

She sighed. "I'm in eternity now, Arthur. There is no death here. I don't age, I don't change. My spirit body will never die—it never *did* die. Those bones you see there are just the remainder of my cocoon after it dropped off the real me. You see, when I was a very young girl, I gave my heart to Jesus, and He gave me eternal life. He wants us all to give our hearts to Him, but after we do, we have to agree to learn to live by the standards He sets for His people. That's the hard part. I've told you all this before."

"So you always looked like this inside, even when your hair was gray? You just had that earthly body wrapped around you?"

"Exactly. And in God's due time the flesh and blood dropped off and went back to the earth it had been created from." This time *she* pointed at the bones. "The *real* me was left. Which meant I had to leave earth, since I no longer had an earthly substance. Believe me, the only hard part was leaving you. The rest of it was pure joy!"

"But here you are again. I can see and talk to you."

She pursed her lips, and said. "This is a *dream*, Arthur. I can appear to you in dreams because there's a special connection with the spiritual realm. I can't come back completely—not till Jesus returns, and we all come back to straighten out the mess down here."

"But I saw you when I died, after the shaman's thugs beat me up." I thought for a second. "Didn't I? Did I *really* die?"

"I wouldn't call it dead. You were in a different mental state, is all, a little closer to death than you've ever been before. But you were dreaming then, too."

"But—why am I seeing you so much these days?"

She frowned then. "You haven't yielded your heart to Jesus yet, Arthur. I prayed my entire life, and you're still fighting it. Jesus loves you, but He can't change His plan. You have to want Him before He can allow you to live in eternity. That's the whole point, the entire thing about faith."

I felt a pang of panic. "But how can I believe in someone I can't even see?"

"My land, you mean all those times I dragged you to church, you didn't learn a thing? He wants you to be reborn in the flesh, to be saved. You know what that means. You just take that first step, just tell Him you *want* to know Him. He'll reveal Himself to you quicker than a button."

"I still remember some of my Bible verses," I said. "Especially the ones about light." A sudden thought hit me. "You used to say we'd know everything when we went to be with the Lord. Do you know everything now?"

She said solemnly, "More or less."

"Then, is a light photon a manifestation of God?"

She shot me a disapproving look. "You don't have to reach the spirit world to figure *that* out. Of *course* it is. So is a drop of rain or a bluebird. God created every particle of the material world, even every particle of your earthly body. Your spirit too, for that matter. You can't even *begin* to imagine the power and majesty of God. Nor the love, or the joy . . . As much as I miss you, I wouldn't come back to this planet for the world!"

"Grandmother?"

"Yes?"

"You know, I try. Sometimes. But there's something here I just can't understand. Why does it all have to be so mysterious and difficult? Why can't God just show up Himself once, just let me know for certain that He really exists? Or let us visit the spirit world once. He expects us to believe something, then makes it impossible for us to do so by hiding everything!"

"But you do see Him, all around you, all the time. And you *still* don't believe, do you?"

I suddenly awakened and felt the same feeling of distress and poignant emptiness I'd felt when I'd fallen asleep. If there was a God, there was an insurmountable wall between me and Him. I lay there, miserable, thinking about my dream, thinking through my problems, wondering why, if there was a God, He wouldn't just step into my life in a very visible way and let me know I could at least turn in the right direction—when suddenly it hit me like a profound revelation! He was all around me! My drapes were open to the morning, and I could see the infusion of golden light as it touched the room, the plants, as it sculpted out each green leaf, each particle of matter. And in that instant I could almost see into the spiritual realm. And I knew in a way I had never known before that the very radiation that lights the world *is* a manifestation of our God, Himself!

God is the light by which we see, the preacher had said. At that moment, a sunshine flooded my soul and I could feel Him again, knew He was real, knew He was with me . . . I fell back into a dreamless, peaceful sleep.

At seven-thirty, the fax machine awakened me with its sharp ring. I sat up, thinking immediately about the dream and the following revelation. My head ached again. None of it seemed real. I slid off the sofa and slowly pulled myself erect, reflecting on whether or not a similar moment might have originated the theory of man's evolution from the ape. Arms dangling, I padded over to the fax machine, letting my malted-milk brown carpet tickle my ankles all the way, then I looked at the first curly piece of paper coming out of the machine. The writing was illegible. I turned it right side up and tried again. It was the first page of the print-outs of Cassie Cardwell's computer disks. When my bleary eyes at last focused, I could see that it was a page of financial transactions for a business in Mexico.

As the pages came in, I woke up fast. Pay dirt! Each page told me a little more of what I needed to know. There were full financial records of all recent donations, of paid expenses and other monetary interactions with an orphanage in Baja. But Ariel had told me this orphanage had gone under with the death of her grandmother Cardwell, more than ten long years before! And these were current records. So either the orphanage had been revived, or someone was using it for a front to transfer money. And I had a hunch that none of the Foundation members were spending any money or energy on feeding hungry orphans.

There were also some more obscure financial records pertaining to a stock transaction of major proportions involving Baja-Pacific Construction and Development. From what I could understand of the records, the company had recently completed a luxury hotel called the Casa del Sol, built at the base of the high blue and golden hills rising up from Bahia del Sol in lower Baja. The hotel had been built on leasehold land, with a $3 million annual fee to the land owner. I turned a page. Angelo had underlined the landowner's name so that it fairly leaped off the page at me. Señor Auguste Flores!

At last I had a paper trail! I waited till the transmission was completed, looked it all over again, then phoned Angelo and shared my exultation by thanking him.

"I got a little more," he grunted.

"Yeah?"

"I phoned a friend at the records office. The major shareholder in Baja-Pacific Construction is—lemme see, I got it written here—it *was* Elizabeth Ann Livingstone but there seems to have been some kind of a transfer—ah, yeah, this Livingstone woman died and now the money has been put into a trust for—lemme see—one Ariel Cardwell."

"Any idea how much the hotel and other property is worth?"

"I'm still working on that but my first guess would be at least 45 mil, and that's American dollars. It's a first-class luxury resort."

I resisted the urge to jump up and click my heels together. "Do me another favor, pal?"

"Anything, for a price."

"Keep digging into the construction angle. See what else you can learn."

"Sure thing."

I thanked him, then went into my spanking new bathroom and took a quick cold shower to get my blood singing as happily as was my brain. Next, I scraped the sagebrush from my face and pulled on a pale green T-shirt with a Lakers logo on the back and a pair of acid-washed Levis. I'd cleaned the cemetery mud from my shoes last night, so now all I had to do was pull on a pair of socks and step into them. That done, I phoned my friendly neighborhood dentist, the low-rent one down the hall from me. He was in and available. I picked up Elizabeth Ann Livingstone's dental files, then grabbed up the jawbone I'd captured last night, and then I stepped briskly down the hallway to the dentist's office.

Fifteen minutes later, my head start on the day came to a screeching end. The jawbone definitely didn't belong to the same person as did the dental chart. There was the little matter of a bridge on the one hand, a few fillings and a crooked tooth on the other. And when I asked the dentist if he could tell me what kind of person the jawbone might belong to, he said that in his estimation it belonged to someone in their late twenties or early thirties, most likely male.

Which meant that, like it or not, I was indeed in the middle of a full-blown murder case. The victim wasn't Elizabeth Ann Livingstone, at least not yet, not so far as I knew. Still—chances were good that the same people who had either duped her or helped her dupe the rest of the world were also responsible for the death of whoever was really buried in her grave. Chalk up one more black mark for the Foundation.

I trudged back to my office, jawbone and files in hand, and dialed Frank Livingstone's number. I caught him in. I told him what I'd found. He was elated that the body wasn't his wife's. I suggested that he wait a day, so I could return the jawbone to the grave, and then he should phone the police and make up some excuse why he wanted the grave opened. "You're going to have to take a little publicity on this, there's no way around it," I said. "But at least now we know that your wife isn't buried there. And by the way, make sure you also phone the funeral director and tell him not to fill in the rest of the grave today," I said. "I don't want to have to dig the whole thing up to put the jawbone back."

He agreed, I hung up, and then I went to the window and sulked for half an hour or so, not because I'd unearthed a real murder but because I was going to have to go back out to the cemetery and return the jawbone. I was standing there like that, feeling sorry for myself, when the phone rang. It was Tony Cacciatore. He said, "You been tryin' to reach me?"

"Yeah," I said. "How you doin'?"

"Not bad."

"Look," I said, "If there's anything I can do . . ."

"Matter of fact, there is."

"Yeah?"

"I don't like phones. Think you could drive up here?"

"Up where?"

"I'm at a church retreat, up in Topanga Canyon. Takin' a little time to figure this thing out."

He gave me directions, and two hours later I'd managed to leave the smog and debris of the city behind me, had navigated the winding road that climbs up out of Malibu, and was pulling in beneath a thick copse of pine trees set into dusty brown earth in front of one of a half dozen well-kept bungalows with dun-colored siding. There was a small horse pasture and barn out back, but I didn't see any horses. A red Ford Ranger sat in the driveway—not Tony's style, he probably had a visitor. I hit my horn once to announce myself, just in case they hadn't heard me drive up. I was just opening my car door when Tony stepped out onto the porch, shielding his eyes against the sun, and called, "Come on in."

I followed him into a simple living room with a plankwood floor. The furniture was the kind with wagon-wheels added in—the tan imitation leather was covered with equally counterfeit Navajo throws. There were some Remington knock-offs on the walls, and a hand-stitched sampler of the Lord's Prayer. Object by object, the room wasn't fancy, but all in all it was a homey place. As I came in, a slightly familiar-looking man rose up out of an overstuffed chair at the far side of the room. He was maybe forty-five and had sandy-colored hair that was already gray at the temples. Trim, lean, dressed in a blue work shirt and matching pants, so that at first I took him for maybe the foreman or a ranch hand. When he turned to look full at me, I saw that his eyes were a clear, cloudless blue with a power in them that gave an impression of distilled lightening.

Tony nodded his head toward the gent and said, "This is the Reverend Irby Howard."

He told Howard my name, too, and then we both stepped forward and shook hands, eyeing each other carefully. In fact, Howard eyed me so carefully that I wondered if he had the same general opinion of private investigators as I generally had of preachers.

I sat myself down on one of the wagon-wheel couches, Howard reseated himself in his chair, and Tony paced the floor back and forth, making me glad that the curtains were drawn tightly shut. Suddenly, he turned and looked at me, and said, "You been sick?"

I was surprised. "Not really."

"You don't look too good. You got problems, too?"

I shrugged. "More or less."

"Somethin' to do with Riggatoni?"

"Not at all. Last I had to do with him was to deliver his message to you. Which you should have listened to."

"That right?" His eyes went sharp and hot.

"Look," I said, "I realize someone just tried to kill you, and I know, firsthand, that's not a very good feeling. But I tried to stop it, remember? I talked to you and warned you and pleaded with you and—"

"Yeah, yeah, never mind all that. Look, somethin's come up. I need to get down to Tijuana. I wanted Irby here to go with me, but he thinks it's a bad idea."

"I've been in the television ministry for ten years," the Reverend said. "People automatically look my way when I'm in a room, wondering where they've seen me before even if they don't recognize me. I'm not the best person to be with if you're in hiding."

"He has a point," I agreed.

Tony nodded reluctantly. "Thing is," he said, "there ain't no reason I couldn't drive down by myself. But Irby here thinks I need a bodyguard. You wanta talk him out of it?"

"I happen to agree with him. I think you should stay planted right here until this thing with Riggatoni gets straightened out. What's the rush to go to Tijuana?"

Tony turned and gave me a bleak look. His shoulders slumped. "Shelby had to go down for a meeting," he said. "He took Rosa with him, he'd promised her she could sing. She disappeared."

I dragged my hand down the lower half of my face as the top half fell into a deep frown. "Not good," I said. "Not good at all. When do you want to leave?"

"Half an hour ago," he said.

"Let me make a couple of phone calls, and we can hit the road."

"Right."

"Thank you," Howard said. "I've made some inquires about you. I feel a whole lot better knowing Tony has you along."

I went into the bedroom where I could have some privacy, and phoned Angelo again. "Hey, old buddy, how would you like to be named as co-conspirator in a murder?"

"My dream come true."

"I *really* have a favor to ask this time. I mean a big one, life or death."

"What's in it for me?"

"Two bills?"

"No sale. That's not enough to pay for my lawyer's first visit."

"It's the Livingstone thing," I said.

"What's up?"

"Someone slipped a ringer into Elizabeth Ann Livingstone's grave."

"Yeah?"

"Yeah. Someone else is buried there."

"Interesting. So whadda ya need?"

"I need for someone to replace the current inhabitant's jawbone into the grave before the police can open it."

"No kidding, little thing like that, you'd think you'd have people standin' in line to help you . . ."

"I could maybe throw in a little sweetener."

"Like?"

"How about a fifteen-minute exclusive interview with hit-man-in-hiding Tony Cacciatore?"

There was a long silence, then he said, "I ain't gonna find anyone stupid enough to do this one for me. I'll have to go out and put it back myself. Throw in another hundred for gas and a shovel. I can get out of my office for a coupla hours around three A.M."

"It's done. You know how to get into my office. The jawbone is in the lower left-hand desk drawer, wrapped in a black nylon windbreaker."

That settled, I again phoned Frank Livingstone, who assured me he'd contacted the director of the memorial garden, who'd agreed to leave things strictly alone till the exhumation could be completed. And no, Frank hadn't yet contacted the police; he'd be glad to wait yet another day.

Next, using a falsetto voice for disguise, I phoned Ariel at her studio. She wasn't in. I left a message that things were moving along fine and told her I'd be in touch. And then I was ready to hit the road.

Chapter

——TWENTY-SEVEN——

Tony sat silently beside me as I wheeled into a self-serve in Long Beach just across the road from a stretch of polluted sand. I ignored the candy wrappers and tissues blowing around my ankles while I gassed up the Beamer. A storm was blowing in from the broad gray Pacific, waves heaving, seagulls circling and dipping and screeching over the dirty gray beach and the black tarmac of the parking lot. It was a good day to leave town. I stuck my head in the car window and asked Tony, "You want anything from the convenience store?"

He shook his head. He had dark bruises under his eyes and his shoulder muscles were so tense they looked like they were made from banded steel. He had a two-day stubble on his face that would have been a beard on anybody else. His hands were clenched into fists and lay defensively on his muscular thighs.

I went into the bright, busy little store, bought a cup of coffee and a package of red licorice for the road, then climbed back into the Beamer, revved her up, and moments later we were on the San Diego Freeway, heading south.

Even early in the morning, the traffic was dense. I focused on driving and thinking. Tony got lost in his own thoughts, and we were just driving past the highway sign that warned us we'd reached the off-ramp to San Clemente when Tony finally spoke.

"Thank you," he said.

It surprised me. I said, "For what?"

"For teaming up with me. Right now, I ain't exactly the social catch of the season."

I shrugged. "Neither am I."

"All the same . . ."

"Look," I said. "I'm just trying to fulfill my obligations to myself as a member of the human race."

"It ain't always easy, is it?" he said. Then he clammed up again for another fifty or so miles, staring out the window and into some dark world of his own.

We were driving across the bridge that spans the San Dieguito River, just outside Del Mar, when he suddenly said, "This is where I did my last hit. For Riggatoni. Some clown who was welshing on his bets here at the racetrack. I wouldn't a done him, Riggatoni or not, but I learned he had a thing about little kids . . ."

I was so startled by this revelation that I jerked my head around to look at him, and almost clipped the fender of a brown '84 Olds before I got back on track. I didn't reply because I was speechless.

"I was thirty years old before I done my first job," he said.

I swallowed hard.

"It ain't true, you know, that you got to 'make your bones' before you can be 'made' by a Family. My old man was a soldier, back when Vito was still running things."

I knew he meant Vito Genovese, one-time crime boss of the entire eastern seaboard and founder of the crime Family to which Tony had belonged until the blow-up that had brought him West.

"I started out runnin' the bag for numbers money when I was seven or so. Time I was eighteen, I'd given up on becoming a priest, and they was lettin' me handle some of my own action. Few years later, they 'made' me and put me up front of a couple a after-hours gambling joints. Neighborhood action, mostly, but we could rake in a bundle on a good night. And no rough stuff. Oh, things happened, but nobody bothered to check with me about it, and I didn't bother to make it none of my business.

"And then, couple a pals of mine—least, I thought they was pals—they started havin' some trouble. They'd been workin' the warehouses out around Kennedy Airport, boostin' furs, jewelry, anything came through that could make them a buck. Did pretty good for a few years but then the Feds came down hard for a while, and they didn't have nothing else goin'. They'd been comin' in, losin' three, four grand a time at the craps tables, now all of a sudden they was sore losers. I seen trouble comin', I told my dealers to lighten up on them, let them win now and again. I thought that loosened 'em up some, they quit beefin' to me, you know. But then some others started tellin' me these two jerks was talkin' to Tony Paulo—he was *capo* of the gambling—about movin' into some gamblin' action of their own. Paulo told 'em forget it, that I'd earned my place. I figgered that was the end of it."

He fell silent again, staring past me and at the traffic whizzing by in the opposite lane. I was silent too. We'd just passed a huge green highway sign that said "San Diego Exit," when he started talking again.

"It was winter. Big storm had just come in, blanketed Jersey, iced up the river, then started snowin' again, and it was up to your armpits everywhere in the city. Action was slow, and these two come in, dropped a few hundred, then said they needed to talk to me. I figgered they was goin' to ask for a loan, no big deal, but they got me alone in the back room and jacked me up, took me out to a car they had runnin' in the alley, and took me for a drive across the river and somewhere way back up in the woods, must a been fifty miles from the closest town. They shot me there. I'll see that gun for the rest of my life, a Smith and Wesson .44 Magnum with a six inch barrel. They unloaded it into me, point blank, one bullet square into my skull, what they thought was insurance." He tilted his head, and touched the side of it, and for the first time I saw a slight indentation, a place where the hair was patched just a bit thinner. "Plastic surgery," he said.

"They left me up there in the woods, figurin' the animals would get me, I guess, strip me down to bones, that the snow would pack me in and nobody would even find the bones till spring. But I come around an hour or so later, and I started draggin' myself; my leg was broken; it was pitch black, and the snow was several feet deep. My shoulder was shattered, and I had bullets in my chest and my skull, one had grazed my lung. I was leavin' a trail of blood, but I was movin'. And I kept movin'. Oh, I'd stop to rest, but I knew if I stopped long I was dead. And I wasn't goin' to die, not me, not that way. So I kept movin', and kept draggin' that leg, and kept coughin' up blood, and just when I thought I wasn't goin' to make it, I seen a light. A farmhouse. And I dragged myself up onto the porch and managed to slam into the door, and then I was gone for.

"I woke up in the hospital, and they kept me there for three months. Police swarmin' all over me, Feds droppin' by to see if I was ready to turn state's evidence against Vito or anyone else in the Family. And I thought about it. Vito hadn't done anything to the scum who tried to clip me. No loyalty there. But my old man was still alive, and he was still in it, and I knew they'd kill him if I talked, so I just laid there and waited, every day, gettin' better and better, and then one day I could get up and walk out.

"To shorten this story up some, I caught them sittin' in their car together, right in front a what used to be one a my gamblin' joints. I used a sawed-off shotgun, blasted 'em right through the windshield, there wasn't enough left a them to identify. And no witnesses. Anybody seen that was afraid to talk. My old man hired me a fancy lawyer just in case and the rest of the Family gave me a pat on the back, but I never even needed the lawyer. I got my gambling joints back and a few more besides, but after that the Family had an occasional hit for me here and there. Didn't matter. That thing did something to me, I didn't care no more. And that's where I was, more or less, till it all came down back East, and then I moved out here, and the rest a my history you already know because you helped write it."

Whew. I'd been transfixed by his story, and quite a story it was. I wondered what I would have done in the same circumstances, and then I wondered why he'd felt the need to tell me. I said, "I never judged you, Tony. It's not my place."

"You thought I was scum."

"I thought you made your living killing people. I don't think anyone has a right to do that."

"I heard you was in Vietnam."

"Yes. I was."

"But that's different, yeah? I never killed anyone, except when it was Family business. Even now, I can look back and see how some of 'em maybe deserved it. Some things you ain't allowed to get away with, no matter who you are." He stopped, thinking again, then said, "But when you kill for the government, that's a different story?" He didn't sound belligerent, just curious.

"No. It's the same. Killing is killing. Unless, maybe, you're doing it to defend your own life or that of someone else who's threatened."

"But the Bible says, 'Thou shalt not kill.' That's one a the Ten Commandments."

"So it is."

"So it's *never* right to kill."

"I don't know. I've never been able to figure that one out. Say someone has a gun and is going for a kid, you have a way to stop it but you have to kill the attacker to do it. What do you do? Either way, you're responsible for someone's death. One way, it's the kid, the other way it's the person who was going to kill the kid. I know which one I'd choose."

"Yeah. I know whatcha mean."

He was again silent. We were on the outskirts of the city now, and the freeway threaded above and through and past the commercial debris of refineries, drive-in theaters, lumberyards, flat gray warehouses, smog-pitted truck-stops, cubby-hole bars, and narrow busy streets with struggling exhaust-covered trees. Eighteen-wheeler trucks backed into loading docks, forklifts scurried around like cockroaches at a banquet. The whole thing was linked together and to the rest of the city by an ugly gossamer of telephone and utility lines.

We exited just south of Chula Vista, stopped at a travel agency and got our visas, then stopped to eat at a Greek food restaurant I'd stumbled across while sitting on a stakeout a few years back. Tony seemed withdrawn, even embarrassed, and I figured he was thinking he'd told me too much and was holding it against me.

But as I dipped a chunk of pita bread into the last of my hummus and polished it off, he suddenly set down his coffee cup and fixed me with a hard look. "I'm gonna have to turn myself in," he said.

I shook my head with disbelief. "For *what*?"

"For all the times I broke the law. It eats at me. I can't figure how to make it straight. Maybe if I give myself up, do my time, it will work out better."

"And who takes care of your mission work while you're rotting in prison?"

He opened his hands wide in a typically Sicilian gesture, and said, "God will work that out."

"You're sure this is what you're supposed to do?"

It was his turn to shake his head. "I don't know. Things didn't work out too bad last time I was in the joint. But on the other hand, I just don't know." He thought for a minute, then said, "The Feds are at me."

That was a surprise. And then I realized I should have known. Riggatoni was worried about more than just the money he was losing because of Tony's demonstrations, although that certainly would have been enough.

"If I ratted out Big Al, he'd go down for twenty to life. That would keep him from comin' at me, which would be good since I don't want to have to shoot it out with him. Plus, I could close his joints down, at least for a while, till the mob found somebody else to front for them. Plus, I could rat out Carlo Testa too, the big cheese himself, shut the whole mob down for at least a few years, save a lot a people a lot a pain. On the other hand, I rat out on botha them, I get to talk about what *I* done. Which maybe I should do anyway, even if I was to leave them out of it." He shook his head. "Hard to figure."

"Hard indeed," I agreed.

"It ain't in my nature to snitch someone off. Guess it's the way I was brought up, dirtiest, lowest thing in the world is a snitch. Hard to figure what to do. I spend a lot of time prayin' about it."

"Keep praying," I said, "Then sit back and see how it works out. Things turned out pretty good when Riggatoni's thugs came gunning for you. If that's any indication of the kind of protection you have these days, I wouldn't worry." I stopped short, amazed at what I'd just said.

"Yeah," he said, his face lightening up a little. "Big Al's boys shot me point blank."

"And they missed you," I said. "Think about that."

"Yeah," he said. "I know." He thought for a minute, then said, "I know it'll work out, but I can't seem to keep it from eatin' at me."

"Tony," I said, "I mean it. Lighten up. If I were you, I'd keep my mouth shut, at least about what I'd done. *Really* keep my mouth shut. There are a lot of people depending on you these days, and you're doing a lot more good on the outside than you probably could in the joint. Go slow for a while, pal, play it by ear, and let the chips fall where they may."

Chapter
——TWENTY-EIGHT——

alf an hour later we were in San Ysidro, buying Mexican auto insurance at one of the stands just north of the border. Which had to be done, because drivers in Tijuana were insane by definition. Every trip I'd ever made to Tijuana, I'd seen at least one metal-mashing accident, most of them involving *norteamericanos*.

And then we were crawling along in one of the twenty-or-so lines of backed up traffic at the busiest border crossing in the world. Finally, a smooth-faced, khaki-clad guard stepped up, did a quick-scan of the inside of the car, and asked us how long we planned to be south of the border. We told him a day, maybe two. He checked the *tourista* cards we'd picked up in Chula Vista, slapped customs decals on my front and side windows, then waved us through and into Tijuana. The million-strong city spread out around us and into dry riverbeds, up across the scorched hillsides and out onto the bluffs and cliffs above the broad blue Pacific, a microcosm of Mexico's population explosion.

When Interstates 5 and 805 merged, Tony gave me directions, and I cut off from the string of RVs and sedans and pick-ups with camper trailers—people on their way to the Mexican mainland or on down the thousand-mile-long highway to see the peninsula. I hung a right, crossed the empty riverbed of the Tijuana River, and then I was square in the middle of the madness. On every side were street hawkers, luxury shops, seedy arcades, bars offering fifty cent margaritas, masses of stalls selling velvet paintings of sleeping burros and nude señoritas and Elvis and anything else the art connoisseur's heart might demand. There were fortunes in turquoise and Mexican silver jewelry, displayed on more dark velvet right outside fine shops selling gold and diamonds and opals. Other shops, posh and tacky alike, sold other Mexican crafts, from tiny Olmec gods to slightly off-center chess sets. Most of the infamous "girlie" bars had been relegated to the side streets during the last "clean-up" of the city. Which meant that now you had to gawk down an alleyway to see bawdy neon signs, lit even in daylight, the barkers out front enticing professional lechers into their lairs. Here on the main drag, still more vendors were selling sandals and cowboy boots and serapes and sombreros. Several street photographers with burros painted in zebra-striping were taking snapshots of various victims from the throngs of grinning *touristas*, while another line of people stood waiting for postcards to be made up. As I passed, a vendor tried to set a small boy atop a burro, which had apparently had enough because it started braying and arching its back, swaying back and forth. The vendor set the boy down on the pavement, grabbed the burro by the bridle strap, and began to resoundingly curse it in fluent English.

The next attraction was a *mariachi* band on the corner, performing amidst a cluster of admirers. Their wide white sombreros were embroidered in bright red, and tiny shards of mirror had been embedded into the fabric so that the sombreros sparkled and gleamed in the brassy sunlight while the musicians strutted and blew on their equally-gleaming brass instruments and bludgeoned their guitars and otherwise made a racket that managed to drown out much of the rest of the city's noise. I had rolled down my window, and now I could smell a fragrant blend of peppers and spices and refried beans. Brilliant colored posters everywhere advertised the bullrings, both the new one and the old, and as I threaded my way through the traffic, a slick-looking *mestizo* with a broad nose and doe-soft eyes leaned inside my window, gave me a limpid, hopeful look, then held out his arm, which was decorated with about a dozen fake Rolex watches. I said no, he snarled something obscene at me and backed off, and then we were turning a corner and were in front of the white Moorish Jai Alai Palace, and the chaos began to thin out a bit.

Soon, the Avenida Revolución became Boulevard Agua Caliente, which bore us past the El Toreo Tijuana bullring, and then, per Tony's renewed directions, we were heading toward the Agua Caliente Race-track. I followed the boulevard a short distance, then turned onto a side street that soon led out of the commercial zone and into the heart of Tijuana's poverty. Here were rusted-out trailerhouses with no electricity or plumbing, lean-to shacks and tin shelters, and pens that held chickens, goats and pigs that rooted in mud-holes alongside naked children. There seemed to be an abundance of dogs lounging in doorways and other shaded places. Laundry was strung between buildings and between poorly-tended utility poles. There was a palpable stench in the air from the outhouses and piled up garbage.

A main building housed the outreach, and there were ten or so surrounding cottages, every building a palace compared to the other structures in the neighborhood. The main building had been erected from plankwood and had an unfinished look about it, but it was set well back on a wide, freshly-mown lawn, and tall jacarandas and cypress provided wide, deep shade against the blazing sun. There was a cross atop the building, a beacon heralding the fact that folks could find refuge here. As we got closer, I could hear the sounds of music coming from within. Tony glanced at his Timex, then muttered something about the afternoon service. We drove up the gravel driveway then cut around back and parked beside a black Jeep Cherokee with California plates and a bumper sticker that said "There's Hope: Jesus Loves You!" Beside it were a couple of rusted out ten-year-old American cars, several motorbikes, and a bunch of rickety bicycles.

We took a side door into the sanctuary and came in near the back of the room, where we sat down on a real pew. Shelby stood behind a rough-hewn pulpit, and he gave Tony and me a slight nod to acknowledge our arrival, then went on speaking. A translator stood beside him, and after every few sentences Shelby would pause, allowing for the Spanish version of his words to reach the hundred or so people who sat listening to him. They were a mish-mash of Mexicans and Americans, some of them teen-agers, some grandmothers, some middle-aged men and women with children.

". . . and the cults always say nice things about Jesus," Shelby was saying. "Some say He's our elder brother, and others say He's Michael the Archangel. The New Agers say He's an avatar, an ascended master. They all say He's a great man, a great teacher, but none of them will admit that Jesus is the only begotten Son of God, the Messiah, come to this earth to take us from the age of law into the age of grace.

"Jesus was God in the flesh. And if someone refuses to admit that, they don't believe the Bible, because the Scriptures spell it out in no uncertain terms. This is where all the confusion comes in. They don't come right out and say, 'Look, we worship other gods, leave us alone.' They'll say, 'Sure, we believe Jesus is the son of God': but they're saying it in the context of their belief that we're *all* sons of God. Ask them if they believe that Jesus was God in the flesh, and if they tell you the truth at all, you'll get a totally different answer."

He paused, shifted positions, then leaned in close to the pulpit, and said in a softer tone, "Which brings us to the point of it all. You can't work your way to heaven. That's another fundamental difference between born again Christians and those who follow cults. Cultists try to redeem themselves by doing works, good or bad, or by enacting rituals, which might even include human sacrifice. It still happens more often than we'd like to believe. I don't need to remind you of what happened a few years ago in Matamoros, when the drug dealers got it into their heads that if they started sacrificing humans they'd be invisible to the Federales. That may seem extreme, but it's typical. They think they have to appease their gods, but the more evil they do, the more the gods need appeasement. It doesn't work. The gods they worship feed on evil. They're disciples of Lucifer, whose goal is to destroy the entire human race so that God can't fulfill His greater plan. Besides that, you can never work your way into heaven, even if you're doing what we think of as good works, no matter how hard you try. The Word says that your righteousness is as dirty rags. That's because we're saved by grace."

There was a murmur of assent in the audience.

"We're saved by the love and sacrifice of the God Who created us and Who continues to care about us. Salvation and eternal life are gifts from God. God understands that we can't even live up to our own standards of goodness, much less to His. And that's why we have to come to Him through faith, have to ask Him to give us a new birth, to take away the old spirit and fill us with the new. And when that happens, when we come to him in humility and with a willingness to turn our lives over to Him and let Him change them to fit His greater needs for the eternal scheme of things, then wonderful and amazing things happen. Your spirit will literally be reborn, it will be as bright and flawless and shiny new and innocent as that of a new-born baby. It's the difference between death and life."

Tony had leaned forward now and was listening attentively. I, too, was hearing every word. I'd never heard Shelby speak before, and his eloquence surprised me.

"Remember when you were a child?" Shelby asked. "When it seemed like the whole world was made just for you and every blade of grass, every bird, sang just for you? Remember when you didn't know about death and sin and evil? That's the way it will be again. Reborn. You'll be refilled with the simple purity that opens up your world and turns it into something shining and new and full of promise. The difference will be that instead of having childlike innocence, you'll have spiritual wisdom. You'll see the evil and the destruction, but you'll understand it in the eternal scheme of things. You won't hate the people who hurt you anymore, you'll hate the being who causes them to hate you and harm you in the first place. That's Satan. Believe me, he's a real being, and a busy one. You'll learn to see your enemies as what they are, creatures in torment, in chains, doing the bidding of a dark god who is at that very moment robbing them of love and of life, of everything wonderful that God wants us all to have, and who will eventually destroy them for all eternity."

He said a few more things, but I stopped listening and started toying, instead, with what he had just said about people being creatures in torment, in chains. I thought about Cassie and Caspar Cardwell, and suddenly I indeed saw them in a different light. If they were actually captives of a dark god—and the gods I'd seen them worshiping sure didn't have anything good about them—then their actions were harming themselves more than me. Thinking about it, I couldn't remember ever seeing them smile, except in that cunning and cold way that people do when they've managed to out-manipulate someone. They were indeed serving a dark god who would destroy them. If the statue of the god, Narayama, was any indication of the spiritual aspects of the phalanx of deities they were worshiping, they were in very real danger of having their hearts ripped out and gnawed on while they were still alive to enjoy the action—in fact, maybe something very much like that was already happening. Maybe their hearts had already been ripped out, their emotions were frigid, stone-cold, totally fixed on dead materialism. Now that I thought about it, I could see it so clearly. Their religion was actually a kind of drug, a narcotic that warded off their fear of death and of dying but even more so their fear of life and of living. And then I made a personal connection to all this and realized for the first time why I'd started drinking so heavily, why I'd spent so many years drugging myself. I hadn't been able to turn my heart to stone like that. And as long as I could feel, I hadn't been able to handle what I saw happening around me, whether in the blood-stained Vietnam jungles or the disintegrating American streets. I'd been too sensitized to it, I hadn't been able to change it, so I'd built a chemical wall. The realization came upon me so suddenly, it was almost an epiphany. The drugs and alcohol had been segments of suicide, grafted into the continuum of my life. And so they were also to others, to the pimps and drug dealers everywhere who were at this moment hawking their wares, to the dealers and users in the streets in Los Angeles, and on to Tod Montgomery as well as every person in the world, of any position, who had to somehow block out their reality, whether through drugs or sex or alcohol or brain-washed obsession with an illusory and inevitably destructive religion, in order to mentally survive.

I shivered with the realization, and Tony glanced at me, his thick eyebrows furled up into a puzzled look. I cocked an eyebrow and shrugged almost imperceptibly, he blinked hard, and then we both started listening again to Shelby.

He was saying, "The truth shall set you free. And the truth is, Jesus said that unless we become as little children, we will not see the kingdom of God. That means we have to be reborn, have to regain the innocence and purity and love. But how do we do that? Some of us have lived through so much, have seen our children starving and sick, have watched them sell themselves in the streets for enough to eat. We've watched death and brutality and violence, and some of us have even done these things ourselves. We've seen it and done it till our souls are frozen and our bodies are deadened and our hearts are like lead. How can we be rid of a burden like that?

"I want to tell you, the true beauty of God's way is its simplicity. John 3:16 tells us, 'God so loved the world that He gave His only begotten Son, that whoever believes in Him should not perish but have everlasting life.' That verse is a summary of the entire Bible. God's word also tells us in Matthew 7:7, 'Ask, and it will be given to you.' So all you have to do is let Him know how you feel. Tell Him, simply tell Him, 'God, I'm tired. I'm sick, I hate the sin and evil I've lived in, I hate the destructive things I've done, and I know they're offenses against You because You don't want to see me or anyone else destroyed. Sometimes it seems like I had to commit sins just to survive. But I'm tired of surviving like that, God. I'm tired of living outside Your will. I offer what's left of my life to You. I ask You to forgive me of sin, to give me new birth and eternal life. Finally, I ask You to guide me as I live the rest of this one, for I've learned I can't do it without You.'"

A thick, elderly *mestizo* had sat down at a piano up front, and now he began playing softly the old gospel song, "Love Lifted Me." The people stood up. Shelby said, "I'm not going to distinguish between those of you who need to ask our Lord, Jesus, into your lives and those of you who have already done so and who just need to reaffirm your commitment or just worship Him. The truth is, everyone in this room needs to be in closer communication with the Being Who created you and Who can solve all your problems. Now don't misunderstand, I'm not promising you that God is like a genie, that all of a sudden, if you ask Him, all your problems will simply vanish. God isn't like that, His job is to see that everything turns out all right in the end, and sometimes that means things get a little bumpy for us here on earth. But I will promise you that if you serve Him, everything *will* turn out right in the end. If you ever doubt that, sit down and read the final pages of the Bible. Speaking of the place where we'll live eternally, Revelation 22:5 tells us, 'And there shall be no night there: They need no lamp nor light of the sun, for the Lord God gives them light. And they shall reign forever and ever.'"

That made me sit up straighter. There it was again, this thing about light.

Shelby then said, "Those of you who wish to talk to the God who created us, for any reason, please come forward to the altar. If you've never committed your life to God before, if you've never asked for salvation and you want someone to pray with you and counsel you, just step to the right side where our brothers in Christ are waiting to help you find the spiritual peace and beauty they know. Don't be ashamed, don't be embarrassed. Each one of us has taken this step at one time or another, we all know the hesitancy and the discomfort, but we also know the aching need to know and be loved by our Creator. That overwhelms everything else in our lives, and it should in yours. Come forward, all of you, let's worship God."

I was standing, eyes closed, the piano player still strumming something evocative and poignant. I was touched by what Shelby had said, but at the same time, I found myself analyzing it. Was I going to get caught up in the emotion of the moment and do something stupid? What would happen to me if I went down there, knelt at the altar, and prayed? Would I suddenly find myself bathed in the light of the God they were talking about? Would I experience a sudden change?

Or what if God decided to turn me into a passive "turn-the-other-cheek" type Christian? What then? What did a Christian do when someone was standing in front of him threatening to shoot his brains out? What did they do when they ran across a drug dealer or pimp who was turning on or turning out a twelve- or thirteen-year-old girl—or boy, for that matter? Would I have to stand and spout Bible verses and turn the other cheek? Would I still be able to burglarize places and take elusive but necessary documents? Lie my way to information? Would I be breaking the commandments, 'Thou shalt not steal' and 'Thou shalt not bear false witness against thy neighbor'? Would I still be able to get the best of someone who was trying to harm me? In short, would I have to become passive and just put up with all the slime and slow death I saw around me? Stand and look pious while the slime-balls stoned me to death?

I thought about it some more, then thought, *Nah*. This Christianity stuff is fine for people who live in nice white houses and work in plumbing shops, for the people in Leave-it-to-Beaver Land. Or for these poverty-stricken and noncombative Mexicans who don't have another hope in the world. But if I started turning the other cheek, I wasn't going to last a day in my business. Which meant that if I went up front and gave my life to Jesus Christ, I'd be giving up. In which case, who was going to find Elizabeth Livingstone? And who was going to find out whose body was buried in Elizabeth Livingstone's grave? And—even more timely—who was going to go out and break the heads that would help us find Tony's missing kid?

While I was doing all this thinking, I was watching the people up at the altar with a jaundiced eye. They were noisy in their worship. Many stood, arms raised to heaven, and prayed and cried out loud. Which should have bothered me, since I'm ordinarily a fairly reserved person when I'm sober. But for some reason it made me feel both uncomfortable and really good! In fact, there was something rolling through the room now, something as strong as the concussion from heavy artillery, but it was invisible, uplifting, beautiful . . .

"Okay, God," I said silently. "I don't understand what's going on here. But I do know that something is happening that I *don't* understand. If You're real—and don't get me wrong, I really hope You are—and You're trying to teach me something, I'm ready to learn. Just don't do it in a way that lets the bad guys win."

That little prayer made me feel a bit better. And then, before I had a chance to think any more about it, the piano player was hitting the keyboard and Shelby was leading all the people in a rousing old gospel song, "Power in the Blood," and the whole room was filled with singing and the sound of hands clapping. People were praising God, and I was suddenly filled with something that felt like the most beautiful light I could ever imagine, something so powerful that I was amazed to see that the real illumination hadn't changed a bit. And then I realized that what I was feeling was holiness. And joy. And something else, too, a Presence: something that there were no words for, just allegories and allusions, and it was a beauty that lifted me up and made me feel love and peace as never before. The feeling suddenly reminded me of something, something not so very long ago—and then I was remembering my experience after my beating by Auguste's henchmen, recalling my journey into the lighted tunnel where I'd met my grandmother—herself a light being—and most of all I remembered the waves of love I'd felt emanating from her. And I was also remembering the even more exquisite love and light at the end of the tunnel—the light to which I could not be admitted. That immense and brilliant love was the same Presence I was feeling now.

I'd thought a lot about my dream or vision in the hospital. I'd wondered if I might have still been hallucinating because of the mescaline. And now, I wondered again if I was having another flashback, if something chemical was actually bursting into my neural receptors and giving me this illusion of joy.

I glanced at Tony, then looked again. If I was hallucinating, so was he, because his face was turned up to the ceiling and his lips were moving in prayer, and a literal halo of light was emanating from his rough-hewn face. I had never seen another person look so saintly.

Whew. Powerful stuff.

I stood and watched all this happen, felt my own feelings and tried to understand them, and then the worship died down some and people began to talk to one another, and then Shelby was striding back to us, a look of joy still on his face, and he surprised me by coming up to me, slapping my hand with a high-five, and saying, "Good to see you, brother."

I managed to get a grip on myself, and said, "We're here to find Rosa."

"Yeah," Shelby said. "Thanks for coming. Let me tell Pastor Machado where I'm going, and we'll hit the road."

"To where?" I asked.

"To see Rosa's ex-pimp," said Shelby. His mood had dropped a couple of levels as he readjusted himself to the business at hand. "He's been down in Ensenada for the day, but he's supposed to be back about now. If anyone in Tijuana knows where Rosa went, that creep will."

He started to turn, but I stopped him. "Excuse me, but aren't Christians supposed to love everybody? I mean, I don't want to be a smart-mouth, but I'm genuinely curious. How can you preach a sermon like that and instantly turn around and bad-mouth someone?"

He looked at me, surprised. "You don't think he's a creep?"

"That's not the point. I mean, I want to know, how can you feel that way about him? You just said that he's a slave to Satan, that it's Satan's fault he acts the way he does."

Shelby shook his head, as if to clear it. Then he said, "Maybe I need to clarify that. We're in a war here on earth. The enemy is Satan. But the enemy is also anyone who is doing Satan's will, which is to destroy humanity. We are indeed supposed to hate the sin and not the sinner, and I don't really hate Garcia. But I sure do hate some of the things he does. And right now, I'm going to go show him just *how much* I hate some of the things he does."

"What about all this 'turn the other cheek' stuff?"

"What about us being the Army of God whose mission is to save people from evil? What about that? And what about Rosa?" He shot me a disbelieving look, then turned and hurried back to where the pastor of the small ministry was tending to his flock. They had a hasty conversation, and then Shelby was back with us. "Come on. Let's roll."

Chapter
──TWENTY-NINE──

We found Pablo Garcia in a spanking new townhouse complete with swimming pool, not far from the Plaza Rio Tijuana shopping center. From the looks of his place, the pandering business was as good as ever in Sin City.

We didn't bother to knock, just went around to the pool then stepped in through the sliding screen door. The pimp was running his blender, mixing up some fizzy orange concoction, and he saw us before he heard us. His eyes went wide, he poised for flight, then managed to get a grip on himself and hit the switch on the blender. The motor whirred to a stop. Garcia fixed Shelby with a tight smile laced through with fear. "Señor Shelby. You surprise me, you creep up on me like a burglar!" He waved his hand toward a white leather sofa, and said, "Please, please. Be comfortable. I think about you, I mean to come to your church, as you offer. But I am a man of many responsibilities, I have trouble finding the time. You want something to drink?"

A cold current of fury ran through Shelby's eyes. "Where is she?"

"She?" Garcia looked around, measuring the distance to the door. I could see how he might be attractive to women, in a weasel-like way. He was tall and trim, and he wore a designer sweat suit in bright gold with black trim. A couple of diamond rings on his fingers were added bait. And this pad would look like a palace to any Tijuana street girl.

Shelby said, "I know you sold her. Where is she?"

Garcia's eyes were wide with disbelief. "But—Señor Shelby—but—this is not so."

But it was. One of Garcia's former "girls" was currently attending the outreach, trying to change her life. Shelby had filled us in on things during the drive. She had given up the street life and was trying to go on to better things. She'd told Shelby everything—Garcia had been trying to find Rosa and bring her back ever since Shelby had rescued her. "There's a man," the girl had said. "A real *diablero*. He hurts the girls, even the pimps did not always make us go with him. But he comes to Pablo Garcia and asks for the little *loco* girl, Pablo tells him she is gone, the man says he will give Pablo one thousand dollars to find her, only her, that she is special to him. Ever since, Pablo looks for her . . ."

"Tell us," Tony said, and stepped forward.

The pimp was terrified, though I couldn't understand why. Neither Tony nor Shelby seemed to be really threatening him. Nevertheless, his face was shrunken with fear.

Tony said, "Where's Rosa?"

"Please. I—the man, he takes her. I do not know where, he only gives me the money."

"How did you find her?"

"I am a poor man with much expense, Mr. Shelby. This man, he offers me much *dinero*, I hire a boy, he watches for her."

"What man? Where is he?"

Garcia was really sweating now. "I give you the address, *sí*? But you no tell Lieutenant Salazar."

"Too late. He's the first one I told."

Garcia turned a muddy white.

"We want some answers."

Garcia evidently decided that he was already sunk, because he started talking.

Originally the *diablero* had spotted Rosa on the strip, after Garcia had decided to act as her "protector." Rosa had also spotted him, seemed to know him, and instead of doing Garcia's bidding and climbing into the man's car with him, she had bolted and run, so that Garcia had to chase her. He had caught her, had dragged her into an abandoned building, where she was hysterical for a full half hour, screaming about snakes and things so hideous that Garcia could scarcely believe them. After that, the girl had been wary, had always watched for the man. And then, Shelby had found Rosa, had taken her away, and the *diablero* had come back, wanting only this one girl, demanding her, finally offering Garcia money if he would get her back, threatening him if he didn't.

Shelby watched with silent fury as Garcia wrote something down and handed it to him. Neither he nor Tony said a word as we walked out the door. As we climbed into the car and drove away, Garcia peered after us from behind the curtain.

I asked, "What was all that about?"

"He's on parole," Shelby said. "He got caught carrying a half-kilo of black tar heroin through the border at Mexicali. He did a year then got out on parole a couple of years back. The Federales more or less look the other way as far as the girls are concerned, but if he steps into anything heavy, he's dead. Five or more years left to do, and in Mexico that's a lifetime."

I finally understood Garcia's fear. "Kidnapping is heavy," I agreed. "You've notified the Federales?"

"One of the Lieutenants, Salazar, is a member of the outreach. He's known about it since the moment she vanished. He's had people looking for her."

"Why didn't *he* put the muscle on Garcia?"

"Politics," said Shelby. "His captain gets a percentage of Garcia's action and is in a position to make trouble."

"So you don't have any recourse to the police?"

"On the contrary, now that we have Garcia's confession, the first thing I'm going to do is call Salazar." Shelby was sitting in the back seat while Tony was again sitting silently beside me. I thought about my earlier reflections on the passivity and of your average Christian and felt a little embarrassed. If I had to be in the front lines—anywhere—I was in good company. I turned to Shelby, "Sorry about my crack earlier."

"No problem." He was intently watching the street signs, his eyes slitted.

"Seriously," I said, "I feel like a jerk." I waited for a comment, but nobody said anything, and I was feeling more stupid by the minute, so I finally just gave it up.

After a few more blocks, Shelby said, "Turn left here. Let's go check out this *diablero's* business address."

He directed me back to the Avenida de Revolución, and then down into the Zona Rio, the ritzy new area just this side of Tijuana's parched riverbed. We cruised along the Paseo de los Heroes, and then, a short distance from the border, we came to a smart little street with elegant white adobe storefronts and red tile roofs, tucked away behind thick jacarandas and flowering shrubs.

"This is it," Shelby said. "Let's check it out."

When they'd both climbed out, I locked the doors, then caught up with them as they climbed a half dozen steps, and then I stopped short and tried to speak, but only a strangled rattle came out.

Tony turned and shot me a strange look.

I managed to cough out, "I don't believe it."

"What's the matter with you?"

"It's impossible," I sputtered. "It can't be happening."

"What's this, you gone nuts?"

"This is incredible," I said, my voice finally working again. "It is absolutely impossible."

Shelby had stopped too, by this point, and had also turned to watch me, a concerned look on his face. "You okay?"

"This is insane. You guys would never believe this in a million years."

"Believe what?"

"This man, this so-called *diablero*," I said. "I know this louse."

Shelby looked unimpressed. "There must be about five million Juan Valdez's in Mexico," he said, "what makes you think you know this one?"

I blinked hard, then stared again at the building. The front door was completely visible now. And, sure enough, the sign was still there: VANCE & VALDEZ, COLLECTORS AND DEALERS: MESO-AMERICAN ART AND ANTIQUES. And beneath it, in fine gold script, it said: ALSO IN LOS ANGELES.

"It's him," I said, "and man, do I have a story to tell you."

Chapter
————THIRTY————

"I t's not coincidence," Tony said.

We were back at the Tijuana outreach, sitting in a simple but clean little living room lent to us by Pastor Machado. He and his family had gone to Ensenada for a meeting that would keep them over the weekend. Shelby was tending to the crew he'd brought down from L.A.

"There ain't no such thing as coincidence," Tony repeated.

"Then explain it," I said. "I'm working on a case, you're totally out of the picture, the only reason I even know you're out of the brig is because Riggatoni wants me to talk to you. And then you phone and ask me to come to Tijuana, and I run square into a big piece of the puzzle I've been wracking my brains trying to put together."

"It's not coincidence, I can tell you that."

"Okay," I conceded the point. "So say it really is God, that He led me to you and then you led me down here. So, why? I mean, what's the point?"

"There's a connection," Tony said.

"Obviously." I was tired and feeling testy. I stood up and stretched. "Mind if I use your phone?"

"Help yourself."

I strolled over and dialed Angelo's home number. His wife answered. I could hear the sound of children fighting in the background.

"Angelo's in bed," she said. "He has to work tonight."

"Yeah. Look, tell him I called, that I may be able to handle the shovel job after all, tell him to forget about it till he hears from me again." I started to sign off, when a thought struck. "Say, Tina, would you mind doing me a quick favor?"

"What else do we live for," she said drily. She'd learned a lot from her husband about how to treat friends.

"You got a phone book handy?"

"Right in front of me. Why?"

"Will you look up a number for me?"

Within a minute, I had the number to Vance and Valdez's antique shop in Los Angeles. I dialed it, a woman answered. I asked for Valdez, she said he was expected back in half an hour, would I like to leave a message. I told her I'd phone back, then turned to Tony, and said, "Valdez is back in L.A."

"You think he took the girl back there?"

"Nobody knows but him."

"Okay," Tony said, "let me tell Shelby. Then we can hit the road."

It was nearing midnight when we turned off Santa Monica Boulevard, then hung a left and drove beneath the *porte-cochere* of a condo complex that looked like an elegant three-story French Chateau. It was set back in wide, well-lit grounds, and as soon as we pulled up uniformed security guards reared their sleepy heads and checked us out.

"Help you?" asked one burly, sixtyish man.

"We need to see Juan Valdez, please. Could you let him know we're here?"

"No point ringin' his place," said the second guard, a wiry little Irishman. "He drove out about half an hour ago."

"You're sure?" My muscles were getting itchy. I'd been promising them some action.

"Absolutely."

"Is his wife in?"

"No wife. He lives alone, 'cept for a lady visitor now and again, if you follow me." He gave me a gnome-like wink. "You want to leave a message or something?"

"Any ladies lately?"

"Hey." He spread his skinny arms wide. "Ain't my business, is it?" He winked again. Then he said, "You ain't a cop or somethin', are you?"

I twisted my face into a grimace, which seemed to make him happy.

I spent a couple of seconds deciding whether or not the security guards were lying to me, decided they weren't, then thanked them and we drove north, taking the freeway to Malibu, where we followed the winding dusty road on up into Topanga Canyon. Tony was silent all the way, thinking hard. When we arrived at the church retreat, the red Ford Ranger sat in front of the ranch house, and as we pulled up beside it, Tony said, "Come on in."

"Can't. Got to run."

"Just for a minute. I want you to hear something."

"Later," I said. I was in a hurry to go get the jawbone and put it back in the grave, plus I wanted to check out the Vance residence and see what was cooking there. Maybe I'd even get lucky and get a lead on Valdez and the girl.

Tony turned and fixed me with a steady look. "You're in the middle of something you ought to know about," he said. "Come in. We got to talk."

I hid my irritation, climbed out of the car and followed him inside. The Reverend Irby Howard was standing in front of a small range, boiling water for coffee. He was wearing a red-and-black checked flannel shirt and faded Levis, with an old scuffed pair of cowboy boots. He looked exhausted. "How did things go?"

"No luck finding the girl," Tony said. He explained what had happened, then said, "Weatherby here is going back over tonight to check Valdez's place and see what he can dig up."

I thought about that. Then said, "That and a couple other things." I checked my watch. Half past two A.M. Tomorrow, for sure, the police would be opening Elizabeth Livingstone's grave. I needed to get that jawbone put back. "Look," I said, "Hate to be rude, here, but I've got other things to do . . ."

"Wait," Tony said. Howard poured three cups of instant coffee into heavy white mugs, then placed them on a red and white checkered tablecloth in front of us. I sipped at mine, then added some fake cream and sugar to cut the strength, while Tony repeated to Howard most of what I'd told him about the caper I was working on, about Elizabeth Livingstone and the Cardwells and their strange religion and all the rest, including Rosa's surprising hysteria when she saw Elizabeth Livingstone's photograph and Juan Valdez's fixation with Rosa as well as his affiliation with the Foundation for the Enhancement of the Human Spirit. As Tony talked, Howard became increasingly agitated. When Tony was done, Howard said, "So the girl is somehow involved with this same cult?"

"Looks that way," I said.

"I see why Tony is concerned," Howard said. "You're in the middle of some serious spiritual warfare."

I spread my hands wide and offered him another shrug. I didn't know what he was talking about.

"It's the New Age religion," he said. "Most of the people who follow the belief system are really well-meaning people. They're just hungry for the supernatural, like most of us are. But they're way off track. A lot of them actually think they've discovered a more enlightened form of Christianity. The religion is highly deceptive, and that's why it's so difficult for many people to understand the sinister side of it. But that's something we need to be aware of because we need to respond to it effectively."

"I don't see anything spiritual about Rosa's abduction." I was a little irritated. I had better things to do with my wee hours than sit here getting a lecture on obscure religions.

"There are spiritual reasons behind everything," Howard said.

I started to make a snappy comeback, then changed my mind and bit my tongue. There either were, or there weren't. Who was going to prove it, one way or another?

Tony said, "Problem is, regular religion has failed too many people. They think God is some warden sitting up in the sky, just waiting for them to do something wrong so He can whack 'em."

"That's right," Howard said. "Too many of our fellow 'Christians' forget about love and try to use the Scriptures as an excuse to try to control the behavior of other people."

"Control freaks everywhere," I murmered, politely. This conversation was all nice and neighborly and everything, but why were they taking up my precious time?

Howard said, "These people miss Christ's point, which is to love and help and guide others toward spiritual salvation and eternal life. People go to church, they don't find what they need, they go shopping everywhere else, from rock concerts to heavy metal to gurus to New Age religion."

"That junk is all stirred up by the religious spirit," Tony said.

"Exactly," Howard said.

I must have gotten a puzzled look on my face, because Howard smiled kindly, and explained. "We believe, Mr. Weatherby—"

"Call me Artie."

"Yes, well, the Bible teaches us that there are actual evil spirits that are in warfare with humanity, trying to keep us from the kingdom of God. One of the worst of these spirits is called the religious spirit. This is the demonic entity who is responsible for all the false religions, all the cults, all the spiritual misinformation. It's also responsible for the bickering and judgmentalism and pettiness within Christian churches, and also the bigoted doctrinarianism that turns so many people away from the Lord. Outsiders see this, and they recognize it for the pettiness it is, and they rightfully want nothing to do with it. In other words, there are a lot of self-professed Christians who don't practice the true Christ-like love that Christianity is all about."

He was right about that. I'd known a few of those people myself. I said, "Must be tough work to pastor a church as big as yours." I looked at my watch again.

"It's not easy. We seat eight thousand now. People are coming back to the churches that preach the truth in big ways. I believe it's the outpouring of the final days before Christ's return. But there's still too much of this judgmentalism to keep me happy. I lose people from my church now and again. And I worry that the New Age religion is swallowing up a lot of these people, without them even realizing what's happening. Like I said, there's a new, surging hunger for the supernatural. For God, really. But people get off track, and they end up with the supernatural, all right. But the dead opposite of God."

"Sounds like pretty heavy stuff," I said. So was a charge of grave-tampering. And without the jawbone, the police would never know who really slept in Elizabeth Livingstone's grave.

I needed to beat feet. I shifted, to get ready to stand.

"Nevertheless," Howard said, "it's vitally important that we don't just place a big negative label on everything associated with New Age, because the hard-core, inner-circle New Agers who know what they're doing from the spiritual point of view use this to discredit everything else we say. The New Agers do some good works and follow some good causes, at least on the surface of things. There's a lot of interest in environmental issues and stopping world hunger. Stopping AIDS, all these things. Unfortunately, they make you swallow the bath water with the baby. To save a whale you have to learn to chant mantras to false gods. To be a truly healthy vegetarian, you have to start practicing Hinduism. You get the picture . . ."

"Yeah, but the Cardwells aren't exactly growing radishes and saving the whales. They're into some seriously strange stuff."

"Right. You went right to the hard core center of the thing. And now you're square in the middle of some very dangerous spiritual warfare."

I felt a cynical disbelief well up inside me. "Sorry, but you lost me there."

"The reason Tony wanted to talk to you is that we're not battling flesh and blood here, but the principalities and powers and spiritual hosts of wickedness who dwell in the heavenly places. You need to know just how dangerous this really is."

I took another hard look at him. "What, exactly, are you trying to say?"

"Look, I know you're not born again, so this may seem a little strange to you, but believe me. These people you've been having trouble with are deceived by the spirit of antichrist. By the spiritual hosts of wickedness."

"This is all a little confusing," I said. *And a little unbelievable*, I wanted to add. What had happened to the good old days, when the bad guys were bad and the good were good, and there was nothing much going on behind the scenes?

"You need to realize that unless these New Age cultists somehow see the truth, it will eventually cost their spirits the eternal life and love that Jesus Christ wants for all of them."

"I heard Cassie Cardwell praying, saying that good is evil," I said, suddenly remembering. "That worried me a little."

"Right. Like I said, you're seeing straight backstage to what the New Age is really all about," Howard said. "You've gone way past the pap they feed most people. Isaiah 5:20 says, 'Woe to those who call evil good, and good evil.' Saying that God is responsible for both good and evil is an old occultic practice which is also at the very center of New Age. It's a way to distort the truth so that evil becomes acceptable, and then anything is okay, from adultery to blasphemy to human sacrifice."

Human sacrifice. I thought about the books Ival Davidson had lent me, about the Aztecs' rituals. "What's all this stuff they're into about sun gods?"

"Demons are often seen as spirits of light. The New Agers think of their spirit entities as beings of light, they call them light bearers or spirit guides, or any number of other things. But they're all the same thing, according to the Bible: demons."

That made me sit up straight. Was this man serious? Forget the vampires and extraterrestrials, now I had to worry about *demons*? Just what I needed to hear when I was on my way to spend a quiet hour or so digging in a grave. Still, one part of my mind wanted to break out into raucous laughter. But some other part of me was saying, yeah, this makes some sense, I could actually see how that might happen. I frowned hard. "So when a spirit guide is talking through someone who's channelling it, I'm really listening to a *demon*?" I thought about Cassie Cardwell, channelling the bloodthirsty Quetz, thought about her basso voice and the near-demented look on her face. I shuddered. I'd been listening to a *demon*?

"Absolutely. At least, if the experience is real. Sometimes the person is just deceiving you on his own, but just as often—maybe even more often—a real demon comes into the person and takes them over. That's why trance channelers often can't remember what was done or said when they were in a trance."

"Could a person be under the spell of a demon at one time, then later do the same voice on purpose?" I was wondering about Sofia, about how she'd duplicated Elizabeth's voice at the seance then had done it again on my phone later that same night. Or had I been talking to a demon then, too?

"It's possible. Once a person gives themselves over to demon possession, I suppose they could later mimic the demon on purpose—if their vocal cords were adequate."

"This is weird," I said. *Demons*?

"Back to the subject of sun gods. A lot of Christian scholars believe that the reason so many ancient deities were considered to be sun gods was because of this manifestation of Satan or Lucifer as a being of this light. Today the New Age holds the sun to be a divine, living being, often called the Solar Father. Lucifer is claimed by the New Age to be a god spirit appointed by the Solar Father to usher in the New Age through the Luciferian Initiation of humanity."

"So what we're dealing with here is just another aspect of Satan worship?"

"Exactly. Except that Satanism is overt, even defiant, whereas New Age is deceptive. Second Corinthians 11:14–15 says, 'For Satan himself transforms himself into an angel of light. Therefore it is no great thing if his ministers also transform themselves into ministers of righteousness, whose end will be according to their works.' Many Christians believe that New Age is the antichrist church—that its worldwide growth is the beginning of a new world order, a worldwide religion, that will usher in the age of the antichrist. The New Age Christ. The false Messiah. New Agers claim that Gandhi, Muhammed, Buddha and Jesus were avatars and that each was therefore a 'christ.' They believe that some avatars are more enlightened than others. In the New Age scheme of things, Jesus is not the Son of God but merely another enlightened avatar. Which basically blows the whole concept of Christianity sky high. A lot of New Agers profess to be enlightened Christians, but you can't have it both ways. The two beliefs are mutually exclusive and totally incompatible."

I was sitting forward on my chair now, listening hard. Who was right here? What made sense? If there really was a spiritual realm—and for the past day or so I'd been seriously toying with the idea that there was—then what was going on there? Was it really a huge cosmic battle between good and evil that somehow brought mankind into it? I thought about the heavy, cloying, decayed feeling I sometimes had when I was around Cassie Cardwell, or Caspar, or their fellow cultists. I wondered about the uncomfortable pall that seemed to have settled down over their opulent house. And then I thought about being with Tony, about being here with Howard. Even in these wee hours of the morning, there was something clean and refreshing about these people, like a clear mountain stream. So—how to choose?

I had to go with my gut instincts. That's the only thing I had. Impressions, scant glimpses of truth, an occasional sip of clear water after the long hauls through the deserts of cynicism and despair and emptiness. There was nothing tangible here that I could hang onto. Even my own cynicism was an act of mental gymnastics that helped keep me from reeling at the enormity of the possibilities here, if what I was hearing was true. Could I really be doing battle with *demons*?

Howard was saying, "Satan comes to us not as a devil but as an angel of light. New Agers report many experiences of communicating during deep meditation or trance with a spirit-being shrouded in light. But this 'angel of light' denies that Jesus is the Christ and guides the individual toward such practices as astrology, spiritism, black magic, and so on."

This made me think of my recent dreams about my grandmother. I felt a poignant twinge of nostalgia for the simple days of Sunday school and fried chicken dinners. When had everything become so complicated?

Howard said, "This thing you've stumbled into is one of the fringe cults. New Age is more or less an amalgamation of a lot of different groups and religions and cults, which all have in common the fact that they believe we can ourselves become gods—that's the original sin, you'll remember. The original act which separated humanity from God. And New Agers believe that Jesus is only another avatar, another wise man, not the true Son of God. Other than that, New Agers are as diverse as can be."

I turned to look at Tony. "So you brought me here to tell me that I'm not just battling a group of loonies, I'm battling Satan himself? *Demons*?"

Tony said, "Exactly. And if I were you, I'd take it seriously."

"Sorry," I said. "I do. It's just that I've had a little trouble getting all this straightened out in my head. I'm not exactly a true believer, you know."

"I know," Tony said, "But you will be. You're too smart not to be. Sooner or later, you're gonna see it. And once it all falls into place, there ain't no way you won't figure it all out."

Chapter

————THIRTY-ONE————

It took an hour to rebury the jawbone in Elizabeth Livingstone's grave. Thoughts of Satanic presences and demons were very much with me and I worked fast.

But thirty minutes later, our conversation about demons was fading into surrealistic memory, and I was arriving in Holmby Hills, where Dr. Vernon Vance and his wife Vera lived in an antebellum mansion that could have been lifted straight off the set of *Gone With the Wind*. I was hoping to get lucky and bump into Juan Valdez, Vance's partner in the antique shops—the *diablero* who had taken Rosa. I'd learned that Valdez wasn't home, and he wasn't in Mexico. Maybe I'd be lucky enough to catch him here.

Besides, I also wanted to get the feel of the house, check it out, see how the psychiatrist and his wife lived. Several times in the past few days I'd had a flashback to the event of my beating at the Cardwell estate, and each time I remembered, in stark relief, the clownish, evil little face I'd spotted behind Caspar Cardwell's while I was drugged and they were questioning me. It had been Dr. Vernon Vance, quietly overseeing everything that Cardwell and the Huichole shaman and the thugs had been doing to me. No doubt about it, Vance was a key player in whatever was happening. Maybe he was also a key player in the disappearance and subsequent purchase of Tony Cacciatore's young friend, Rosa.

I parked a couple of blocks from Vance's house, then hiked back and scaled the high iron fence. After a while, when no pit bulls or dobermans showed up, I padded around a bed of what was probably belladonna and stepped up to a lighted window.

I found myself peering into a sitting room carpeted in wine-red, with a lot of glass tables and brass lamps and white upholstered furniture. The walls were chocolate brown and held a gold-framed collection of nineteenth century Mexican art. There was a cut-crystal ashtray beside one of the chairs, and in it a cigarette was burning. As I watched, Vera Vance came into the room. She was wearing a filmy white peignoir and satin nightgown, and was barefooted. Her platinum hair was tousled, and I figured she was having trouble sleeping. As I watched, she poured something amber from a crystal decanter into a matching glass, then swilled it down. She sat in the chair, curled up her legs, and touched a TV remote. I heard the sounds of CNN come on. Now here was a fairly normal domestic scene. Insomnia.

I watched for a few more minutes, then lost interest and crept up to the next window, where dim illumination came from a night-light in a kitchen. It was modern, spotless, empty of all life save a tabby cat lapping at a bowl in the corner. I moved on.

By the time I'd made my way around the house, I'd seen everything from a darkened solarium to a faintly lighted swimming pool to the six-car garage, but I hadn't seen a sign of Juan Valdez, or the girl—not even of Vernon Vance.

He was probably tucked away upstairs for the night. No lights on there. And no point in rousting him out.

I was turning to leave when another light snapped on downstairs, not far from the room where Vera Vance had been watching TV. I detoured there and peered through a window.

I was looking into a large office, plush but efficient, obviously a place where real work got done. There were file cabinets and a couple of computers and a fax machine, a typewriter and other office equipment. And right beneath my nose there was a wide table covered by an architect's miniature rendition of a complex of buildings.

It was a temple compound. The gray-white stone had been aged to look like it had been buried beneath harsh earth for countless centuries, and it was framed by a rich green sea of miniature jungle.

A tall pyramid-shaped temple loomed above the trees. Steep stairs ascended the front, conjuring up images of bloodied victims being dragged to the altar of sacrifice by gold-bedecked Aztecs for sacrifice to bestial sun-gods. Numerous stone gods were placed like totems throughout the compound. Small crystals glittered here and there upon the miniature, perhaps added as some sort of New Age blessing.

A plaza spread out before the miniature temple, and on both sides were long blue ponds of water. Grass covered much of the area. And to the right was a huge stone palace, no doubt the dwelling of a high priest or ancient king. This building was also pyramidal, though not so sharply angled as was the temple. Half a dozen lesser buildings completed the compound, all of them also made from the weathered stone.

And to the left, off into the jungle, was a long strip of tarmac that had to be a landing strip. Which was especially odd, since ancient Indians didn't fly airplanes.

Vera Vance was rummaging in a desk, searching for something and totally oblivious to my presence. I moved to a better angle and examined the temple. I could see now that there were tiny people here and there, just as in an architect's rendering of a modern building. Some of the people were wearing modern dress, some were dressed as ancient Indians, some wore masks and robes.

Vera took a small black address book out of a drawer, then flipped off the light and left the room in pitch blackness. I stepped down from my perch, thinking about the odd temple. What *was* it? A tourist mecca, populated with people dressed as ancients in order to lend authenticity to the vacation spa? An Aztec Disneyland?

I moved back to my original spot and watched Vera Vance sit back down in the chair and light another cigarette. She poured another heavy slug from the decanter into a glass, then she opened the address book, picked up the phone, and dialed.

She drummed her long red fingernails on the table while she waited, then she started talking into the phone. I strained to hear, but the window was too thick. But as I watched, her face began to contort into first amusement, then suddenly into rage. She said something into the phone, then slammed it down, rose quickly from the chair, threw the address book across the room, then moved swiftly up a flight of stairs I could barely see through the angle of the doorway.

A light went on in an upstairs window, and then another light came on, this one in a small half window that I figured was a bathroom. I cooled my heels. The small light went out and I could see distorted portions of her silhouette as she moved quickly around the room. Her motions were agitated.

I watched a while longer, then the upstairs light went out. I watched through the front window again, waiting for her to come back into the lighted sitting room, then I started as the light directly above me went on, then another light outside the front door almost illuminated me in dead center.

I jerked back into the shadows just as a pair of headlights beamed around the corner and turned into the driveway. I shrank farther back into the black foliage. A white Mercedes cruised up the driveway then stopped at the front door. Caspar Cardwell climbed out of the driver's seat, went to the front door where Vera was already coming out, two small suitcases in her hand. The night was clear and silent, and their voices floated to me on the faint sweet breeze.

Vera's voice was caustic. "I can't understand why these things must always be done at the last minute. Vernon said he'd contact me . . ."

"The world doesn't revolve around you, Vera. The offering is ready. The stars are in alignment, there's no point in waiting till the equinox."

He placed her bags in the back seat of the car, and she climbed into the passenger seat. Caspar closed the door behind her, climbed in, and the big car purred as he hit the gas, then made a clean loop and roared away.

I was shielded by a row of trees and had already hit a dead run as they turned the corner. By the time I was back in the Beamer and had her revved up, their taillights were fading into the night. I caught them a few blocks past Wilshire, and tailed them to the Santa Monica Airport, where they bypassed the commercial section and tooled into the gate wherein lay the ritzy private planes of the rich and famous.

I parked well away from their line of vision, then gum-shoed along after them, staying well inside the shadows of all the multi-million dollar flying toys.

Cassie had been in the car with Caspar. Now the three of them climbed into a large, snow-white, twin-turbine bird with a strangely shaped body and seven sleek portholes on each side.

The pilot had her warming up, and an attendant carried on several small suitcases, then the door was folding shut, the plane was already in motion, and they were turning, moving down the runway.

I watched for about two minutes as they waited for clearance, then taxied away and flew swiftly into the night. I watched till their lights vanished, trying to get a fix on the direction they were taking, then I raced back to my car, climbed in, peeled rubber out the gate and hit the freeway doing eighty-five.

I broke the speed limit all the way to my office, cursing to myself all the way—though I didn't know what I could have done to stop them, or even if I should have stopped them. My answering machine was blinking red, awaiting my arrival. I hit the playback and collapsed to the sofa, then heard the click as the first message came on.

"Mr. Weatherby?"

I froze.

The voice was still husky, still soft, but the scratchy quality was gone. It was her all right, the real Elizabeth, the voice so evocative that for a moment I again saw the mesmerizing pain in her dark-green eyes, again saw her pale, heart-shaped face and the flowing white dress.

"I'm so sorry," the voice on the recording said. "I wish I hadn't tried . . . But no matter what you've done so far, you have to stop now. Please. I beg you. They—they're going to kill Frank unless I go back. I have to go back. I'm afraid for Frank, please check on him, he's so helpless. And tell Thomas thank you for hiding me. I should have known better. They always said they'd kill Frank, or even Ariel, but after a while, I—I began to think they were just saying that to control me. But now I know they'll do it. Please, forgive me for getting you involved in all this. Take care of Frank and Ariel, don't let them be hurt . . . and thank you, too, for trying. I really am sorry."

There was a click then as she hung up the phone, and I sat there rigid and stunned.

She was going back to where? To La Casa del Sol? To Serpent Mountain? And what, if anything, did this have to do with the sudden exodus I'd just witnessed?

Thomas, she'd said. Tell Thomas thank you. So he'd been helping her! I grabbed my windbreaker and started out the door, then had another sudden thought. I backtracked and grabbed up my phone, dialed Angelo, and paced back and forth while I waited for it to ring once, twice, and then Angelo was on the line. I said, "Hello, old buddy. What's up?"

"Nothing important. You get your jawbone back in the ground?"

"Indeed. Anything new with the financial data?" I was trying to keep the anxiety out of my voice.

"Nothing real important. I was planning to work on it some more about the crack of dawn, give me something exciting to keep me awake tonight."

"Forget it. I have something new for you to do."

"What is this, Weatherby, I'm your new stand-in while you're on vacation or something?"

"It's important, Angelo. Life or death important."

He was suddenly serious. "Yeah? So, shoot."

"How do I get a flight plan on a plane that just took off?"

He thought a minute. "I know one of the honchos at the FAA."

"Can you get it from him?"

"Most likely."

"I'll be right here at my office phone while you do just that. Move fast."

"Hold it. Not until I know what gives."

"Can't really tell you, but I'm getting closer to something. And whatever it is, it stinks. It started with the Livingstones and Cardwells, but it keeps getting bigger. It has something to do with Mexico, with Auguste Flores, the hotel development and the orphanage. And, I think the Cardwells just abducted Elizabeth and took her back down there. If they did, I wouldn't give two cents for her life right now."

"That's reason enough," he said and hung up.

I paced the floor, looked out over the city lights, worked on getting an ulcer, and had just about exploded from the frustration of waiting when the phone jangled and I picked it up in mid-ring. "Yo."

"Your plane was registered to the Foundation for the Enhancement of the Human Spirit. Flight plan has them headed for Guaymas, on the Mexican mainland, clear across the Sea of Cortez from the hotel and orphanage. Must be the closest airport, they'll probably take a boat back."

"Maybe not. Maybe they filed a phony flight plan, just enough off to cover their tracks. I'll check with the hotel—La Casa del Sol—and see if there's a landing strip there."

"Anything's possible."

"Angelo, I need another favor. Things are moving fast, and while I'm gone I need someone checking into background on Juan Valdez and Dr. Vernon Vance." I gave him their home and business addresses, told him what I already knew about them, then thanked him profusely when he agreed to drop everything else and go to work on it. As an afterthought, I said, "And by the way, I'd also like for you to check into Dr. Gates. He was the medical examiner here in the city about ten years ago, handled Elizabeth Livingstone's supposed death, last known address in Newport Beach."

"Consider it done."

I made three more phone calls: one to the Foundation's Mexican hotel, one to a pal who was a pilot, and another to Tony Cacciatore. And then I rocketed out of my office building, leaped into my Beamer, slammed my pedal to the metal, and burned rubber all the way to Clover Field.

Chapter

───── THIRTY-TWO ─────

Like Angelo, Lou Rickerby was an old Vietnam buddy. And like the handful of others with whom I'd survived the war, our bonds were fused in blood. A favor asked was a favor done, and Lou had his Mooney TLS fueled up and ready by the time I sped into the bumpy parking lot. Moments later, Tony screeched Howard's Ford Ranger in beside my Beamer.

Lou didn't ask questions and I didn't offer any answers, but we all three knew we were flying into trouble. The air inside the little four passenger plane fairly crackled with it, like faint lightning forewarning a terrible storm.

I didn't want to go to Mexico. I wanted to go home, shut out the world, sleep all day, then fry a burger and watch the Lakers game on TV. On the other hand, I wasn't going to spend the rest of my life knowing I might have helped the girl, helped Elizabeth, but hadn't even tried.

I glanced over at Tony. He was riding shotgun, belted in and sound asleep. I thought about him. I respected him deeply. Whatever came, he wasn't afraid to dig into the front trenches. I was glad he'd decided to move over to the right side, and I was glad he was with me on this one.

I looked at the back of Lou's head. He was watching the dark sky, monitoring the instrument panel. Back in Nam, I'd once seen him bring a chopper in under such heavy shelling that a sparrow couldn't have landed in it. But Lou did, and he'd lifted us up and out, away from Charlie and certain death.

Lou sensed me watching him and grinned. "Nice time to drag me off to Mexico, Weatherby. Lakers are playing tonight."

"Yeah," I said, "I know. I miss all the good ones."

We talked for a while about basketball, then talked aviation, and then I dozed off.

When I came to, we'd been in the air for just over an hour and the first pale stain of dawn was outlining the steep spectacular peaks of the Sierra De Juarez Range. By the time the sun was full up in the sky, I'd taken the controls and we were cruising at 250 knots and 22,000 feet, soaring over the even more spectacular peaks, plateaus, and canyons of the Sierra San Pedros while the sun glinted off the broad blue Pacific to our right. Lou and I chatted amiably about other times and people.

Tony was still napping off and on. He'd wanted to comb L.A. to find Rosa, but I'd convinced him that by coming to Mexico we were just taking a slight detour. Here we had a chance to finally get some questions answered and maybe learn something that would help us zero in on the missing girl. Valdez alone knew where she was. Valdez was probably here, or on his way here.

At an average 250 knots, we were in the air for nearly three hours, flying beneath the hot Mexican sun and above the brown, green, and golden mountains. After a while I started having trouble staying awake and Lou took back the controls. When I awakened, we were flying low over a dusty little village spread out near to vast chalky dunes and expanses of what appeared to be snow. We had reached Guerrero Negro with its huge salt mounds and mines. There was a tiny thread of runway, and Lou showed off his speed brakes by bringing the Mooney in for a sharp descent and a smooth landing.

It took us three-quarters of an hour and a couple of American five spots to locate the man who handled the fuel pumps, another half hour to refuel, and then we were zooming off again, heading toward our final destination, back north and across the peninsula toward the tiny village of Bahia de Cortez. The Mexican equivalent of the FAA had assured me that there was a serviceable landing strip at the hotel. So our true destination was the stony beach where La Casa del

Sol—the House of the Sun—the mega-million-dollar hotel resort designed, financed, and built by the Foundation's victims and friends, sat waiting for us in mysterious splendor.

The hotel was apparently on the same site where Elizabeth Ann Livingstone's mother had once supported an orphanage sheltering some five hundred Mexican children. Cassandra Cardwell's records had told me that some really big money was being funneled through the supposedly defunct orphanage. I was still trying to figure that all out. *Cherchez la cash.* When all else fails, figure out what's happening with the money, and the rest of the caper will always fall into place.

Yes indeed, there were answers down here. Including the answer to the mysterious appearance, then disappearance, of Elizabeth Ann Livingstone.

As we approached the coastline, I was increasingly certain of that. I felt my neck muscles tensing up, felt my fists flex involuntarily, felt every little nerve and brain cell and fiber of my being coming fully alive. And then we banked out over the sea and broke down through the clouds, and there it was.

I was surprised by the truncated, gleaming white, five-story pyramid set next to the indigo waters of the Sea of Cortez. I had expected the Foundation's hotel to be a larger version of the miniature Aztec temple I'd seen at the Vance residence last night. Nevertheless, the place was breathtaking. The green and golden hills of the Sierra del Sol jutted sharply up behind the buildings. Beyond these foothills, other and unapproachable mountains towered, capturing the indigo of the sea and the azure of the sky amidst the rich, thick browns and iron-reds of the earth. At the highest altitudes, there were cappings of dusty green forest. The Aztecs had believed that the sky was once water, that it had been poured from above to be captured in basins and ponds, rivers and streams, so that now the sky was empty of all save the gods. Looking at the sea's colors brushed into the shadows of the surrounding land, I could see where they might have gotten that idea.

Chapter

——THIRTY-THREE——

We circled the hotel then approached from the sea. We'd expected a narrow, rutted landing strip, but a first-class runway long enough to accommodate a Lear jet stretched out beneath us, skirting the narrow rocky swathe of land between the sea and the rugged hills. It stopped a hundred or so feet short of the manicured green-velvet grounds.

Several Lears were parked beside a hangar with a gleaming tin roof. And beside them sat the large, snow-white, twin-turbine bird with its strangely shaped body in which the Cardwells and Vera Vance had sailed away.

The small control tower was empty, which explained why we'd descended into the landing strip without so much as a radio crackle asking who we were or what we were doing. Lou taxied the Mooney over to a long row of Cessnas, Pipers, and other numerous aircraft, then parked and locked the plane. If the number of aircraft was any indication, we'd arrived at the right time. There were enough people here that with any luck we could get lost in the crowd. For a while . . .

We walked past the Lears, then around the Cardwells' plane, and Lou paused in front of the rounded white nose, reached out, and patted it respectfully. "A P180 Avanti," he said. "It's made out of aluminum, a flying dream. If I had one of these babies, I could take charters anyplace in the world." He looked wistfully at the sleek white nosecone with its two small wings protruding like truncated catfish whiskers.

"So buy one," I said.

"Sure. When I have an extra four mil or so."

We moved on down a pathway that cut beneath thick cypress trees, through an emerald swathe of golf course, then on to the back of the hotel. Lou was still thinking about the Avanti. He said, "Only way I could afford one of these babies would be to move drugs, and I don't want *anything* that bad."

Tony had been silent, measuring things, looking over the terrain, thinking and sometimes praying. Now, he gave Lou a curt nod. "You're smarter than most." He turned to me. "So we're here. Now what?"

"Now we try to find Elizabeth." I detoured around a bush, then pushed open a small wooden gate that admitted us to a lush garden between the sea and the hotel. I said, "We just act like we belong here and learn what we can."

Lou said, "So when someone asks why we're here, what do we tell them?"

On the way in from Guerrero Negro, I'd told him enough of what was happening to keep him out of trouble. But I'd left out the part about the seances and violated graves and ancient Aztecs, figuring he'd think I was back on the junk if I tried to tell him everything. Now, I said, "There's some kind of spiritualist convention going on here. Let's just roll with the show and see what happens. Ignore the obviously inane, the patently insane, and stay ready to pull out fast."

Tony shot me a hard look. "You really think this is going to work?"

I shrugged. "You never know till you find out."

There were about fifty people in the lobby, all of them coming and going and fussing about. We blended in with the crowd and nobody paid much attention as we checked into a $250-a-night suite with twin beds in one room, a king-sized in the other. They threw in a Mexican-tile tub, a balcony overlooking the sea, and room service. I paid the dapper little *mestizo* man behind the front desk with cash, then said, "Cassie Cardwell said to ask at the front desk for the events calendar. So—what's up?" I kept looking around, hoping to see someone I knew—like Vance or Valdez.

He looked puzzled. "This hotel is mostly for the pilgrims, *señor*." He looked worried and tapped his pen against the counter-top, as he again read our names. "I do not see you on the list here. Though you know Mrs. Cardwell, perhaps you have found the wrong place? There is wonderful deep sea fishing further south. Perhaps you need to fly on to Cabo San Lucas?"

"La Casa del Sol," I said, stretching lasciviously. "House of the Sun. This is where we want to be, all right."

"Then you are a pilgrim?" He was still frowning and looking over a long list.

"Cassie Cardwell told us to check with you and you'd fill us in on the happenings here."

In spite of his frown, he was fawning, ingratiating, just in case. "*Señorita* and *Señor* Cardwell have already arrived. They are at their *hacienda*. Perhaps I should ring them and tell them you are here?" His hand was crawling toward the telephone.

"Don't bother," I said hastily. I whipped out a five dollar tip and used it to intercept his hand. "Just give us directions, and we'll toddle on over and say hello."

"I'm sorry, but that is not possible without first getting permission." He was looking at the money in his hand, hesitant . . .

"Don't worry about it then," I said. "We'll rest up and touch base with them later."

A man and woman, both very blonde and with tropical tans, waited impatiently behind us. The *mestizo* was already pushing the desk register toward them, hinting for us to move on. There was an activities desk set up at the edge of the lobby. Beside it were posters that advertised several New Age seminars, one on reincarnation, another on trance channeling. There was a small cocktail lounge off the lobby and a large, well-appointed empty dining room with a velvet rope hitched across the door. The hotel looked pretty tame.

At that moment a cluster of middle-aged women came into the plush lobby, all of them wearing sun-dresses and sandals. One woman was saying, "And Betty really *must* learn not to give those children money."

"But Mable, they seemed so hungry . . ."

"Of course," Mable replied. She was about forty and plump, with hennaed red hair. She wore a bright green dress with a full skirt and a halter top, and her skin was red and leathery from years of too much sun. "But that's their karma. You'll learn. We all determine our own destiny. There's no such thing as bad fortune, everyone asks for what they get. If they're here in this God-forsaken country starving, that's because that's what they decided to do before this incarnation. They must have felt like they needed to learn something this way . . ."

"Well, it just seems like such a shame," the other woman said. She shifted her purse from one side to the other, then added, "By the way, do you know if Judy and Jewel are going to be in the advanced seminar tonight?"

"I believe Judy is going to spend a few more days at the research center," Mable said. "Dr. Vance is very interested in the entity she's just started channeling . . ."

Vance! He *was* here! I craned my neck in their direction, trying to hear more, but they'd all clustered inside the elevator now, had pushed the button, and the door slid shut. I watched the indicator as the elevator lifted them up to the third floor, then stopped.

"By the way," I said to the desk clerk. "I heard there used to be an orphanage down here."

"Yes?"

This man wasn't going to volunteer much information. I pressed on. "I used to know a woman who was raised here."

He said politely, "Her name, *señor*?" He kept looking around us at the people backing up in line.

I said, "Maria Elena. She works for Ariel Cardwell."

His eyebrows moved a notch upward, and I thought I saw a quick flash of recognition, but he hid it and said, "Her last name?"

"Sorry, afraid I don't know."

"Well, there was an orphanage, *señor*. I myself grew up there. But it has been changed, now, into a place for the psychic research. The children no longer come."

"The Research Center is in the building where the orphanage used to be?"

"*Si*. The large white building over behind the salt water swimming pool. But you should know that all the buildings here have now been integrated into the hotel."

That explained a lot about Cassie Cardwell's overlapping and befuddled financial documents. But *why* were they still using the orphanage's name in those documents? Why not be overt about it? Nobody was going to hide this hotel from anyone who was looking, that much was certain. Not that anybody seemed to be trying to hide it. Though a lot of people apparently arrived by air, there was a narrow highway that led back between the tall hills and to the Transpeninsular highway and quite a few cars in the parking lot. There were no guards or guardposts. And we'd sailed right into the landing strip, had checked right into the hotel.

I wanted to ask a lot more questions but decided I was pushing it. So I took the three room keys he was handing us and brushed past the arriving and otherwise milling guests. Then we took the elevator to our fourth floor suite.

Chapter
─────THIRTY-FOUR─────

W e were all tired and hungry, and certainly not up to doing battle. Besides, we still had to work out a battle plan.

So we spent an hour or more showering, then eating huge plates full of delicious enchiladas and stuffed tortillas that we'd ordered up from room service. When the food came, I automatically switched on the TV, wanting to check the news. But all I could get were pictures of surf and shore, the sea washing in hypnotically while Muzak played in the background. I changed channels, and there was a video playing, a tutorial on Eastern religions and what they promised the Foundation's participants. I took a bite of enchilada, changed channels again, then sat up straight and almost choked!

On the screen, a man sat on an elaborately carved throne that seemed to be made from pure, burnished gold. It was engraved with cherubs and saints and also with the intricate geometric carvings typical of Aztec art. His feet were on a matching purple-upholstered footstool with gold claw feet. Purple satin draperies covered the wall behind him, and in the center of the wall was a huge gold Mayan calendar. The man on the throne wore a mask of a human skull, in an ancient Indian stylization that included a protruding red tongue. He wore a gold loincloth and the rest of his stringy body was covered with shards and parts of human bones, a whole one hanging here and there, and his oily black hair was studded with starlike eyes. Paper rosettes protruded from his head. Behind him, sitting on more purple satin, were two fat tarantulas that probably held enough poison to kill everybody in this room. They were held to a tiny golden pole by two tiny gold chains.

Tony grunted.

Lou said, "What in the world . . . ?"

I held up my finger, then turned up the volume.

Then froze.

Auguste's hypnotic monotone emanated from behind the mask. He was saying, ". . . in a garden filled with flowers, where the hummingbirds dwell, Narayama waits for you, Narayama waits for you, Narayama waits for you to sip the nectar of life eternal, he waits for you to sip the nectar of constant pleasure, he waits for you to tire yourselves of these futile earthly doings and take the step that brings you to him, he waits to offer you the abundance of his delights. Here on earth we sleep and dream, here on earth we wither . . . like grass in the springtime we wither, like the spring flowers we wither, but Narayama, all powerful, all knowing, offers you the way of constant pleasure, the way of eternal delights."

He kept repeating that same chant over and over again.

Tony looked at me, a new horror in his eyes. "These are the people who run this joint?"

"That's one of the men who tried to kill me."

Lou shot me a worried look, then we all fell back to watching the televised horror, watched the repetition of Auguste, dressed in a mask different than the snake mask he'd worn while trying to kill me, as he swayed hypnotically and chanted lies as old as the earth.

The lie. The big lie. Its hot, fetid breath swept into the room like a gust off the boiling Sea of Cortez, capturing my breath, searing my brain, and suddenly I closed my eyes and saw the deep atrocity of Narayama, a dead stone god, rising up on Cassie and Caspar Cardwell's patio, ruling over other dead gods with ghastly, blood-stained grins. Death. This was the god of death, professing to offer life. Another enormous, cosmic lie.

A horrible realization sliced through me like lightning. I had been believing that same lie in a slightly different form these many years. I had been believing in death. And I had been wrong. Dead wrong. I felt a sudden panic, a vast sense of insecurity, as if there had been a sudden, slight molecular shift that had realigned everything, had left everything ever-so-slightly distorted and ungrounded, even me.

There *was* a reality beyond this one. In that moment, I knew it with a certainty that belied anything I had ever known before. But I also knew, in that moment, that a cosmic evil lay there: something foul, fetid—a thing that robbed people of their health, stole children, and used them for pornography or Satanic sacrifice, destroyed families and love, caused AIDS and other physical suffering. What existed beyond this perceptual wall of physical reality was evil, pure and incarnate. And it was at that moment manifesting itself through the man they called Auguste.

Tony was watching Auguste closely. There was a glitter of anger in his black eyes. "That's the most evil man I've ever seen," he said. Evidently he'd been feeling the same thing I had.

"Coming from you, that's saying a lot." I was being flippant, trying to hide my discomfort.

Tony shook his head in disgust. "People I come from, we got reasons. But *this* man!" He opened his mouth, started to say more, then clamped it shut, realizing the words were beyond him. He studied Auguste carefully for another moment, then said, "He's demon possessed."

Lou shot him a skeptical look. I felt a shudder run through my soul. I said, "What makes you say that?"

Tony said. "I look at him, I get an unclean feeling, like something spiritually decayed and rotted has come into the room."

I thought about that. I'd felt the same thing in varying degrees ever since I'd first stepped into the seance room at Cassie and Casper Cardwell's pink mansion, but I'd never really articulated it, even to myself. I looked harder at Auguste. I was indeed looking at something hideous and decayed, something beyond the physical that was merely

286

manifesting itself through the shaman. It wore an imbecilic toothy grin and breathed eternal death and decay.

Demons. I'd progressed from the "ghost" who'd brought me into this caper by handing me a five thousand dollar check, then on to Cassie and Caspar and the ancient spirits, and now all the way to demons.

And yet my skepticism had faded. There *was* evil in this universe, and an evil beyond anything that could emit from just humanity. I couldn't see it or grasp it physically, yet looking at Auguste it again became tangible to me, and in an unmistakable way.

Which was surprisingly good news, as I thought about it again. Because evil is only one side of a coin. Evil requires good, by definition. Without good as a reference point, the term evil has no meaning. So—if absolute evil exists at the supernatural level, then absolute good must also exist there. Good, as in God.

Which meant that maybe Tony hadn't gone totally off the deep end after all. Tony claimed to have spiritual enlightenment and inferred that he could actually see beyond the material and into that warring spiritual world where the Maker of this universe fused and forged an eternity that would banish, once and for all, every form of evil. There was a world, he said, a world beyond this one but which nevertheless contained and molded this one. For a split instant, as I thought about it and contrasted it to what I saw in Auguste, I had a sudden glimmer of it, too. It astonished me with its clarity and immensity, and I wanted with every fiber of my being to see more. But at that moment the camera suddenly cut to a woman—Dr. Winch!—who was standing behind a podium in front of high white draperies. My sensations vanished into surprise and curiosity.

She was saying, ". . . the end of our meditation for today. I leave you with this. You are your own god. There is no other being. The great god Mictlantecuhtli, whose avatar just inspired you, calls us to overcome our fear of what we call death, to realize that the end of this earthly existence will usher us into the age of Narayama, lord of the House of the Sun. We come and go on this earth, but always there is that beautiful reality beyond this one, where we can enter the world of constant pleasure, the world of eternal delights. Once there, we can choose whether to come back as the beautiful hummingbird or as an avatar, as the eagle who soars above these beautiful and sacred hills, or as the fish that leaps freely in the sea."

Lou said, "What *is* this junk?"

Tony said, "Shaddup and listen. We got to figure this thing out."

Dr. Winch said, "You are all already gods. You are perfected. Your only mission here on earth is to better understand yourselves, and once that is done you must take the Fifth Step, the holy step that will take you back to the true House of the Sun."

Suddenly I knew where we were. Approaching Step Four, which was the absolute commitment of everything to the Foundation—and perhaps to the evil spiritual beings who were behind all this. And I knew clearly, too, what Step Five would be. Suicide—but not before all earthly possessions had been turned over to the Foundation.

The immensity of the revelation of the true depravity of what these people were doing hit me like a physical blow. I couldn't have explained the sudden insight to anybody else. It had either come from outside me or from some far remote place in my own unconscious mind. I forced the disturbing insight back and said, "Time to put a stop to this, gentlemen. I say we start by checking out the psychic research center to see what Vance is up to."

"Shaddup," Tony said again. He was leaning forward, his eyes hot as he peered at the TV.

"Tch," I said. "Testy."

Tony shot me a hard look. "Don't you realize that what this dame is sayin' is the basis for the whole ball of wax? You want to find Elizabeth, you want to find Rosa, shut up and listen."

Dr. Winch was saying, "Without self-understanding and completion this world will never improve, for the only way things will get better is if we choose, from our spiritual positions, to quit coming back as criminals and poor people and sick people. We must learn all there is to know about the cosmos, and then we can choose wisely, we'll no longer need the lessons to be learned as the human dregs of this earth." She paused.

Tony muttered, "Wish I'd heard all this garbage when I was still workin' for the mob. I coulda convinced myself I was doin' my victims a favor, that they'd set it all up themselves."

A thin high flute was playing in the background of videoland now, and Dr. Winch took a little bow. "Thank you for worshiping with us," she said. "The seminar tonight will be conducted by Señorita Esther Martinez, Director of our Foundation branch in Mexico City. Afterward, a small string quartet made up from our visitors from Calcutta will entertain. I will be back day after tomorrow, and for now I wish you blessings and wisdom."

"Okay," Tony had turned to me. "This is just what I thought it was."

"Which is?"

"Which is a true mess that we ain't gonna straighten out without some prayer." Whereupon he knelt right there against the bed, looked to the ceiling then closed his eyes, and began to petition God as if God were another person, maybe hidden just beyond the panels in the ceiling.

Lou looked at me, embarrassed. He seemed to not know where to look. I shrugged my shoulders. Lou and I had both been privy to the ministrations of the lieutenant in Vietnam who had led the little group we called the "Born Agains," and who had talked to us at length about Jesus dying for our sins, about eternal life, about salvation and a thing he called "the baptism of the Holy Spirit." I explained to Lou, "Tony believes the same things as The Loot in Vietnam, remember him?"

Lou furrowed his brow as he fished about in his mind. When he'd snagged the memory, he grinned, "Then whatever it is we're doing here just might work!"

Tony asked God for wisdom. He asked God for protection. And then he stood, completely unembarrassed and completely composed, adjusted his waistband, and asked, "Okay, what next?"

Hopefully, I said, "When you were praying there . . . you didn't get any directions? No sudden revelations?"

"Not at the moment. Don't mean I won't."

I shrugged, feeling a little embarrassed. I said, "Then *I* think it's time to pay a visit to either the Cardwells' *hacienda* or Vance's lab."

Tony said, "The *hacienda* seems like as good a plan as any."

We went out the service door of the hotel. We weren't going to look like "pilgrims," no matter how hard we tried, so we had to keep a low profile instead. We toured the grounds, careful to stay away from the other people clustering or walking here and there. After about fifteen minutes we hit pay dirt. The Cardwells' sprawling white adobe house was set some distance from the hotel building and was fenced off from the rest of the hotel grounds. It was sheltered from view by a large, jagged outjut of rock and dozens of jacaranda trees, and its huge plate glass windows were flush with a cliff that plunged straight into the crashing sea.

Tony scaled the ten-foot corrugated fence on our side of the yard and had just started to drop inside and to the lawn when something snarled loud enough to freeze our blood and stop us all dead in our tracks. Tony jumped back down just as two Rotweilers came tearing from the far side of the house and slammed into the fence, once, twice, and then a hound the size of a nightmare, straight from Baskerville Hall, came crashing from the same side of the house and also lunged into the fence, trying to batter it down. We were already moving, backward, fast, and now we turned tail and did a three-way sprint. I heard voices shouting behind us, but they seemed to be calling the dogs.

Okay. If we were going to visit the Cardwells', we'd either have to go in the front door, or bring along some tranquilizer guns.

When we were well away from the house, we stopped for a parley and decided to forget the Cardwells for the moment and check out the old orphanage. If, as we'd overheard in the hotel lobby, Vance was currently conducting psychic experiments there, maybe we'd be lucky enough to catch him hard at work. Maybe even working on Elizabeth.

Something had to break for us here, before the Cardwells and friends realized we were here and sent the boys with guns. *If* we could just get lucky . . .

We padded over to the compound, then killed a few minutes arguing about whether to slam in and take Vance down physically or just spy and see what was up. We had just decided on the sneaky approach when Vance himself suddenly solved our problem by walking straight out the front door and down a pathway six short feet from where we were hidden. He was wearing white slacks on his short, lean legs, and a blue and white flowered shirt with a lot of gold chains shining at the opened neck. His pointed clownish face had a dark, dreamy expression, but a closer look told me that the dream was a nightmare for anyone but him. As he came out, a cloud slid across the sun so that a sudden gloom seemed to accompany his appearance. He was walking smartly, several people in tow. All of them seemed intent on some urgent purpose.

We stayed behind our hedge till the entourage had passed, then followed. There were three men I didn't recognize with Vance, all of them fawning on him. From their looks and mannerisms, I guessed that they were professionals of some kind, perhaps psychologists or sociologists or maybe even medical doctors. Sofia, the woman I'd met at the Cardwells' seance (the one whose husband had advised her to sell everything and take the Fourth Step) was also in tow. Her bleached blonde hair was matted and dirty, she was wearing a flowing white gauze dress that came nearly to her ankles, and she looked like she'd packed on another fifty pounds. Her face was furrowed with distress, and even from my distance I could see she had that dazed look in her eyes of a deer caught in headlights. Two other equally blowsy and distressed women were also rushing along a few steps behind Vance, and they also looked unhappy and dazed.

We slid through the trees and foliage, following them. When they reached the turn-off to the Cardwells' *hacienda*, Vance said something to the others and cut off from them, headed for the house. The others turned toward the hotel and kept walking.

We followed Vance. He went around to the front of the *hacienda*, said something into an intercom planted into the high white stucco wall, and the tall wooden gate swung open. He entered, latching it behind him and shutting us out again.

I was tired of walking. I'd stepped on a sharp rock and my left foot was beginning to bother me. I glanced at my watch. The Lakers game would just be starting. There was cold iced tea in my fridge.

Lou said, "This isn't working out."

Tony squinted, angled his head, and said, "Shaddup. I hear something."

I could hear it too, then, a motor of some kind, coming closer. We melted into the greenery beside the narrow path.

A golf cart came into view, then another. Both were driven by young *mestizo* men wearing the pale sky-blue jackets of the hotel. They passed us, then stopped at the front gate. The first one got out and spoke into the intercom. We were too far away to hear what he said.

The second young man got out too, and they both stood expectantly beside the closed gate. Insects buzzed around my head, and I could see a small iguana climbing up a tree behind Tony. I wondered if there were snakes in the foliage. Surely there were snakes. I wondered what kind of snakes. And I wondered about Elizabeth. If she was here, she was probably inside the Cardwells' house, looking at this semi-primitive world through those pain-filled, dark green eyes, the shadows growing deeper around her. I could see her curled, perhaps, in a corner, watching her world disintegrate through the machinations of these hard-faced people and unable to do anything about it.

After a long moment, another young *mestizo* man came through the gate. He was lean and muscular, and he carried a small suitcase in each hand. He handed them to the blue-coats, and went back inside. They loaded the luggage into the golf carts.

This was repeated several times, till about eight suitcases were stashed inside the carts, and then the young man came through the gate again. But this time he stepped to one side and held it open.

Cassie came through first. She was wearing a green and white striped pantsuit and carrying a large white handbag. Caspar came right behind her, wearing white from stem to stern. Next came Vance, with his blue-tinted hair and his sharp, hungry little harlequin face. Next came his wife, Vera, wearing an orange and black pant suit and a turban over her hair.

A hot wind suddenly roiled up off the sea, whipping at Cassie's white jacket, causing Vance to duck his head and lean into it. Vera grabbed her turban and held it on as they boarded the second golf cart. The wind charged the air with the same smothering pressure I'd felt the night of my first seance, when the sea breeze had stopped, the temple bells had pealed through the still air, and the hungry wind had swept in from the sea, rushing the Cardwells and their fellow worshipers to their destiny. This was that same dark wind, and instead of carrying the sweet, salt taste of the sea, its breath held the fetid scent of ancient decay.

Everything was loaded now. The people had climbed into the golf carts too, their facial expressions dark and hungry and purposeful as the wind. The attendants revved up the golf carts, and the Cardwells and Vances were spirited away.

Tony said, "They're taking the lam."

"Right," I said. "They'll be headed for the airport. Let's beat them there." I was still wondering if Elizabeth might be inside the house, perhaps under armed guard there. But the urgency of these people's departure was making that possibility increasingly remote. Something was up, something big, and whatever it was, it wasn't here.

We broke through foliage, I dinged up my hand as we scaled a rocky patch, and then we were on the airfield. We ducked behind a hangar and were already waiting when the golf carts, which had followed winding paths, rounded a green bend and rolled onto the asphalt roadway beside the airstrip. They made straight for the Avanti, which was sure enough already running. The attendants slammed the suitcases into a baggage compartment as the foursome boarded. The door folded shut, and the plane started moving.

We could see two figures in the double windshield as the Avanti's nose came around. A flash of recognition hit me as I spotted the pilot. It was the big-boned *mestizo* chauffeur who'd had the pleasure of kicking in my head while I'd been wasted on peyote. I squelched an impulse to storm the plane and return the favor, man against Godzilla, and then the plane turned at just the right angle to give me a full-on view of the person riding shotgun, and my furious impulse evaporated into pure rage! It was Valdez, his face pressed to the porthole as he watched the ground slide past. I touched Tony's shoulder and pointed. "That's him," I said. "Valdez. Our *diablero*." Tony gave me a curt little nod.

The Avanti was taxiing down the runway toward the sea, gaining speed, and then it was off the ground, then up, turning in a long, slow loop, gaining altitude and heading inland, up over the looming green mountains.

We were already inside Lou's little Mooney by the time they'd made their sweeping turn out over the sea. Now, as they gained altitude and turned inland, we were also taxiing down the runway. Lou timed it so that they were small on the horizon as we lifted off. In our smaller craft, we could sail straight toward the mountains, so we gave the Avanti room, watched it climb above the horizon, and then we were in the air behind it, coming up strong.

"If it flies too high, we're going to lose it," Lou said. "My cap is twenty-five, they can top thirty."

"Maybe we'll get lucky. Looks like they're staying fairly low."

"Problem is the fuel," Lou said. "We could make it all the way back to Tijuana without refueling, but not much farther."

I was sitting up straight, peering forward after the gliding white bird, keenly alive in every cell and nerve and fiber. I said, "We'll take it as far as we can."

We were directly over the mountains now, flying low to avoid the towering buildups of soggy cumulus. Already, several heavy curtains of rain slanted into canyons and darkened the mountaintops. The terrain beneath us grew wilder and wilder, with sheer peaks spotted here and there by lush forest and narrow jagged canyons blanketed with thick, tangled underbrush.

There was a light chop in the air, approaching turbulence, and we only had glimpses now and again of the Avanti, so white was it against the banks of clouds. But finally we saw it dropping beneath the cloud-cover, then circling above a sheer-sided cone-shaped mountain topped by a near-flat plateau. The Avanti flew in low and slow—they were obviously checking things out—and then it circled again, tilted to adjust for the wind, and then it was down beneath the treetops, landing.

We circled to the left of the plateau and came all the way down out of the clouds with a rush that felt like a roller coaster ride. Looking down, I felt my stomach drop and the sudden sense of falling. We were above a thousand-foot-deep abyss with rust-red walls and boulders the size of buildings. Lou gave the sleek Avanti plenty of headway as we followed it back in and over the cone-shaped mountain, above the plateau. The mountaintop was perhaps a mile across and a half-mile wide, and though there were hillocks and other irregularities in the terrain, for the most part the plateau was flat and thick with jungle.

We dropped down, following the same path that the Avanti had taken for landing, then flew in low to see where they'd gone.

I leaned in over the instrument panel, my chin pressed against the black plastic casing as I peered at the green forest below. I was hoping that we didn't lose so much speed and lift that we couldn't zoom upward again if we didn't like what we saw.

I spotted the temple first, dead ahead, a jutting ziggurat, complete with a shrine on its sawed-off pinnacle, materializing out of the ancient past and looming sharply above the thick, tall trees. And then we were past the landing strip and over it, zooming close in over the temple, startling the fifty or so people who had been moving through the plaza and into or out from the palace, across and beside the pools of water which were gray today with the coming storm. Some of the men wore shirts and slacks, others wore the robes and headdresses of Aztec priests. Some of the women were dressed in shorts or slacks, in blouses and T-shirts. Others wore summer dresses. Seeing the strange mixture of ancient and modern made me blink hard and shake my head to clear it, but when I opened my eyes the people were still there, behind us now as we swept up and banked, ready to make another circle and take another look.

It was a jewel of ancient architecture created from aged chalky-gray stone that looked as if it had been buried beneath harsh earth for countless centuries. It was set in an emerald sea of jungle. The mountain walls fell off sharply in every direction, and from what I could see from the air I was pretty certain that the only way in or out was the long gray landing strip.

It was the temple compound I had seen, miniaturized, in Vernon Vance's home.

Serpent Mountain.

I felt a shudder run up and down my spine and something dark and malignant seemed to fill the air, making it suddenly and suffocatingly cold.

Just as in the mock-up, the tall, weathered temple stood at the rear center of the compound. It was a steep, five-story pyramid, with several ledges to each story that added an even steeper angle to the height. The temple loomed above the trees and was crowned with a roof comb that jutted into the sky. Steep stairs ascended the pyramid's front, conjuring up images of bloodied victims being dragged to the crest of the temple by gold-bedecked Aztecs as sacrifices to some ancient sun god. Numerous sculptures of angry-faced gods were placed like totems throughout the compound. I could see a huge prostrate carving on a ledge about three stories up the temple. It looked like a creature half animal, half man, in a back-bend. It was an altar of sorts, and the center—where the figure's heart might be—was partially scooped out. I had seen these in Ival Davidson's books; they were the sacrificial altars, and the inversion was where the living heart was lain, awaiting the dark appetites of the gods and priests. I got just a glimpse of the atrocity, just a glimpse of deep stains that might have been centuries-old blood, and then we were past again, beginning to gain altitude.

The radio had been on all this time, and now it crackled to life. "You have entered restricted air space, you have entered restricted air space. Identify yourself, identify yourself, do you read?"

Lou shot me a questioning look, and I shook my head.

The radio kept ranting. I leaned forward and shut it off.

And then we were swooping away again, and several little clusters of men with rifles were running to positions within the compound, shielding their eyes, looking up at us, already aiming, while others were shaking their fists into the air, and Lou was saying, incredulously, "You want to land?"

Tony snorted, and I said, "Not at the moment." I was busy loading one of our own rifles.

"What *is* this place?" Lou asked, banking away, gaining altitude. Something that sounded like a tiny "crack!" came from beneath us, and then another one, and then Lou was banking straight up, into the clouds, leaving the angry men with their deadly weapons beneath us, and then we were taking a heading south and east, already well away from the temple of Narayama.

I said, "Gentlemen, you just saw Serpent Mountain. The *axis mundi* of the Cardwell empire."

"You think this is where they've got the Livingstone woman?" Lou asked.

"It's possible."

Lou shook his head. "Trying to land there is suicide. They've got more artillery than the VC."

"True," I said.

"You want to go back to the hotel?"

I thought for a moment, then said, "Bad idea. They'll be in contact by radio. We'd better fly back down to Guerrero Negro and refuel again. See what we can learn. Maybe there's another way in."

Tony grunted. "We can at least check it out."

297

Chapter

—————THIRTY-FIVE—————

In Guerrero Negro we refueled the plane, then found a little *posada* that fixed us up with clean rooms, a few palm trees for shade, and a view of the hot brassy sun setting over the broad gray Pacific. The storm had stayed behind us, and there were seagulls diving for fish against the translucent sunset. An iguana sat in the deepening shadow of a jacaranda, checking us out through the opened patio door. We cleaned up and ate some decent grilled swordfish in the three-table dining room, then went to the small bar nearby, a place called Pepe's Cantina.

The interior of the cantina was such a cliche of unruly Mexican nightlife that it might have been staged by Tod Montgomery. Raucous music ripped your eardrums, lung-scalding marijuana and tobacco smoke clogged the air. A *mestizo* with a quivering paunch wrapped in a filthy T-shirt and a filthier apron stood behind a long polished bar, pouring shots of booze for men who were shouting and cursing and laughing. When we walked in, the men at the bar who could still see turned and fixed us with hostile stares. The Mexican *machismo* is always at the boiling point when it's been heated up with tequila. But then, I guess that's true for all *machismo*. I'd even been that way myself a time or two and I have a couple of scars to prove it.

The three of us sat down at a rickety table. Tony folded his arms and leaned back, watching with pursed lips as the denizens of the cantina proceeded to rot their bodies and brains.

The waitress' body had sort of settled down on itself, so that her waist and hips were thickened with all the meat that should have been in her shoulders and chest. Her face was chubby, but surprisingly pretty. Lou wanted a tequila slammer, but I talked him into a soda instead since we weren't sure when we'd have to fly again. As for me, I'd been off the juice for a number of years, and Tony and I both ordered sodas, too. The waitress looked contemptuous when she took our order. As she walked away, the man sitting at the next table, who had been watching us furtively since we'd come in, said in slightly accented English, "Are you here to watch the whales?"

I shook my head, baffled.

"In the lagoon," he said. "The whales are giving birth. It is the big thing to see here, except for our salt mines." He laughed again, mirthlessly. He was a big-boned man with the haggard look that comes to men everywhere in the world who are trying to make a buck the hard way. He was wearing worn Levis and a faded blue T-shirt with one sleeve rolled up to hold a pack of Camels. He had a gold crucifix on a thick chain around his neck. His muscles were thick and sinewy. His hands were huge and the short nails were surprisingly clean.

"That right?" I was looking past him, checking out the room, looking for someone I could learn something from.

"I have a brother who can take you to the whale's lagoon," the man said. "Very cheap. It is only seventeen miles south of town."

"We need to go a little farther than that," Tony said.

The man dragged his chair over to our table, looking around suspiciously as if he was about to engage us in some vast and dangerous conspiracy. Once settled, he gave us a sly grin, and said, "I can perhaps be of help?"

"We need to travel north, up into the mountains," Tony said. "We'll need a Jeep part of the way, maybe a burro for the rest. You know anybody who can fix us up?"

"Where do you weesh to go?"

"The Sierra del Sol, up out of La Bahia del Cortez," Tony said. "And we need to get there right away."

"But you have the airplane?"

Lou and I both shot him a look. News traveled fast here.

"We can't land it where we want to go," Tony said.

The sly look was replaced by one of veiled contempt, with an undertow of disgust. "You perhaps have something to do with La Casa del Sol? The beeg resort the rich people took from the orphanage?"

Tony said, "We can afford to pay you, if that's the question."

"Ah, *señor*, there are many people in Mexico who have money, though there are many more who do not. Me?" He offered the hint of a shrug and a shrewd smile. "I wish to be one *weeth* the money, but for the moment I am one without."

"We could fix that," Tony said.

I tried to give Tony a look, but he ignored me.

"You are here to do the business?" The man asked.

Tony looked steadily at him.

"I mean," the man said, "you wish to perhaps make some kind of deal, maybe? Do some shopping? Maybe the *chiva*, or the *coca*?" Again he waited for some spark of interest to appear in any one of us, his low-browed face moving slowly as he searched each of our faces in turn.

"We want to go up north," Tony said. "Nothing else."

"Ah," the man said, leaning back now in a posture of relaxation. "This is very mysterious, is it not? Three *Norteamericanos* who suddenly appear in a nice new airplane but want to instead travel on burros? Men who could no doubt live in the finest hotels in Acapulco but who instead choose to come to our poor little town and then wish to vanish into our desolate mountains?"

"We're looking for the Treasure of the Sierra Madre," Lou said wryly.

"Ah. You have the sense of humor, *señor*. Humphrey Bogart, *si*? I saw that movie many, many times. The men who made that trip, they all died, did they not?"

"Look, let me put things up front," I said. "If you're selling drugs, count us out. That's not what we do."

300

The man's face changed so fast that it startled me. Whereas before he'd been oily and ingratiating, he was suddenly sharp and hard and furious. His body tightened up like a rattler's, and there were shards of hard ice in his eyes as he said, "That is good, *señor*. Because I do not like the *narcotrafficantes*. They do not have so very much trouble with the *chiva* and *coca* here in Baja Sur as we do across the gulf on the mainland. Here, an honest man can still live, as my father and brother still live. So if you are here to make the deal, I advise you, please fly across the sea. There are many who will be happy to accommodate you there. But not here. Here, the people can still live cleanly."

Tony grinned. I realized then that he'd already had it figured out. I said, "You're from the mainland?"

"I was born here in Guerrero Negro, but now I am from Guadalajara. I am a *Federale*. Emilio Aragon. Here, I am on special assignment. In Guadalajara, I put the *narcotrafficantes* behind bars. Unless I can shoot them first."

I put out my hand for a shake. "Artie Weatherby," I said. "Private peeper from The Big Smog. And this here is Pastor Tony Cacciatore, who runs a church outreach in Tijuana. And this is our buddy and pilot, Lou Rickerby. We're looking for someone who disappeared from Tijuana, a young girl."

"Ah," said the Federale. His eyes grew keen and his face took on a feral look. "And your investigation has led you to Baja Sur?"

I nodded.

Tony was eyeing Aragon carefully.

The man thought a long time, studying us. And then his shoulders sagged, and he said cheerlessly, "We have a problem too, señor. Here in Guerrero, and also on the mainland." He made an elaborate shrug. "We have also had several disappearances."

He had our attention. Tony leaned in closer. "When? Who?"

"Young people," The *Federale* said. "Three of them, and not the sort who are likely to be involved with criminals. Not drug dealers, nobody has ever even imagined these young people doing anything criminal. A true puzzle. That is why I am here. Our government was asked to send someone to investigate."

"Any luck?" I asked.

"*Nada.* I have been here five days, and I am beginning to wonder. Perhaps it is not the drugs that are our biggest problem these days. Perhaps there is a new evil here."

"Such as?" I asked.

The man measured me carefully. "You recall the tragedy at Brownsville? The Witch of Matamoros and the *narcotrafficantes* who believed they could become invisible to us *Federales* by sacrificing humans?"

"I remember it well," I said. Shelby Knight had also mentioned it recently. Though it had been a while back, it had rocked both the United States and Mexico. Mass graves had been found on the Mexican side of the border, along with altars and other signs of ritual sacrifice. Several young people had been lured from Brownsville, at least one had been ruthlessly murdered. The Mexican authorities had finally cornered the two ring-leaders in a hotel room in Mexico City, and the leader had shot himself. His partner, the woman they called the witch, had been busted. The various confessions had included details on why the sacrifices occurred—they'd believed the ritual sacrifice of human beings made them invisible and invincible during their illegal drug dealings. The witch was doing life now in a Mexican penitentiary, but all of us had long had a feeling that there were more out there like her and her little crew. Take it from me, after eight long years as a heroin addict I can guarantee you that anyone who has the stomach for dealing drugs won't think twice about overt slaughter of one of their fellow human beings. Especially when their mind-set is compounded by the drugs themselves.

"Ugly," Lou commented.

"Yes," the man said. "And now we are concerned that a similar group may be acting here. First, a young girl disappeared in Guadalajara. She had just attended a church service with her boyfriend, he left her for only a moment and when he came back she was gone. She has not been seen again. And then several people vanished from this very town . . ."

"What kinds of people?" Tony asked. He'd leaned forward and his face was keen with interest.

"No special kind, *señor*. Two teenaged boys, one sixteen-year-old girl, one man who was twenty-three. All of them suddenly and suspiciously gone . . ."

Tony said, "I mean, what do they all have in common? Anything? For instance, do they all belong to the same church?"

The Federale leaned back and studied Tony carefully for a moment, apparently reconfiguring this new slant on the issue. Then he said, "Yes. That is indeed a link. They are all members of Christian churches." He frowned. "Though that does not make them so unusual in Mexico. Most of us are Catholic, as you must know. And these people, their Christian denominations were all different. The girl from Guadalajara was Catholic, the two boys here were members of a Baptist mission that does a small part to take care of the children left homeless when they closed the orphanage in La Bahia del Cortez. The others were members of our little Pentecostal church . . ."

Tony shut his eyes and his face twisted up in a grimace. I could see his lips moving. He was praying again.

I shifted uncomfortably. It seemed to me almost sacrilegious to pray in a *cantina*.

But then Tony opened his eyes, and said, "It's started."

The *Federale* was watching him intently. "What has, *señor*?"

I said, "Yeah, *what*?"

"'We do not wrestle against flesh and blood,'" Tony said, "'but against principalities, against powers, against the rulers of the darkness of this age, against spiritual *hosts* of wickedness in heavenly *places*.'"

"Ephesians 6:12," said the *Federale*, surprising me. He smiled warmly. "I am also a Christian. And I agree, we are battling nothing less than absolute evil."

I said, "*What's* started?"

"The 'cleansing,'" Tony said. "The beginning of a holocaust against anyone who believes that Jesus Christ is the true Son of God."

I was looking at him like he'd gone nuts.

Tony said. "What we got here is a splinter group—people who are screwy enough to do anything. And whether they know what they're doing or not, it's started."

I was totally bewildered.

Tony said, "The Bible predicts it. In the latter days people will be slain for the Word of God. Add that into this: most New Agers believe there's going to be a "shift" that will bring in a New Age. They blame the Christians for everything that's ever been wrong on earth, and they claim that before this shift can happen, the Christians gotta go. They want to send us into the spirit world to 'rethink our attitudes,' then they'll fix it with their gods so's we can all be reincarnated, come back and be just like them."

Suddenly I was thinking of Step Five. The ultimate experience. Suicide, death, human sacrifice.

Tony said, "We gotta get up onto that mountain."

I agreed. But suddenly the last thing in the world I wanted to do was go back to Serpent Mountain. Because suddenly I knew that the very ultimate evil waited there.

Chapter

THIRTY-SIX

The *Federale*'s brother fixed us up with a battered Jeep with rust-spots and chewed upholstery and all the gear we needed. As the few forlorn lights of Guerrero Negro fell behind us, the night turned heavy and humid. Driving into the black vortex, I had the sensation of suffocation. But soon a clean, salt breeze swept in from the sea, and then a golden glimmer of moon came out from behind the clouds to join the faint diamond scattering of stars. There was no other traffic for a thousand miles on the empty, endless highway that bore us north and east, toward the opposite coastline and the Foundation's hotel.

The first faint pallor of dawn caught us winding through a short mountain pass at the skirt of deep, high cliffs. Tony was at the wheel, and Lou was sacked out in the back. I poured coffee from a thermos into styrofoam cups, and passed a cup to Tony. The Jeep hugged the curves as the morning sun etched out the hills and foliage, and finally we spotted what seemed to be the inland side of Serpent Mountain. As we approached the conical, green-capped peak, the hum of two small aircraft set us alert and staring upward. Tony yanked the wheel, and we spun off the road and under a cover of tall brush and trees where we hid as the two planes circled the top of Serpent Mountain, then landed.

Half a mile further down the road, a rutted dry riverbed intersected the road. Tony twisted the wheel, we took a sharp left, and we found ourselves on a baked-mud flat that carried us to the very base of the peak. We hid the Jeep behind a copse of *manzanita* brush, then covered it with a bower of sage branches and other dried twigs to hide it from the air. Then we strapped on our backpacks and weapons. Lou and I waited impatiently as Tony offered up a prayer, and then we started the long and difficult ascent.

By mid-morning the temperature had hit ninety, and by noon, when we were just over halfway up, the sweat was streaming down our faces, and our shoulder and arm muscles were throbbing from the work of chopping through undergrowth and thick, snake-like vines with our machetes. The footing was bad. The rocks were sharp and many were loose. The tendons in my legs were aching and trying to cramp up on me. The mud from yesterday's rain had left parts of the mountain slick and difficult, and with every foot we gained, the pall of oppression seemed deeper, as if something dark and sodden and invisible was tightening its grip on the mountain.

Three-quarters of the way up, a squall blew in from the Sea of Cortez, and suddenly the curtain of rain that had been on the eastern horizon was on us, a waterfall, so heavy that we couldn't see a foot ahead. We pulled a small waterproof tent out of one backpack and huddled under it to wait it out.

We ate cold tortillas and some canned refried beans as the deluge slashed and bruised the mountain around us. We were damp, but comfortable. Everyone was silent, awed by the fury of the storm and by the uncertainty of our task. The rain raged, pounded, flooded across the terrain and down the mountainside. I was glad it had come, glad for the rest, and—oddly—I felt a strange sense of peace for the first time since we'd reached Mexico. What had been a die-hard belief that there was nothing beyond this life had slowly warmed into a willingness to tinker with the possibility that there was indeed a God. And, at the moment, I was content to more or less accept the probability that I was indeed in the hands of a Being great enough to send this storm or stop it, to design and think into being black holes and galaxies, One who could shake the very planets, guide the paths of comets and moons, divide the seas. I knew that this deluge, if God were in the mood, might become a nightful of rain, then a canyon full, then could cover the very world. There was something about the wildness here that made the concept plausible. And if that were so, I was content in the knowledge that God Himself would send me some kind of ark.

And yet, at the same time, I sensed that this was no more than a mild reprieve before the true storm, that just outside this circle of comfort made up in equal parts from physical exhaustion and mental exploration, there lay a vast impending evil . . .

After about an hour, the rain stopped as suddenly as it had come. We drank some hot chocolate cooked on a sterno can, then folded the tent, unfolded our aching muscles, and again began our ascent.

The storm had brought the sensual scent of rain-freshed loam. But the going was really tough now, every step slick, part of the ascent made on our knees, all three of us grabbing onto branches and the tentacles of strange, forbidding plants. Finally, at well past four P.M., we were almost at the top and the sun was low on the horizon. We reached a small ledge just beneath the crest, and Tony sagged to the ground and dropped his backpack. "I gotta rest."

I squatted beside him. We were all three mud-caked and totally exhausted. Lou pulled a rain poncho out of his gear and spread it on the ground, then stretched out on it, his backpack behind his head. "We can't get into the compound anyway till after dark," he said. He'd bought a straw cowboy hat at the little store where we'd purchased our supplies and it had become soaked with the first rain. Now, it was misshapen and comical, as he pulled it down over his eyes.

The sweat had dried into dirty streaks on my face, and my muscles were starting to stiffen before I finally managed to doze off a bit, in spite of the flies that kept buzzing my face. Tony was taking an hour's watch, after which he would awaken me and get some shut-eye himself. We'd been up for the better part of forty-eight hours now except for an occasional nap, and without regeneration we weren't going to be much good in any real pinch.

I must have been dreaming because at first I thought it was just another fly, an especially large one, but as I tried to reach up and swat it the buzzing turned into a roar. Tony said, "Hey," and I shot up straight to see a sleek Cessna Caravan coming in low, circling the plateau. There was still just enough daylight for me to realize that it was a red and white job that I'd seen parked beside a hangar at the hotel.

"More visitors," Lou said. He'd also been awakened by the sound. This was about the fifth plane we'd seen fly in since we'd started climbing the steep slope, all of them prop jobs. Evidently the landing strip was too short to handle even a small jet.

"Busy little place," I said.

Tony agreed. "Somethin's up." He gestured toward the temple compound. We could just see the top of the temple and twinkling electric lights had come on against the growing dusk, outlining the jutting comb and the sheer sides of the pyramid.

I opened my canteen, and now I wet my whistle before I said, "So whadda ya think? Time to make a move?"

"I have a bad feeling," Tony said. "There's not much time."

"Then we go," I said.

We moved slowly, taking nearly an hour to get through the expanse of trees and underbrush between us and the compound, timing ourselves to pace the setting sun. We had almost reached the compound when a sudden rhythmic drumbeat froze us in our tracks. A distant primitive chanting had begun.

We waited breathlessly, all of us shot through with the eerie sound. But as the chanting continued and became more frenzied, we moved on, seriously intent on our purpose now, though we were still uncertain as to what that purpose was.

After a minute, we came to a thick, ten-foot stone wall that enclosed the grounds. Lou and I had learned our combat training in the Vietnamese jungles, Tony had learned his in the darkest city streets. We'd left our rifles in Lou's plane, opting instead for more manageable handguns. Now, all three of us had our weapons ready in case something—man or beast—loomed up out of the darkness to test our training. But nobody seemed to be on patrol. As we scaled the rough wall, the sounds of the ritual grew louder. I glanced at Tony. His face was furrowed with distress.

We came in single file around the back of a one-story stone building with steel-barred windows, then stopped short at the sudden nearby sound of a low, mechanical whine. I aimed my flashlight through the bars and saw two huge generators. More lights had gone on in the complex: the second generator had just kicked in.

We inched around the building, careful to stay well back in deep shadow, and now I could see the plaza that spread out in front of the temple.

The tiles were polished gold, reflecting the tiny carnival lights of the temple and palace as well as the rows upon rows of flickering torches that lined the walkways. The moon was hidden behind newly gathered clouds, and the long obsidian ponds reflected the black sky as well as the flickering golden light. The torchlight and electric light also shone and reflected in the huge geodes strewn throughout the compound so that the entire scene had a shimmering, dream-like quality. I could see now why these people needed so much money. Even without the movies and publications and other expensive prose-lytizing projects, this place alone could swallow up a hundred million dollars in a flash!

A motion caught my eye. I turned and looked up. Then looked again, not believing my eyes. Caspar and Cassie Cardwell stood on one of the palace balconies, dressed in white robes, wearing towering golden headdresses, regally watching the milling action in the plaza from an appropriately deified distance. I felt a wave of repulsion so deep that it nauseated me. I toyed with the idea of going in after them, jacking them up and seeing what I could learn, then decided against it. All things in good time.

Tony and Lou were close on either side of me, all three of us in deep shadows with our backs to the hard stone and watching intently, guns still ready.

Something—someone—had come out in front of the temple, and now stood behind and slightly above the sacrificial altar I'd seen from the air. The being was robed in black, and wore a diamond collar that came from his chin to his shoulders, made a V down between his breasts then continued in a wide belt around his waist. Diamond cuffs also glittered, and he wore a conical headdress that was equally bejeweled, and crested in huge red and black macaw feathers.

I shivered. Something dark seemed to be settling down over the temple, over the complex, into my lungs. It was a suffocating cloud of palpable evil that hit me with such force that I had to struggle, for a moment, to get my breath.

Slightly behind and above the black-clad being was a huge statue *identical* to the one I'd unveiled on the Cardwells' white marble patio, but twice the size. This statue also rose from a writhing base of serpents into a cloak of stylized feathers set with glittering diamonds and other precious stones. The body and face held elements of the carvings of ancient Aztecs, Sumerians, Babylonians, Hindus and even ancient European art. This was the Light Bearer, half serpent, half man, covered in shining gold leaf.

Narayama.

The embodiment of all the demon deities from all time who had ever had a hand in the horrors that had eternally assailed the human race.

I looked back at the embodiment of Narayama. A red mask covered his face, and where his mouth should have been there was a large, black bird's beak. Curved down from that were fangs that might have belonged to a huge serpent. His fingers dripped with diamonds and at their tips were gold claw-like objects that resembled razor-sharp talons.

Two lesser priests stood beside the altar, one on each side, holding basins. They wore turquoise robes with gold loin-plates, belts, bracelets and collars, and the hideous snake-masks I'd first seen when I was flat on my back on the Cardwells' patio being interrogated by the similarly-masked Auguste.

The drum-beat suddenly changed. A procession was coming past the squat one-story building beside the palace. First came Auguste, wearing the same death's head costume he'd worn on his TV show. Behind him came four lesser priests, all of them hideously and variously masked and carrying ceremonial torches.

And then came the *piece de resistance*: a smaller white-veiled woman borne prostrate on a golden litter carried on poles across the shoulders of four muscular young men in loincloths and gold collars and more snake masks. They were almost staggering beneath the weight of it all.

My breath came short.

Tony went rigid. Lou muttered a curse. The veiled person's head lolled back and forth slowly, and her body was limp. I'd have bet my next ten years that she was drugged.

The crowd grew frenzied, chanting over and over again: "Hail Narayama, hail Night Drinker, we send to thee this day a messenger. Hail Narayama, hail great spirit, we send to thee this day a messenger . . ."

Unless I missed my guess, in a few moments these people were planning to honor my ghostly client, Elizabeth Livingstone, by placing her atop the altar and using her in their grisly, cannibalistic ritual sacrifice.

The procession was nearing the lower temple steps.

"Hail Night Drinker," screamed the mob. "Hail Narayama, Hail great sun god. We offer you our flesh, we offer you our earthly life. We send you a messenger, that you might spill thy water of precious stones . . ."

The procession stopped in front of the temple. Auguste continued on up the steps, then stopped to stand in front of the being who was impersonating Narayama. The drumbeats and chanting stopped. The shadowy ghosts cast by the flickering torchlight and the faint illumination from the temple lights outlined the steps and altar. The men carrying the litter began to move up the temple steps. Narayama lifted a bejeweled dagger and stood, poised, behind the altar.

The universe seemed to stand still in that moment as I wondered helplessly what to do to stop this horror. And then, swiftly, a humid breeze from the dank sea three thousand feet beneath us rubbed its back against the mountain like a hungry ocelot then coiled around it, stirring brush and trees, then roared with a rush up the mountainside to send a harsh gust through the compound, blowing out fully half the torches and scattering leaves.

"The generator," Tony muttered.

"It might work," I agreed.

"I'll go." Tony replied.

"You'll need help." Lou said, and they were gone.

I was left standing alone. I gripped the .38 Chief Special that was still in my hand. A good gun. But not good enough to take out the great god Narayama from this distance, and certainly not good enough to take out everyone in the compound who was involved in this atrocity.

I watched the smoke rising from the still-lit torches of the people who now surrounded the twisting white-clad figure on the funeral bier. Already, the other torches were being relit. The litter had been set down on the first temple ledge and the men were lifting the figure, carrying her up the steps to where Narayama stood hungrily, Auguste slightly beneath him and also waiting. They gently placed her on the sacrificial altar. The people began a hungrier and lower chant.

I had to move. I slipped through the shadows, then hunched down and shot swiftly along the murky edges of the compound to the back of the temple. Suddenly it was so dark that I had to feel my way. I was in a narrow passage between the temple and the jungle. The night-grind of insects made a background, now, for the distant demented chanting. The cold stone ledges towered above me, there was a smell of damp mulch and fetid decay in the air. And with every step forward, a weight grew on me as if someone were pumping my blood full of lead. At the periphery of my hearing, the gnashing of insects became a distorted song. Not human voices, but the voices of all the incantations, all the screaming victims who had ever been part of such evil human sacrifice. It was a cacophony of horror, lingering at the distant edges of the chanting and shouting that emanated from the demon hordes at the other side of the temple. I felt a coldness I had never felt before. Every muscle in my body ached. My body grew infinitely heavy.

Fighting past the heavy pall, I gripped the stone and began to climb the wide ledges, coming up the back, moving as quickly as I could without attracting attention to myself. Who knew how long it would take the cultists to offer up all the incantations and do all the ritualistic motions that prepared them to take another's life? It could be an hour, it could be seconds. Time was running out, not just for the person on the altar, but for all of us.

Finally, I knew I was on a level with the sacrificial altar where the evil had already begun. I edged with my back along the clammy stone, coming around the side then all the way toward the front so that only a corner shielded me from the priests, the altar, and the victim. I was still deep in shadow and I had my gun out, ready to aim, as I carefully stuck my head out to see. I froze. Auguste was standing above the white-clad figure with his obsidian knife raised, knuckles whitened as he got ready to plunge the metal into her breast. Someone in the crowd saw me and screamed, pointing, and Auguste, eyes glazed, turned in slow motion to look at me just as the two priests dived for me. I had my finger on my trigger, was actually beginning to squeeze, when suddenly the electricity died and night swallowed the scene at the same instant as another and stronger gust of wind blasted through the compound and struck out the torches, every last one. I missed my shot, heard it zing off of stone, and then people were shouting and screaming, milling in pitch blackness, and there were other shots fired, everywhere it seemed. I lunged forward, seeing only the faint white milk of the veiling in front of me. Then I had her, had the veiled figure in my arms, and was feeling my way and tripping over the altar and people, and I shoved someone and heard a scream as that person fell. Then, I was trying to get around to the back of the temple again so I could safely descend into oblivion instead of running the armed gauntlet of all the black frenzied forms who milled, crazed now, in the plaza beneath me.

There were more gunshots, more shouting, and though I was at the back of the temple now, someone hit me from behind. I managed to swing the white-clad figure around and knocked him off balance with her legs, I heard him fall, too, cursing all the way to the ground. I moved swiftly, beginning the descent with one arm still around the veiled person I was holding. She had come around enough to stand on her own, and though she didn't know where we were, she was letting me guide her downward. I said, "Are you okay?"

A faint moan came from beneath the veiling, then heart-rending sobs.

I ignored proprieties and touched her ribs, her back, her abdomen. I didn't feel any dampness, no warmth that felt like blood. I'd gotten to her before they'd managed to make the first stab wound. I was zinging with relief, and then I was off the temple tiers, on firm and even ground, carrying her again, running through the trees, zigging and zagging and not knowing how close I was to a drop-off or any other catastrophe. Then, miraculously, the quarter moon slid from behind a cloud and I could see the hulking shape of airplanes ahead. I was running toward the landing strip.

The sound of gunshots came from behind me, closer now, and then suddenly the lights blazed on inside the compound and the whole mountain turned ink-black against that evil, brilliant light. I wondered if they'd nabbed Tony and Lou, and then I heard someone huffing through the trees. I stopped short, crouched behind a rock, lowered the woman to the ground beside me, then quickly checked my .38.

Something touched my shoulder. I spun and rammed my gun into someone's gut, before a man whispered, "Hey, get a grip, pal!"

"Lou?"

"You were expecting maybe Satan?"

"Him or his henchmen. Where's Tony?"

"Don't know. It was too dark, too much confusion. I picked out your shape coming through the woods and managed to follow you and hold them off. You got the woman? Is she still alive?"

"More or less." I leaned over and touched her. She murmured again. Drugged heavily. She didn't even know what was going on.

I pulled back the veil.

And froze.

It wasn't Elizabeth!

"So now what's up?" Lou asked.

"Wrong woman," I said shortly.

"You've got to be kidding me."

"Nope. This isn't who we came after. But all is not lost. This little girl disappeared a while back from Tony's outreach in Tijuana. Her name is Rosa."

"I don't believe it."

"Well, believe," I said. "Because here she is, and Elizabeth is nowhere is sight."

"Okay, whatever, we saved her. They're regrouping. What now?"

"We can't climb off the mountain," I said. "We'd never make it in the dark, plus they have too many people after us now, they'd catch us for sure."

"Which leaves me hot-wiring airplanes."

"You can do that?"

"Can and will." He turned, and in the faint moonlight I saw him looking with longing at the Avanti. But then he shook his head, said out loud, "Too hard," then reared up and made straight for the Cessna Caravan.

They were coming through the brush, carrying flashlights and relit torches, scores of them, the crowd that had stormed Frankenstein's castle, except that this time, they were on the monster's side. I had dragged Rosa into the plane and was waiting for Lou to start it. I was still outside, standing beside him as he tinkered with the engine. And then suddenly it purred to life, and he said, "Hop in."

"You go, take the girl, I've got to get Tony."

"You're nuts. They'll get you both."

"Can't go," I repeated. "Not without——"

"What's keepin' ya?" Tony growled. He was coming out of the bushes.

I managed to gape only as long as it took him to make one stride, then I said, "You. Get in."

He grunted, climbed in, and once inside said, "I was wanderin' around out there thinkin' I'd probably fall off a cliff when I heard the airplane engine come to life right beside me."

"That was a piece of luck," I said.

"I keep tellin' ya, luck has nothin' to do with it. I was prayin' for all I was worth."

Lou opened the throttle and the plane started to move. There was barely enough moonlight to see the outlines of the strip, but enough, with luck *or with prayer*, to bring her around and take off.

But just as Lou brought the tail around and lined her up for take-off, three shapes came running along the edge of the strip. Narayama was in the lead. He was still wearing his black robe and diamonds, though he'd thrown off the hideous mask. He braced, raised his arm and fired an Uzi. It made a ratta-tat-tat, and in the moonlight his face was open and feral and bare to the world.

It was Vernon Vance.

Tony sucked his breath in through his teeth. I sensed his sudden rigidity and rage.

Vance was a poor shot, even with an Uzi. The shots went wide of the plane, but he stilled himself, aimed, and started to fire again.

Tony tensed up like I'd never seen him, even when he was on trial for the charges I'd help bring against him. He said, "That maggot." He aimed and fired. Our plane was moving fast now, but nevertheless I could tell he'd deliberately sent his shot wide.

I fired till I ran out of bullets. My others were in the rucksack I'd dropped on the temple steps.

"That's Vance," I said. "Big cheese psychiatrist who, along with Cardwell, is behind most of this. If you want to shoot him, that's okay with me."

"That ain't no psychiatrist," Tony said, taking another bead at the rapidly receding group. "That's Carl Cooper. He's a free-lance con man, used to run up against the Families once in a while. I had a chance to clip him, must of been fifteen or so years back. I didn't take the job. Figured he didn't deserve to die for somethin' so small as a little stock swindle, even if he did mess up some Family action. Goes to show, maybe I shoulda done the job, kept him from goin' on to bigger things."

I wanted to ask Tony a lot more, but at that moment, as we were accelerating for take-off, a smaller Cessna was suddenly coming in behind us, and it seemed to have more maneuverability on the airstrip because it swung around and was coming up fast. And then we were in the air, and Lou yelled, "Hang on." We made a swift little loop, barely clearing the treetops, and then I was craning my neck, looking beneath and behind me, and the other plane was lifting off too, but low, something was wrong, and as I watched, the belly of the fuselage scraped the treetops and caught the little plane. It somersaulted, bounced against the forest, then ripped into the trees with a blast of thunder and a ball of flames that lit up the entire mountainside.

Tony and I watched for a long time, the fire growing tinier and tinier behind and beneath us, and finally he broke the torturing silence, "At least we got your woman."

"Not exactly," I said.

He looked at me oddly. "Then what's that wrapped up like a mummy back there?"

"*Your* woman," I said. I'd strapped her in so she could partially lie down, and now I turned and shined my flashlight on her sleeping face.

Tony blanched, then looked at me wide-eyed, then shook his head in amazement. Then he shook his head again and said, "Rosa? You got Rosa? I can't believe it." He grinned. "Man, this is great. God certainly does work in mysterious ways."

Chapter
———THIRTY-SEVEN———

We flew the pirated Cessna into the airport at Guerrero Negro, then found the *Federale* who'd been looking for the missing kids and told him everything that had happened, including where to find his brother's Jeep. He was furious at the idea of a bunch of rich American cultists making use of his bailiwick to violate everything he believed in, and you could see, too, the beginnings of a sick worry that maybe his own people hadn't been lucky enough to get away. He immediately started planning a raiding party to look into the temple compound, as well as the hotel, and by the time we took to the air in Lou's Mooney TLS, government planes and choppers were already flying in from the Mexican mainland.

We'd had the village doctor look at Rosa, but he didn't seem to know or understand much. Still, she had come around enough to convince us that she didn't need immediate medical care, so we flew her back to Clover Field, then drove her downtown to Tony's mission. Now, she was tucked away in her own bed, after having received a house call from a top-notch physician who donated time to the mission. She had indeed been drugged, had a few bruises, but she'd make it. Though she still couldn't tell us why Valdez had picked her out of the thousands of Tijuana street girls.

Tony and I were sitting with Shelby at the table in the huge kitchen, hashing over the past few days. "Those people have to be nuts to believe all that garbage," I said.

"People find excuses every day to kill others," Shelby said. "Look at all the wars that are fought because of differences in religious beliefs—or for economic gain, for that matter. Here, you have a little of both. The ancient Indian thing is just an excuse."

"I'm going to have to go back down to Baja," I said. "To find Elizabeth. I should have stayed there and gone in with the Feds, but Aragon didn't like the idea of carrying along a civilian."

"We'll pray about it," Tony said. "See what happens."

Ever since we'd flown out of the temple compound, I'd had a growing premonition that I would never again see Elizabeth Ann Livingstone alive. In fact, our raid on the compound, though it had freed Rosa, had probably put Elizabeth in more jeopardy than she'd been in before. My throat constricted when I thought about it. "Look," I said. "I don't know if I believe in God or not, there's too much that doesn't make sense, but just in case it might work, could we pray for her safety right now?"

We could. We did. And when we were finished, I didn't feel a bit better about things. But after I'd left, as I was driving back through the smog and soot and traffic to my office, the world started looking a bit brighter. If there really was a God in heaven, maybe it wasn't entirely my fault that I hadn't yet found Elizabeth Ann Livingstone.

Suddenly I remembered that there was one more little matter that had gotten lost in the shuffle. I reached over and unlocked my glove compartment. The videotape that Ariel had boosted from her mother's safe was still there. I took it out and put it in my lap, so I wouldn't forget it again.

Back in my office, I turned on the television and VCR, then shoved in the tape. It was at the end. As the machine rewound it, I leaned back on the chintz sofa, propped up my feet on the coffee table, and stared at the ceiling. A ship's horn blew mournfully in the harbor, and the traffic sounds were a long way off and melancholy. I wanted to talk to Christine. She was the only one who understood my loneliness, who knew why I had to keep on fighting all my hopeless battles.

I picked up the phone and dialed her father's home number. He was the special agent in charge of the L.A. field office, and he'd know where she was, how she was doing. He could at least tell me she was okay and tell her I'd asked about her. But the answering machine came on, so I hung up.

And then the videotape clicked, it was rewound, so I hit the PLAY button on my remote, then leaned back, and a sudden, inexplicable fear grabbed me. I stood up, shook my head, and just then the tape began to play.

We were back at Serpent Mountain, but this time the temple was in the early stages of construction, though the first three tiers had been completed and the sacrificial altar was firmly in place. The same bevy of masked figures stood there: the snake masks, the other priests, the avatar who played Narayama. The tape was grainy and now and then there was a place that went white, but I could tell from their movements and sizes that they were pretty much the same people who'd been there just yesterday. Vernon Vance in his hideous mask and black robes—though there didn't seem to be near so many diamonds as when I'd last seen him. Auguste, resplendent in his hideous costume of bones. There were others, all masked. Elizabeth, in fact, was the only one not masked, and she wore a black robe. Her face was dazed. She looked at the stars—for it was night—and seemed to follow along as they chanted: "Hail Narayama, Hail Night Drinker, we offer thee a messenger . . ."

I felt like somebody had poured lye down my throat. The smothered feeling was back. I didn't want to see the rest.

Elizabeth clutched an obsidian knife. She stepped forward, and the amateur photographer who'd been handling the VCR cut away from the scene for a moment and got a close-up of the stone steps, and when the shot zoomed in again, Elizabeth was standing above a limp young man who was laid backward atop the altar. Elizabeth looked once at the camera, and I could see that her eyes were empty of life. And then she stepped forward. I watched in horror as the grisly ritual sacrifice unfolded before my eyes.

"Hail Narayama, Hail Night Drinker. Hail, great god of the Obsidian Underworld. We come to thee asking for all wisdom and life and love . . ."

And finally the tape went mercifully blank. I fast forwarded it, but that was it, nothing more to see. I felt sick.

But I knew now.

I knew why Elizabeth had come to me. She'd set me up. She'd needed the kind of help that others in her little clique weren't about to give her, so she'd combed through the phone book, had picked a gumshoe at random, and it had happened to be me.

But there was still a lot I didn't know. Like why she'd tried to dig up her own grave, then stopped, and why her feet had been bared and muddy when she'd come to see me.

I was musing on those and other matters when the phone gave a shrill little yelp that made me nearly jump out of my shoes. I walked over to my desk and grabbed it up. "Yo. Weatherby Investigations."

It was Angelo. "Glad you made it back," he said dryly. "I thought you were going to leave me alone in the middle of this mess."

"What's up?"

"What's down is more like it. Dr. Gates, for one. He went down in a twin-engine plane last night, down in Baja. Flying in the mountains near the Foundation's hotel, where he'd been on vacation for a month or so. He was with one of your weirdos, some writer named Dr. Deborah Winch."

So, Gates must have been in the plane that tried to chase us out of the temple compound and instead crashed. This small world was getting smaller and smaller.

And Angelo had more. A lot more. Frank Livingstone had had his wife's grave opened. The body had even been identified, to everyone's surprise. The jawbone belonged to a man named Bernie Barker, a small-time con artist out of Las Vegas who had first been busted at the age of twenty-one, something to do with a voodoo cult in New Orleans that had convinced several people they had to cough up a hundred grand apiece to keep from being visited by Baron Samedi, the Haitian equivalent of the Grim Reaper. When they'd given up the money, a member of the group had then convinced them to drink a certain potion—which had been laced with arsenic. No witnesses left to talk, and Barker had walked.

Barker's next bust had been in Houston, just over ten years ago, for running a securities scam on some rich widows. He had offered up the man behind the scheme in lieu of a jail sentence. The Feds had taken the bait and had busted and jailed the partner: one Carl Cooper, stock swindler, purveyor of non-existent oil leases, financial scammer, religious *fakir*, and con man *par excellence*.

"Wait a minute," I said. "Did you say Carl Cooper."

"Right."

I frowned. Could this be the same Carl Cooper Tony had recognized—the one who was posing as Vernon Vance? "Angelo, can you get a photograph of the man whose body was in the grave?"

"Got one right here on my desk, just waiting for the morning edition."

"How about Cooper? You got anything on him?"

"You're in luck. I just got in a pic from the Houston Globe."

"Can you fax copies of both?"

"Don't see why not. Hold on, I'll have to copy them first, the fax won't take photographs."

After a minute I heard the shrill beep of my fax receiving, and then the paper came through. I uncurled it then held it up. Carl Cooper was indeed the same man as Vernon Vance. And Barker was the man I'd just seen Elizabeth plunge a knife into on videotape. Man, I was doing it again. Lifting up rocks, from under which every weird critter in the world was skittering out and into the light of day.

Trouble was, the body in the grave had been put there by two professional bullets to the head, not by several stab wounds to the chest from the hands of Elizabeth Livingstone. Which left a lot unexplained.

I picked up the phone and dialed Angelo again. "Old buddy, you ain't gonna believe this."

Angelo's voice was breathless. He'd scented the size of the story, and he was coming alive. "What is it?"

"This is off the record."

"For the moment."

I told him about the videotape. And I told him about the two bullet holes I'd seen in Barker's skull.

We threw around the possibilities, and then he told me some more.

A week before the Houston Securities scam trial, Barker had disappeared. Without his testimony, Cooper walked.

"Cooper was already setting up shop here in L.A.," I said. "In fact he must have been busy here even before the Houston trial."

Angelo said, "I'll check it out."

And then I told Angelo about Mexico, about the hotel and the temple compound, about Rosa disappearing from Tijuana and the people who had vanished in lower Baja—all of it. I needed to pick his brain now and see what things looked like from a fresh angle.

But sometimes he was sharper than I wanted him to be. He said, "So—what was Elizabeth Livingstone's role in all this?"

I could see him in my mind, eyes fiery, pencil poised.

"I haven't quite figured that out yet," I said. Which was mostly true. "But look. Think about it this way. Vance is a scammer. As Cooper, he was about to go down for a long time if Barker testified against him. Furthermore, he was going to lose everything he had set up here, and my guess is that he already had Elizabeth Livingstone's money in mind, if not in hand. They must have already set up the scheme to get Elizabeth's money by making it look like she was dead. They already had a grave, why not plant Barker there? Who was ever going to look? And no body, no crime. I know, nobody saw Vance shoot Barker, but it had to be him."

"But why did they make it look like Elizabeth was dead?"

"I'm still working on that one."

"Okay, let's say that's the way it was. But it doesn't answer a lot of questions."

323

"No, but it gives me a better handle on who's running the bigger thing."

"Which is?"

"Elizabeth's money is where it started. Vance was needing new territory, a new game. He comes to L.A. with a set of phony papers, and a phony background, marries well, and the wife turns him onto this group of weirdos who believe they can conjure up spirits with crystals, or whatever. Or maybe he picked them himself, and the wife was target number one—a way in. Talk about a bunch of birds waiting to get plucked. Whichever way it happened, if this is the same joker I saw pretending to be the god of the universe, he's wearing diamonds from stem to stern. We're talking mega-millions here, just for the taking. Some of the oldest, biggest money in Smog City, all up for grabs if this schemer can only convince them he's got the key to eternal life."

"And he was getting away with this?"

"He was. He managed to convince them that he was holier than any of them, and he took over the reins. He even managed to scam Elizabeth into turning over her family home as the Foundation's headquarters. Then when she wouldn't play ball anymore—and still had all that money sitting, waiting to be spent—he started putting heavier pressure on her. Who knows what he did to get her to fake her own death—or to take part in that macabre little scene they have on videotape. Dr. Gates was in on it all, and with the city medical examiner in the game, anything could have been faked. Elizabeth was never dead. Frank saw her at the bottom of the stairs, but she wasn't dead. He only thought she was because the doctor said so, and Gates drugged him when he started putting up a fuss. These people seem to be able to do a lot with drugs. Mostly peyote. Believe me, I know."

"Yeah, but man, for ten *years* they had her under wraps?"

"Probably drugged. Every day, I'll bet. The question is, why did they keep her alive at all? The answer has to be that somehow they couldn't get the money without her, and they couldn't get it away from her. She must have been sharp enough to set it up so that they couldn't get to it unless she signed for it or something. Which is no doubt what saved her life. They'd threatened to kill her husband and niece if she didn't play ball, so she did."

"This is the biggest scam I've ever heard of."

"It gets better. My theory is that somehow Elizabeth finally got fed up. She got away and came to me, wanting me to find something out for her. I don't quite have that one put together." I did, but it wasn't time yet to tell Angelo. "Anyway, I've apparently thrown a real monkey wrench into the works."

"So what now?"

"So now we get to Vance and find out what we can."

"Watch your step, Weatherby. This man sounds deranged."

"He is, but he's vulnerable."

"How so?"

"He's a victim, too."

"Meaning?"

"Meaning that someone bigger is running what he thinks is his show."

"Who?"

"That's spiritual, old buddy, and at this point I wouldn't expect you to understand."

Chapter
——THIRTY-EIGHT——

I stared at my newly painted beige ceiling and let my mind drift back to the first day, when Elizabeth Livingstone had walked into my office tracking cemetery mud onto my brand new carpet. I mulled over everything she'd said, even got up at one point and opened the wall safe then took out the recording of her conversation and replayed it.

And then I was replaying tapes of conversations and encounters and events in my mind, rehashing everything that had happened since that peculiar day, from the violated grave to the sinister ritual at the Temple of the Sun. Finally, I again watched the videotape, looking carefully at the sacrificial victim's face, at his opened eyes, and then I knew the rest of it . . .

And I knew, too, that I had to get some shut-eye, that the old body was folding up on me. There was still a lot to be done, but I wasn't going to manage much if I fell asleep in the middle of it. It ticked me off. Sam Spade and Philip Marlowe never had to sleep when they were working a big case. Why me?

On that note I did fall asleep, and was dreaming about a cartoon gumshoe, a caricature in large shoes and a trenchcoat with a huge fedora pulled down over his ears, a sort of Daffy Duck type character but without a face. He and I were burrowing our way through tunnels full of Aztec gold and ancient bones, looking for something, looking and looking, and I had the feeling we'd almost found it when the phone jarred me awake. I grabbed up the receiver just to shut it up, then managed to grunt something into the mouthpiece, and then heard, "*Señor* Weatherby?"

"Snzraffle."

"*Señor* Weatherby?" The voice came across the line again, and this time it jangled something inside my brain and rewired some connections, because I sat straight up and said, "Yo."

"This is Lieutenant Aragon, in Guerrero Negro. I wanted to let you know. We raided Serpent Mountain. We discovered a well there that had become a mass grave. We believe at least ten persons have been sacrificed, maybe more. Our people are still bringing bodies up."

"I'm very sorry to hear that."

"*Si, si*, but it is not your fault. On the contrary, you have no doubt saved many lives by discovering this evil place. We have arrested one American, a Juan Valdez. We have also arrested a Mexican man named Auguste Flores. But the problem we have is that other than these two, none of the people whose names you gave me are still here. Nor are they at the hotel. We have taken many people into custody, but still . . . "

"Ain't that the way it goes," I said. "The action is started by the big-shots, the small-fry take the heat. So—how long ago did Vance and his fellow piranhas leave?"

"From what we are told, they departed shortly after you fled their presence," he said. "They did not file flight plans, but we feel certain they will return to Los Angeles. We have already contacted your *policia* there, they have agreed to arrest them so soon as we can present them with the papers. But that will take several days, *señor*, and in the meantime, so far as we can tell, there is no trace here of the *señorita*, the one you had asked me to watch for . . ."

"Elizabeth?"

"*Si*, that one."

"Thanks," I said. "And I mean thanks. If they're here, we'll get them."

"If I can be of help . . ."

"You have been, buddy, more than you'd ever believe."

My mind told me to go out and make things happen, my body told me just a few more hours of rest. I listened to my body, and it was around four o'clock A.M. the next time the phone rang. I picked it up, irritable now, and heard Ariel.

"Weatherby—you've got to come right away. It's horrible—"

She was talking in a rapid-fire staccato that I could barely understand.

"Whoa," I said, "Slow down."

"It's Tod," she said. "He's stoned, and he's furious. Mother and Daddy just flew back from Mexico, they're acting horrible, they tried to force me to sign away everything Aunt Liz left me and when I refused they came right out and told me. They've already used up a lot of it, they've embezzled to pay their own expenses, the Foundation has ruined them. Everything is mortgaged or sold. And Tod is—I mean it seriously, he's going to kill someone. He's saying his life is over and they've destroyed him, and he's threatening to kill them. Can you get out here right away?"

"You're at the studio?"

"At Mother's," she said, her voice catching. "Please hurry."

I left burn stripes in my carpet, did a "roadrunner" down to my car, and then I was on the freeway, honking and darting in and out of the light traffic and averaging eighty-five all the way.

I'd just come off Sepulveda and turned onto Santa Monica when I spotted them. Two bozos with hard faces and football-player shoulders driving a black '91 Buick Regal. They were keeping well back, working the early morning traffic like pros, but anyone in the world can spot a tail when only one car is on the job. I slowed down and acted like I was turning left, watched in my rearview mirror as they adjusted their position accordingly, and then, tires screeching, I hung a hard right into a side street and gunned it. The chase was on.

They came right behind me, not bothering to mask their intentions now. And as they got close, I recognized one face, the heavy, squared jaw of the Mexican chauffeur/pilot who'd taken the lead the night they'd mashed me into mincemeat. He was bringing up a Luger, firing, and then I was in and out of traffic, clipping a fence then regaining control, and then I was back on the boulevard, shooting across three lanes of traffic, the other cars careening and swerving around to miss me and the Buick.

A yellow cab sideswiped the Buick, which ran up onto the sidewalk and clipped a light pole, and then the Buick was back in the street again, fishtailing for about half a block. They were still after me, but I'd gained some time.

I careened around a corner, made another quick right, then I spotted the lot of a BMW dealership. It was closed down for the night, the office dark and a single streetlight hanging in front of the rows of used cars. I wheeled the Beamer in, right between a lemon yellow Porsche and a dark green late-model Mercedes, then leaped out and grabbed the huge white sign from the front window of the car behind me—BEST BUY: $19,995.00. I stuck it on my windshield and ducked just as the front end of the Buick screeched around the corner, leaving half its tire tread on the pavement. The chauffeur was leaning out the window, gun ready, looking back and forth every which way for my car. But he missed me. Looked right at me and scanned on past, his brain not processing the fact that the car he was chasing had transformed itself into a used ice-gray Beamer on sale for $19,995.00.

I waited maybe five minutes and sure enough, they came back down the empty boulevard, slowly this time. I was outside the car, behind the Porsche, my gun ready for action. But again they cruised on past, identical looks of bewildered disgust on both their faces.

As soon as they turned the corner, I jumped into my Beamer, fired up, and followed them. I'd read a story once about a hunter in Wyoming who'd been after a grizzly bear. He'd been tracking the varmint, following the footprints, when suddenly he'd realized he'd backtracked on himself. It didn't take him long to figure it out. The bear had doubled around, and was now tracking him! That man didn't waste any time getting out of the forest.

I'd liked that story, and now I tried to reverse the odds like that every chance I got. The worm turns, as they say. They'd given up on me, and didn't have a clue that I was watching them from behind a little black VW bug that was behind them. But when they passed Sunset, I peeled off and returned to my original goal. Ariel was waiting. Time later for the chauffeur.

I turned north on the coastal highway, then sped to the house. The gate was open and I squealed my tires around the corner, screeched to a halt on top of the flagstones, and raced up the pink stone steps.

The front door was also open, and the lights were burning in the large room with the marble tiled floors and cathedral ceiling. I raced into the room, my .38 out and ready, then left tread marks on the tiles as my sneakers brought me to an abrupt stop. Tod Montgomery stood there, a Colt .45 automatic in his right hand, his left hanging limply. He was wearing white flannel slacks and a blue blazer with a gold crown on the pocket, but his hair was mussed and he had a wild growth of beard. He brought the Colt around to aim at me as I came in, but when he saw who I was, he turned back. He was blubbering, hysterical, but his gun hand was steady and the aim was level. "You've ruined me," he said. "It's your fault, my production studio is lost, you've destroyed everything I ever wanted . . ."

In front of him, in the eye of the storm, stood Cassie and Caspar Cardwell. Beside them stood Vernon Vance. Ariel was backed up against a far wall, her face white and her hands clutched to her chin.

"You . . ." Cassie hissed when she saw me. She went stiff and her claws came out like talons. She started to step toward me, then stopped as she realized that Montgomery's gun was following her. She stepped back beside her husband, her eyes darting back and forth between me and Montgomery, unsure whether her hatred of me supplanted her fear of the gun. Caspar just stood there, his eyes dark with hatred as he looked contemptuously at Montgomery.

Vance remained dapper and cool, oozing confidence. He had a contemptuous little smile curled into his clownish face and his quick, dark eyes kept darting around the room, though they held a sense of senile vagueness. His blue-black hair was blow-dried and neat. A heavily jeweled watch adorned his wrist and he actually glanced at it, as if this scenario was interfering with some far more important function for which he was late. Diamonds glittered on all his fingers. He had about two thousand dollars worth of suit on his back, and his shoes were spit-shined black Italian leather. Actually, he looked like this was nothing more to him than a minor annoyance, even though he had his hands in the air.

Ariel sobbed, "Weatherby! Talk to Tod, make him stop!"

I turned to Montgomery. "If you shoot these people, they're going to bleed real blood. And they won't get up and walk away when the take is over."

Montgomery's head turned slowly, and he gave me a dead look. I knew then that he wasn't running any games on anybody and he wasn't just zonked out on drugs. He'd snapped and was genuinely dangerous. He turned back to the Cardwells. "I used to make movies. I used to create amusement and entertainment, and now you've reduced me to a mere purveyor of garbage and slime and filth. I went through all this because I believed something better was ahead. But now I see, there will never be anything else, never, this is hell, this is what hell is all about. This—"

His hand was flexing, his eyes had narrowed. His gaze had fallen full on Cassie and he was about to empty a chamber square into her chest. I dived at him, hit him just as he squeezed the trigger and the gun roared, and then I was in a strange hallucinatory stop-framed place where people were shouting and screaming and the gun went off again, even as I fell, dragging Montgomery to the floor with me. He was crazed, coiled like a steel cobra, whipping away from me and again getting off a round while I grappled with him, got hold of his trousers, nearly pulled them off as I literally climbed up his body and fell on top of him. The gun was high in his hand now and going off again. Then someone was pulling me up from behind by my collar, and I heard it tearing away from the shirt as I spun and looked square into the face of the Mexican chauffeur I thought I'd ditched on Santa Monica Boulevard. They must have picked me up and followed me here.

I brought back my fist and hit the bozo square in his leering face with everything I had. Everything. He flew backwards and bright red blood exploded from my hand. I stood poised, ready to punch him again, but he was out cold. My hand was numb for just an instant, then it began throbbing. I looked at it. It was still balled into a fist. I brought it back and looked again. Half a dozen of the man's teeth were deeply embedded in my knuckles, which streamed blood. I wondered about rabies, and then I heard a small noise—the room was horribly silent now—and I spun around, looking for the chauffeur's partner. But he was cowering in the shadows at the side of the room near to the balcony window, and as he saw me turning and drawing a bead on him, he flung himself out the door then took off at a dead run, crashing into the huge statue of Narayama as he fled, sending it smashing to the marble tiles with an earthshaking thud, and then he was over the balcony wall and gone.

My stomach was in knots and my adrenaline was still pumping, keeping me primed for more trouble. I fell into a karate crouch, my .38 in my hand now, and slowly scanned the room, ready for whatever came next.

Montgomery was crouched on the floor, his head in his hands, sobbing, while Ariel knelt beside him, a dazed look in her eyes as she picked up the gun he'd dropped, then held it dangling on a finger at a distance, looking at it with revulsion. Cassie had collapsed onto a pink sofa, her eyes wide with shock. She was whimpering and blood was pouring through the chest of her mustard-colored dress. Caspar stood over her, looking at her coldly, saying something I couldn't quite hear in an accusing tone of voice.

And Vance was dead.

He'd taken most of the bullets that Montgomery had intended for Cassie, though I was sure that had Cassie gone down. Caspar and Vance would have been next in line anyway. Vance was sprawled on

332

the floor, flat on his back, a look of surprise on his death-frozen face. He looked like a rag doll that had been possessed by some hideous demon and now, with the demon gone, all that was left was the crumpled clownish rag with its dyed and blow-dried hair.

Their demented, narcissistic little world had just collapsed like a house of cards in a strong gale. It was over. I went to the telephone and dialed the LAPD, looking down at my tooth-studded knuckles as I talked. I grabbed somebody's cotton jacket and wrapped my hand in it as I walked over to Ariel and said, "You'd better do something about your mother, if you can. The ambulance is on the way, but she's in bad shape."

She was a gutsy little girl, and as soon as I spoke she snapped to life and took charge, getting her raving father out of the way and trying to help Cassie. Montgomery was still on the floor, whimpering, his eyes looking into a faraway place that made me shudder and to which I hoped and prayed I would never have to go.

The rest of the early morning was like a grainy newsreel. The police came. The medical examiner arrived and inspected Vance's body, and then they brought the stretcher and took him away, leaving the chalk outline etched onto the marble-tiled floor. Cassie had already been taken away by ambulance and Caspar was sitting talking to a detective, who was scribbling furiously, getting down Caspar's version of the events. Ariel was also being interviewed. Montgomery was in cuffs, sitting alone at one side of the room, waiting to be taken downtown. I found a discreet place to make a phone call, fulfilled my promise to Angelo by giving him the scoop, and then I went back in and waited until the police were ready for me, then I gave them my report. By the time I left, dawn was approaching and I was filled with near-mortal exhaustion.

Chapter

───THIRTY-NINE───

Back at my office, I took a cold shower and even shaved. But the fatigue stayed with me. Still, I couldn't sleep.

I paced for a while, then opened the drapes and sat down on the edge of my desk and looked out over the cold gray dawn bruising the cold gray Pacific and the cold metal loading cranes and ships across the street. Elizabeth was here. In the city, somewhere, still alive if I was lucky.

I could wait.

I'd wrapped a clean cold towel around my fist. The bleeding had stopped and the throbbing had turned into a painful ache. I'd have to get to a hospital, have a surgeon remove the teeth from my knuckles, see if any nerves had been severed. But there would be time enough for that later. Now, I still had things to do.

I waited.

The ships' horns tooted across the street and five stories below, the sea muffling the mournful sounds and turning them hollow. Later that evening, the sky lightened from steel to pewter, traffic sounds in the streets below picked up and the eighteen-wheelers started blowing their airhorns as they pulled in to and out from the loading docks, picking up cargo containers. About six-thirty, the sun came up and the smell of freshly brewing coffee began to waft up from the greasy spoon downstairs, and then came the smell of frying bacon.

Still, I waited.

At eight forty-five, the tap came on the door. It was light and brief. I stayed in my chair. Someone turned the knob, and then the door opened a crack and she stuck in her head, saw me, and said, "Mr. Weatherby?"

"At your service." I didn't bother to get up this time, just waited for her to come in. She was wearing a forest green designer suit and a creamy white blouse. Back in the upper crust. Emerald earrings set off her emerald-green eyes, which were still filled with pain, though the sallowness had left her face. Her legs were neatly shod in nylon, and on her feet were expensive brown pumps.

I waited till she'd settled herself carefully in the apple green client's chair, and then I leveled a look at her, and said, "Why?"

"I—I had no choice. There was no other way."

"You set me up," I said.

She fumbled with the gold clasp of her Italian leather designer purse and her eyes got wet. "Would you have believed me if I'd told you the truth?"

I thought about that, then shrugged. "Probably not."

She gave me a little up from under look. A poignant smile flitted across her face, then was gone.

"Why me?" I asked. "I'd never even heard of you before."

"I picked your name out of the phone book because your office was the closest to where I was at the time."

"I see." Just as I'd figured. So much for any theories of my reputation preceding me. I stretched lazily, and said, "You want to tell me about it?"

"You still wouldn't believe me. Nobody would."

"Try me."

"I—I can't tell you. I'm sorry, but—"

"No matter what they had over you, sooner or later it's going to come out. It's over. The whole ball of wax. People are dead here, people are dead in Mexico. Somebody is going to start talking, and when they do the next one in line will want to give his side of the story, and then the next one, and after that it's going to be a waterfall of snitches, everybody climbing over each other to be the first to kiss and tell. The local police are going to find out, the Feds will be in on it, and the *Federales* in Mexico are already holding about half the loonies from Serpent Mountain. So the question isn't whether or not the truth is going to come out, it's whether or not your version of it is going to get aired. So I'm going to ask you again. You want to talk about it?"

"Oh, dear God," she said, and it wasn't a curse, it was a prayer.

"I know this isn't going to be easy, but take all the time you need." I leaned back in my chair ready to listen.

Her eyes went empty as she looked into the depths of another, darker world. I waited. After a while, she blinked and refocused on me. She looked like a frightened child. She said, "You have to finally reach the point that you'd really rather be dead."

I nodded like I knew what she was talking about.

"Because you might be, you see. Dead, I mean. I thought I would be. I believed that was what it would cost me this time—my life." Her eyes went wide with realization. "But I'm here, aren't I? I mean— well—now I know, this is what I should have done from the beginning. But I was so confused, it was so hard, and then they began to use the mescaline . . ."

I waited for her to tell it in her own way. I wanted to hear it all.

She was looking down, studying her nails. She started nervously chipping at her plum-colored nail polish with her right thumbnail. There was a little tremor in her hands. "I still don't know if I'm sane," she said. "Do you have any idea what mescaline does to you?"

"As a matter of fact, I do."

"The real trouble started when I gave them Mother's house," she said. "I had been in the Foundation—then out of it. And I really didn't want to give up the house. But I felt guilty because Mother had left so little to Caspar. And Casper and Cassie kept at me, constantly, wearing me down, not giving me a moment's peace. I thought the house might be enough to make them leave me alone. Then Vance joined the Foundation. Cassie and Caspar believed he was a very important avatar from the very beginning. Oh, he was cunning. I even believed, for a little while . . ."

She continued talking, her voice an almost monotonous drone. But the words were anything but boring. After a moment, I could see it, live it right along with her.

She'd been hurt, lost. She'd recently learned of her husband's infidelity with Cassie, her mother had just died. She'd been empty and vulnerable, and she'd gotten more involved with the Foundation again. She'd been down to Mexico, had watched the initial planning phase of Serpent Mountain and the hotel staging area, La Casa del Sol. At first, she'd been as fascinated as the rest of them at the prospect of building a temple that would be their doorway to pure spiritual truth. But then they started going through all the money her mother had left Caspar, and then they insisted that Elizabeth shut down the orphanage and integrate the buildings and funding into their project. More and more, Elizabeth realized that she was helping to tear down everything her mother had lived for and believed in. And she began to have nightmares.

On her last trip to the orphanage, when she'd told the administrators that she was closing it down, she'd overheard Cassie and Vernon Vance talking about sacrifice. The debate had ended with both of them agreeing that if they were to do things right at Serpent Mountain, that is, in a way that would really stir up the ancient spirits, they might indeed have to offer up human sacrifice. Elizabeth had been sickened at what she'd heard, and her eyes had suddenly been opened. These people were so obsessed that they would stop at nothing.

The day after she'd flown home, the pastor of her mother's church had come to call on her. She'd been attending church once in a while, but still maintained an interest in the Foundation. He'd sensed that she was in some deep spiritual trouble.

She listened to him, had prayed with him, suddenly her vision had cleared and she'd seen the cultists for exactly what they were, so she'd broken off with them, just like that, in one day and out the next. Cassie and Caspar had been outraged. Not only because they thought she was rejecting them and what they so firmly believed—and they did believe, there was nothing fraudulent about that—but because she controlled a good deal of the money they needed to build their temple retreat.

They'd confronted her and threatened her and then, when that hadn't worked, they'd abruptly changed their tactics. They'd phoned her and told her they wished her forgiveness, that they were wrong, that she should be allowed to believe in anything she chose. Caspar had invited her to dinner, wanting to reconcile their differences. He was her only brother, and she'd accepted.

The mescaline may have been in anything—wine, food, even on the tip of the cigarettes she then smoked. She had hallucinated wildly, had "freaked out," was the word the kids used. Days had passed, maybe weeks, and she was aware of being down in Mexico again, and then she recollected parts of a plane ride back. And then she'd awakened in the Cardwells' turquoise and black living room, staring out at the statues—she hated those statues—and they'd turned on the television and shoved a videotape into the VCR.

"I've seen the tape," I said.

Her eyes widened with horror. "Dear God," she said. "How could I have done it? Even drugged, under any circumstances, how could I have killed someone?"

"You didn't," I said, but she was looking beyond me and didn't hear me.

"They said they'd kill Frank if I did anything at all," she said. "At first they threatened me with that. And they said they'd kill Ariel. After Mother died, they were the only two people in the world I really cared about. Except the children at the orphanage, of course. But Cassie and Caspar knew how to pull my strings, especially then, when I was emotionally so very low . . ."

They had worked on her, told her over and over what would happen if they made the tape public. There was no way anyone could prove they were also in the picture—they were well masked and nobody spoke, the chanting had been in unison and therefore unusable for voice analysis. Frank would be ruined, Ariel would be ruined, Elizabeth would go to prison, it went on and on.

Finally, the pressure was too great. "They really wanted the excuse to kill Frank," she said. "Perhaps Ariel too, I'm not so certain about that. By then, I'm not sure there was very much human left in either Cassie or Caspar. I—I believe they had become demon possessed." She shot me a little look to catch my reaction. I nodded. I had come to the conclusion that that would explain a lot of what had happened.

"They couldn't just bleed me for money without alarming Frank. I'd always handled my own money, but he would have known something was wrong, he's very financially astute. They knew that he'd have to be disposed with. I wanted desperately to save his life, so I came up with my own scheme. We'd fake my death and I'd disappear, go with them to Mexico and live in seclusion and give them a certain amount every month. It seemed so ridiculous, but it was a chance. I thought maybe I could go along with it for a while and then things would change, surely they couldn't continue their nonsense forever and I was certain I would find a way out sooner or later, even if there is no statute of limitations on murder.

"I came up with a plan whereby I hid my money inside a revocable trust and buried it inside Ariel's trust. I set up a branch trust—my name was only on several well-hidden documents—so I could also tap into the money. And then we doctored the documents Ariel saw so that amounts that said thousands were actually in the millions. The Mexican property is there, it's worth $45 million, but Ariel's trust reads it as only $45,000. The Foundation's lawyers helped me do it. I knew enough to not let them totally cheat me. It was clever and skillfully done."

One of the problems, Elizabeth continued, was that when Ariel's trust matured she was going to find out that everything was mixed up. Caspar and Cassie knew that. As Ariel's twenty-fourth birthday approached, they started putting more and more pressure on Elizabeth to simply give them everything, and she had realized her time was running out.

At that same time, Valdez had picked up one of the many young girls he constantly pursued and brought her to Serpent Mountain. Everyone had known about his perversions, but the others didn't care, and Elizabeth, herself essentially captive, was in no position to help anyone else escape. The Foundation members believed that good and evil were merely different faces of the same thing and therefore nothing was really evil. The logical extreme of that was there were no barriers to anyone's appetites, and things kept getting worse and worse.

Elizabeth had tried to befriend the girl, who had been terrified of everything. She was a simple and credulous girl.

"She was afraid because of the name, Serpent Mountain, but also because at the rituals they were always explaining how the Rain Mother was a serpent who lived in the sea and gave birth to the Rain Child, who turned into baby serpents that fell to the earth when it rained. It was all mumbo-jumbo, but it terrified that poor child. She seemed so intelligent at first, but then they started giving her mescaline, too. It disorients you so, and seems to make you terribly passive. I suppose that's why they use it, and then too, there's an esoteric thing about it because it's used by the shamans. Auguste has plentiful access to it . . ."

Elizabeth's interest in helping the girl had been noticed, and the girl had been placed under wraps, though she was still on the mountain. And then Elizabeth overheard more veiled conversation and realized the girl was to be the next sacrifice. So far as Elizabeth knew, no one else had been sacrificed on the mountain since the night she had plunged a knife into the breast of the young man on the videotape. Even in her semi-drugged state, the idea of another sacrifice apalled her. Sickened and terrified, she'd helped the girl get away by bribing one of the younger Mexican guards with a huge amount of money, at least she had managed to do that much. But the whole thing had nauseated her, had made her realize just how deranged the entire operation had become. And so she'd started planning her own escape.

"I had no cash, of course," she said, "I'd had to steal a letter of credit for the young man who helped Rosa."

I sat up straight. "Rosa?"

"Of course, the young girl Valdez brought to the mountain. I stole the letter of credit from Vance's suite in the palace and gave it to the young man so he could draw on my hidden funds. And thank God, they got away. It took me almost two more months, but so did I."

Rosa! Of course. Why hadn't I put it together while she was telling me? I thought about Shelby Knight finding Rosa on the streets in Tijuana, thought about how Valdez had also tracked her there, then had paid the pimp to kidnap her from the church so they could take her back to the mountain. Of course. They had another reason to want her dead, by then. They didn't want her to ever be able to talk about all she had seen in their unholy compound. I thought about my bumping into Tony Cacciatore after his several years in the joint, and I thought about the violent sacrifice that we had interrupted at the temple. There was a Hand in this far larger than mine. An Intelligence that surpassed anything I could even imagine.

Elizabeth looked weary. Her eyes were lifeless again. "I walked down off Serpent Mountain," she said. "I thought I was committing suicide."

I thought about that mountain. She had indeed risked her life if she'd come off it alone.

"I finally just waited till the middle of the night, then walked away. I walked all the way to the Transpeninsular Highway, hiding in the brush in the daytime when they sent the planes to look for me. It took me three full nights. By the time I got there, my sandals were shreds. I threw them away. I caught a ride to Tijuana with a man and woman who were delivering produce from their small farm in El Arco. I told them I'd come south with a boyfriend and we'd fought. They were sweet people. I plan to send them something as a way of thanking them. But I had to lie to them because I knew everyone would be looking for me, and I didn't want to leave a trace of my escape.

"In Tijuana, I caught another ride, this time with a trucker who was bringing someone's furniture north. He gave me five dollars for food, then dropped me at a truck stop near the airport, and from there I took the bus to Bel Air. I broke into the house."

"Why didn't you just go to your husband for help?"

She shook her head quickly. "You don't know Frank. He would have done anything to help me, but he's just no good when it comes to things like this. He's too confrontational and he never knows what he's confronting. He would have gotten us both killed."

She knew where Frank stored family things, and she'd gone straight to the attic, where she'd found her possessions and even her old checkbook. But she'd heard a noise before she had a chance to find and change her clothes. She'd fled the house.

"I have a question," I said. "Why the check? And why did you date it ten years ago?"

"I suppose I had some idealistic idea that Frank might have left my account open. That you'd actually be able to get money out, if the check was dated before my death."

"But it wasn't dated *before* your death. It was ten years ago to the very day of your death."

Her eyes went wide. "I—I got mixed up. My mind was focused so much on the past that day, I suppose it was unconscious . . ."

I waved it away. "Never mind. That little slip got me interested enough to get me started. I suppose the rest was destiny. Look, I have another question."

"Of course. You must have many more."

"Why did you change your mind about shaking my hand that first morning?"

She frowned. "I'm sorry. I know that was rude. But I hadn't been touched in a friendly way by anyone for so very long, every bit of human contact I'd had was exploitative and often very abusive. I—I simply couldn't bring myself to touch anyone in a friendly fashion. I know that must seem peculiar—"

"Not at all," I said. I remembered how it had been when I'd first come back from Vietnam. "What about now? Are you going to go back to being Mrs. Frank Livingstone?"

She looked sad. "I don't know. I really don't. So much has happened, and it's going to take time for me to even begin to heal at the emotional level. Ten years is such a very long time. And there will certainly be legal repercussions. I did, after all, kill a man, even if I was under the influence of drugs."

I narrowed my eyes and studied her. "What about the grave? Why did you go out and dig it up first thing when you got back?"

She looked startled. "How did you know?"

"The mud," I said. "Not to mention that you left bare footprints all over the place out there. I wiped them out before the police opened the grave."

"Yes, Thomas told me that was happening. I'd been staying with him, you know, until Vance's thugs found out where I was. I managed to get away before they could hurt Thomas. I phoned you, and left a message on your machine, so you'd at least know you could stop trying to figure everything out."

"It was a little late for that. Why did you set me up to begin with? Why didn't you just tell me the truth?"

"I—I don't know. I did it on an impulse, I wasn't thinking clearly. I suppose I wanted to point you to that time in the past when it all started, I was hoping somehow you could unravel it and make it all go away, make things go back like they had been before I got lured into all the madness."

"I guess I can buy that. But back to the grave. Why did you dig it up?"

"I think I was deranged. All the time I was down there, they held the sacrifice I'd committed over my head. Every time I'd rebel, start talking about getting out, they'd bring it up. Cassie had told me they'd buried the man I'd killed in my grave. She thought that was ever so funny. It haunted me. I thought about it and thought about it, and they did give me so many drugs at first, until I finally realized that if I was just passive and took what they dished out they didn't drug me, and then they eased up. But the idea of that man being in a grave, in the family complex, with my name on the tombstone—I don't know how to explain it, but it was a true horror to me.

"And then, after a time, I started telling myself it had never happened. The mescaline causes such vivid hallucinations, and I'd had so many, so much was so very mixed up in my mind, and I finally began to convince myself that the sacrifice had never even happened. I suppose it was some sort of denial mechanism that helped keep me sane. I wasn't even sure if I'd really seen a videotape. It kept eating at me more and more, and finally, when I got back here I was so desperate, so certain that they were following me, that they'd find me right away, but regardless of what happened I wanted to see, just see if the body was really there. I went to the cemetery after I'd broken into Frank's house. I walked all the way. I was so very tired. But when I got into the complex, the gardeners had been working there. They'd left shovels and trowels and other implements. I was suddenly determined to know the truth. I started to dig, and I dug and dug for what seemed like hours, and then I must have collapsed, because I awakened just as the sun was coming up and I was spread out in that grave—ugh! You can't imagine the feeling! I was terrified, shivering, mud-stained. And there was still a lot of dirt on top of the coffin. I got out of there. I was at my wits' end, Mr. Weatherby. I found your name in a phone book at a public phone not far from the cemetery, and I decided on you because you were close by. I sat in the park and waited till I thought you'd be in, and then I phoned you. It was all I could think of to do. If I'd gone to the police, I'd have had to tell them everything, and they still wouldn't have believed me. Just as you wouldn't have, but after I met you I knew you'd at least try to find out . . ."

"You didn't kill that man," I said.

Her eyes went wide with disbelief. "But his body was in my grave! Thomas said Frank had opened the grave and they found the corpse!"

"Yes, but the man had been shot. Twice, in the head. I know you didn't watch that videotape very closely. They probably played it for you just once, then went to work on you while you were still in shock. But I can tell you, that man was already dead when you stabbed him. Stone, cold dead. And right there on the videotape you can still see the matted blood where one of the bullets went in that killed him. You can tell by his eyes. Believe me. That evidence would stand up in any court of law. They might be able to bust you for mutilating a corpse, but never for killing a man."

She was looking at me with astonishment.

"It's true," I said. "Ten years is a long time to believe a lie of that size, but I can assure you, it *was* a lie. They've duped you all along."

She wept. Just unraveled right there and sobbed and sobbed, till I finally figured she'd let out enough, and I went around the desk to her and pulled her to her feet. I wrapped her in my arms, and said, "I'm going to phone Frank. I think it's time for you to go home."

"Oh yes, please," she sobbed. "You have no idea, staying there with Thomas, oh, he's such a sweet old man, but I could see the house, I felt so left out of the world, so alienated, so unwanted, and so unclean."

"It's over now," I said. "Except for some very nasty publicity, of course. Your brother is going to jail."

She stopped crying instantly, jutted her delicate jaw out and looked up at me. "Good."

"Ariel is going to need help."

"She's my daughter anyway. Cassie never was a mother to her."

"And I'll be billing you for expenses," I said, holding her at arm's length and giving her a charming grin. "This has been a very expensive caper."

She smiled back through her tears. "If only you knew," she said. "Call my husband and tell him I want to come home."

Chapter

FORTY

We phoned Frank, then I drove Elizabeth out to the house and watched the reunion. They were hesitant, uneasy with each other, but I could see real love there. It was going to work out.

I felt restless, like I always feel at the tail end of a caper. I'd been running on adrenaline for too long, and now there was nothing much to spend it on. That old feeling of alienation was coming back, and I felt strangely at odds with the world. I started back to the office, then on an impulse decided to whip by the mission and see what was happening with Tony Cacciatore.

Shelby was at the pulpit, and about thirty people were listening to what he had to say. They seemed to be mostly winos and other derelicts, people who had come in for the shelter and free lunch rather than the sermon, but Shelby wasn't letting that hold him back a bit.

I slid in beside Tony on the back pew and said, "What are you doing here?

"Can't hide out forever." He grinned, then added, "Glad you came. I need to talk with you."

He motioned for me to follow him into his dinky little office and the minute he shut the door he was deadly serious. "Riggatoni tried to hit me again last night," he said. "They was evidently watchin' for me to come back. One a his punks tried to run me off the road and gun me down, but he hit the corner too fast and rolled his car. Cops tell me he was D.O.A. Too many people are dyin', pal."

"At least it's the right ones," I said.

Tony shot me a disapproving look, then said, "Anyhow, Shelby's takin' over here till I get this thing straightened out. It ain't just me. Riggatoni has really been puttin' the pressure on my people this past few days. I gotta put a stop to it."

I had a sudden dark premonition, but Tony evidently saw the look cross my face because he added, "It ain't what you think. I'm out of the shootin' business. I'm goin' over to the Feds."

I cocked an eyebrow. "You cut a deal?"

He nodded. "But they seem to think that no matter what I give them, I'm going to have to do a little time. Don't worry about it, I can do it standin' on my head. There's always prison ministries to keep me busy."

"I'll be happy to act as a character witness," I said. "And if there's anything else I can do . . ."

"Matter of fact, it would be good if you could sort of help Shelby keep an eye on things. There's goin' to be some heavy action comin' down once I start talkin'. People might want to get even, and I'm goin' to be under wraps for a while. If Riggatoni can't get to me, he may try to get to my next in line just so's there's some kind of a payback. You know how the game goes."

"I do," I said. "I'll help you as much as I can."

"I got to be downtown in about ten minutes," Tony said. "Might as well get things moving."

"I'm going to miss you, buddy."

"I'll let you know what's up, soon as I get settled. Maybe we can get together, talk this thing over some more."

"It will be my pleasure. And by the way, this thing with Elizabeth Livingstone?"

"Yeah?"

"She's back and she's fine. I'll explain it next time we see each other. And she's going to have a bunch of land down in Mexico that I suspect she may never want to see again. Think your people might like to take over an orphanage down there?"

"I'll talk to Howard soon as I can, but right off the top of my head I'd say the answer is yes."

"I'll see what I can do," I said.

I walked out the back door, wondering if Tony had made the right choice, and feeling strangely empty. I climbed in my car, and then, suddenly, I was driving, just driving, wrapped tight, not caring where I went, just needing to move.

I drove along the Harbor freeway till I hit the coast, then turned south, leaving the empty, endless network of chaos that was the city. When I was past the gridlock of traffic, I hung a right on a little-traveled road, and came to the ocean. I parked and locked my car, then started walking down the beach, barefoot, cuffs rolled up. The day had turned murky and dark, and for once I had the whole shoreline to myself.

As I walked, I thought. Something was wrong with my life. Vitally wrong. The beach was turning stony, and I came to a short rocky promontory upon which stood one lonely, wind-gnarled tree. I found a perch on a weathered outjut of gray-brown rock, then sat gazing out at the roiling sea. The air was cool yet heavy. The tide was coming in, and the silvery whitecaps were lapping high up on the rock. Out at sea, a gray curtain of rain was moving toward shore, slowly drinking up the pewter-blue of the remaining sky.

I was tired of the emptiness of my existence. I had been for years. I'd tried to fill the vacuum with booze, with heroin, with war, with women, even with money. But everything I tried just ripped another chunk out of my soul and made the vacuum grow deeper. And now, for some reason, it had suddenly grown so large it was swallowing me up entirely.

I didn't want to go on like this. Sure, I was good at what I did. I was a knight errant, I helped people. I had just unraveled a caper that had stopped a lot of very bad people from doing some very bad things. But I was tired of the loneliness, tired of dealing with it all, tired of seeing and battling the decayed underbelly of the world. I was *so* tired that I thought, for a moment, about just stepping off the rocky outjut and into the crashing sea.

What else was there?

Ah, but maybe there was something else. Maybe what Tony had found? The concept still seemed almost foolish to me. Something for children and old women to believe in. But I had to consider where Tony had been when I'd first met him. It wasn't just what he was doing, but what he *was*. He'd carried the stench of death with him, so deeply had he become mired in his hellish existence.

And now, Tony epitomized light. Maybe even the light I'd wanted all my life to understand. And He epitomized life. And—yes, even true, selfless love. And in that instant, I knew what was missing in my life, what I wanted. I'd tried everything else. Why not check this out?

I looked up at the gathering storm, and said aloud, "God, if You're there, if You're real, please help me. I can't do it by myself. I can't figure it out, I can't live like this anymore. God, fill me up with whatever it is that You are. Give me back a purpose. Give me wisdom, God. Let me understand what this thing is I'm caught up in, why I'm here, what exists beyond all this."

I waited a minute. The storm clouds were drawing tighter, and a bolt of lightening shot through the blackness on the far horizon. I felt a quick sensation of fear. Was I going to miss out again? I lifted my face heavenward, and said, "If You can do this, God, if You can bring me to life again and let me believe in You again the way I did when I was a child, and show me what this whole thing is about, then I'll serve You, just as your Word says I should. Because that's what I really want to do, God. It's just that I can't get past this cynicism, I can't get past this disbelief. I *want* You to be real, God. Who wouldn't want it to be true that salvation and eternal life are ours because You sent Your Son to be a sacrifice in our place? *I* want it to be true that an all-powerful Being really cares what's happening to us down here. But I just haven't been *able* to believe in You. Too much still doesn't make sense. But please, I know maybe it's wrong to even ask You this—but I don't know any other way except to be honest. You'd know if I was lying anyway. Please, show me somehow that You're real, and let me believe in You again."

I stopped then and waited again. Just waited, just as I had waited earlier in the day for Elizabeth Livingstone to show up. I'd known somehow that she'd be there. I wasn't so sure about God.

And indeed, after about half an hour, the wind came up and the storm reached the shore. Raindrops began pelting my face, which I wouldn't have minded, but the tide was lapping furiously, almost at my toes now. I stood, disappointed, ready to leave. I was totally defeated.

Then suddenly it happened. It was so simple, I was astonished. Nothing changed on the outside, I was still my old thorny self. But inside a sudden joy and certainty flooded through me, and I instantly knew that I had been stripped clean and purified, filled with a white holy light that somehow illuminated the world in a whole new way. This was what they meant, this was *The Light*! Not a physical light at all, but something totally new. I was filled with a silken calm. Saturated with peace and a new certainty of my importance in this universe. In that instant, the stormy sea gleamed like a moonstone, the rocks and stones were sculpted out with a whole new beauty, the rain was fresh oil falling on my face. Every molecule in my universe had come to full, vibrant life. But I was still the same old Artie Weatherby. Amazing.

It wasn't what I'd expected at all. There were no sudden revelations, no great burdens to instantly pick up and lug around, no devastating guilt trips about things I had done before. Nevertheless, I was reborn and I knew it. Everything was bright and shiny, and in that moment I knew that I was privy to something golden and pristine and wonderful.

I was wrapped in amazement as I moved, somewhat unsteadily, through the rain and back to my car, almost expecting the sudden epiphany to leave. But it stayed, the new illumination keen and perfect as it carved every object in a new beauty.

And then suddenly I saw it all. The whole, devious thing. All my life, beneath everything else I'd known and done, I'd been buying a lie. A con game of cosmic proportion, the biggest lie ever devised. There *was* something beyond this reality. I couldn't see it with my eyes, but I could feel it with a deeper perception than anyone could have ever had with just the physical senses.

But now I had taken the first steps into a new and incredible discovery, not only about myself but about the universe itself. And I knew in that instant that no matter how difficult this walk with God would prove to be, no matter where it took me, I had finally found the purpose of my existence, and I was never again going to be desperate or self-destructive.

But even as I felt that, I knew a deeper and keener sense of alienation than I'd ever felt before. Filled with this new light, the darkness in the world around me had become a deeper and uglier thing than I had ever seen or sensed before. I hadn't stepped out of the combat arena: I'd stepped *into* it! But now I had a new Partner in my quest to rid the world from evil. And I knew with a complete, tranquil certainty that this was a partnership that was going to work.

About the Author

J.M.T. Miller is a professional writer and author of several books. She began the Weatherby Mystery Series with Ballantine Books in the late eighties. *The Big Lie* is the first in the series to feature protagonist Artie Weatherby confronting the truth of Christianity.